Phillip Hewitt

Lamb.

"Can't stand t
softly. "That your p   aphne got down in the
gutter to wallow around with people you think are
too bloody low to lick your boots."

Lamb lowered his voice even further, so that he
was almost whispering. But the pub was so still that
the venomous sound seemed to fill it to the furthest
corners.

"Your family tried to destroy me, Hewitt," he
snarled. "Well, they're stuffed now, aren't they?
Them, and you, and everyone else round here who
screamed for my blood, and talked their heads off
to the cops while my wonderful family just stood
back and did bloody nothing. But now I'm here,
and you'll know I'm here, every breath you take.
You'll think you're in hell. And you know what? It's
going to get worse, and worse, and worse. . . ."

* * * * *

Lamb
to the
Slaughter

Jennifer Rowe

BANTAM BOOKS
NEW YORK • TORONTO • LONDON • SYDNEY • AUCKLAND

All characters in this book are entirely fictitious
and no reference is intended to any living persons.

*This edition contains the complete text
of the original hardcover edition.*
NOT ONE WORD HAS BEEN OMITTED

LAMB TO THE SLAUGHTER
*A Bantam Crime Line Book / published by arrangement with
Allen & Unwin*

PUBLISHING HISTORY
*Allen & Unwin edition published 1995
Bantam edition / September 1996*

ISBN 0-553-56820-5

Published simultaneously in the United States and Canada

*Bantam Books are published by Bantam Books, a division of Bantam
Doubleday Dell Publishing Group, Inc. Its trademark, consisting of the
words "Bantam Books" and the portrayal of a rooster, is Registered in
U.S. Patent and Trademark Office and in other countries. Marca Reg-
istrada. Bantam Books, 1540 Broadway, New York, New York 10036.*

PRINTED IN THE UNITED STATES OF AMERICA

RAD 0 9 8 7 6 5 4 3 2 1

Lamb
to the
Slaughter

One

'It's happened. They're letting him out.'

Her husband's voice was loud, and near, but Dolly Hewitt didn't turn around. She pressed her stomach against the gleaming sink, and held tightly to the potato she was peeling. She stared down at her hands. Wet. The thin fingers streaked with smears and lines of dirt from the potato skin.

'Did you hear me?'

She nodded. She could hear the harsh breathing of the man in the doorway behind her. She made her hands move again. The peeler scraped at the potato, sliding over the bumpy red-brown surface, failing to cut cleanly. She frowned, and changed the angle of the peeler. It was important to get all the skin off. He complained if the mashed potato had brown bits in it.

'A free pardon. That's what is said on the news. I heard it in the pub.'

Trevor Lamb, convicted five years ago for the murder of his wife, was today granted a free pardon ...

Dolly had heard it too. His *wife*. They hadn't even said Daphne's name.

'A pardon. The man kills our daughter, does five bloody years in gaol, some bleeding-heart lawyer writes some book and the bloody governor says fine, okay, fair enough, you poor suffering bastard. All you did was kill your wife. You're free to go.'

He paused. 'Well? Haven't you got anything to say? Just going to stand there like a stuffed mummy?'

She licked her dry lips. 'They say he didn't do it. Trevor Lamb.'

It was hard for her get her tongue around the name. She hadn't spoken it for five years. Her voice sounded strange to her. Cracked and faint. She went on looking at her hands. Suddenly they seemed strange to her, too. Like someone else's hands. They were old and wrinkled, like little claws. And the nails were ridged and ugly. She stared. She used to have such pretty nails. She remembered. When did they change? How long had they been like this? Surely, only yesterday . . .

Or was it Daphne's hands she was remembering? Daphne's smooth, capable little woman's hands, helping with the washing up, leading Emperor to the stable, tilting a milky bottle to feed a motherless lamb, turning the pages of a magazine, feeding the chooks, brushing her mother's limp hair back from her forehead, out of her eyes. *Don't frown, Mum. You'll get wrinkles.*

'Didn't do it? Of course he bloody did it.' Her husband's voice roared around her ears, coarse, full of hard rage and pain. 'I should've killed the bastard. I knew it. I should've killed him then. That idiot brother of his reckons he's coming back here. To Hope's End. Tomorrow. And I'll tell you what, Dolly. If he does. If he does . . .'

Dolly Hewitt stared at her hands. Wet brown claws among the potato skins in the sink.

The man made a stifled, growling sound. And left her.

Annie Lamb eased her vast bulk down on the verandah step and poured sweet sherry into a teacup. 'Cheers, Trev,' she said aloud, and filled her mouth. She swilled the sweet liquid deliciously around her bare gums before letting it slip like warm honey down her throat.

It was still hot on the verandah, this late afternoon, but not nearly as hot as it was inside the house. There you could hardly breathe. Even the flies had given up the ghost. They were just crawling around.

Bloody scorcher, Annie thought to herself, flapping the loose top of her flowery dress to cool herself off. A bloody scorcher. Hope it's nicer tomorrow, for Trev.

Sweat was trickling down between her huge breasts, tickling like ants. She rubbed at it, then noticed a torn magazine lying on the verandah boards, right next to her hand. She took another drink. This time she swallowed it straight down.

She heard a slight scuffle under the steps, and thought vaguely of snakes. Her toes, bare and wide in rubber thongs, curled. But then she realised it was only Jason.

'I can see up your dress, Grandma,' he said, and guffawed with fake cartoon laughter.

'I'll tan your hide for you, you cheeky little bugger,' Annie retorted automatically. 'Get out of there. Where's your mum?'

'Gone to the pub. She and uncle Punchy went. Before. And Uncle Keith and Lily. And Grace.'

Annie took another drink. 'No one said anything to me,' she mumbled. So they'd all gone off and left their old mum to rot. Today, of all days. She was supposed to cook the tea all on her own, was she?

'You were asleep,' said Jason. He wriggled out from under the verandah and made a face. 'You were snoring. It sounded disgusting.'

'Is that so?' Annie rubbed her mouth. She looked around at the front yard of the house, the familiar litter of rotting wood, kids' toys, rusting car bodies and bottles. It's a sad old place, now, she thought. Was a time it had more life. When Miltie was alive. And the kids were little. My word, the old place jumped in those days.

The kids. Nine of them, she'd had. Not counting the miscarriages. Three of those. Or was it four? No wonder she'd put on a bit of fat.

She squinted at the yard, peopling it with the ghost children of the past. She frowned with concentration, getting them in order. It was important to get them in order. Otherwise she sometimes forgot one.

There by the old cow bail was Bridget, the oldest, freckled face serious, long brown plaits swinging, ordering all the others around. Then there was Mickey, knobbly-kneed with bright red hair. No one knew where that hair came from. Miltie had given her a few hard looks after Mickey came along.

Annie grinned to herself. Those were the days.

'Grandma?' It was Jason again. She waved him away impatiently. She wanted to finish this.

There was Johnny, little and dark like a monkey,

balancing on the home fence, or what was left of it. And Brett, sandy and solid like his grandfather, watching him. There was Keith, big for his age, the image of Milton, frowning at Bridget. And by the tank was Cecilia, pink and pretty with tangled fair curls, playing with a bald doll, in a world of her own.

Somewhere at the side, under the old windmill, were Trevor and Rosalie, the twins. Always together, those two, tumbling like puppies. And finally, there was Paul. Quiet, watchful little Paul. Her baby, last of the brood.

She'd have had more, but Milton wasn't keen. Wasn't keen on much at all after that last spell in gaol. Except sitting around in the pub, drinking beer. Hardly came near her. Lost his confidence, she always thought.

So little Paul was the last. Paul. Punchy, they called him now. She never should have let him go in for that boxing business. The money wasn't worth it.

He was still at home, anyhow. That was one thing. More than you could say for most of the others. One by one they'd drifted off and left her.

They didn't know where Mickey was. He could be dead, for all she knew. Disappeared after a fight with his father at sixteen, and never came back.

Bridget—her big girl, her firstborn—was the next to go. Thanks to that interfering bitch Dolly Hewitt filling her head with a lot of shit about bettering herself. Bettering herself? Who was Dolly Hewitt to decide what was best for Bridget? Just because Dolly had been a schoolteacher and had a la-di-da voice, and hooked that rich bastard Les Hewitt for a husband, did that make her God Almighty?

Annie filled her mouth with sherry, gulped it down.

Bridget was married to some tight-arsed newsagent up north. She had kids, but she never came down to Hope's End. Sent a card at Christmas. *Love from Bridget, Brian, Holly and Therese.* That was all they ever heard of Bridget. Didn't even know her address.

Brett was a wanderer. He came back now and then. When he ran out of money. He'd been in the nick quite a bit. He'd always had bad luck, Brett.

Cecilia had gone off to the city the year after her father and Johnny were killed in the ute. Same year Rosalie had Jason, as Annie recalled. Eight years ago. Or nine. Cecilia kept in touch at first, then got religion. Some oddball thing where they shave their heads and don't eat meat. Seemed a shame. Cecilia had such beautiful hair. And she'd always had a good appetite. Anyway, they hadn't heard from her for years.

So now the family had shrunk to Annie, Keith and that hard little tart Lily he was shacked up with, Rosalie and her two kids, Grace and Jason, Paul . . . and Trevor.

Annie shifted on the step. She'd almost forgotten. Tomorrow, Trevor would be back.

'D'you know your Uncle Trev's coming home tomorrow?' she asked Jason. He was just a kid, but he was the only person she had to talk to at present.

'Course I do,' he sniffed, and spat on the ground, like an American baseball hero. 'Mum said. That's why they've gone to the pub. To celebrate. They made me stay here, to tell you. Get you to come. When you woke up.'

She stared at him. He looked a bit blurred around the edges. Sherry's not the best in the hot sun, she thought. I should remember that.

'Why didn't you tell me, then?'

'I tried to, but you wouldn't listen,' the child whined. 'You just waved at me.'

Annie screwed the cap on the sherry flagon and carefully pushed the empty teacup behind the verandah post. She stood up, pulling her dress down where it stuck to her sweaty body.

'Well, we'll go now, then,' she said. 'Bugger tea, eh?'

'Bugger tea,' he nodded, brightening up. 'We can have chips at the pub. To celebrate.'

She nodded, and began picking her way across the yard, her thongs flip-flopping on her heels. Jason danced around her, urging her to hurry, but she didn't bother. It wasn't far to the pub. And there was plenty of time.

'Floury' Baker, the Hope's End publican, had a full house. The locals had started drifting in soon after the four o'clock news. He'd been expecting them. The Lambs, of course. Well, Keith, Lily, Punchy and Rosalie were regulars anyway. But now utes and banged-up Fords crammed the dusty roadside opposite the pub, noses buried in the shade of the pepper trees, tails burning in the sun. There were even a couple of tractors, and Bull Trews' Bobcat. It looked like everyone in the district had had the radio turned on at four. Everyone had heard that Trevor Lamb was getting out. And suddenly they'd all felt thirsty.

'Heard he was coming back here. How does big Sue feel about that?' leered Bull Trews, jerking his head in the barmaid's direction. He pushed two empty glasses across the bar and began feeling for money. 'Two middies, thanks.'

'I wouldn't know,' muttered Baker. He didn't wonder how Bull had heard Lamb was coming back to Hope's End. News spread around here like spilt machine oil. One minute it was a small puddle. Next it was all over the place. He pulled the beers, slammed them down onto the draining grate, filled them up again and pushed them across the bar. He swept Bull's pile of coins into his hand and turned to get the change. There were no tips in the Hope's End pub.

Bull Trews only had a few front teeth, but he showed them all as he turned away with his drinks. 'Betcha looking forward to tomorrow night, Sue,' he yelled. 'Been a while, has it?'

Sue Sweeney, buxom and sweating behind the bar, ignored him. But her cheeks, neck and plump cleavage, already red with the heat, began to burn.

Floury remembered how she'd looked when the radio report came through. And when, just after, Punchy Lamb came in shouting that the Lambs had had a phone call, and Trevor was coming home.

She hadn't gone red, then, but pale. Dead pale. He'd thought she was going to faint. And it wasn't because Les Hewitt was in the pub, either. Though God knows it was a nasty enough moment, watching Les's face close in, and his fists double up, as Punchy went on and on, grinning like he'd just won the lottery.

There was nothing you could say to Les. He'd just got up and left, leaving his glass half-full on the bar. Going home to tell poor Dolly, probably. Or just getting away quick, before he did something he'd regret.

There was a sour, heavy feeling in Floury's stomach as he lumbered around, pulling beers mechanically, taking money, pushing over change. Every now and then he'd look secretly at Sue, working feverishly, tense-mouthed and bright-eyed, twin patches of dark sweat spreading under the arms of her tight, yellow blouse.

Not that he cared about Sue. Not any more. She could do what she liked with Trevor Lamb. Why not? She did it with everyone else.

Six years ago, when she'd first come here, he'd cared. Not about her, maybe, thinking back. But her big, soft tits, her heavy, clinging thighs, her willing, experienced mouth— God, he'd cared about those.

Sue Sweeney did things for him and to him that Cheryl wouldn't have dreamed of doing. God, by the time he and Cheryl had been married six months it was as much as he could do to get her to let him pull her nightie up on a Saturday night. And then she'd just lie there with her eyes shut, waiting for it to be over. No wonder, considering what she was. But he hadn't known about that till she left. Then it had hit him like a truck.

That whole thing had shattered him. Made him feel like half a man. Everyone had heard about it, too. Annie Lamb saw to that, however much Keith tried to shut her up. Every farmhand and fencer within cooee of Hope's End sniggered about it, behind his back. They never said anything to him, of course, when they came into the pub. But he knew, by the looks on their faces. Curious. Superior. Pitying. That's the poor bastard whose wife . . .

After a while he'd realised that he had to get someone to replace Cheryl behind the bar. He couldn't manage on his own. So he advertised. And along came Sue Sweeney.

He thought she'd be a good barmaid when he hired her. And she was. Much better than Cheryl. Cheryl had never really liked pub work. She used to get sharp and bad-tempered on pension days when the place was full. Sue was different. She liked a crowd.

She settled in behind the Hope's End bar as if she'd been born there. She wisecracked with the locals as if she'd known them all her life. And in the room he gave her, the one built over the old stable he used as a garage, she quickly taught him a thing or two. Within a fortnight he was counting himself lucky that Cheryl had gone. He thought he'd finally found out what life for a man could be.

It was like a porn movie come true. He was like an old brown dog with a bitch in heat all to himself. He went

around in a dream for months. Made a fool of himself.
Couldn't keep his hands off her.

She got bored with him after a while. She wanted to
ease off. There were all sorts of little hints and signs. He felt
it, but wouldn't admit it. If he'd held back a bit it might have
been different, he thought later. But he was drunk with her.
Out of control.

He started buying her things in town. Little glass vases
and jewellery and scent. Flowers, even. She said she didn't
want them but he pressed them on her, going to her room
night after night, after closing time. He could see himself
now, crossing the yard, hurrying up the stairs to the room
over the garage, with his latest offering in one hand and his
throbbing cock, so to speak, in the other.

She must have been sick of the sight of him by then.
Wondered what she'd got herself into. But she never told him
to piss off. She took what came laughing, like she took
everything, good and bad, in those days. Took whatever he
had to give those nights, pushed him down on the bed,
ripped off her gear and climbed all over him, while he buried his face deliriously in warm, scented tits, belly, thighs
and bum.

He'd realised since that she was making a game of it.
Keeping herself interested. Paying the price. Maybe she
thought he'd chuck her out if she knocked him back.

Then Trevor Lamb started making a line for her. He'd
only been married to Daphne a year and a half then, if that.
And Sue and Daphne had got pretty matey as well. But that
didn't stop him. Or Sue, as it turned out.

Floury remembered the night he'd caught them. He'd
gone out the back, into the yard, for something. To get another keg, maybe. He never could remember.

It was the sight he could remember. Sue Sweeney bent
over, with her hands against the pub wall, skirt bunched up
round her waist, white skin gleaming in the dark. And
Trevor Lamb, slim and black-haired, gripping her hips with
hard, brown hands, pumping away at her like a machine.

They'd heard him. He'd probably groaned aloud.

Floury's stomach churned. Even now the memory made
the sweat pop out on his forehead. The agony of it. The
shame. Sue, looking around, her mouth making an *o* of
shock, then trying to say something to him while there she

was bent over bare-arsed and pinned to the wall. Trevor Lamb grinning, white teeth shining, hips thrusting, never pausing for a second.

'Just on the vinegar strokes, mate,' he'd leered. 'Give us a chance, will ya?'

Floury had turned on his heel, then, and gone back inside. He went on serving drinks like nothing had happened. He didn't turn his head to look at Sue when she came back to the bar a few minutes later. Inside him something had shrivelled, like a weed touched by fire.

Sue stayed on. Why not? She was a good barmaid. Why cut off his nose to spite his face? He wouldn't ever talk to her about what happened. He just left her alone.

She went on seeing Trevor Lamb. On the quiet, because of Daphne. But he'd often see Trevor slinking out of the flat over the garage late at night. Fair enough. It was nothing to do with him.

Then Daphne was dead. Little Daphne Lamb. Daphne Hewitt, that was. And Floury had stood on the street with everyone else and watched Trevor Lamb being driven away, across the bridge, out of town. When he turned back to the pub there was Sue, standing by the door, looking like she'd been smacked across the face.

He'd never talked to her about it. Never talked to anyone. Left the talking to other people. Most of them thought Lamb had done the murder, no risk. He was a bad bastard. Everyone knew that. Some thought he hadn't, or said they thought he hadn't. All the Lambs for a start. Well, you'd expect that. The Lambs always stuck together.

He and Sue had had to testify at the trial. They'd had to go to the city for it. He'd had to close the pub for a day and a half. Didn't matter much. Most of the regulars were in the city too, for the same reason.

Sue wore her blue suit and white blouse in court. With navy-blue high-heeled shoes, and a little gold brooch pinned to the lapel of the jacket. The same outfit she'd worn to her job interview with him. She looked nice in it. But she still got a hard time from the prosecution. She got made to look like a slut. Trevor Lamb's whore. Fair enough.

No one gave Floury a hard time. His evidence was all about times when people arrived at the pub and left again. Nothing much was made of anything he said. He was glad he hadn't had to give important evidence against Lamb. Or for him, either. It would have been bad for business either way, the mood the locals were in.

And it wasn't necessary. It was plain as the nose on your face that Lamb was for the high jump. Obvious right from the start. He looked like real bad bastard up there in the dock. Like a thug, for all his good looks. The best his defence could do was say that some thief must have crept into town and killed Daphne. Her diamond ring was missing. But most people round here knew that Daphne's jewellery had all been sold to pay bills and keep Trevor in beer. And anyhow, no stranger had drifted into town that night. If one had, everyone at the pub would have seen him coming across the bridge. That theory was never going to hold water.

Then Dolly Hewitt told about how Trevor had given Daphne a black eye and a cut lip once, and a sprained wrist another time, and that just about finished it. Trevor denied laying a finger on Daphne, but the prosecution had the doctor from Gunbudgie in to testify as well. So that was that.

Floury had hoped Trevor Lamb would rot in gaol and then in hell. And now he was coming back.

TWO

Keith Lamb, Rosalie Lamb and Lily Danger sat outside the pub, on the log that served as verandah seating. It was their usual spot. Everyone else knew it, and kept away. They'd sent Punchy in for more drinks, but he'd been gone awhile.

'Jesus, it's hot,' said Lily. 'It'll be like the hobs of hell in that caravan tonight. We should be sleeping at the shack. It's much cooler closer to the creek.'

Keith didn't say anything. Lily knew why they couldn't sleep in the shack. The shack was Trevor's, and Rosalie's. Always had been. Dad had given it to them when they were kids and the place was just an old wreck with a leaky roof. As far as Mum was concerned, that ended it, even if the shack was quite liveable now. With electricity and everything.

'Lying empty for five bloody years while we swelter every summer and freeze every winter.' Lily wasn't going to let it alone.

'Well, it won't be empty tomorrow night, will it?' he heard himself saying. He drained his glass, to stop himself saying any more.

It was beyond him how Lily could even want to move into the bloody shack. Bloody. That was about the size of it. The place would still stink of blood to him, whatever Mum and Rosalie had done to clean it up.

He'd said that to Lily once, and she'd sent him up gutless. Called him a wimp. But she hadn't seen what he'd seen in that kitchen five years ago.

Trev had, though. And Trev was set on moving back into the place. Straight off, too. He'd told them when they talked to him on the phone this afternoon. Right after saying that Jude, the lawyer who got him off, was bringing him home tomorrow, and there was going to be a TV show about him.

They hadn't heard his voice in years. It was strange. He'd sounded different. Talked like a professor, or something. He made Rosalie write down what he said, as if otherwise they were going to forget what he wanted them to do.

Maybe it was that university course he did in gaol. Or spending too much time with that Jude Gregorian bloke who was bringing him home. They seemed to have got pretty thick over the years. And Jude, Saint Jude, one of the papers had called him, had a plummy sort of voice.

They hadn't even heard of Jude Gregorian till a few years ago. That was when he'd turned up in Hope's End with a letter for them from Trev. The letter said Jude was some lawyer who wanted to get Trev out of gaol. Said it was okay to talk to him.

It hadn't seemed likely he could do much. He hadn't looked too prosperous. Skinny, foreign-looking bloke. But they'd all talked to him anyway. He'd been good for a few drinks.

Then he'd gone and they'd more or less forgotten about him. Till Trev sent Rosalie a copy of this book called *Lamb to the Slaughter*. Jude Gregorian had written it, and it was about Trev. Trev's letter said that Jude reckoned the book might help. Start a campaign going, or something.

They'd all read bits of the book. Even Mum. It gave you a funny feeling, reading about things you knew, people and places and things that had happened, printed in a book. Their names were all there. Even young Jason got a mention, because he was with Rosalie and Grace when they found Trev knocked out in his car, and Daphne dead.

That was all in the first few chapters, though. After that it got to be hard going. Lots of stuff about times, and fingerprints, and all the tools and junk that had been tested for being the murder weapon and weren't, and all that. Then stuff about all these other murders, where the cops had lumbered the wrong person. Keith hadn't bothered reading all that. Everyone knew what the cops were like. It was no news to him that they set blokes up.

You didn't really have to read the book to know what

this Jude bloke was going on with, anyhow. It was all written on the back cover, under his picture. He thought Trev
hadn't killed Daphne, and he thought he should be let out.
Thought Trev got lumbered just because the judge and jury
didn't like the look of him. It was no more than Mum had
been saying ever since Trev got done.

At the time Lily reckoned this Jude Gregorian was just
big-noting. Using Trev to make a name for himself. And
money. People who wrote books got paid for it, didn't they?
And whatever he'd told Trev, there was no way some lawyer's book could get a bloke out of the nick when he'd been
sent down for twenty years for murder.

Keith had seen Jude Gregorian on TV a few times over
the years since then. Once talking about Trev, and other
times talking about other things. You couldn't understand
half what he said. Wouldn't know if his arse was on fire.
That had been what Keith thought of him when he first
met him, and nothing that had happened since had changed
his mind.

But people in the city thought different, it seemed. In the
end it all happened just like Jude had told Trev it would.
People started getting all stirred up about Trev being in gaol
when there hadn't been any proof he'd done anything.

Not round here, though. People round here had made
up their minds one way or the other a long time ago, and no
book by some poofy city lawyer was going to change their
minds. Or stuff on TV, or in the papers. Or questions in
Parliament.

There was a big petition, it said on the radio. No one in
Hope's End was ever asked to sign a petition. The last petition round here was when Les Hewitt got one up ten years
ago, for a new bridge over the creek. And that had been
about as useful as tits on a bull. All that happened was that
the council sent a couple of blokes to nail the old timber one
back together.

It was falling to bits again in six months, of course. Timber was rotten. One day someone'd go right through that
bridge. That was the only way anything was ever going to be
done about it.

But the petition about Trev did better. A lot better. And
it turned out Lily was wrong about Jude Gregorian. He
hadn't been bullshitting. It took a few years, but in the end

his book—plus the talk, and the petition and the TV interviews and everything else—got Trev out of gaol. And tomorrow he was driving Trev back to Hope's End.

That was the reason for the instructions. Trev wanted them to fix it for Saint Jude to stay at the pub overnight. Plus get a separate room for the ABC tart, who was coming to do something or other about the TV show, and would be staying a few days.

Jude Gregorian and Verity Birdwood. God! Who'd have names like that? Trev spelt them out to Rosalie. Made her read them back to him, as if it mattered. Took her four or five tries to get them right. And what for? Floury Baker wouldn't care what their names were, as long as they paid the tab.

Mum had been disappointed. She'd expected Trev to come and stay in the old house with her and Punchy and Rosalie and the kids. At least for a while. But she reckoned she understood why he wouldn't.

'He wants to settle back into his own place, his old place, after all those years away,' she said. 'They're like that. Your dad was. And you know how Brett always is when he comes home. Won't sleep in the house. Likes his old spot in the corner of the verandah. Mozzies and all. It's his, see. What he remembers.'

Rosalie said she didn't know how he could do it, all the same. She said the thought of the place made her sick now. She'd gone in with Mum to clean it up after the cops were finished with it. But she'd never set foot in it again after that.

Keith hadn't either.

It wasn't like blood worried him normally. He'd slaughtered lambs, plenty of them. Butchered them, too. He'd even worked at the abattoir for a while, once, when he'd been married. Yvonne had badgered him into it. Sick of living on dole money, she said. Sick of living in the old house with Mum and the others.

So for a couple of months he'd worked up to his knees in blood and guts. He hadn't minded that. It was turning up every day that gave him the shits. Being ordered round by a soft-bellied bastard who thought he was scum. He didn't worry too much about the other. The lambs dying. The sound and smell of it. The skinned bodies, dripping on his boots. That's what the beasts were bred for. It was just a job.

But Daphne lying there on the kitchen floor with her

head caved in—and the blood, in a sticky pool, slowly sinking into the old boards . . . God, that was something else.

And Trev had seen it, too. But he was coming back. To live in the shack. Just like nothing had ever happened there.

Trevor always had been a tough, mean bastard. It was like when he and Rosalie were born he got all the hard, and Rosalie got all the soft. Look at her now, staring at the creek like she'd never seen it before.

Always in a dream, Rosalie. You'd wonder how she'd got herself pregnant. Twice. And no father for either of the little bastards. Well, none she'd put a name to. Lily said once that Rosalie probably couldn't remember who'd done her over. She probably slept through the whole thing, both times.

He'd laughed. But then he'd felt a touch of anger. Lily shouldn't talk about his sister like that. She wasn't any genius, but she had a good heart, Rosalie.

'We should have been using the shack all this time,' Lily said, tossing her head so that the little gold crosses dangling from her ears flicked against her jawbone. It was a thing she did when she was irritated. 'All you had to do was tell your fat cow of a mother to stick it. Just tell her we were moving in. We could have set ourselves up. Been comfortable.'

'Too late now,' mumbled Keith.

'Why? We could move in tonight, before Trevor gets here. What's he going to do, throw us out?'

'Yes,' Keith said simply.

He watched her disbelieving sneer. She didn't know Trevor. Thought she did, but she didn't. Trev'd been on his best behaviour when he met her at the pub the day she turned up in town cuddled up to that baldy feed-truck driver who'd picked her up.

She gave that bloke the arse. Wouldn't leave with him. Liked it better at the pub, she said. No wonder. Everyone had just got their dole money, and it was payday for the farmhands. She never had to buy a single drink for herself all afternoon, all night.

Trev went after her like everyone else. He must have decided he needed a change from old Sue Sweeney. And Lily was young. Real young. Spiky blonde hair with black roots, tight little patterned pants disappearing up the crack in her bum, skinny singlet affair with nipples poking through, a tattoo of a bluebird on her wrist.

When it came to closing time it turned out she didn't have any money anyhow. Didn't have anywhere to sleep. Trust Lily. She had plenty of offers, but Floury said she could have a bed upstairs if she wanted. It was no skin off his nose. The rooms were all empty, as per usual. And she was good for business.

She'd told them she was sixteen when they asked her, but she could've been even younger. Even now, after five years, Keith wasn't sure. She'd hardly changed at all, except for a few little lines under her eyes and a new tattoo she got herself in Gunbudgie a couple of years ago. Another blue-bird. On the inside of her ankle this time.

Her age was one of the things she'd never told him. She'd never told him where she came from, either. Said she wanted to forget it. All he knew about her really was her name. Lily Danger. It suited her, but sometimes he wondered if she'd made it up.

It was like she'd never existed before she came to Hope's End. Just appeared, looked about for a bit, then latched onto Keith, whipped her tail, and wriggled under his skin.

But that was after Trev had gone. Lily never had a chance to find out what a bad bastard he could be when he wasn't trying to get his end in. Her first night in town was the night Daphne was killed. And the next day Trev had been arrested and taken away. She'd never believed he killed Daphne. That was about the only thing she, Mum and Rosalie had ever agreed on.

'Are you scared of Trevor, or something?' Lily smiled, a cat's smile. 'He's six years younger than you, too, isn't he? Same age as Rosalie? Might still have a bit of life left in him. Hey, maybe I took up with the wrong brother. What d'you reckon?' She went on smiling, running her fingers through her boy-cut hair.

He looked at her. 'Guess we'll find out tomorrow, eh?' he said. He turned to look for Punchy with the drinks, bellowing at him to hurry, hunching his shoulders against her mocking laughter.

Rosalie Lamb sipped her beer and stared at the dirt of the road, the grey timbers of the bridge, the slow-moving water of the creek.

She was aware of Keith and Lily arguing beside her, her daughter Grace giggling with some bloke, her leg tucked up behind her as she leaned against a verandah post, Punchy laughing loudly at some joke inside the pub door. It was like flies buzzing. Dull, familiar, meaningless.

Trevor was coming home tomorrow. After five years, coming home.

She'd thought she'd never see him again. Twenty years—that had seemed like forever. She hadn't been able to imagine him turning up in Hope's End after twenty years—a middle-aged man with grey hair. And her on her way to looking like Mum, probably, by then. Except she'd keep her teeth. No matter what else she lost.

She looked down at her bare legs, stretched out in front of her. The hems of her old checked shorts were cutting slightly into her thighs, making the soft flesh bulge. There was a patch of tiny blue veins on one of her calves. She'd got that when she was carrying Jason. There was another one high on her right thigh, at the side, but it was hidden under the shorts. Like the stretch marks. Jason had been a big baby. Not like Grace. She'd been small. Small and neat and perfect, like a doll.

Rosalie turned her head to look at her daughter. Grace was fingering her glossy black hair, arching her back against the verandah post so that her small breasts stuck out through the thin cotton of her skimpy dress. The boy with her, bare-chested, jeans hanging low on his hips, watched her, still and intent, while the beer warmed in his hand.

She'll be at it soon, if she's not already, Rosalie thought vaguely. I should do something about it. Condoms. She knows about them, from school. Plus the pill, maybe, whatever Mum says. Still, it seems young. Fourteen. I was only a year older than that when I had her. But it was different for me.

Different for me . . . Her thoughts veered, scattered.

'There's Mum and Jason,' she heard Keith say.

'Great.' That was Lily, sour as usual. Lily the bitch. Why Keith kept her around, Rosalie didn't know. Or why Lily stayed, for that matter. She never acted as though she loved Keith, or even liked him much. Not in public, anyway. What they did locked up in the caravan at night was another matter.

'She's got him by the balls,' Mum said sometimes, when Keith and Lily had got up from the table at night and gone, leaving them with the greasy dishes to clear away.

Punchy would grin, and pat his crutch. 'By the balls,' he'd echo.

Jason and Grace would snort with laughter.

'Don't you kids laugh at your uncle,' Mum would mumble, aiming a half-hearted swipe at them and missing by a mile. 'You get out to the kitchen and start clearing up. Go on!'

The kids wouldn't go of course. No one really expected they would.

'She's a prize bitch,' Rosalie would spit, full of hatred for Lily's sharp little face, boyish bleached hair and taut, skinny body. She'd had five years of Lily, and it was five years too many. She despised Keith for putting up with her.

Mum would shrug, draining her glass, pouring another. 'Ah, well. Poor old Keith. Got to have someone, hasn't he?'

'Why?' Rosalie would grumble. 'I haven't. Punchy hasn't.'

'Don't you worry about Punchy. Punchy does all right for himself, don't you, love?' Annie Lamb winked at her youngest, who grinned uncertainly, gnawing a chop bone.

'What about me?'

'It's different for women. And anyhow, you've got the kids,' Annie would say, as if that ended it.

But it didn't. Not for Rosalie.

Three

A world away from Hope's End, Verity Birdwood packed a bag. She had mixed feelings about this job. Had had mixed feelings for weeks, ever since she was asked to do it.

'Birdie? Beth. Listen, mate, aren't you a friend of Jude Gregorian's?' That was how Beth Bothwell had started, as soon as Birdie picked up the phone. Typically straight to the point.

'I used to be,' Birdie had said cautiously. 'We did law together. But I haven't seen him for years. If you're thinking you can use me to get a Trevor Lamb interview for you, you're . . .'

'It's practically a certainty anyway, Birdie. We know Jude favours the ABC. He told Ziggy at the last press conference. We just need to clinch it. And I thought a personal apporoach . . .'

'The other networks'll be waving chequebooks, Beth. And they'll back off if he does something with you. Unless you're happy to be second cab off the rank."

'Of course we're not. We've got to be first.'

'Well, you're stuffed. Whatever Jude thinks, I can't see Trevor Lamb knocking back big bucks to do the ABC a favour.'

'That's the beauty of it, mate. Lamb doesn't need money. But he wants respectability. And that means us.'

'What d'you *mean* he doesn't need money? That's bloody ridiculous, Beth. He hasn't got a bean, has he? Doesn't his whole family live on social security?'

'More or less. But what I mean is, he doesn't need money *now*. He's going to write a book. That's what Jude told Ziggy. Jude organised the contract—I forget who with—one of the multinationals, anyway. Lamb's got some huge advance. And later on there'll be serialisation rights, TV rights, and—'

'Beth, if Lamb's writing a book he won't talk now. You know that. He'll waffle. He'll keep all the good stuff for the book.'

'I'll take what I can get. And that's Trevor Lamb, home again in Hope's End after all those years unjustly locked in jug. The tragic antihero. Free at last. Breathing the sweet, country air. Yellow ribbons round the old gum tree. The old pub looks the same. Dear old Mum . . .'

'Beth, have you *seen* Trevor Lamb's mother?'

'Birdie, stop being negative. Just do it for me, will you? Get in touch with Gregorian. Set it up. Tell him we won't interfere with the actual homecoming. We'll send you to research the piece, so everyone will feel comfortable before the crew arrives. A nice, gentle piece. That's all we want.'

'What if Lamb isn't released?'

'He will be. It's a dead cert.'

'What if he refuses to go back to Hope's End? Why should he put his head in that noose, just for you?'

'He wants to go back *himself*. That's the point. Think I'd have suggested the going home thing if he didn't? He wants to go back to Hope's End, move back into his shack, and pick up life where he left off. They're keeping it quiet, but that's what Jude told Ziggy . . . Birdie, are you there?'

'He's going to *live* there? In Hope's End? In the house where his wife was murdered? With her parents living a stone's throw away, and them and half the rest of the town thinking he should have been lynched?'

'That's the reason he's doing it. He wants to rub their noses in it. That's what he's like. A conceited, aggro prick. A real, dyed-in-the-wool bastard. God, Birdie, where've you been? A man who'd beat his pregnant wife to death is capable of—'

'Beth, he's supposed to be innocent!'

'Oh, well.' Birdie could almost see Beth shrugging her square shoulders. 'Whatever. Innocent or guilty, he's still a bastard. You can tell just by looking at him.'

'Should be a fun job.'

'You'll do it then? Good! Ring me as soon as you've spoken to Jude. Home or at work. Okay? Thanks, mate. You're a ripper. Bye.'

So that was that. Birdie had hung up with the strong feeling that she'd let herself in for something she'd regret. And yet—she couldn't deny she was fascinated, too. She'd always had her own ideas about the Trevor Lamb case. And, of course, there was Jude.

Jude. She'd looked up his number and called straight away, before she lost her nerve. It was something she never liked—ringing up people after a long time, just because you wanted something.

Jude was in his early thirties now. He wore well-cut suits, and sober ties. For television interviews, anyway. How many times had she seen his lean, dark face on TV lately, arguing some case or putting some point? He sat on government committees, he ran a busy practice, he went to court, presumably, in a wig and gown. Yet he still argued with all the fervour of the young idealist she remembered. Still lashed out at supercilious opposition in flaming anger. Fiery eyes, gesticulating hands, leaning forward in his chair, his heart on his sleeve and his ferocious intellect undimmed—on TV he was the Jude she'd always known, unchanged.

Was he still like that really?

She'd been rather relieved to find him unavailable. 'In court,' the woman who answered the phone said, in rather hushed, reverential tones. Birdie had left her name and number, hung up, and gone out to meet a client of her own. A woman who wanted her teenage daughter tracked down.

But he'd rung back, at seven that night. She could tell by the background noise that he was still in the office.

'Birdie!' His voice was warm. Just the same.

'Hi, Jude. Thanks for calling back.' She'd hesitated. Didn't quite know the best note to strike, now he was actually there, at the end of the phone. But he'd taken it out of her hands. As, she remembered, he almost always had.

'What d'you mean, "thanks for calling back"? Of course I'd call back. How the hell are you? How's work?'

'Pretty good. You?' She cursed the automatic response. Stupid question. Everyone knew how work was with Jude

Gregorian. Saint Jude. Patron lawyer of hopeless cases. And with Trevor Lamb's release . . .

'Great! You know it's almost a certainty Trevor Lamb's going to be out by the end of the month.'

'Yeah. I heard it was on the cards. Congratulations, Jude. You finally did it.'

'Yeah. It was a hard slog, but we got there in the end.'

Typical of Jude to put it that way. 'We got there.' As if he and he alone hadn't been the driving force that had pushed the Free Trevor Lamb campaign to its (still potentially, but fairly assuredly) successful conclusion.

'*You* did it, you mean, Jude.'

'Oh, well . . .' His voice trailed off awkwardly. Birdie grinned to herself. The guy really hadn't changed. He'd always been as embarrassed by praise as other people were by criticism. Couldn't take a compliment to save his life.

But he was fast on his feet. He recovered quickly. He was doing it now.

'Hey, Birdie, it's great you got in touch. It's so good to hear your voice. Can we have lunch?'

Again, she found herself hesitating. She could almost hear Beth's voice hissing over her shoulder. *Yes! Great! You're in! Say yes to lunch. Chat, chat. Bottle of wine. Old times. Work the interview idea in at the end. You'll have him, then. How can he refuse?*

But she couldn't do it. Not with Jude. She couldn't bring herself to see him after all this time on what amounted to false pretences. Being devious and 'professional' with Jude would be like being devious with herself.

'I wanted to talk to you about Trevor Lamb,' she heard herself saying bluntly. 'About an interview.'

'Ah—yes, of course.' She could almost see him settling back a little in his chair, adjusting his mind-set. Personal to professional. She was conscious of a faint, sinking feeling of regret. Whatever happened now she'd shifted something delicate. Intruded on her own past. Changed an intact, remembered relationship, for good.

She hadn't thought of that, quite, when she'd agreed to phone him. She hadn't, till this moment, realised how important was the small chunk of her consciousness labelled 'Jude Gregorian and me.' It would have been better, far better, to leave it set in amber.

'But listen, I didn't think you worked for the ABC any more,' Jude was saying. 'I was sure I read . . .'

So he knew what she'd been doing. Now it was her turn to adjust. He'd always been so single-minded. She'd imagined he'd have been too caught up in his own doings to note the odd newspaper paragraph mentioning her name.

He'd thought she was wasting her talents when she was a full-time ABC researcher. What must he think of her now she was a private investigator, half the time working hand in glove with the police he so despised? Detective-Sergeant Dan Toby, the cop with whom she was most frequently linked, had actually worked on a couple of the cases Jude had later taken up. She could just imagine Jude's opinion of Dan.

Yet he'd still sounded pleased to hear from her. She hadn't been imagining the genuine warmth in his voice.

'I still do freelance research, as well as the other,' she said quickly. 'Mostly for the ABC. They mainly use me for documentaries now. They want to do something with Trevor Lamb. Well, you know that. They asked me to try to firm it up with you.'

Because we're old friends. Because we're part of each other's pasts. Because they thought I might have influence over you. They're using me as a tool to get what they want. They don't care about you, or me, or Trevor Lamb. They just want an interview that'll rate, and unlike the commercial channels they can't pay for it. They're expecting me to manipulate you into agreeing.

'Ah—right.'

He understood perfectly.

There was a short pause. Birdie waited for the hedging to start. The mention of other offers. The promises to think about it, discuss it with Trevor, get back to Beth or Ziggy in due course.

'Well—all the more reason to have lunch, eh?' said Jude. 'We could talk about it then. See what we can work out. Unless you're too flat out, or anything.'

She was dumbfounded. 'No. I'm fine. Lunch is fine.'

'Great! Let's make a time. Hold on.'

She heard the flipping of pages. He was looking in his diary. She glanced around for hers. It was buried in a sea of paper. Still, it didn't really matter. She had no appointments that couldn't be cancelled or reorganised.

'Birdie?' His voice was slightly muffled, as though he was holding the phone against his ear with a hunched shoulder. 'How about the day after tomorrow?'

'Sure. No problem. Where?'

'The Greek place? Twelve-thirty? Or—is the Greek place okay with you? Would you rather—'

'Oh, the Greek place's fine. Fine. But are you sure it's still there?'

He laughed. 'I go there at least once a week. And every time, I think about you.'

She wouldn't have dreamed he'd given her a thought for years.

He was talking again. 'Birdie, I've got to go. My appointment's arrived. All right? See you at the Hellas, twelve-thirty, Thursday.'

'Yeah. Good, Jude. See you then.'

After he'd hung up she'd sat for a minute or two, staring at the phone. Lunch with Jude at the Hellas. It would be like being caught in a time warp.

She jumped as the phone rang again. She answered it cautiously.

'Birdie? Beth. Listen, sorry to hassle you, but I just can't wait. Have you spoken to—'

'Just hung up, as a matter of fact.'

'Well? Well? What did he say?'

'He didn't commit himself. But we're having lunch on Thursday.'

'Yeah? Great! Birdie, you're a treasure. We're in!'

'Not necessarily, Beth. We're just having lunch, for God's sake.'

'You'll get him, mate. I know you will. Chat, chat. Bottle of wine. Old times. And then . . .'

'Beth, I've got to go. I'll call you Thursday. After lunch. Okay? Bye.'

Birdie hung up without waiting for the end of the other woman's surprised farewell. She ran her hands through her mass of curly chestnut hair, then took off her glasses and threw them onto the desk in front of her.

Despite her protestations, she knew Beth was right.

They were in. Jude was going to give her the interview. Over lamb with rice, and a glass of wine, and memories, on Thursday, at the Greek place.

And she had a sinking feeling in the pit of her stomach, just thinking about it. For lots of reasons.

Four

Birdie tossed another shirt into her bag. How many had she put in already? How long was she going to be away? Three days? Four? Beth had said four. Birdie had thought three would be enough. More than enough.

Jude was going to be there, in Hope's End, on day one. Delivering Trevor Lamb to the bosom of his family, introducing her around. But he was going to have to drive back to Sydney early the next morning. He was due in court the following day.

After he'd gone she'd be on her own with Lamb—and his family. She wasn't looking forward to that. She'd spent more than enough time with them, second-hand, lately. For the last couple of weeks, waiting for the pardon to be granted, she'd been refreshing her memory on the Trevor Lamb case.

The bound transcript of the trial and Beth's bulky folder of notes and newspaper clippings lay beside the bag. She'd take those with her. And *Lamb to the Slaughter*, of course. She'd just finished re-reading that.

There was a sense in which she hadn't needed anything else. It was a very good book. She'd been even more impressed with it this time around.

Lamb to the Slaughter was a showcase of all that was impressive about Jude Gregorian—that rare ability to combine passion, idealism, logic and attention to detail. Though unapologetically heartfelt, it was scrupulous. It begged no questions. It suppressed no inconvenient facts or impressions. It made the reader understand why the jury had convicted Trevor Lamb, then carefully explained why it had been wrong.

And it was all the more convincing, paradoxically, because Jude Gregorian plainly didn't like Trevor Lamb. He didn't like him any more than the cops, or the judge and jury had done. It was just that he didn't think dislike was a good enough reason to gaol a man for life.

For Jude, Lamb was an innocent. An unpleasant, drunken, brutish innocent, but an innocent nonetheless. In his view the man was propelled into conviction and imprisonment as callously and inevitably as a fat lamb is carted to the abattoir. Not because of what he had done, but because of what he was. Trevor Lamb's personality and reputation had convicted him, rather than the facts of the case. There wasn't a shred of proof that it was he who had killed his wife. The evidence, such as it was, was wholly circumstantial.

The book set it all out, point by point, mercilessly exposing both the flimsy foundations on which the prosecution's case rested, and the dismal failures of the defence. Most tellingly, Jude had compared the Lamb trial to other notorious trials over the past century in which circumstantial evidence had been sufficient to convince a jury to convict, but after which the convicted accused had proved to be, or been judged to be, innocent. He argued that in every one of these cases the personality, reputation, colour, class, religion, or moral standing of the accused had influenced the police, judge and jury far more than was ever admitted, right or reasonable.

Jude made no excuses for Trevor Lamb. If he detailed Lamb's background—the poverty, the recidivist father, the eight brothers and sisters, the truncated schooling, the family's barren cultural tradition of alcohol, ignorance and petty crime—it was simply to fill in the picture of the man. No one knew better than Jude that it was possible for boys to grow to manhood in distressing or poverty-stricken conditions without becoming criminals, bullies, brutes and drunks. His own family history, confided to Birdie many years ago (over lamb with rice, and a bottle of wine, at the Greek place), had made her almost ashamed of the resentment she still occasionally felt for the debilitating loneliness of her own comfortable, middle-class childhood.

Loneliness? A feeling of difference from her peers? An awkward, unresolved relationship with her mother? What was that compared to the dark, desperate world of the little Armenian boy the other kids called Louis the Fly? With the father, hard hand rendered helpless at last, dying of lung cancer in the front bedroom, and the mother, slaving away on her sewing machine, at piecework, far into the night? Both of them pinning all their hopes on their bright-eyed boy, because there would be no other children? Dying within a year of one another, leaving the child in the cold, slippery hands of the state? Without a relative, a friend, a cent. With nothing. Except hope, ambition, determination and a passion for justice.

She had never felt so self-indulgent, so middle class, as she had that day, when lunch stretched into late afternoon, and Jude talked on and on, across the littered table.

But in a way it had made her understand why it was that two such different people could, at bottom, have so much in common. Why they had drifted together and formed an alliance. Neither of them fitted in. He and she had been oddities together at law school. Both of them had been regarded by most of their peers as unsophisticated, unrealistic and naive.

But their differences had emerged in the end.

Birdie's reaction to the pragmatism and elitism which sickened both of them had been to withdraw from it. She'd qualified, because she didn't like giving up. She refused to be defeated by the smart, smooth, alien other. But then she had abandoned the law without a backward glance.

Jude, by contrast, and characteristically, had charged full tilt at the profession. He wanted to turn it on its head. To challenge it. He wouldn't compromise. He insulted the wrong people. Earned a reputation as a hot-head. A troublemaker. A risk.

Struggling along on occasional legal aid cases, with too much time on his hands, he'd become fascinated by the Trevor Lamb case. To him it represented everything that was wrong with the legal system. And he'd written *Lamb to the Slaughter*. The book that changed his life. And Trevor Lamb's, as it turned out.

Birdie stuffed a spare pair of shoes down into the side of her bag, trying not to crush the shirts, and failing. She glanced at her watch, and sighed. It was getting late. She should call Dan Toby now. Right now, before he left the office. He was going to perform when he heard what she was doing. But there was a chance he'd be a bit more moderate in the office than he would be at home, where there was no one to hear him rave.

She wandered along the corridor to her office at the front of the house. She sat down at her heaped desk and picked up the phone. Then she put it down again. She wasn't looking forward to this.

What had gone wrong with her life? Lately, she seemed to be continually doing things she didn't want to do. She was always on the back foot, somehow. How had it happened?

It's Jude. You should have said no to Beth in the first place. You should have refused to ring him. Why didn't you?

I don't know.

Yes you do. It was because you were curious to see what he was like now, after all this time. You couldn't resist the chance to make contact when it was offered. When you could tell yourself you were doing it because Beth wanted you to. You thought he'd say no to you, and that would be the end of it. You miscalculated. Got it wrong. Now you're stuck. You've only got yourself to blame.

True. Unpalatable, but true. Gloomily, Birdie picked up the phone again, and dialled.

'You're *what*?!'

Birdie held the receiver away from her ear and gazed into space for a moment. She imagined Dan Toby on the other end of the phone. He would be leaning forward on his desk, his face red, pulling savagely at the knot of his tie.

Of course she'd known he'd react like this. Of course. But she'd had to tell him, hadn't she? She couldn't just leave him sitting at the pub waiting for her tomorrow night. Anyway, he'd have found out sooner or later. Better to get it over with.

The furious voice buzzed impotently into the air.

'Birdie! Are you there? Birdie!'

A piercing whistle from the phone. Dan was losing his cool. Further losing his cool.

With a sigh Birdie put the receiver back to her ear. 'Yes?' she said politely.

'Did I hear you right? Did you say you were going to Hope's End?'

'You know I did, Dan. That's why you're yelling. You're upset.'

'Of course I'm bloody upset!'

Birdie winced and put the receiver down on the desk. She looked moodily at the papers scattered there. Mostly bills, some with unpleasantly brief messages. She'd better find a way of paying at least those before she left. Write the cheques tonight. Drop them into a post office on her way to—'

'Birdie, pick me up! *Pick me up!*' quacked the phone.

Birdie ignored it. She began reading one of her other letters.

'Dear Ms Birdwood. Congratulations! You have been chosen to receive ABSOLUTELY FREE, our newest and most outstanding-ever offer . . .'

She sighed, plucked the paper from the desk, and dropped it in the general direction of the overflowing bin.

The voice from the phone went silent, then abruptly changed tone. It became bluff and reasonable. 'Okay, mate. I'm not shouting. All right? Now, stop being childish, will you?'

Birdie grabbed the receiver. 'You're the one being childish, Dan,' she snapped. 'And I haven't got time to argue. I'm in the middle of packing. I'm going to Hope's End to research a profile on Trevor Lamb for the ABC. They asked me to do it, and I'm doing it. End of story.'

'Why you?' The voice was dangerously quiet.

'Because I'm a good researcher, I suppose.'

'Balls! It's because you're on with the bloody dangerous, bleeding-heart, crim-loving shark, Jude Gregorian, isn't it? He set it up for you, didn't he?'

'Dan, is anyone in the office with you?'

'No. Milson went out when I whistled, looking like he had a wooden spoon up his bum.'

Thank heavens for small mercies, thought Birdie. She toughened her voice. 'Now look, Dan. You can stop being bloody offensive. I don't have to answer to you. I don't have to explain anything to you. I just rang to tell you why I can't meet you for that drink tomorrow night. So I'm telling you. I can't meet you because I won't be here. I'll be at Hope's End, God help me, with Trevor Lamb and co. Don't think

I'm looking forward to it. I'm not. I deserve sympathy, not abuse.'

'Balls! If you didn't want to do it, you wouldn't. I know you. You just can't resist it, can you? Can't wait to meet the big celebrity. It's a bloody disgrace. The man's an animal, Birdie. He beat his wife to *death*. Poor little girl half his size, pregnant—'

'Dan—'

'And what does he get for it? Five years of free room and board, a university education, and at the end of it, TV interviews, plans to write a book, women writing to him asking him to marry them, everyone patting him on the back saying how wonderful he is. The world's gone mad.'

'Dan, you're missing the point. Trevor Lamb's been let out of gaol because he *didn't* murder his wife. He should never have been convicted in the first place.'

'Balls!'

'Stop saying that! Haven't you read the papers? Didn't you read Jude's book?'

'Yeah. I read it. Well, most of it. It didn't convince me. Didn't convince anyone I know.'

'That's because you only know cops.'

'Lamb was guilty as sin. You could smell it.'

'*Smell* it? What are you talking about? Since when has your nose been a legal argument? We're talking about gaoling a man for life, here, Dan. And for that there has to be no reasonable doubt. You know that. There has to be proof.'

'He was covered in her blood.'

'So would you be if you'd found her lying there dead, and rushed over to her and touched her. And that's what happened to Lamb.'

'So he says. He's lying. If he was innocent, why did he run?'

'He was going for help! What else could he do? He was drunk, and shocked. He crashed the car on the track in the dark. That's why . . .'

'That's why he got nabbed, Birdie. He was running, believe me. He just didn't run far enough. He mucked it up. That sort always do.'

'Well he's never changed his story. Not for a minute. Not through the trial, or any time afterwards.'

'That type learns to lie from the cradle. It's like breathing in and out for them. God, did you see his family in court?'

'I saw pictures. But that's my point, Dan. Jude's point. Didn't you read—?'

'Yeah. I read the bloody book. I told you.'

'The man was convicted because the jury didn't like him. It's as simple as that. There wasn't a shred of hard evidence against him. The weapon was never found. The shack was full of fingerprints and footprints. Everyone in town had been along that track and into the place by the time the cops got there.'

'So?'

'Daphne Lamb was alone in that shack from five in the afternoon till eleven at night. *Anyone* could have killed her.'

'Who did, then? If it wasn't Trevor Lamb, who was it?'

Birdie was silent. Toby pressed home his advantage.

'If your mate Jude, patron bleeding saint of hopeless causes, was so sure Trevor Lamb didn't kill his wife, why didn't he find out who did?'

'He wasn't interested in proving anyone guilty. He just wanted to free someone he thought was innocent. A victim. That's why he got interested in the case in the first place. That's what Jude's like. That's what he's always been like.'

'Well, you'd know.'

Birdie gritted her teeth. There it was again. She knew he was fishing. She knew she shouldn't rise to his bait. But she couldn't stand the idea of appearing to acquiesce in the assumptions he claimed to be making. The very thought made her unpleasantly hot. She could feel a dull blush spreading over her cheeks.

'Dan, for your information I'm not "on" with Jude Gregorian, as you put it,' she heard herself saying. 'I'm not on with him, I never have been on with him. We're friends. That's all. I'm hanging up now. I'll talk to you when I get back from the bush.'

'If you ever get back, Birdwood. That place isn't called Hope's End for nothing.'

'Goodbye Dan.' Birdie hung up. After a moment's thought she turned on the answering machine. Just in case.

She left the study and wandered back to her packing. The little house seemed very quiet. Usually she liked that. But this evening the quiet wasn't restful. Somehow, even with the answering machine on, she felt besieged.

There was the risk that someone might call in, when they couldn't get her on the phone. Beth Bothwell, for example, bursting with unnecessary last-minute reminders, arrangements, instructions. Even Toby himself, trying to barge in, wanting to go on with the argument, refusing to let her have the last word.

She hunched her shoulders defensively, thinking about that.

The gaping bag lay where she'd left it, beside the built-in cupboard that housed her spartan wardrobe. She threw in a few pairs of socks. Then she remembered she'd packed some already and took them out again, replacing them with flat brown sandals. Jude had told her it would be very hot at Hope's End.

Later, she'd call her father. She usually let him know when she was going away, though he'd never asked her to. She'd tell him she was going to Hope's End. Unlike Dan, he wouldn't comment. There'd be no demanding curiosity. No pushing. No tension. No threat.

Suddenly she was seized with the urge to go and see him. They could have dinner. At his house, or the restaurant where he usually ate when he was alone. Thick, white napkins, silver and crystal, flowers, good food. The chance to relax with the one person who accepted her absolutely for what she was, and asked nothing of her but a similar tolerance.

She walked quickly back to the study, picked up the phone and dialled Angus Birdwood's office number. He would still be there at this time, for sure. He never hurried home.

Of course, he might have a function to go to tonight. He often did. A business thing. During the week it was always a business thing with Dad. Meetings with his few close friends were reserved for Saturday golf, Sunday lunches.

'It's Verity, Madeline,' she said, as Angus's secretary answered. 'Is my father in?'

'Putting you through.' As usual, Madeline wasted no time on idle chat. She'd been Angus's personal assistant since Birdie was at school, but they'd never exchanged more than a few stock phrases in all that time.

The phone went dead. Birdie imagined Madeline sitting

at her spotless desk in the hushed anteroom where she spent her days. She had always had the vague suspicion, unsupported by a shred of proof, that under that mask of efficient courtesy Madeline disapproved of her. Thought, perhaps, that it was a pity Angus Birdwood's daughter was not more fitted by profession, looks and temperament to life in the fast lane. Angus was a widower without apparent inclination for remarriage. An acceptable daughter would have been a career asset. A sparkling hostess for media parties. An astute arranger of politically-useful dinners. A charming companion at cocktails and first nights.

In her wildest dreams Madeline wouldn't be able to picture Birdie in such a role.

If Madeline had wild dreams. Which Birdie doubted.

Of course, if Birdie had stuck with the law, it might have been different. Madeline would have approved of a barrister. Maybe. As long as she took high-profile cases, and won them, and went to a good hairdresser.

'G'day, kid.' Angus's quiet voice hummed on the line. Birdie's besieged feeling ebbed.

'Hi. I'm going away for a couple of days. Was wondering if we could have dinner tonight? Before I go? Are you free?'

She found herself crossing her fingers, like a child. Firmly, she uncrossed them. Enough was enough.

'Free as a bird, kid. Pierre's do you? Seven-thirty?'

'Great.'

'See you then. I'll be looking forward to it.'

'Thanks, Dad.'

The line went dead.

Birdie went back to the living room and put on some music. Loud, so she could hear it in the shower.

As she pulled her respectable, going-out-to-dinner-with-father-at-Pierre's clothes—black pants, cream silk shirt, black shoes—from the built-in cupboard, Mozart filled the open spaces of the empty house, and flooded her mind.

She put the clothes on the chair beside the cupboard, then crossed the room to pull the curtains shut, screening off the little courtyard with its nodding greenery and scuttling, next-door cats.

She wouldn't think about Hope's End or Trevor Lamb till tomorrow morning, she promised herself. She wouldn't think about Jude Gregorian, or miscarriages of justice, or desperate entanglements, or poverty, or loss, or victims, or wasted lives and chances.

Or death.

But when she trailed back from the shower, padding barefoot on the silky polished boards, the *Requiem* was playing. And she pulled on her black clothes, wishing she'd chosen another CD, wishing she'd never seen *Amadeus*, and wishing more than anything that she could get the question out of her head.

Toby's question.

If Trevor Lamb didn't kill his wife, who did?

Who did?

FIVE

The sign reading 'Hope's End' was pointing straight downwards, into a patch of spiky brown grass. But beside it a barren strip of bitumen ran off the main road, heading straight for the yellow-brown hills, then curving, shimmering, into oblivion. There wasn't any other track in sight. This must be the one.

Birdie pushed her foot down and swung the car into the side road. Paddocks marked off with wire fences stretched away on either side of the road, and in the distance she could see one or two houses, some outbuildings, and an idle tractor. But there was no sign of life except for a few knots of sheep nibbling under scrubby gum trees, and the odd crow wheeling in the dark blue sky.

It was very hot. She could feel the heat beating down through the roof of the car, in through the windows, up through the floor.

Left off the highway, the guy in the service station at Sassafras had said as she paid him for petrol and her lunch—a can of Coke, and a chocolate bar. ' 'Bout ten minutes along from here. You'll see it. You go along there and 'bout another ten minutes you'll get to a fork. You go right. Right. Left's a dead end. 'Bout *another* ten minutes you'll get to Hope's Creek. Cross the creek and you're in Hope's End. Brake fast, or you'll miss it and end up in the scrub. Road peters out further along.'

He'd looked at her curiously as she tucked the receipt into her wallet. (This time, she'd promised herself, she was definitely going to defeat her own apathy and claim full expenses.)

'Nothing much up that way,' he'd said after a moment.

She smiled briefly and turned to go.

He stared. 'From Sydney, are you?'

She nodded.

'Would you be one of the film people, about Trevor Lamb?'

'Yeah. That's right.'

He nodded, slowly. 'Shocking thing, that,' he said.

She wasn't sure if he meant it was shocking that Lamb had been gaoled, shocking he'd been released, or simply shocking that the ABC was doing an interview, so she said nothing.

She brushed through the long strips of plastic that hung in the doorway baffling the flies, and went over to her car baking quietly in the sun beside one of the three petrol pumps. She swung the car door open and stood back, letting the hot air gust out. Opened the can of Coke, and drank.

'You want to watch it, love.'

The man had followed her outside. He leant against the door jamb, squinting at her in the glare. She looked at him enquiringly.

'Funny place, Hope's End,' he went on.

'So I heard,' she replied, sipping Coke.

He smiled, brushed at a fly.

'Funny place,' he repeated.

Birdie made herself smile back at him, and slipped into the car. It was still baking hot, but the smell of it was familiar and comforting. She swung the door shut, tucked the Coke can between her knees and started the engine.

The man lifted his hand in farewell as she turned back onto the road, and drove away. He didn't move. After a minute or so she glanced in the rear-vision mirror. He was still standing there, looking after her.

Right at the fork. Lucky he'd told her that, because where the bitumen finally disintegrated into what appeared to be *three* rambling dirt tracks, there was no sign at all.

Birdie looked at her watch, and turned the car to the right, taking it slowly over the unmade road. It was still only twelve-thirty. She had plenty of time. Jude had said he and Trevor Lamb would be stopping for lunch on the way, arriving at Hope's End no earlier than two o'clock. She'd left early. She'd felt too restless to hang around at home once she was up and dressed. And she hadn't wanted to stop for lunch. The thought of sitting in some highway steakhouse staring out at the traffic, or, worse still, getting trapped in some quiche and alfalfa-sprout-ridden 'country' cafe, with rabbit traps on the walls and 'distressed' pine furniture, was unappealing to say the least. She supposed it would be different if you'd been eating prison food for five years.

The dust puffing up from under the car's wheels had begun drifting through the window. She rolled it up, then changed her mind and rolled it down again. The dust was preferable to being locked in with the heat. Thick bush rose on both sides of the track. Dust coated the grassy tufts that clung precariously to the dry verges. At least that showed that people did indeed drive this way. Sometimes.

She slowly rounded a bend, and the dust in the air thickened. Why was that? Was a breeze blowing across the undulating paddocks that had now taken the place of bush on her right-hand side? No. The trees that clumped here and there were perfectly still. Not a blade of grass moved.

For a second she was unnerved. Then she snorted with disgusted laughter as she saw a small vehicle emerge from concealment in a dip in the road ahead and chug on up the hill. Some sort of farm machinery, going at a fair bat, too. She was travelling in its dust.

'Some detective,' she said aloud. She saw a thin patch of shade ahead, where a gum tree leant over the road, and pulled up there, as close to the steep verge as she dared. She would wait until the dust had settled. She turned off the car's engine, and wiped her sweaty hands on her jeans.

Now, faintly, she could hear the thudding motor of the vehicle that was just reaching the brow of the next hill. It was a funny little machine. Like a large-scale kid's toy. And actually, she realised, she knew what it was. It was one of those small earth movers. A . . . 'A Bobcat,' she said aloud, with satisfaction. Obscurely, she felt that being able to give the thing a name put her more in control.

She leant back in her seat. She didn't feel too hot. Well, she felt very hot, in fact, but she didn't feel well. Everything seemed slightly unreal. Her head felt thick. Maybe the Coke and the chocolate hadn't been such a good idea on an empty stomach. Slowly she realised that her vision was blurry, too.

It was as though she was seeing everything through a haze.
What was . . . ?

She blinked, trying to ignore the tiny jab of panic. Then
a thought occurred to her. She took of her dust-filmed glasses, polished them vigorously on her shirt, and shoved them
back on her nose. The world came back into focus, fresh and
clear. A miracle cure.

Another triumph for the great detective. She tried to
sneer at herself, but found herself laughing. The relief was intense. For a moment she'd really thought . . .

She started the car again, and eased it back onto the
road proper. The dust hadn't quite settled, but she couldn't
wait any longer. She needed this trip to be over. Even if at the
end of it was Hope's End.

Sue Sweeney glanced at the clock on the wall, wiped the bar
with an automatic hand. Nearly one o'clock. Trevor was due
in an hour. He wouldn't be on time, she told herself. Whatever old Annie thought, he wouldn't be on time.

She imagined him walking into the pub. Meeting her
eyes, across the heads of the crowd. She'd be casual. 'Hi,
Trev,' she'd say. And smile. 'Great to see you.' And he'd
say—

'Four more, thanks, darling.'

She took the glasses Punchy Lamb pushed towards her.
He grinned at her happily, leant against the bar, hitching at
his belt. Standing like that he looked almost normal.

Poor old Punchy, she thought. Like a little kid. Like
Jason. Then she corrected herself. No. Not like Jason. Jason
was a smart-arse little bastard. Punchy was nice. Loud,
sometimes. But underneath, a real gentleman. Not a nasty
bone in his body.

Funny that the only male Lamb you could say that
about was simple. Ironic, really.

Punchy passed over the money, watching the head brim
over the glasses as Sue topped them up.

'You want to go slow, Punchy,' she warned him. 'You
don't want to be too pissed when Trev and that lawyer arrive. And the TV woman.'

His grin broadened. 'Mum's pissed already. We're
celebrating.'

'Well, just you be careful, all right? We don't want any fights today. Floury wouldn't like it.'

His brow puckered slightly. 'I wouldn't fight today, Sue. Trev's coming home today. We're celebrating.'

She gave up. Why spoil the poor bloke's fun?

'Here you are, then,' she said briskly, lifting the foaming glasses onto the bar.

She watched him collect them in his huge hands, carefully spreading his fingers so he could carry all four at once. He backed away from the bar and made for the door.

She'd known Punchy Lamb for a year before what Annie called his 'accident'. He was a big, powerful kid then, with a reputation for being good with his fists. A real looker, too. But he was already a bit slow. Too many knocks in pub brawls.

Sue had seen a few of those in her first year. Punchy never started them. It was usually Keith or Trevor taking offence at something someone said, hoeing in, knowing Punchy'd back them up.

He always did, too, of course. Had done, Floury said, since he was fourteen or so. And maybe if it had stopped at that he'd have been all right.

But then he started doing bouts at shows round the place. And that finished him. He won a bit of money at first. Sue remembered him coming into the pub, hands full of cash, shouting the whole place, everyone patting him on the back. He thought he was going to turn professional, make a fortune. He used to boast he'd build a new house for the family when that happened. Put in a swimming pool. Maybe buy back all the land his dad had sold to Les Hewitt over the years.

Daphne tried to stop it. And she might have finally done it, too, if she hadn't been killed. Punchy had a lot of time for Daphne. Listened to her. She told him it wasn't worth it. Told him he could get brain damage, letting himself get knocked around like that.

But the family thought different, of course. Old Annie Lamb was just about busting with pride. Kept saying how chuffed Miltie would have been seeing little Paul come good like this. And the others liked the money coming in. Even Rosalie.

Daphne was the odd one out. Well, she would be. It was crazy, a girl like that being mixed up with the Lambs.

The pub was filling up. Guys still coming in. No one leaving. It was a weekday, but a lot of people were hanging round long past their normal lunchtimes. Waiting for a glimpse of Trevor Lamb.

They weren't his mates. Trev didn't have mates—he didn't want them. He didn't need them.

When Sue had first come to Hope's End she'd realised straight away that a lot of people didn't like Trevor Lamb. Didn't have much time for any of the Lambs, but Trevor especially. Not that they ever said, while he or his brothers were around. They were too chicken for that. They just kept quiet.

But after he was taken away it was different. Sue had heard them talking over the years. A lot of them said straight out Trev should have been hanged, or shot like a dog, instead of just put in gaol. He'd always been a bad bastard, they said. The worst of the lot of them. They thought he was having it easy. And none of them had really believed he'd be let out. Right up till yesterday, and the four o'clock news.

But he had been. And they wanted to be on the spot to see him. Wanted to be able to say they'd seen him. They call women gossips, Sue thought. They say we're curious. Well, women are nothing to these blokes. Drifting in all casual, nodding at each other, pushing their hats back on their heads, standing around with glasses in their hands, pretending it's just another day, just another lunchtime. Who do they think they're kidding?

Sue pulled beers, took money, gave change, wiped the bar, watched the clock. Soon . . . soon . . .

And then what?

She didn't know.

Once, years ago, just after she started her thing with Trevor Lamb, she'd been standing on the old bridge at dusk. And she'd seen a fox, slinking through one of Hewitts' paddocks, from one patch of cover to another. After new lambs, probably. But at the time Sue hadn't thought of that. She'd just seen the solitariness of it. And the—completeness. As she watched it, it stopped and turned its head. It seemed to look straight at her. Its eyes were shining.

It stood stock still for a moment, then lost interest in

her, and went on its way. Ears up, tail down. Going just so fast, and no faster. Knowing what it was, where it was going, what it wanted, and nothing more. A being without conscience.

It had suddenly come to her that Trev was like that. And the thought had given her a shuddering thrill, right up from the tops of her thighs, through her belly to her chest and throat.

The warm blood flooded her face as she stood there on the bridge, looking down now at the fast-moving water. She'd felt shaken, shamed, and shocked. She'd thought she was attracted to Trevor Lamb's brooding looks, hard muscled body. She'd thought that in taking up with him she was seizing life with both hands as she always did, joyously drinking it up. If she'd felt any pricks of conscience about Daphne, or Floury for that matter, she'd turned her attention away from them. Following the creed. What happens, happens. Anything for love.

But now she understood that love had nothing to do with it. Understood why she'd never found a man she'd really cared about. Any man who hadn't finally bored her, however vaguely fond of him she was.

Whatever she'd told herself all these times, in all those towns, with all those men, she hadn't been looking for love at all. She could see that now. She'd been looking for excitement, and danger, and the thrill of shamed fear she'd just experienced.

That's why she couldn't stop thinking about Trevor Lamb. He gave her something she must have craved all along. A man who didn't need her. Didn't respect her. Didn't need or respect anyone. Who had no conscience, or honour, or any sense of other people's needs or rights. Who was bad. Bad all through.

Sue shivered with an almost superstitious dread. She hunched over the bridge railing as the trees' shadow deepened over her shoulders. And self-loathing flooded her. What was wrong with her? How screwed up was she? She should get out of it. Leave Hope's End and move on.

But even as the thought crossed her mind, she knew she wouldn't do it. She didn't have the will. She would wait, as she always had, all her life, for something to happen.

Leaves and twigs floated under the bridge, half-submerged

by the darkening running water, spinning helplessly in circles as they were caught in tiny eddies. She felt as though she was being dragged along with them, out of control, pushed by currents she could barely understand.

A feeling of doom settled over her, there on the bridge, the night she saw the fox.

It had lifted, of course. Almost as soon as she went back to the pub, into the light, the familiar chiacking of the locals, the sounds and smells she knew. But it had never really left her. Just moved to the side of her mind where she could always catch a glimpse of it if she wasn't concentrating on something else.

Then Daphne was killed. And Trevor was taken away. And even that wasn't enough to make her leave Hope's End. She'd stayed, when she should have gone. When there was no point in her staying. When her staying could only destroy her.

And now Trevor was coming back.

Sue looked up. Became aware that something was happening outside. The men at the bar were looking towards the door. Her mouth went dry.

But it was too early. It couldn't be him. And she couldn't hear Annie's voice calling out. Or Punchy's. Or Jason's. It couldn't be him.

Bull Trews came swaggering self-consciously into the pub, carrying a worn black leather overnight bag. Close behind him was a small figure in blue jeans and a limp, dust-smeared white shirt with rolled-up sleeves. A woman, with curly brown hair and glasses, a bulging brown handbag slung over one shoulder.

A reporter? Sue wondered. There weren't supposed to be any reporters. The idea was that Trev's whereabouts were going to be kept quiet as long as possible. But everyone round here had found out. Why not the press? It was their job, wasn't it? To poke their noses in where they weren't wanted.

Floury didn't move from his place behind the bar. Just watched, wiping his hands on a towel.

'Floury, you old bastard, you finally sold a room,' bellowed Bull, jerking his head at the woman behind him. 'But I want commission. Ten percent. This sheila followed me up the track. Couldn't resist me fatal charm, see?' He thumped the bag down in the middle of the floor, and looked round him, grinning.

The pub was almost silent now.

'Yeah?' drawled Floury.

The small woman looked in his direction, and moved towards him. Men eased back to let her pass, flicking their eyes over her, their faces carefully expressionless.

'G'day. I'm Verity Birdwood,' the woman said casually. She grinned up at Floury, and ran her fingers through that mass of hair, tucking it behind her ears. 'From the ABC. Booked in here for a couple of nights. I hope.'

Well, what a turn-up. Sue had never been so surprised in her life. She'd been expecting some cool, high-powered glamour girl. Or one of those dark vivacious types, all nose, eyes and teeth, full of opinions about woodchipping and abortion and all that.

Anything but this nondescript, almost scruffy little person. She looked like a librarian. Not that Sue knew many librarians, she had to admit. Only the one she'd had at high school. Mrs Binkie. Blinky Binkie. Binkie had had this thing about turning over pages carefully. She'd demonstrate, almost every library period. 'Take the top right-hand corner of the page gently-but-firmly between finger and thumb and tu-urn,' she'd go. You'd have thought those old library books were precious antiques, or something, the way she went on.

This woman didn't look like Mrs Binkie, of course. But she looked like someone who read a lot. Well, maybe that was the specs.

She isn't Trev's type, anyway, Sue found herself thinking. And not likely she's on with that lawyer bloke, either. He'd want someone fancier than her, by the look of him. Although . . . she slightly narrowed her eyes, looking more closely at Verity Birdwood, leaning on the bar, talking to Floury. She looked as though she knew what she was doing, anyhow. She looked . . . in control. That was it. Like she didn't need to impress anyone. And her hair was quite nice. In a way.

The two of them—Floury and the woman—suddenly turned in her direction. Caught staring, Sue smiled widely.

'Will you do the honours, Sue?' asked Floury, using his genial country publican voice. 'Show the lady all the doings?'

'Sure,' she said agreeably, keeping her eyes firmly turned away from the clock.

The small woman picked up her bag, nodded pleasantly at Bull Trews, and moved down to Sue's end of the bar. Again the men shifted their positions almost unnoticeably, to avoid contact.

'The stairs are back here,' Sue said to her, pointing.

They moved out of the crowded room together, towards the back of the hotel building. Sue swung open the door marked 'Guests Only', revealing the narrow stairs, and stood back to let Verity Birdwood through.

'You watch yourself, Sue,' Bull Trews bellowed from the bar. 'Don't you let that city girl go teaching you any bad habits! You got enough already.'

Gratified guffaws and the buzz of male talk echoed after them as they climbed the stairs. Honour had been satisfied.

'Take no notice of them,' growled Sue, embarrassed for herself and for them. 'They're idiots. Showing off. Shouldn't even be here, most of them. They've come to gawk.'

Verity Birdwood looked back at her, and grinned good-humouredly.

But Sue, suddenly staring straight into cold, intelligent, amber eyes, found she couldn't smile back. Because all of a sudden she was back on that bridge, years ago. Looking into the eyes of the fox. The fox.

Her stomach turned over. Here was another one. Another solitary. Another calm, ruthless one. Dangerous.

The woman above her looked slightly puzzled, turned away again, and climbed the last few stairs to the first floor. Sue followed quickly, feeling her cheeks flush.

What a fool she was! What a prize gink! Letting her imagination run away with her like that. There was nothing to fear from this woman. She had foxes on the brain, that was her trouble. And she was all stirred up about Trevor.

That was all there was to it.

But at the corner of her mind, the darkness stirred.

Six

Birdie sat on the edge of the double bed and levered off her shoes. She lay back. The bed creaked dismally. The bed-cover, a hectic mass of lime green, black and white triangles, smelt like a second-hand clothes shop.

The small room was stifling. Subdued noise from the drinkers below floated up and through the window, which faced out towards the road. But little air seemed to come with the sound. It was too still outside.

She let her eyes drift around the room. There was nothing much to see. Small, freestanding wardrobe, white-painted chest of drawers on which lay a folded, striped towel, mottled oval-shaped mirror on the back of the door. On the walls, lines of large pink roses climbed relentlessly to the ceiling on a white trellis set against a background of pale green faintly spotted with rusty blotches. Obviously the wallpaper predated the bedcover by quite a few years. Birdie tried to decide which period she preferred, and decided the roses just nudged it in.

She stared up at the sloping ceiling, where fine cracks zig-zagged around the scalloped china light fitting in a spider-web pattern. She took off her glasses. The roses and the cracks receded into a pleasant haze.

I can't just lie here, she told herself. I have to get up, change my shirt, go down. Meet the Lambs before Trevor and Jude turn up. That was them, for sure, sitting outside the pub, on that big log. There couldn't possibly be two women in Hope's End who look like Annie Lamb. And some of her kids were with her. Rosalie, I'd say. Keith. And Paul. The brain-damaged one. I should've gone up to them as soon as I got here, really. If it hadn't been for that Bobcat bloke I would have. But anyhow, I'll do it when I go down. Buy them all a drink. Get them on side.

She didn't move.

Her mind drifted to thoughts of Sue Sweeney and Allan Baker. 'Floury' Baker. She'd read their evidence in the transcript of Lamb's original trial. The newspaper articles, and Jude's book had mentioned them, too.

Floury Baker looked just about as she'd imagined him. One of those big, almost flabby, fair, red-faced blokes who don't say much. And she'd recognised Sue Sweeney from the newspaper photographs. Her hair was the same—auburn, waving thickly to her shoulders. She'd gained a bit of weight over the five years. In the face, and around the waist. But she was less brassy than Birdie had expected. And more vulnerable-looking in the eyes and mouth than the photographs had indicated.

'Are any of the Hewitts down there?' Birdie had asked her, at the top of the stairs.

The other woman had stared, her eyes widening slightly so that the whites showed above the round, hazel-green pupils. 'No,' she said.

'Do you think they'll come?'

Sue Sweeney had shrugged her plump shoulders uncomfortably. 'I don't know,' she mumbled. 'Mrs Hewitt wouldn't, for sure. She never goes out. Not anywhere. Since . . .' Her voice trailed away.

Since Daphne was killed.

The words hung in the air, unspoken. Sue fidgeted, pulling at the plunging neckline of her blouse.

'What about Mr Hewitt? Or the brother—Phillip, isn't it?'

'Les might come. You can never tell with him.' Her brow furrowed. She plucked at her blouse. 'Phil'd be still at school now. Won't get off till three-twenty. After that . . .'

'School?' Birdie searched her memory. Five years ago Phillip Hewitt was just finishing high school, wasn't he? So . . .

The other woman saw her confusion. Explained. 'He teaches here, now. At the primary school.'

'Oh, yes, I remember now. I read that somewhere. Where's the school?'

Sue waved a hand vaguely towards the front of the building, as she led the way along the corridor. 'You wouldn't have seen it. Tiny little place. It's off the main road.'

'I wouldn't have thought this place was big enough to keep a school going.' Birdie was keeping her talking.

'It's not. They reckon it's closing down next year.' Sue Sweeney stopped at a door marked three. A key poked from the lock. She turned it, swung open the door, displaying the room beyond. Light and heat streamed out into the corridor. Inside the room, dust motes swirled in the air, making it look hazy. 'Always been a one-teacher school, they say. Used to be bigger. Was bigger when Dolly Hewitt taught there. 'Course, she had quite a few of the Lambs.' A small smile crossed her face. 'That must've been a picnic.'

'Phillip Hewitt'll have to move away, then.'

'Good thing, if you ask me,' said Sue. She crossed the room, to the window. 'I'll just get you some air.' The muscles of her strong arms strained against the sleeves of her ruffled blouse as she heaved the stiff window up as high as it would go. 'Soon as he finished his training he asked for the school. So he could be near his mother. She . . . he thought he should stay around. Because . . . you know, since . . .'

Since Daphne was killed.

Birdie watched as the other woman walked over to the door, preparing to leave. 'Bathroom and toilet down the end of the hall. You have to share with the others—Floury and the lawyer bloke who's coming with Trevor. Floury's in one. Mr Gregorian'll be in two. Four's empty. The locks work. There's another toilet downstairs, in the yard.'

'Why do you say it'd be a good thing if Phillip Hewitt moved on?' Birdie wasn't interested in bathrooms.

She shrugged again. Wasn't it obvious? 'He's going crazy there. Kids drive him crazy. This place drives him crazy. He—shouldn't be here. It's killing him. It'd kill anybody like him. This place . . .' She stopped abruptly, made a well-practiced comic face, shook back her hair. 'Anyhow—I'd better get back to the mob. You're all right?'

'Sure. See you later, then.'

'Oh, by the way. We don't do breakfasts. But you're welcome to make your own in the kitchen. Just use what's there. Floury doesn't mind. Tea and coffee too. Biscuits. Anytime. Help yourself.'

Business completed, Sue escaped, shutting the door behind her. The scent of her make-up base, shampoo and perfume lingered in the room, more obvious, somehow, now that she'd gone.

Birdie watched the glittering dust motes swirl in the air, stirred up by the movement of the door.

Since Daphne was killed.

This place . . .

It was strange that Sue Sweeney had stayed on at Hope's End after the going-over she had at the trial. The scarlet woman. The victim's friend, carrying on with the victim's husband. Wonder how she felt about Trevor Lamb coming back? Would they take up where they'd left off? Maybe she was wondering the same thing. She seemed very tense underneath all that jolly barmaid stuff. That look on the stairs—almost scared.

But maybe that didn't mean anything special. The whole atmosphere of this place was tense. You could feel the suppressed excitement, however casual all those men downstairs acted. Well, no wonder. Quite apart from the fact that Lamb was coming back, vindicated and free, everyone here must be wondering if there was going to be trouble. If Les Hewitt was going to turn up, for example.

You can never tell with him.

Birdie thought about that for a minute. Then, forcing herself to admit she was just diverting herself, delaying the inevitable, she put her glasses back on and heaved herself off the bed, noticing with foreboding that the mattress remained indented where she'd lain.

She pulled a clean shirt from her bag, found the sandals she'd put in as an afterthought. It was very hot. The room was stifling. As she changed, convincing herself she already felt cooler, she heard the sounds of two more cars rattling over the bridge and turning into parking spots outside the pub. Uh-oh. Had Trevor and Jude arrived before time?

Swearing softly at herself she went over to the window to look, ducking her head under the brown blind that seemed fixed in its half-open position.

But the four new arrivals were all strangers to her. She watched them hitching at their belts, pushing back their hats, clumping across the road to the pub in their elastic-sided boots. *More audience. The theatre's filling up.* The thought popped into her head, making her blink.

Yes. It was as if all those people down there were waiting for a play to start. An avant-garde production, where the actors took their places among the audience till it was time for the show to begin.

Most of the cast were here already. They were only waiting for the leading man, and his minder. Then everyone would find out if what they were going to see was comedy or drama.

Suddenly eager to get downstairs, Birdie grabbed her handbag and thrust it over her shoulder. She let herself out of her room, and locked it behind her, stuffing the key into her jeans' pocket. Not that it was probably necessary to lock up here. And there was nothing in the room worth stealing anyway. But people were curious. And the habit of ensuring privacy was strong.

She made for the dark stairway, pleasantly conscious of a small surge of excitement in the pit of her stomach. The heavy, bemused feeling that had loaded her down for weeks seemed suddenly to have gone.

Comedy or drama? That was the question. Most of the cast was already here. Most of the audience. And it could be that unknown to her, or even to themselves, some members of the audience were going to be part of the play themselves, once it began.

And what am I? she wondered then, moving down through the dimness towards the light and noise of the bar. Cast or audience?

She wished she knew.

Birdie threaded her way through the crowd in the bar and slipped into the open air, murmuring apologies as she squeezed past a bare-chested boy and a heavily made-up, black-haired girl standing close together in the doorway. In unison, as though joined at the hip, they swayed aside to let her pass. The light dazzled her, and she felt instinctively for her sunglasses.

A sharp-faced little boy wearing baggy shorts and a huge black t-shirt with a skull on the front, sidled up to her, a knowing smile hovering on his lips.

'You the ABC tart?' he smirked.

'Jason!' shrilled a voice from the corner of the verandah. 'Get back here.'

The boy's eyes flickered, but he didn't move.

'Well, are ya?' he persisted.

'You could say that. Are you Jason Lamb?'

He looked startled, as though he hadn't expected to be recognised. Then a gratified expression crossed his face, and he turned and bolted away to peer at her from the safety of the old tank that stood beside the pub, near where his family was sitting.

'She knows me name!' Birdie heard him hiss. Someone, a woman, hissed angrily back at him, and he subsided into watchful silence.

Birdie walked towards the Lambs. Keith, dark, medium height, forehead deeply furrowed between heavy black brows, slouching unsmiling by one of the posts that supported the lean-to roof. Near him, a very thin girl with close-cropped white-blonde hair, tossing aside a cigarette with a quick, jerky movement, her long silver earrings swaying. That would be the improbably-named Lily Danger. Blue singlet, lots of black eyeliner, skin-tight patterned leggings, bare feet. A fairly exotic figure in this crowd.

She hadn't been named in the newspaper reports, and hadn't given evidence at the trail. But Jude had mentioned her in his briefing. Birdie hadn't noticed her before. Maybe she'd just arrived. Beside her, Paul Lamb, tall, black-haired and powerful. Very good-looking, too, despite a broken nose. But grinning foolishly, gripping his beer.

Birdie took them all in with one casual glance, nodded to them, then turned her attention to the monstrous figure sitting on the log against the wall.

'Mrs Lamb, I'm Verity Birdwood from the ABC,' she said, holding out her hand.

'Mrs Lamb!' Jason snorted with derisive laughter, skulking in the safety of the tank stand. 'Listen to that! Mrs Lamb!' He let out a hyperactive howl, and swung violently on the old wood, never turning his face away from the scene under the lean-to. Birdie thought of *The Exorcist*.

Annie Lamb wiped her palms on her enormous bosom and shook Birdie's hand limply. Her fingers felt like warm, uncooked sausages. 'Bugger of a day, innit?' she said, slurring the words.

Birdie nodded. 'A real scorcher.'

Annie Lamb grinned, showing a full set of bare gums. 'We've had worse, 'course,' she croaked. 'Hundred times worse.'

She was leaning forward, knees well apart, feet in rubber thongs planted firmly on the verandah boards, glass of beer in her hand. Her thin, yellow-grey hair was scraped back into a rough ponytail, secured by a pink ruffled band, but long wisps had escaped and hung limply around her ears. She was wearing a sundress patterned in mauve, green and pink: a vast, shapeless garment that still seemed too small for her. The flesh of her arms, strangely white compared to the coarse redness of her face and neck, bulged enormously from the sleeveless top

'Haw, haw!' jeered Jason. 'If it was a hundred times worse we'd be dead. Wouldn't we, Mum? Mum? *Mum?*'

The woman sitting beside Annie Lamb stirred. 'S'pose we would,' she murmured.

' *Course* we would!' Jason made no effort to hide his contempt.

The exchange seemed to remind Annie of the social niceties.

'This is me daughter, Rosalie,' she said, jerking her head at the woman. All her movements were slow, and each one was accompanied by a groaning little grunt, as if it was an effort. She munched her gums together almost continuously when she wasn't actually talking. It was the toothlessness that made her look so extraordinary, Birdie decided. She tore her eyes away from Annie and focused on Rosalie, who was smiling at her in a vague sort of way.

Rosalie? It was difficult to find the rather fey, slim creature of the newspaper photographs in this mature-bodied, vaguely pleasant-looking woman with the blurry features, weather-beaten skin and shoulder-length, permed brown hair. Five years had made a great difference to Rosalie. She looked far older than her twenty-nine years. And there was something very detached about her, Birdie thought.

'Pleased to meet you.' Again that murmuring, listless voice. And while the lips smiled, the eyes seemed far away.

Five years ago, one early morning, Rosalie had found her brother's wife lying on her kitchen floor, with her head smashed to pulp. Then, stumbling along the track towards the pub, and help, she had found her brother, slumped over the wheel of his wrecked car, covered in blood. And later, she had screamed and screamed as her brother was taken away.

Had she given up, then? Or had the process of Rosalie Lamb's detachment from life begun long ago, and simply accelerated over the last few years as motherhood, life, and Hope's End wore her down?

'I'm Punchy.' The tall, good-looking son was reaching over and pumping Birdie's hand.

'She can see that, if she's got eyes,' drawled Lily Danger.

'You watch your tongue, you little bitch!' Annie Lamb's raised voice was startling in its sudden violence. Her already flushed face darkened to scarlet.

Unmoved, Lily smiled, cat-like, and tossed her head so hear earrings flashed in the sunlight.

'Keith Lamb,' said the sombre man beside her, ignoring the exchange absolutely. He made no move to hold out his hand.

'I was going to get myself a drink,' Birdie said, deciding to provide a diversion. 'How about joining me? ABC can afford it, eh?'

'Yeah!' Annie drained her glass and held it out, good humour immediately restored. 'Betcha life. 'Nother beer, thanks, love. Watcher say your name was?'

'Verity Birdwood.'

Jason screeched with laughter. Lily Danger smirked. Birdie was suddenly seized by a violent urge to leap across the verandah and knock their heads together.

'People usually call me Birdie,' she murmured, taking Annie's glass.

Annie beamed. 'Good-oh,' she said. She smacked her lips. 'Anyhow . . .'

Taking this as a hint, Birdie turned to go to seek refreshments. Immediately everyone else drained their glasses. Punchy lumbered forward, expertly gathering up the empties.

'I wanna Fanta,' bawled Jason. 'Hey, Berdie, c'n I have a Fanta?'

Birdie nodded shortly.

With Punchy clinking close behind her, she walked towards the pub door.

'Grace,' Punchy said urgently. 'Grace, come on, drink up. It's Birdie's shout.'

'What?' It was the dark-haired girl Birdie had seen on her way out. She glanced at Birdie, flicked her hair back, and quickly downed her beer.

The boy with her did the same.

They both stacked their glasses into the pile Punchy was already carrying, then looked away.

So that was Grace. She looked much older than Birdie had expected. More like twenty than fourteen. At fourteen she shouldn't even be drinking in a pub. But presumably that wasn't an issue in Hope's End. Especially if you were a Lamb.

Birdie moved towards the bar. Again the crowd of men eased back, giving her room.

'In luck are ya, Punchy?' someone said, behind her. There were a few half-hearted laughs.

'Six—ah—seven beers, please. And a Fanta,' Birdie said to Allan Baker, stolid behind the bar. Wordlessly he reached for clean glasses, began filling the order. Birdie felt for her money, wondering how she was going to justify her expenses. No way were receipts going to be the order of the day here. She'd just have to make Beth take her word for it.

She glanced at the clock on the wall. Nearly two o'clock.

'Saw Les Hewitt earlier,' said Bull Trews, edging closer to her, but speaking to Baker.

'That right?' growled Baker, apparently concentrating on the beer tap.

'Yeah. Big north paddock. Cutting out a lamb.'

The beer foamed up, spilled into the metal grate below the glasses.

'That right?'

'Yeah—' with a sly, sideways look at Punchy, '—must've decided he may as well get in for his chop while there's still a few about. Got a way of going off, prime lambs, at Les's place, by all accounts. Funny thing, that.'

Punchy turned slowly to face him. 'What you on about?' he growled. The flesh of his face seemed to swell. His huge hands doubled into fists.

Bull Trews mimicked surprise, unconvincingly. 'I'm not on about nothin' mate,' he said. 'Not even talking to you, am I?'

Floury Baker hurriedly pushed four brimming glasses

forward. 'Here,' he said to Punchy. 'You take this lot, mate.
Lady can take the rest.'

Punchy hesitated.

'Go on, mate,' said Baker. 'Bull didn't mean nothing.
Did ya, Bull?'

Bull Trews shook his head. 'Didn't mean nothing,' he
mumbled. 'I was just talking.'

Punchy slowly uncurled his fists, reached for the drinks,
and gathered them up. Then, with another lowering look at
Bull, he turned and lumbered away towards the door.

Floury finished serving Birdie in silence, his mouth a
hard line. He put the remaining four drinks on a round metal
tray, and watched as she took it, moving carefully away from
the bar.

'You bloody idiot,' she heard him say to Bull Trews in
an undertone when she was a few paces away. 'You want to
get yourself killed?'

'I c'n handle meself, mate,' whined the other man. 'Anyhow, he wouldn't've done nothin'. Not with Trevor coming
back any tick of the clock. He wouldn't wanna—'

'You joking? You've seen him go off. You know what
he's like. You bloody idiot. You keep away from him. You
don't say nothing to him. Hear me?'

Regretfully, Birdie moved out of overhearing range, balancing her tray. She was nearly at the door when Jason's strident voice screeched from the verandah, easily penetrating
the low hum of male voices.

'They're here! They're here! Uncle Trev's here! Hey,
Mum! Hey Grandma! Uncle Trev's here!'

The pub fell absolutely still. Then, casually, slowly, men
began drifting forward, pressing Birdie with them in a gentle
tide, out through the narrow doorway, and into the sunlight.

In a body, the Lambs were moving out to the road,
Annie lumbering in front, Jason capering and shrieking
around them, urging them on like a dog mustering sheep.
Real dogs roused themselves from their places in the dirt or
in the backs of their masters' utes, and barked.

A new Volvo, its pristine white exterior frosted all over
with a film of yellow-brown dust, reached the bridge,
slowed, and rattled across the old timbers. It drew up outside
the pub, parking parallel, blocking the road.

Jason ran to open the passenger door, grinning all over his face. The other Lambs hung back, waiting.

A man got out. Dark, medium height, wearing sunglasses. Skin pale in the strong light.

He stared around, unsmiling, as if taking everything in in one long look. The old pub building, the men lounging against the verandah posts, Sue Sweeney and Floury Baker drawn to the door as if by an invisible string, his family standing motionless in the dusty road. Even Birdie, tray clutched in her hands, watching.

'Trev!' Annie's voice cracked the silence as she lurched forward.

For the first time, Trevor Lamb's grim mouth relaxed into a half-smile.

'G'day, Mum,' he said.

And braced himself, as she engulfed him in her arms.

Seven

Annie Lamb's voice, reminiscing, telling stories, raucous with beer and excitement. Punchy's laughter. Jason's catcalls as other kids stared from the road. Lily's earrings, flashing. Trevor Lamb, sitting on the log, brooding and superior, saying little. Rosalie, standing looking at the creek. Jude, propped against the verandah rail, smiling, smiling. The sun, low in the western sky, but still baking the road. The occasional revving of an engine as a car or truck backed out of the pepper trees opposite and drove away, clattering over the bridge, accelerating away in a cloud of dust. Heat. Flies. Sweat prickling at the back of the knees. The smell of beer, dust, car exhaust, sheep, the creek . . .

Birdie moved to let Punchy through with yet another tray of empty glasses. He was going for another round. She'd lost count of how many there'd been already. Lost track of time, too. Lost track of everything except the need to stay upright, when all she wanted to do was lie down somewhere, anywhere, and sleep.

How long had this been going on? She blinked at her watch, frowned, lifted her wrist higher. She couldn't quite see the numbers, somehow. But it must be late. She remembered seeing kids riding bikes down the road, bags on their shoulders. A cream and brown bus, rattling over the bridge. Remembered registering then that school must be out. That was ages ago. An hour, at least. Maybe two. So . .

'Drink up, Birdie,' roared Punchy. 'Jude's shout.' She roused herself to shake her head, pointing to her half-full glass.

'Piker!' he jeered, grinning delightedly. 'C'mon!'

His smile was very sweet. She found herself smiling back at him. She liked him quite a lot. Or was it the beer?

'I can't, Punchy,' she said. 'I really can't. I hardly had any lunch, and . . .'

'Going back up the house after this one,' he said, anxiously. 'Barbecue. You know? So you better—'

'Hey, Punchy, what's the hold-up?' Annie craned her neck to see. 'Dyin' of thirst up here, we are.'

'Birdie's being a piker. Reckons she's pissed,' Punchy yelled.

'I didn't say that!' Birdie heard herself protesting. 'I just . . .'

'Don't look pissed to me, love,' hooted Annie Lamb, narrowing her eyes against the sun. 'Come on. Drink up. Watcha holding up the works for? We gotta get back to the house, get the barbecue on, 'fore it gets dark. It'll be a bugger otherwise.'

'Just let him do it, Birdie,' called Jude. 'You can't get out of it. What does it matter? No one's going anywhere. No one's doing anything. Relax. Enjoy.'

He was laughing. But there was something slightly forced about his voice, and even at this distance she could see the tension behind his eyes. She suddenly realised that underneath the bonhomie he was as uncomfortable as she was. The haze induced by sun, alcohol and boredom lifted a little, as she considered this.

The traces were slight. Maybe she only noticed them because she knew him so well. But they were there, all right. It reminded her of times when he'd had to socialise at law functions in the old days. Fish out of water. Square peg in a round hole. Putting on an act to cover it up, where she never could, or would.

She hadn't picked up on it before. At first, watching, fascinated, as Trevor Lamb accepted his mother's tears and embraces, Keith's perfunctory handshake, Punchy's adoring backslapping, Rosalie's confused kiss all with the same, ironic half-smile. Then, witnessing the triumphal procession to the verandah, the half-hearted greetings of the watching men, their sidelong glances as he kissed Sue Sweeney on the mouth, and her cheeks began to burn. Undergoing her own introduction to Trevor Lamb, by Jude, under the family's watchful eyes. Meeting Lamb's dark, almost sneering, stare with a level look of her own. Coping with the instant feeling of dislike, masking it, suppressing it. Then, relegated again to the sidelines, slowly lapsing into a dream of mindless discomfort, as the minutes stretched into hours on the pub verandah, and the beer flowed in an endless stream, swelled by Jude's money, and her own.

She'd seen Jude as one with them—the Lambs. He was the conquering hero, right? The man who'd fought and won, righted a great wrong, brought the prisoner home. Wasn't this the climax of his triumph?

But now, in this belated moment of clarity, she saw it wasn't. Of course it wasn't. Understanding, she looked at Jude in the old way, for the first time since he arrived. Saw him register it, shrug, almost imperceptibly, and smile. She grinned back. Sympathy flowed between them. The climax of Jude's triumph would have been at the moment formal notice of Trevor Lamb's release came through. It was the triumph of an ideal, of his obsession with seeing justice done. Trevor Lamb himself was almost irrelevant—always had been—to Jude's quest.

This—all this—was the aftermath. The necessary tidying up. And with it, for Jude, came the hard slog of dealing socially with people with whom he had nothing in common. And facing, yet again, inevitably, the fact that he hadn't saved the tragic antihero of the newspaper sob-stories, but a real man without much to recommend him—except his innocence.

'Okay, Jude,' she said. 'It's your money.'

'That's right. Good on ya!' beamed Punchy. 'Drink up!'

'I'll finish this while you're gone,' she promised.

Satisfied, he went on his way.

Annie Lamb clambered to her feet. 'I gotta have a pee. I'm busting,' she announced. 'Want to come, Rosalie?'

Rosalie shook her head.

'No point holding on, y'know,' her mother warned. 'You c'n bust your bladder that way. I know a woman— Angie Shaw, Porky Shaw's sister, held on all the way from Sydney to Melbourne once, 'cause she was with a mate of Porky's and she was embarrassed to say—'

'Like, ladies don't pee?' jeered Grace, arching her back against the verandah post, thrusting out her breasts.

Birdie saw Trevor Lamb look, half-smile.

Saw Rosalie's forehead crease, her vague eyes darken.

'Anyhow—' Annie's voice rose. She was determined to finish her story. 'Anyhow, she held on too long, and in the end she all seized up and couldn't go. Tried everything, she said. In agony. They had to have the doctor to her. And when it finally came out it came out all black. Black!'

'Oh, gross!' howled Jason.

'Better go with Mum, Rosalie.' Trevor smiled lazily up at his sister.

'Go yourself,' she retorted childishly.

Annie laughed and flip-flopped heavily towards the pub door. The old verandah boards shook. Birdie hastily drew up her knees, to get her feet out of the way.

'Always the same, the twinnies,' Annie said as she went by. 'Loving each other up or fighting like cat and dog. Never in between. Kids!' she smiled benignly, gummily, and disappeared into the dimness of the pub.

Background info for the researcher, thought Birdie. Must make a note. Headed, The Twinnies.

She saw Jude say something to Trevor, then move from his place and come towards her. She looked up enquiringly. 'Feel like stretching your legs?' he murmured.

She nodded, and scrambled to her feet. As she did so her shoulder bag knocked over the glass of beer she'd stowed on the floor behind her. Well, that took care of that problem, anyway.

Upright she felt worse than she had before. For a moment, everything seemed to spin. She grabbed at Jude's arm, to steady herself.

'You've got to give up the grog, Birdie,' he teased, holding onto her. 'Got to learn to say no.'

'Can't help myself.' Slowly Birdie's head cleared. The world settled back into place. Suddenly very conscious of the warmth of Jude's hand through her thin shirt, she laughed, and moved forward, away from him. They had rarely touched in the old days. Touching wasn't part of her relationship with Jude, whatever everyone else thought.

Maybe that was the trouble.

'Where are we going?' she asked, as they stepped onto the road and turned their backs to the red sun.

'Just up to the bridge or something. Can't stay away

long, or they'll get insulted. I just had to give myself a rest. Don't know about you. How are you coping?'

'Not too badly. Though I'd rather be up to my neck in pig swill, plucking live chickens.'

'Sounds like a great idea.'

They walked. Birdie looked at her feet. Dust filled her sandals, settled between her toes. The sun burned her back.

'Do you really have to go tomorrow?' she asked him. She wouldn't have asked if it she was quite sober, she realised. But she wasn't sorry.

'Yeah. I wish I didn't, with you here. But I have to go. I've got to be in court Wednesday. That was organised long before I knew when Trevor would get out. Before I was even certain he *would* get out.'

Jude paced. He was watching his feet, too. 'Not that I wanted to stay here longer than I had to anyhow,' he added, as if compelled to be completely honest with her. 'Look—my job's over, isn't it? No need for me to hang around.'

'You don't have to explain it to me, Jude. If I were you I wouldn't have come at all.'

They reached the bridge. Automatically they moved to the railing and leant over it, looking down at the sluggish water.

The railing creaked dangerously. Both of them jumped backwards.

They looked at each other and laughed.

Back at the pub there was an echoing laughter. Maybe someone had been watching them. And maybe not. Maybe the Lambs had forgotten all about them, and were laughing at something else.

'I had to come,' said Jude, after a moment. 'Trevor had to get back here somehow.' He ran a thin, nervous hand through his hair. It was a gesture Birdie remembered. 'And—I don't know—I felt sort of responsible for him. Having got him out, I didn't feel I could just leave him flat. Now he's here, I can leave him with a clear conscience. Well, in a way. I don't think it's the best place for him. Far from it.'

'You aren't his keeper. And he wanted to come here, didn't he?'

'Yeah. It's a worry.'

Birdie remembered what Beth had said. 'You mean

because he wants to rub people's noses in it? The people who thought he was guilty? The Hewitts, and so on?'

'Partly. Well, that was it at first.' He pointed to the paddock across the creek. 'That's Hewitt land. Part of it. Property's huge. Trevor's shack's actually on the border. If he wanted to, he could see Les Hewitt every day. Yeah, the crowing's part of it. But on top of that he's been a bit—odd, lately. Keyed up.'

'Well, that's pretty natural. Waiting for the release. Looking forward to getting home.'

'No—it's something more than what's natural. Natural for Trevor, I mean. Which isn't what's natural for most people, I admit.'

Jude strayed to the railing again. Looked down, but didn't lean over. Birdie watched the back of his head, waiting.

'I've been noticing it for a couple of weeks,' Jude said, finally. 'He's planning something. He's decided something. He's pleased with himself. I know him so well.' He grimaced. 'I should, after all this time. On the way here, he hardly said a thing. Which is unusual for him. He usually can't wait to talk. He's got opinions on everything going these days.'

'I heard he is planning to write a book.'

'Oh, sure. Yeah. Got a brand new computer in the back of the car for exactly that purpose. I told him I'd set it up for him before I left. But it can't be that. He's been planning that for months.'

Birdie put her hand on his shoulder. Breaking the rule again. She felt the muscles stir under her fingers.

'You did all you had to do for Trevor Lamb, Jude,' she said softly. 'He's free. You can let him go now. In fact, you've *got* to let him go. He is what he is. He'll do what he wants.'

'I know that. I know that. But—'

He turned to her, his face deeply shadowed in the failing light. He looked, at that moment, very young. Like he'd looked when they were both very young together.

'Yes?'

'I messed him around, Birdie. I—I was so—so full of it. I yapped at him all the time. I encouraged him to matriculate. Do the uni course. All that.'

'But that was good, wasn't it?'

'I guess it was. I mean, yes, of course it was. But I—I didn't realise he'd want to come back here, when he was out. He hardly had any contact with his family while he was inside. I thought he wanted to make a fresh start. I didn't know that what he wanted most was to come back here and take up life basically where he'd left off. And now—'

'Hey! You blokes! Don't ya want ya drinks?'

Punchy's voice roared from the pub. They turned, and saw him standing there, silhouetted on the verandah step, waving at them.

They waved in answer, turned, and started walking back the way they'd come.

'He doesn't fit in any more,' Jude said. 'You can see it. He thinks he's above it all, now.'

'Well he isn't, as far as I can see,' said Birdie bluntly.

'But that's what he thinks. And so he'd almost be better off if—'

Birdie stopped.

'Listen, Jude,' she said rapidly. 'Whatever you've done, whatever Trevor is or isn't, it was his decision, in the end. He's decided every move he's made. You're not responsible. None of us is responsible for anyone else's life. Isn't that right?'

'Of course it is.'

'So?'

He laughed. Soft, relieved laughter. 'So I'm a wanker. Okay?' His teeth gleamed as he turned towards her. 'Listen, Birdie, how come you never got in touch?'

'How come *you* never got in touch?'

'I thought it was up to you.'

'Why?'

'Because—oh, I don't know. Because I didn't want to pester you. Bore you. You and the law—well, you loathe all that, don't you? I thought you disapproved of me.'

'I thought you disapproved of *me*. And besides, you're the one who got famous. I only got—sort of—infamous. The rule is, the famous one calls.'

He laughed again. 'And the infamous one waits. That it?'

'That's it, I guess.'

'Well, now I know,' he said lightly.

They reached the pub and stepped up onto the verandah, carefully not touching.

'About time you bloody turned up!' beamed Punchy. 'We're going. Got a barbecue, up home.'

'Not yet we haven't.' Keith drained his own glass in a gulp.

'You better get up and start it then, Keith,' said Annie. 'You and Punchy. Get the chops out of the fridge. Trev and the rest of us'll be along shortly.'

'Let's go now,' whined Jason. 'I'm hungry. Mum? Mum?'

Rosalie sighed.

'Mum?'

'Shut up, Jason.' Grace was slurring, her dark eyes slitted, her mouth loose. Yet again she dipped her head to the glass in her hand, and drank.

Trevor Lamb stood up, stretched. 'Too early to eat for a while. Jude and I had a big lunch on the way. Anyhow, I want to go to the shack. Jude's got to set up the computer for me. You lot go back to the house, get things started. Eat if you want to. Jude and Verity and I'll come on when we're ready.'

'She's called Birdie, not Verity,' said Jason sulkily.

Annie stared at Trevor, mouth hanging slightly open. 'Why don't you leave the shack, son, come on home with us?'

'I will, Mum. Later. Coming, Jude?'

He nudged his way past Annie, stepped over Grace's outstretched legs, brushed past Lily Danger. She looked up at him with a malicious smile.

'Had enough of your family, have you? Join the club.'

He put out his hand and cupped it around her cheek and jaw. A proprietorial gesture. 'You'd better be careful, young Lily,' he said. 'I've been watching you. You might get what you're asking for, one day.'

'You reckon?' She met his eyes, ran her tongue over her lips.

His fingers tightened.

Punchy whistled. Keith stirred, but said nothing.

Trevor dropped his hand. As it fell, it lightly brushed the girl's breasts. She held his gaze, smiled her closed-lips smile. On her face, the marks of his fingers showed pale, darkening to red.

Trevor stepped off the verandah, onto the road. Then he

looked back over his shoulder. 'Come with us, Rosalie,' he said. 'The shack. Like old times.'

Summoned, chosen, Rosalie stood, and walked unsteadily to the road. She took care not to look at Lily Danger as she passed her.

'What about tea?' Annie complained. 'Rosalie?'

'The potato salad's made. Grace can butter the bread.'

'You must be joking,' muttered Grace, glaring after her mother.

'You'll do what you're told, you lazy little bugger!' screeched Annie, jerking forward and lashing out at her with all the sudden violence of deflected anger. But Grace pressed back against the verandah post, and the stubby palm batted empty air.

Trevor was walking towards Jude's car, with Rosalie trailing after him. Neither of them looked back.

'Looks like we're off, then,' Jude said to Birdie, feeling for his car keys.

'You really want me to come with you?'

'Only if you want to,' he said. 'But it'll be a good chance for you to get a look at the shack. Won't it?'

She fidgeted. 'I just have to go to the loo. Can you wait?'

He nodded and she darted off, before he could say anything about holding on or black pee. But halfway through the pub door she realised he wouldn't have embarrassed her like that, anyway. Unlike Dan Toby, who wouldn't have hesitated.

Birdie had braced herself to face the covert attention of the pub crowd. But only Bull Trews and three other men still stood at the bar. The dim little room was almost empty. With a jolt of surprise she realised that a lot of people must have drifted out and away through the afternoon without her quite noticing.

But when she thought about it, it was obvious. The road opposite the pub had been packed with cars and trucks. And she'd seen how few were left. She just hadn't registered, somehow.

Behind the bar, Floury Baker nodded to her as, bemused, she walked quickly towards the back of the pub. She tried to gather her scattered wits. Why hadn't she noticed the dwindling crowd? What had happened to her this afternoon?

She usually noticed things like that automatically. Her mind seemed to have gone blank. Turned off.

She shook her head and followed a short corridor that led out to the pub's back door.

She stood on the small porch beyond the door, and looked for the toilet. The yard was a barren square of dirt trodden hard as paving, with patches of rough grass here and there. Boxes and crates of empty bottles were stacked against the pub wall. Pepper trees lined the other boundaries, their trailing feathery fronds weeping forward, thick and dense. Nestled into their shadow, over to the right, was a small two-storeyed outbuilding—an old garage, or the original stable, with a flat at the top, Birdie guessed, by the look of the rickety stairs that led from the yard to a green-painted door set into the side of the top floor.

For a moment Birdie couldn't see anything else, and then she realised that right beside her, its side wall forming part of the porch, was the traditional small weatherboard outside lavatory.

She stepped outside and rounded the corner. There was the door, facing out into the yard. As she reached for the doorknob there was a rush of water and the sound of a bolt being drawn. Then the door was swinging open to reveal Sue Sweeney, still straightening the back of her skirt.

Birdie stepped back. Sue looked up, and gave a little shriek.

'Oh!' she exclaimed. 'Oh, sorry, you gave me a shock. Didn't know anyone was here. You waiting for the loo?'

Birdie nodded.

'The one upstairs is better,' said Sue, wrinkling her nose as she came back out to the yard.

'Oh, it doesn't matter. I have to leave with the others, so I just wanted to—'

'Are they leaving?' Sue asked quickly.

'Going to eat, I think.' No point in going into the details.

Sue nodded, a vacant look on her face. Stood back to let Birdie into the lavatory.

But when Birdie came out, she was still in the yard, looking up at the sky. Her face was pale in the dusk. Her bright lipstick had worn off during the afternoon, and her nose was shiny. She walked over to Birdie.

'Just having a breath of air,' she said unconvincingly. 'Think I might as well have some tea myself now, if the Lambs are going. Take my break while things are quiet.' She brushed her hair back with her fingers. 'They'll be back later, do you reckon?'

'I don't know. I'm just following them around. Doing what I'm told.'

'Yeah. Sure. Well, see you.'

'See you.'

Birdie followed the other woman inside, and watched as she went behind the bar to talk to Allan Baker. Sue was disappointed. Of course she must be. That was something else Birdie had barely registered. After that kiss on the verandah, Sue had gone back into the pub, back behind the bar. But Trevor Lamb had gone to sit with Annie on the log. All afternoon it had been Punchy who'd gone in to the pub for drinks. Trevor hadn't stirred.

She'll keep.

She remembered Trevor saying that to someone—to Punchy, or to Keith, maybe, after an hour or two. In answer to a muttered question or suggestion. There'd been sniggering all round afterwards. At the time Birdie had wondered who they were talking about. Now she thought she knew.

Hope she tells him to go to hell, she thought savagely. She didn't often identify with other women just because they were women. But there was something intensely, brutally male about this place that stirred partisan feelings. The other women—Annie, Rosalie and Lily—and even fourteen-year-old Grace—seemed to have worked out their place in the scheme of things, and accepted it, each in her own way. They mightn't be happy in it, but they'd accepted it.

Sue was different. She was still struggling, wanting, trying, looking for something better. You could see it in her face.

Birdie stepped out onto the verandah. The Lambs were still sitting where she'd left them. Punchy waved. She lifted her hand in response.

'You better hurry up,' Jason said enviously, pointing to where Jude's car waited on the other side of the road.

Trevor Lamb was lounging in the passenger seat, head tilted back against the headrest as though he was dozing. Rosalie crouched on the far side of the back seat. She saw

Birdie, and said something. As Birdie watched, Trevor turned his head to look. His face, still masked by the sunglasses, was expressionless. But Rosalie looked troubled. Trevor had been kept waiting.

Good, thought Birdie irrationally. She stepped off the verandah and crossed the road. Taking her time.

Eight

They could have walked to the shack if they hadn't had the computer to deliver. It would have taken ten minutes, at most. Jude had pointed this out in *Lamb to the Slaughter*. But, despite the fact that she'd studied the map he'd supplied in the book, Birdie was still a little surprised to find how near to the pub was the dim gap that marked the start of the track that led to Trevor Lamb's home. She hadn't noticed it when she arrived, though she'd parked very near it. It was well-disguised, screened by the pepper trees on one side, and uncleared bush on the other.

Anyone entering that gap in the trees would be hidden from sight of the road very quickly. The track curved to the left almost as soon as it began. Tall trees and thick bush lined it on both sides, arching overhead.

Jude's quite right, thought Birdie, as the car bumped at walking pace along the dim, leafy tunnel, light from the headlights streaming forward into the gloom. Anyone could have slipped down this dim alley, reached the shack, killed Daphne Lamb and hurried back, unnoticed.

Anyone? Who?

Jude wasn't interested in that question. He had been simply interested in showing how wide were the possibilities, given the scenario and timing. In showing that Trevor Lamb was not the only possible suspect for the murder of Daphne.

Daphne. Sue Sweeney had talked about her. In fact, she was the only person Birdie had met so far who had mentioned her name. To everyone else, even Jude, Daphne had become, it seemed, an almost forgotten symbol. Her murder was the occasion of Trevor Lamb's martyrdom. That was all.

But Trevor Lamb was alive, at least. And free at last,

thanks to Jude's passion for justice. Daphne was dead. Dead at twenty-two. Where as the justice for her? Did no one care about that?

The car crept along, negotiating twists and turns, bumping over the deeply-rutted earth. Then the track seemed to come to a dead end. Jude stopped. The sound of the creek filled the air. A great gum tree rose like a dark sentinel in front of them. Jude pointed. 'That's where you pranged, Trevor,' he said.

Trevor turned his head to look. 'Nearly there, then,' he said.

Jude eased the car forward again, twisting the wheel sharply to the right, and Birdie saw that they had reached not the end of the track, but a ninety-degree bend.

Around the bend the track straightened. Trees lined it like a deliberately-planted avenue, strangely formal and impressive. The car's headlights picked up a dark shape directly ahead. A sloping corrugated iron roof, a chimney, a small verandah jutting out. The shack.

Trevor leaned slightly forward. 'Sure the electricity's on, Rosalie?' he snapped.

'Yes. I told you. Grace went down and checked it this morning. She says everything works.'

'Grace, huh? Why didn't you check it yourself?'

'I don't like coming here.' Rosalie's voice was very low.

He turned in his seat to stare at her. 'Don't like coming here,' he repeated slowly. 'Is that right?' He gave a low laugh. 'But that was our place, Rosalie. When we were kids . . .'

Rosalie looked out the window. At the dark scrub, the trunks of the marching trees. 'We're not kids any more,' she said flatly.

'Grace doesn't mind the shack,' said Trevor, still staring at her, as if willing her to meet his eyes. 'Made my bed for me, she said. Put some beers in the fridge. Batteries in the old transistor. She told me she likes the old place.'

'She doesn't know what she's talking about.'

He turned back to face the front, with another half-laugh. 'She seemed to know exactly what she was talking about, Rosalie. Little Grace. Not so little any more, eh?'

Rosalie closed her eyes.

He sank back, pointed. 'Pull up in front, Jude,' he said

off-handedly. 'That's the key I've got. Let's just hope Gracie wasn't bullshitting her old mum about the power.'

Rosalie bit her lip. 'Trev, the electricity's on. I told you.'

He continued as if she hadn't spoken. 'Wouldn't have surprised me if that old bastard Hewitt had ripped the wires out. It's the sort of thing he'd do. Just because he paid to have the power put in. Tight-arsed bastard.'

'I would have told you,' murmured Rosalie. 'Anyhow, far as I know he's never been near the place. Dolly Hewitt and Phillip came, that's all—to take some things.'

'What things?' The question was sharp, almost a bark.

Rosalie jumped, very slightly. 'Things. You know. Clothes and things.'

'You mean Daphne's stuff?'

'Yes.'

'What did you let them do that for?' Trevor's voice was rising.

Birdie saw Rosalie's fists clench in her lap. 'We didn't *let* them do anything. They just did it. The cops let them in, and they did it.'

'There'd be a list of what they took, Trevor,' said Jude quietly. 'We'd have it in the files. It would only have been small personal things.' He guided the car into the clearing in front of the shack, and stopped.

'She was my wife, you know,' said Trevor Lamb, still in that injured, hectoring voice. 'Anything of hers was legally mine. Like the shack. Legally mine. They had no right to trespass. You should've stopped them, Rosalie, you half-wit. Protected my rights—'

'You were in bloody gaol for *killing* her, Trevor!' screeched Rosalie, suddenly flaring out of her lethargy, the whites of her eyes startlingly white in the dimness of the car.

Trevor said nothing.

She beat her fists together in an agony of frustration. 'Rights? You didn't have any rights. *We* didn't have any rights. What's the matter with you? Are you crazy, or something?'

'Shut up, Rosalie.' The voice was low and threatening.

'I won't shut up. You're acting weird. You're acting crazy. You're crazy anyway, wanting to come back to this place. What do you think you're trying to prove? Don't you remember? The blood in the kitchen—the blood—'

With a choking sob she wrenched at the car door, finally heaving it open and almost throwing herself out into the clearing. She leant against the car roof, panting and crying for a moment. Then she stumbled away, around the back of the car and into the bush.

'Happy homecoming,' murmured Trevor sardonically.

Jude glanced at him. 'Will she be all right?'

'Who? Rosalie? What could happen to her?'

Something happened to another woman alone, right here, five years ago.

'It's getting dark,' said Jude. He shrugged uncomfortably.

'You reckon someone's going to rape her by mistake? No risk, mate. Once they got up close they'd run a mile. By God she's gone off since I saw her last.'

The savagery of his contempt was stunning.

Jude said nothing. But even from the back seat Birdie could sense his withdrawal. His fight to contain his dislike.

Trevor Lamb felt it, too. It seemed to please him. He grinned, and reached over to grab the back of Jude's neck. Deliberately making contact, daring the other man to recoil. But Jude didn't move.

'Rosalie and I go back a long way, mate,' Lamb purred. 'Don't you worry about her. She can look after herself all right. She's been running round this bush all her life. Knows every rabbit track round the place. The old house's just up the hill, isn't it?'

As if to underline his point a faint light suddenly glimmered through the trees. Somewhere, not far away, a house had come to life.

'That's them. They're home,' said Trevor Lamb. He opened his own car door and got out. Looked at the dark, closed little cottage hunched in the clearing. Verandah. Two mean little windows on either side of a battered front door. He took a deep breath. 'I said I'd come back, and I did,' he muttered. 'I told those bastards.'

Jude wet his lips. 'Listen, Trevor, you've made your point,' he said carefully. 'But—given everything—if you don't want to stay up at the house with the rest of them, don't you reckon it might be better for you to put up at the pub, with Birdie and me—at least for tonight?'

'Why would I want to do that?' Trevor's eyes narrowed suspiciously.

'You'd be more comfortable. You'd have company.'

'Mate, I've had enough company to last me a lifetime. You ever been in gaol?'

'You know I haven't.'

'Then get off my back.' Lamb strode across the clearing, towards the shack.

'Jude, let's just do this and get out of here,' murmured Birdie, throwing open her own door. She felt as though she was suffocating. Trevor Lamb was poison. A poisonous mixture of arrogance, paranoia, vanity and savage selfishness seemed to ooze from his pores like bitter fumes. She watched him cursing as he fumbled with the key to the door.

Jude heaved himself from the car and went around to the boot. He looked very tired.

The door to the shack opened with a wailing squeak, and a light was switched on. They heard Lamb's shoes clunking on a hard floor. Then the window in the next room lit up. He was prowling the shack.

Jude lifted a large box from the boot, and began carrying it towards the open door. Birdie took a smaller box and a package of paper, and followed. She had no wish to help Trevor Lamb. But she had even less wish to stay in this place one moment longer than necessary. And short of staying huddled in the car there was nothing else to do.

She wondered, as she crossed the dusty clearing, how she was going to be able to cope with the next few days. With Lamb, without Jude.

The man's an animal, Birdie . . . Lamb was guilty as sin. You could smell it.

Since when has your nose been a legal argument?

Smart-arse talk. Easy enough in her house in Annandale, where the streetlight shone through the front window and the air was full of the sounds of people, police sirens and planes roaring overhead.

Different here in this dismal clearing where trees loomed above them, trapping the hot air, and the only sounds were the sluggish trickling of water, and sheep and their doomed lambs, calling to each other now and then in the paddocks across the creek.

Jude elbowed his way through the door, which squeaked miserably again. 'Where do you want the stuff?' Birdie heard him say.

'On the table there,' called Lamb from somewhere inside the house. 'Just push the other junk off.'

Birdie climbed the single step, crossed the narrow verandah and moved inside.

She blinked in the yellow light. The room was bigger than she'd expected. Stained white walls, rough wooden floor, light bulb in a paper shade swinging from cobwebbed rafters, already attracting the moths.

Jude brushed past her and went outside again. Going for the rest of the computer equipment. The big box he'd brought in stood on the wooden dining table near the window. A red-flowered tablecloth, a small, white transistor radio and some china salt and pepper shakers shaped like red, white-spotted toadstools had been pushed to one side to clear the space. Birdie put her packages down beside one of the toadstools. Stared around.

A kitchen-dining room. By its size, it took up one entire side of the little house. At the back, there was a bolted door that probably led to the yard outside. The back was the kitchen end of the room. It was efficiently, if modestly, organised. There was a sink with a cupboard underneath, an electric stove behind which spatulas, spoons and tongs hung on a rack, a refrigerator, a small dresser with ripple-glass doors, a red flip-top rubbish bin. Beside the stove was a side table, its top covered with stick-on plastic patterned with red cherries, a matching red curtain hanging like a skirt around its legs.

Daphne. In the Hope's End pub, she didn't exist. In the clearing outside, there was no trace of her. But here she was everywhere. In those brave, bright cherries, that red curtain. In the red-checked tea-towel hanging on a hook screwed into the side of the sink cupboard, the blue mug upturned on the sink, the salt and pepper toadstool shakers, the single-page calendar pinned to the wall, marked in black pen.

On the floor, in front of the stove, the boards were darkly stained. They had been washed, by the look of it. But nothing could take that darkness away. Nothing ever would. Birdie became conscious of the smell of the place. Old dust, old wood—and something else. Something that, like the stain on the floor, would never quite disappear.

Drawn across the room almost against her will, she turned her eyes away from the floor and went to look at the calendar. It was a give-away, from the Christmas issue of a women's magazine. Down the side was a photograph of a sulphur-crested cockatoo holding a sprig of wattle in its claw. The months were set out in rows. Four rows of three.

The January days were neatly obliterated, each with its own black cross. February had been begun, but never finished. After Wednesday the ninth, the crosses stopped. On the night of the tenth, Daphne had died. So the calendar she'd marked so carefully remained mostly blank. She never reached the anniversaries she'd circled and labelled in tiny printing.

February 16 Mum's b'day, March 22 SS b'day, May 3 My b'day, August 10 P's b'day, September 8 Dad's b'day, September 24 M & D anniv., November 12 T's b'day, November 14 Auntie P's b'day . . .

There was something very personal about these brief notes. Daphne had marked the things that mattered to her. Birthdays, her parents' wedding anniversary.

Birdie squinted at the messages. SS was probably Sue Sweeney. Sue and Daphne had been friends. P, presumably was Phillip, Daphne's brother. T was Trevor. Auntie P was a mystery. A family member Birdie didn't know about. Interestingly, none of the Lambs, except Trevor, featured. Maybe the Lambs didn't celebrate birthdays. Or maybe Daphne had given up including them on her list of dates to be remembered.

May 3 My b'day. That was the saddest note of all. Daphne had never reached her twenty-third birthday. Unknowing, marking off her calendar each morning, or each night before bedtime, she'd been counting off the days to her death.

Like the lambs under the trees in the Hewitts' paddocks. Doomed, without knowing it.

I'm getting maudlin, thought Birdie, turning her back on the calendar. None of us knows when we're going to die. We're all marking off the days, for God's sake, in one way or another. But this place . . .

This place.

Jude came struggling through the door with a bulging plastic bag and the last two boxes, and set everything down carefully on the edge of the table. At the same moment Trevor Lamb came striding in from the next room.

'Lights all work, anyhow,' he announced. 'Bloody miracle. Window broken out the back. Bolt on the back door's stuck. Water's rusty, but it'll come good.' He walked over to the sink and turned on the single tap. Water flowed out sullenly, drumming on the stainless steel, gurgling down the drain. He nodded, as if satisfied.

He crossed the stained floor without a glance on his way back to the table. Then he stuck his hands in his pockets and surveyed the sharp-edged, shiny white boxes with a bitter smile, as if appreciating how out of place they looked in their new surroundings.

'Now you know how the other half lives, don't you?' he said softly, turning his eyes to Birdie.

'You're a bit short on power points,' she said, refusing to be embarrassed into reacting more extravagantly. She could have said, gushingly, that the shack wasn't so bad, that the kitchen was cosy. She could have said, more aggressively, that she knew writers who worked happily and well in far more primitive circumstances. She could have asked, moreover, to which 'half' Trevor Lamb meant he belonged, in view of his possession of a huge publisher's advance and thousands of dollars worth of computer equipment. But this would have been, as Beth Bothwell would have said, 'counterproductive'.

'I'll get that fixed. For now we've got extension cords here somewhere,' said Lamb, turning away. 'And some double adaptors. Did you bring them in, Jude?'

Jude flicked the plastic bag. 'Yes. Will we set the stuff up here?'

'I said so, didn't I?' Lamb started pulling at the boxes, pushing tablecloth and toadstool salt and pepper shakers impatiently aside. The salt rolled and fell to the floor, bouncing on the boards. Birdie bent quickly and picked it up. She was absurdly relieved to see it hadn't chipped.

She held the little object for a moment, fingering its smooth surface. At the table Trevor was heaving the printer from its box. Jude was working quickly, pulling out computer and keyboard, reaching for leads.

Get on with it, Birdwood. What's wrong with you? You're here to work. Just do it.

'Do you mind if I have a look around?' she said aloud. 'I need to know the layout. So I can give—'

'Help yourself. Won't take you long.' Lamb didn't even look up.

Birdie turned to leave the room. Then, on impulse, she spun back, picked up the pepper shaker and took it, with the salt, to the other end of the room, out of harm's way.

Trevor was right. A tour of the shack didn't take long. Beside the kitchen-dining room was a small sitting room furnished with a battered couch and a single armchair, both drawn up in front of the brick fireplace that took up much of the side wall, a rickety side table covered with a limp, embroidered white cloth, and a cane magazine rack, stuffed full.

It was a dreary little room. But Daphne's attempts to make it homelike were apparent. The walls were white. A vase of dusty dried flowers and seed pods painted gold stood on the mantelpiece above the fire. A bright cotton rug disguised the couch's original cover, and cushions filled its corners. A flimsy lace curtain tied back with ribbon decorated the window that looked out to the front verandah. Pictures from magazines, neatly mounted on black cardboard, were pinned in groups to the walls.

Pictures from magazines. A calendar from a magazine. A full magazine rack. Daphne had liked magazines, apparently. In fact, Birdie realised, many of the small touches in the house were reminiscent of magazine articles about decorating on the cheap. 'Clever Decorating on a Shoestring.' 'Give Your Home an Instant Face-Lift.' '101 Great Ways to Beat the Budget Blues.'

Two more doors opened into the back of the house on this side. Through one was a bathroom: a tiny window looking out to the trees, an ancient claw-footed bath, deeply stained by a dripping tap, a chip heater, a piece of dry, cracked yellow soap in a plastic basket and a rubber bathmat. Nothing of Daphne here.

Through the other door was the bedroom. And, strangely, it was also almost devoid of personality. Except for the lace curtains at the window, and the flowered bedspread on the old double bed, neatly made, presumably by Grace, there were few signs that this room had been inhabited by a woman.

Daphne's mother and brother had come and taken
Daphne's personal things, Rosalie had said. They seemed to
have confined their attention to this room. And they seemed
to have done the job thoroughly, as though determined to
leave nothing of hers, however small, in the room the married couple had shared.

Nothing lay on the small oak dressing-table. Not a pin,
not a thread. There were no women's clothes in the dark
little wardrobe, door hanging open on its hinges. On each
side of the bed was a fabric-covered box doing service as a
bedside table. One was cluttered with a big glass ashtray,
three boxes of matches, cigarette papers, a couple of shoot-
er's magazines. The other, nearest the window, was bare, except for a reading lamp.

Birdie eased open one of the dressing-table drawers. It
was empty. And so, when she looked, were all the others.

Phillip and Dolly Hewitt had packed Daphne's intimate
belongings, all her bits and pieces, useful and useless, into
boxes and suitcases, and taken them away.

How they must hate Trevor Lamb, Birdie thought. How
certain they must have been of his guilt to remove every trace
of her like this.

How did they feel now? Were they still so certain? Or
had they started to wonder if Jude Gregorian, smart city lawyer, was right? If, all along, someone else was their daughter's murderer? Someone else in Hope's End, hiding guilt
behind a lazy greeting, a familiar face?

Birdie turned off the light and backed out of the room,
suddenly oppressed by its closed deadness, its desolation. She
could hear Trevor and Jude talking in the kitchen, and went
out to join them. They had the computer set up now, with
the printer beside it, paper loaded, ready to go.

Jude straightened up as she came in, glanced at her
briefly.

'Seen enough?' he asked, with forced cheeriness. 'Done
the grand tour?'

' 'Course she hasn't. Dunny's out the back,' grunted
Trevor Lamb. 'Dunny, laundry, tank, clothes line . . . God,
she's hardly started, has she?'

'I'll come back tomorrow, when it's light, if that's all
right,' said Birdie.

'If that's all right,' he mimicked unpleasantly. 'Sure. Do what you like. I'll be here.'

Jude glanced at his watch. 'Listen,' he said, 'I think you're right now, Trevor, so I might leave you. Go back to the pub. I'd like to have an early night. Got to drive back tomorrow. So—'

Lamb raised his eyebrows. 'Aren't you coming up to Mum's?'

'Well, I was going to, but it's getting late. And anyhow, I thought you might rather . . .'

The other man looked up sharply. 'No, I wouldn't rather be on my own with them, if that's what you're going to say. And they're expecting you. It's all organised.' His mouth twisted and his voice rose. 'If you can't face spending any more of your precious time with the low life, just say so. You can just push off. You don't need my permission, do you? You can just take your little girlfriend and your fancy car and . . .'

Jude put up his hands, palms out. 'Don't start that bullshit with me, Trevor,' he said quietly. 'All right? Just don't start. You know I'll come with you if you want me to. It's your night.'

Lamb held his gaze for a moment, then suddenly relaxed, and grinned.

'Just let's do a print test,' he said, in a more normal voice. 'Then we'll go. Have a bite. A few beers.'

Jude handles him very well, thought Birdie, slipping quietly through the front door and into the relative freshness of the evening air.

She heard tinny radio music, someone flipping through stations in bursts of static, as she stepped down into the clearing and walked across to the car. Trevor had turned on his transistor.

The car was still warm, but she sank into the back seat gratefully, pulling the door shut after her and curling up in the darkness. He handles him well, she thought again. But all the same Trevor's going to get his way, whatever Jude wants, however he feels. Jude's still in there now. And we're still going to the Lamb's to eat. Thanks to that little scene we're committed. For quite a while.

She closed her eyes. A mosquito whined beside her ear. Across the creek, out in the darkness of Hewitts' paddock, a lamb bleated, and its mother answered. From the Lamb house there was a whooping yell. Punchy, probably, keeping the celebrations alive. From the shack, a singer wailed remorselessly about her lost love. Or, rather, 'l-er-erve'.

Birdie sighed. It was going to be a long night.

Nine

A dog was chewing at a lamb's head over by the house step. Coming upon it suddenly, Birdie looked at the half-eaten chop on her paper plate, had an appalling thought, and immediately felt extremely sick.

'Aren't ya hungry, love?' Annie Lamb loomed up at her in the darkness, a bone in her hand.

'I probably ate too much bread,' said Birdie weakly, forcing her eyes away from the dog.

Annie laughed heartily, gnawed at the bone. Fighting down waves of nausea, Birdie watched, fascinated. Had she managed to eat a whole chop? How could she, without any teeth?

'Lovely and fresh,' Annie said, winking. 'Punchy only killed it last night. Nothing like prime lamb, is there? Fresh?'

She wiped the corners of her mouth delicately with the tips of her fingers, and threw the bone to the dog. It looked, but then turned back to the lamb's head.

'Spoilt bugger,' she said. 'Got the brains and all this time. Thinks it's bloody Christmas.'

The barbecue fire flared as Jason threw his plate into the flames. Fat spat and hissed. Orange flickers lit up faces, greasy fingers, fencing wire and dusty ground littered with crushed beer cans. A radio blared unrecognisable music.

'Give us another beer, Jason,' Annie called. 'And one for Birdie. She's dry.'

'Only one left,' said Jason, before Birdie could protest.

'We're going back to the pub now, Mum,' said Trevor. He was standing by the barbecue with his arm round Rosalie's shoulders. Amazingly, she was smiling.

'Right you are,' Annie said comfortably.

Keith walked over to the house step and kicked at the lamb's head. The dog growled, and he kicked it, too. It yelped.

'It's all right,' Annie said. 'Punchy buried the ears with the guts. Turn off the house light, will you? If we're going now.'

They turned away. Birdie took the opportunity to tip her plate and toss the chop in the dog's direction. It nosed at the meat, then, with an air of having unwelcome work to do, picked it up in its jaws, got to its feet and loped off into the darkness. Presumably to bury the prize in preparation for some future, leaner day.

'Seems we're going back to the pub,' said Jude's voice in her ear.

Birdie jumped slightly. She hadn't heard him approach. And she felt guilty about the discarded chop.

'I heard,' she said. 'How can they go on drinking?'

'Practice,' he said with a grin. 'So, did you enjoy dinner?'

She grimaced and jerked her head at what remained of the lamb's head. 'I think I'm going to turn vegetarian,' she said.

'You're in the country now, mate.' Jude peered at the head. 'Ears gone,' he commented.

She shuddered. 'What's this obsession with the poor thing's ears?'

'You coming, Jude?' bawled Punchy from the gate. A car engine revved.

'Coming!' Jude fumbled for his keys

'I'm going in your car, Jude!' screamed Jason.

'No you're not!' snapped Grace from the darkness. 'You're going with the others. I'm going in Jude's car with Mum. Uncle Trev said.'

'It's not fair!' whined Jason. 'I don't want to go in our car. I want to go in the good car.'

'Stay home then.'

Birdie and Jude began walking out of the yard, kicking aside beer cans as they went.

'What's with the ears?' persisted Birdie.

'Sshh. Keep your voice down,' Jude muttered. 'The lambs' ears are marked. It's like the brand on a cow.'

'So?'

'So—it's fairly important to hide the evidence, isn't it? In case the police come round. Which in the case of the Lambs happens with monotonous regularity.'

'You mean—they *stole* the lamb? And killed it? And we *ate* it?'

He laughed quietly. 'What did you think? See any stock round here? The Lambs haven't farmed for twenty years. And now they couldn't even if they wanted to. Les Hewitt's got all the decent grazing land they ever had. Milton sold it off to him bit by bit to make drinking money.'

'Milton. Trevor's father?'

'Yeah. The Lambs' land used to go all the way down to the creek at the back of the house, and over the other side for quite a way. The paddocks you can see from the pub used to be theirs, for example. It was Milton's father's property originally. Anyhow, it's all gone now. All but the home paddock, and a narrow stretch that slopes down to the shack. You can look at it in the morning.'

The Lambs' station wagon screeched past them, horn blaring, heading for the main road.

'Beatcha there!' howled Jason, leaning out the window.

Trevor, Rosalie and Grace were already installed in the back seat of Jude's car. Trevor was sitting in the middle, his arms draped over the two women's shoulders. Grace was giggling self-consciously at something he'd said.

Birdie climbed wearily into the front seat. By her watch it was only nine, but as far as she was concerned it could have been three a.m. Maybe once we get to the pub I can just ease myself away and up to bed, she thought. Her stomach growled. She realised she'd hardly eaten anything all day. But she didn't feel hungry any more. Just vaguely ill.

Jude started the engine, and switched on the headlights. He had them on high beam, and as he swung the car around, the house and yard were sweepingly illuminated as if by searchlights.

Rotting timber, rusting roof, collapsed outbuildings, car bodies and junk. The house shape distorted by the lump of the caravan parked at its side. Down the hill, at the back, tussocky, rock-filled paddock falling away to dark scrub. And across the creek, beyond the trees, the silver pastures, the neatly-grouped trees, the well-filled dams that belonged to the Lambs no longer.

Trevor Lamb made a low sound—half-laugh, half-sneer. 'What a dump,' he muttered.

'I'll say,' Grace agreed. 'No one ever does anything to clean it up, either.' She wriggled smugly in her corner.

'No one's stopping you, if you want to make a start, Grace,' snapped Rosalie. 'I've got enough on my hands, cooking and washing for the lot of you. God knows, I've tried to get you and Jason to clean up the yard often enough.'

'I've got better things to do,' said Grace, smothering a pretended yawn.

'I'll bet you have,' Trevor leered, cutting off Rosalie's sharp retort. 'You'll have to tell me all about it one of these days.'

Grace giggled again. Rosalie said nothing.

The car bumped down the track, turned left into the main road through Hope's End. Less than a city block away shone the lights of the pub. The Lambs' station wagon was parked under the pepper trees, with several other cars.

As Jude's car approached, a small, wild figure came running from the pub verandah. Jason. Jude slowed, and finally stopped in the middle of the road, to avoid running him over. The boy's grubby hands gripped the edge of the open window. He poked his head into the car. His avid face was still smeared with tomato sauce and flecks of charcoal. His eyes were dark with excitement.

'Hey Uncle Trev, Phillip Hewitt's here,' he gasped. 'He's in the pub. He's really pissed. Are you gonna have a fight? Are you gonna beat him up? Are you? Are you?'

'I don't know, Jason,' drawled Trevor Lamb. 'Have to see, won't I? Mind you, I don't usually fight with girls. I'd rather do other things with them.'

Jason howled with laughter and tore back across the road to the pub again, probably to relate this piece of wit to the others.

'Bloody little animal,' muttered Rosalie, looking after him.

'Needs a good kick in the arse,' said Trevor. 'Like a few people round here.'

'You mean Lily,' giggled Grace. 'But Lily's got no bum, practically. If you tried to kick her you'd miss. Lily looks like a boy.'

'I suppose you think you haven't got that problem, little

Miss Hot-Stuff,' said Trevor. There was a scuffle and a de-lighted shriek from Grace.

'Anyhow, I didn't mean Lily,' Lamb went on. 'I meant that little poofter Hewitt. I'd like to kick his arse for him. Except he'd probably like it.'

'Should hear Jason sending him up,' screeched Grace, by now very full of herself. 'He's such a dork. He writes *poems*. Really hopeless poems, Jason says. Don't rhyme properly, or anything. He writes them at lunchtimes. Once Jason got one of them and put it in the teachers' toilet.'

'Very clever,' growled Trevor. Suddenly he was grim, dis-playing one of the lightning changes of mood that seemed to characterise him. Rosalie, too, had become absolutely still and silent.

Jude parked and turned off the engine, but made no move to get out of the car.

'We don't want any trouble tonight, do we, Trevor?' he asked casually.

'Probably not,' said Trevor Lamb. 'Depends on Hewitt, doesn't it?'

He elbowed Rosalie, who obediently slid out of the car. He followed her, with Grace close behind him. Grace slammed the door roughly. Together the three of them crossed the road, Trevor swaggering, hands in pockets. Cries from the verandah greeted him.

Alone in the darkness of the car, Birdie and Jude stared at one another.

'Once more unto the breach, dear friend,' he said.

'There's going to be a fight.'

'I doubt it. Phillip Hewitt isn't up to it.'

'That's Trevor's story,' said Birdie, looking over towards the pub. 'Doesn't mean it's true.'

'It's not just Trevor's story. I know Phillip. Well, I feel I know him, after all this time. He's a pretty classic case. Phys-ically weak, sensitive, introverted, close to his mother, doesn't get on with his father—all that.'

'Even worms turn, Jude. God knows, I've seen that hap-pen often enough. You must have, too.'

'Yeah. Guess I have.' They sat in silence for a moment. Finally Jude stirred. 'His sister being killed was a disaster for him. It's because she died that he came back here to teach. That school—it's a zoo. It must be torture for him.'

'That's what Sue Sweeney said.'

'Did she? When?'

'When I first arrived. When she was showing me my room. We were just talking.'

'I never got her to talk much.'

'You're a man.'

Jude laughed. 'Men are her specialty, aren't they? So I hear.'

'That's what she probably thought. That you'd heard. From Trevor, and everyone else. She probably had her guard up with you. City boy. Looking down your educated nose at the town tart.'

'I wouldn't have thought she was that sensitive.'

Birdie raised her eyebrows. 'I rest my case,' she murmured. She swung back towards him, and their eyes met.

'I wish we were somewhere else,' said Jude softly.

Birdie's stomach turned over. She managed to laugh, as though she thought he was joking, pushed at her door, and almost stumbled out into the shadow of the pepper tree.

What are you scared of? Scared he's coming on to you? Or scared he isn't?

She waited, clutching her shoulder bag, while Jude closed and locked the car. He took his time, and when he'd finished and was standing beside her she was feeling calmer.

They crossed the road, Birdie walking carefully, looking straight ahead as if she was interested in what was happening in the pub. She didn't want to meet Jude's eyes again. Didn't want their hands to brush together. Or maybe she did. But she didn't want him to *think* she did. In case—

As they reached the pub step they saw that the verandah was empty. For some reason everyone had moved inside. Voices inside the pub were raised. Punchy waved to them from the doorway, mouthing, grinning and beckoning.

'You're a murderer! A murderer!'

The voice rose, a wail of accusation and despair. Then there was a shout, and the sound of breaking glass. Grace's squeal of excitement and Annie's laughter screeched out into the night.

Jude swore under his breath. 'Do you want to disappear?' he murmured to Birdie. 'You could go round the back, get in that way, go upstairs.'

She shook her head.

'He wasn't going to leave it alone.'

They both spun towards the voice. It was Rosalie. She was leaning against the tank stand at the end of the veran-dah. They could barely see her in the dark.

'He hasn't changed,' she went on dully. 'I thought he had, but he hasn't. I just forgot what he was like. He talks different, now. But inside he's the same. Just the same.'

'I don't want any trouble here,' roared Floury Baker's voice from inside.

Rosalie hunched her shoulders, and turned away.

Ten

Birdie sidled up to the pub door. Punchy grinned at her, and obligingly made room so that she could stand beside him and peer in.

Trevor Lamb was standing at the bar, shaking drops of beer from his hand. Broken glass scattered around his feet. Beer puddled the bar counter, and dripped to the floor.

A metre away from him stood Phillip Hewitt, bleary-eyed, his face sickly white. His arm was outstretched in front of him, hand cupped as though he was still holding the glass that had been swiped from his grip.

Daphne's brother had hardly changed at all in five years. Thin, nervous-looking, the good clothes that seemed a little too big for him, the tremulous mouth, the prominent Adam's apple, the thick, straight, shiny fair hair flopping over the forehead, the big blue eyes with their long, black eyelashes. Birdie recognised him easily from his photographs. But the photographs had flattered him. In the ones she had seen he appeared romantically good-looking. The sensitive young man. The tormented poet. Hamlet. Romeo. But here, now, in real life, the same assembly of features produced the impression of a caricature.

It was a vivid tableau. Phillip ashen, Trevor sneering, the puddle of beer spreading between them, Floury Baker frowning behind the bar, Sue Sweeney, further along, her hand frozen on the beer tap. It was as though they were in a charmed circle. People had moved back, giving them room. Annie Lamb, Keith Lamb, Lily, Grace and Jason were in a group together. Six or seven other men were leaning against the wall, watching, and occasionally glancing at Punchy, massive by the door.

'Now will you piss off?' snarled Trevor Lamb.

The boy's lip twitched, but he didn't move.

'Trev, I'm warning you, mate,' rumbled Floury Baker. 'I don't want the cops here, and I don't want the place wrecked. I'll close up if you give me trouble. I'll do it. I've done it before. You ask Punchy.'

'So I'm supposed to stand here while this little poofter abuses me, am I? Supposed to just put up with it?'

'He's had one too many, Trev. Just leave it.' Baker looked meaningfully at Phillip Hewitt and almost imperceptibly jerked his head towards the door.

'I won't go. I'm not drunk,' slurred Phillip Hewitt, white to the lips. He looked wildly around the pub. His voice rose, and cracked. 'Why don't any of the rest of you say anything? You were happy enough to talk last month. Last week. Yesterday. Why not now?'

It was excruciating to watch the men shifting, angling their bodies very slowly, minutely, towards each other and away from him. Excruciating to watch the faces become sunbrowned masks: thin-lipped, blank-eyed, shutting him out.

'Go home, Phil,' said Floury Baker quietly.

'Yeah, get out of it,' shouted Annie Lamb, fists clenched. 'Trev's home. He's free and clear. For good. The court said so.'

'My sister's dead.' Phillip Hewitt's voice was trembling. 'She's dead. Because of him. Because she married him.'

He looked with loathing at Trevor Lamb.

Lamb smiled. 'Can't stand the thought she did that, can you?' he said. softly. 'That's what none of you can stand. That your precious Daphne got down in the gutter to wallow around with people you think are too bloody low to lick your boots.'

'That's right!' cried Annie, stepping forward, red-faced.

'Well she did it,' Lamb went on. 'She did it because she wanted to. And she liked it. God, you bet she did. Where do you think the kid she had in her belly came from? You think she was the Virgin Mary?'

Phillip stared at him, panting, as if hypnotised by those cold, dark eyes.

Lamb lowered his voice even further, so that he was almost whispering. But the pub was so still that the venomous sound seemed to fill it to the furthest corners. It was then that Birdie realised just how drunk he was. He was one of those people who could consume vast quantities of alcohol without obvious effect, so that strangers, like her, were deceived into thinking he was unaffected in any way. But all the time, drink by drink, the strings that restrained the beast inside the man were loosening. And now, with this last beer, and faced with a quaking victim, the rigid self-control she'd sensed in him was giving way.

'Your family tried to destroy me, Hewitt,' he snarled. 'Your bastard of a father. And your crazy, screwed-up mother. Because they thought I was shit. Well, they're stuffed now, aren't they? Them, and you, and everyone else round here who screamed for my blood, and talked their heads off to the cops while my wonderful family just stood back and did bloody nothing and I went down the mine.'

He glanced over his shoulder, at Annie, Keith and the others. His face was closed now. His eyes were cold.

'Is he talking about us?' mumbled Annie. 'Hey!' Her face crimsoned with anger. 'Hey, is he talking about us?'

Keith's eyes narrowed. The crease between his brows deepened. 'What did you expect us to bloody do about it, mate? You had a bloody lawyer, didn't you? It was his job to get you off. Not ours. He was the expert.'

Trevor's lip curled. 'He was the dregs. And that suited you, all right, didn't it?' he said, flicking his eyes from his brother to Lily Danger, standing beside him. 'Suited you to have me out of the picture. Have things your own way, be boss cocky in the henhouse without me queering your pitch.'

'Don't you talk to your brother like that!' screeched Annie. 'How dare you talk to your brother like that? After all we've done for you, you—'

'Done? What've you done, Mum? Blown your mouth off to the press for a few drinks and made everything ten times worse? Yeah—well, you did that. And what else? Bugger all. Didn't write to me, did you? Didn't come and see me. Not you. Not any of you.'

Annie's lip started to tremble. 'I'm not well enough to—'

'Don't give me that. You're strong as a horse. You couldn't be buggered, that's all. Too busy staring into the bottom of a glass to think about your son rotting in gaol.'

He looked away from her, his voice trembling with bitterness. 'No one came. Not Keith. Not Punchy. Not even

Rosalie. And I know why, too. Because it was easier without me, wasn't it? You liked it.'

He stood motionless, his face working, as if fighting for control. Then abruptly he threw back his head and drained his glass. He grimaced, and pushed the glass across the bar towards the impassive Allan Baker. 'Just like Floury here liked it, because he hates my guts,' he added casually. 'Because I'm twice the man he is, and he knows it. Because he's like Keith. Can't hold a woman, however much of a slag she is.'

Birdie felt her own cheeks grow hot as she glanced at Sue Sweeney, standing at the end of the bar. Sue's fingers were gripping a white towel. She was staring glassily ahead, looking at no one.

Floury said nothing. But neither did he fill Trevor's glass. He just stood, his hands planted on the bar, massive and immovable.

Trevor laughed. 'Big man,' he said. He turned back to Phillip Hewitt.

'But I'm not in gaol any more. I'm here, you stinking little shirt-lifter. And I'm staying. You'll know I'm here, every breath you take. You'll think you're in hell. And you know what? It's going to get worse, and worse, and worse . . .'

Birdie felt Jude move beside her. He walked forward, into the pub, till he was standing just behind Trevor Lamb.

'Trevor,' he said in a low voice. 'That's enough. There's no point in going on with this.'

Trevor didn't look around. But his face registered that he'd heard. Agin, that half-smile curved his lips.

'This is Jude Gregorian, Phil,' he said. 'The lawyer who got me out. He's pretty cluey, Jude. But even Jude doesn't know everything. You know I've got a degree now, don't you? A BA, just like you. So gaol wasn't all bad, was it?'

At last he broke that hypnotising stare, and looked down at the empty beer glass. He picked it up, and held it thoughtfully up to the light. It was as if he was trying to make a decision.

'Gaol gives you a lot of time to think, you know,' he said, after a moment. 'That's another good thing about it. Gives you a lot of time to work things out.'

He put down the glass, and leant against the bar. His gaze swept the room. As at the moment of his arrival, he

seemed to take in everyone's face in that one, long look. His
smile broadened.

'So I read a bit, and thought a bit, and I worked a few
things out. And when I'd done that I decided what I was going to do,' he went on, almost conversationally. 'I was going
to wait a while. Going to save it all up for the book. You
know. Big surprise? But what the hell.'

He feels invulnerable, thought Birdie, staring at him in
fascination. He's drunk on power as well as booze. What
hideous genie has Jude let out of its bottle, putting him back
on the streets?

She glanced at Jude. He looked intent. Wary. Jude
wasn't shocked by Lamb. By the violence, the megalomania.
No, he wouldn't be. He knew the man too well. But he was
puzzled and taken by surprise all the same. He didn't know
what was coming.

'I was going to wait,' Lamb repeated. 'But now I'm here
I dunno—I don't think I want to wait. I've waited too long
already. Months. Ever since I knew I was going to get out.
Since Jude told me it was a sure thing. Give me something to
think about, didn't it? Something to look forward to.'

'What d'you mean look forward to?' screamed Annie.
'Isn't coming home something to look forward to, you un-
grateful sod?'

'What's he talking about? What's he been waiting for?'
Jason's voice rose at the back of the room. Someone—Grace
probably—shushed him.

Punchy stirred at the doorway. Birdie glanced up at him.
He looked bewildered. But he didn't speak.

The little room seemed to simmer with tension. Smoke,
light and the smell of beer and sweat billowed outwards
through the door on waves of heat.

Everyone was staring at Trevor Lamb. It was like looking at a painting. A tableau that told a story, seen through a
yellow haze.

Trevor, the centre. Behind him, Jude, dark and watchful.
Next to him, Phillip Hewitt, paper white, fair hair flopped
over his forehead, pupils dilated till his eyes were almost
black. Behind the bar, Floury Baker and Sue Sweeney,
widely-separated, faces totally blank, unreadable. Then, together, behind Jude, the Lambs: Annie Lamb, her red face
shiny with sweat. Keith, deeply frowning. Grace, looking

frightened, licking her painted lips. Jason confused, standing on his toes, craning his neck. Lily Danger, a smile just curving the corners of her mouth. And at the back of the room, lined up against the wall, the silent audience of tan-faced men. Checked shirts, elastic-sided boots, hard hands clutching glasses of warming beer.

No one moved.

Birdie's eyes were watering. She felt someone moving up behind her and looked quickly over her shoulder. It was Rosalie, staring vaguely, as though she was sleepwalking.

'You don't get it, do you? Dumb bastards,' said Trevor Lamb. He laughed shortly. A dead sound. 'Why do you reckon I came back here? Because you're so great? Because this arsehole of a place is somewhere I want to be? You think I'm insane?'

He drew a deep, slow breath. 'I'm back here because I've got something to tell. And I want to see all your faces when I tell it. I'm going to let you into the secret. Going to tell you what I know. Going to tell everyone. The cops. The press.'

'Tell what? What's he going to tell?' whined Jason. Everyone ignored him. 'Mum?' he called. 'Mum?' He looked around for his mother, but failed to see her behind Birdie at the door. Rosalie made no move to attract his attention. Just stood, motionless.

'Come out where I can see you, Jason,' ordered Trevor Lamb.

Jason hesitated, then sidled to the front.

Trevor fixed him with a black stare, and smiled. 'I've been in gaol for killing your Auntie Daphne, Jason,' he said. 'You know that?'

Jason nodded, open-mouthed.

'But now I'm out. They've decided I didn't do it after all. That I was set up. Right?'

'Yes,' Jason muttered. Again, he looked around for his mother.

'Well haven't you wondered, you ignorant little bastard, who did kill her, then?'

Jason wriggled uncomfortably. 'No,' he mumbled. 'Well, yes, I guess. Sort of.' He snuffled and wiped his nose with the back of his hand.

'Trevor,' said Jude sharply. 'What . . . ?'

Trevor Lamb leant forward, still looking at Jason, his smile fixed. 'Well, I'm not wondering,' he breathed. 'I know. And I'm going to tell. What d'you think of that?'

Jason stared, wide-eyed. His mouth gaped.

Trevor laughed. Now he gave the impression of enjoying himself immensely. 'But not tonight,' he said. 'Tonight I'm going home. To bed.' His eyes flicked around the room, lingering on the women, one by one. 'Anyone wants to come and join me, I'll see she has a good time. I haven't forgotten how to do it.'

With a strangled sound, Phillip Hewitt made for the door.

'Not you, Phil. I'm not a convert yet,' snarled Lamb. 'Never took to it.'

Birdie had a glimpse of Phillip's gleaming white face and tormented eyes as he pushed his way past her. Where was he going? she wondered. Home? To the bastard of a father and the crazy, screwed-up mother? Had he come here tonight on their behalf, or on his own? What was he going to tell them?

Trevor watched him go. Then, with a lightning change of expression, he turned, and held out his hand to Jude. 'I mightn't see you in the morning before you go, mate,' he said. 'Depends if I get lucky, eh?'

'Trevor . . .' Jude began. But the other man shook his head briefly. 'Don't worry. I'll call you in town tomorrow night. And I'll look after Verity. She's going to get a lot more than she bargained for. She's going to do all right.'

He and Jude shook hands. He winked at Sue Sweeney, standing flush-faced behind the bar, then strode a little unsteadily to the door. As he passed Birdie he placed a proprietorial hand on her shoulder. 'See you,' he murmured.

He looked impassively at Punchy, grinning uncertainly, and at Rosalie. And then he was moving off the verandah, across the deserted road. In less than a minute, the shadow of the trees had swallowed him up.

The Lambs closed in on Jude after that. Led by Annie they surrounded him, demanding to know what Trevor was talking about, what he'd meant, what Jude knew. At least—Birdie corrected herself—Annie demanded. Punchy simply echoed. Grace shrilled incoherently. The others—Keith, Lily,

Rosalie and, for once, Jason—simply stood by, listening, watching.

The tan-faced men had begun drifting to the bar. After-show drinks. Or is this only intermission? thought Birdie wildly, watching them passing over their glasses to Floury Baker, putting down their money.

Suddenly she wanted a drink herself. Not beer. It was possible she'd never drink beer again. But Scotch. They had a bottle. She could see it at the back of the bar. A small Scotch with ice. That would be civilised. And welcome. She eased herself away from the door jamb and moved warily behind the crowd of Lambs to reach Sue Sweeney, at the other end of the bar.

Jude had raised his hands, palms out, in that familiar, peacemaking gesture. 'I'm sorry. I don't know,' she heard him saying, as she edged past. 'I really don't know. Trevor didn't tell me anything. Look, I know you're upset. I don't blame you. I'd never have brought Trevor back here if I'd thought—'

'He'd have got back here on his own. He's crazy,' said Rosalie dully. 'He doesn't care what he does. He's always been like it. He was born like it. And gaol's made him worse.'

Annie wagged her head violently. Her huge body quivered. 'Don't you start making excuses for him again, Rosalie!' she exclaimed. 'He's not crazy. He's wicked, that's what he is! What he said about us. His own family! After all we've done for him. After how we stuck by him! He didn't even give Sue here the time of day. After what they were to each other. If I was her I'd of scratched his eyes out. Well, I wash my hands of him. That's what I do. I wash my hands of him.'

'Looks to me like he's the one who's doing the hand washing,' smirked Lily Danger.

'Forget that shit,' growled Keith. 'He says he knows who killed Daphne. Well, who was it, then?'

'Don't be stupid all your life,' sneered Lily. 'He's just big-noting. How could he find out any bloody thing, where he's been? He's sending you all up gutless.'

Keith was silent. But the furrow between his brows deepened.

'He knows,' whispered Rosalie. 'Or at least he thinks he does. He wouldn't have said what he did otherwise.'

'God, he leads you all around by the nose,' laughed Lily. 'Got you all worked up, hasn't he? Don't you see that's what he wants?'

'Shut up, Lily,' said Keith roughly. 'You don't know him.'

Her eyes flashed with anger. 'I want another drink,' she said.

'Get it yourself,' he said, turning his back on her.

She jerked her head, so her earrings gleamed and rattled, and walked over to the bar, pushing in front of Birdie. 'Give me a beer,' she said to Sue Sweeney. She jerked her head at Keith. 'He'll pay. Later.'

Sue looked over to where Floury Baker was serving, and caught his eye. He gave the slightest suggestion of a nod. Whether Keith agreed to pay or not, he wanted Lily to have her drink. It was the line of least resistance.

'Good old wage slave, aren't ya?' jeered Lily, as Sue put a clean glass under the beer tap. 'Had to get his permission, didn't ya? Couldn't just give me the bloody drink.'

'It's not my money paying for it,' said Sue. For a moment she watched the beer foam rising in the glass. Then she looked up. 'Not yours either,' she added. She made no effort to conceal the contempt in her voice.

Lily's face twisted. 'You slag,' she hissed. 'Trev was right about you. You fat old slag.'

She pushed the foaming glass across the bar with the tips of her fingers. Her cheeks were bright red, but she stared the other woman straight in the eye. 'At least I work for a living so I can pay for my own beer when I want it, Lily,' she said loudly. 'Slagging's just a hobby with me. With you it's a full-time job.'

Annie swung around to look and, amazingly, screeched with laughter. 'Go it, Sue!' she roared. 'Give the little bitch hell!'

Grace giggled.

Jason let out a piercing catcall. 'Give the little bitch hell!' he mimicked. 'Give her hell!'

Lily bared her teeth. 'Keith!' she shouted.

Keith stared straight through her. She ran over to him, grabbing his arm. 'Aren't you going to say anything?' she shrieked. 'Are you just going to let them insult me, you gutless wonder?'

Keith reached over and disengaged her hand. 'You started it, Lily,' he said heavily. 'You finish it.'

She almost spat at him. Then she whirled, surveyed the watching men, caught Birdie's fascinated eye for a split second, and stormed out of the pub.

'Good bloody riddance,' Annie yelled after her. She looked back at the bar and saw the abandoned beer still sitting there. She reached out a huge arm and grabbed it.

'Waste not, want not,' she said, raising the glass to Sue with a gummy grin. 'Cheers, Susie Q!' She drank, smacked her lips with satisfaction, and drank again.

Birdie moved to the bar, feeling for her money. Sue Sweeney, gripping the edge of the counter, slowly recognised her presence.

She frowned slightly, turned and reached for some scraps of paper beside the phone behind her. 'Some woman's been ringing you,' she said. Her voice was distanced. Her mind was very obviously elsewhere. 'Sounded urgent. I told her you weren't here. She said something about your phone not answering. Your mobile. She wanted you to ring her, soon as you got in. I said I'd tell you.'

Birdie looked at the three notes. Beth Bothwell. She sighed.

'Want to ring now?' asked Sue, gesturing at the phone.

Birdie stuffed the notes into her pocket. 'Nah!' she grinned. 'I'll do it later. Right now, I just want a drink.'

She'd rethought her small Scotch with ice. She'd decided to have a double.

Eleven

The roses on the wallpaper climbed up, up, going nowhere. Moths fluttered around the light. They were going
nowhere, too. Birdie lay on her bed, her head slowly swimming, her body limp. It was a rather pleasant feeling. Pleasant, too, to be clean and cool from the shower, barefoot and
wrapped in a cotton kimono instead of encased in jeans and
a shirt. Pleasant that Sue had found her some peanuts to eat
with her Scotch. Her double Scotch. The peanuts had been a
bit soft. But she'd enjoyed them.

There were sounds of voices on the road outside. And a
slam, as if a door was shutting.

Floury's closing up, Birdie thought dreamily. The Lambs
are going home.

As if to prove her deductions correct, the light glowing
through her window from the pub below suddenly snapped
off. And a car engine roared.

Birdie smiled. Just for that moment she was perfectly
happy. It was blissful to be cool, undressed, at peace, and
alone. It was even blissful to have the sharpness of her mind,
for the moment, blunted. And that proved something she'd
always thought. Relief from any intolerable stress or physical
misery was the greatest, most profound happiness of all. It
mightn't last long before minor, everyday dissatisfactions di-
luted its effect, but while it lasted, it was wonderful.

She rolled over on her side and with one hand languidly
rummaged in the big leather handbag that lay beside her on
the bed. If she could find a barley sugar or two in there, her
cup would be full.

Wallet, keys, calculator, dictaphone, notebook, address
book, mobile phone . . . I must ring Beth, she thought,

remembering the messages ... batteries, comb, Band-Aids, numbers of pens, two packets of tissues, loose change, torch, spare pair of glasses, three stamped, addressed envelopes ... ah, those bills she'd paid! She'd forgotten to post them. She'd have to remember to do it tomorrow.

One hand went on scrabbling in the bag, while idly Birdie switched on the phone with the other. She watched the lights begin to glow. She really should have left the phone on today. Then Beth would have been able to get into her, instead of driving herself wild, leaving messages at the pub.

But old habits die hard. Birdie had the mobile phone so she could ring other people whenever she liked, and wherever she was. She didn't particularly want other people to ring her, whenever *they* liked, and wherever she was.

The phone began to ring.

Birdie stared at it. The coincidence seemed to her so extraordinary in her present mood that she toyed with the idea that she was imagining the sound.

But the phone was ringing all right. It must be Beth, she thought hazily. Who else would ring her at eleven o'clock at night?

'Hello?'

'Birdie! At last!'

It was her father. Birdie was so startled that she sat bolt upright.

Mistake. The bedsprings couldn't cope with the sudden movement. She jerked forward, then fell backwards with a shocked squeak. Her head spun violently. She closed her eyes and lay extremely still.

'Dad,' she managed to say weakly at last. 'What's wrong?'

'Nothing. What's wrong with you?'

'Nothing.'

'You sound awful.'

'I'm fine.'

Typically, he made no further comment, just got on with what he wanted to say. 'I've been trying to ring you all day, kid. Heard something this morning. Thought you'd like to know.'

'Yeah?' Birdie frowned, trying to collect her wits.

'Yeah. Just journos' gossip. Nothing we can broadcast. Yet. Might be nothing, ever.'

'Should you be telling—?'

'Give us a break. It's no big secret. Whole town seems to know about it—or will, by tomorrow. But I thought where you are it'd be different. And you can never be sure your mates in the ABC are on the ball. Big story about discrimination against visually challenged orphan ethnic whales might be taking up all their attention today.'

Birdie smiled, but didn't rise to the bait.

'Beth's been trying to ring me today, too,' she said instead. 'Been leaving messages downstairs, apparently. What's up?'

'We're on a mobile, so I won't name names,' Angus Birdwood said. 'But the word is, your interview subject's got some new information on the matter that put him inside. Today a few of his—ah—colleagues have let it be known that over the last few weeks he's been hinting, very broadly, that he's looking forward to stirring the pot. When he's ready.'

'In fact, he seems to have decided he's ready now.'

'You mean he's said something?'

'Yes. Tonight. In front of the whole town, such as it is. Anyhow, he's sleeping on it now. We're waiting for the next instalment.'

'Birdie, you—'

There was a tap on the door.

'Dad, there's someone at the door. Just a sec.'

Birdie slid carefully off the bed and went to the door, the phone in her hand.

'Yes?' she called softly.

'Birdie, it's me, Jude.'

Quickly she opened the door. Jude was standing there, propped against the corridor wall. He looked exhausted, but grinned weakly. She beckoned to him and put the phone back to her ear as he came into the room. 'Dad? It's all right. It's just Jude.'

'Just Jude, huh?'

Birdie felt the tips of her ears grow hot. She pushed the door shut and leant against it, watching as Jude wandered to the window, hands in pockets, and peered around the edge of the blind.

'Well, I'd better go, Dad,' she said. 'But thanks for calling. I suppose it means we can look forward to a whole troop of journos turning up here, then? From your lot at least?'

Jude looked around, and raised his eyebrows.

'Don't know about that, kid. Not sure they even know where Lamb is, yet.'

Birdie smiled to herself. Naturally her father wouldn't have said anything.

'Anyway, News makes those decisions,' Angus went on. 'I just run the place.'

'Well, look, I'll keep in touch.'

'Do that,' said her father quietly. 'And Birdie? Keep your phone switched on. Will you?'

'Sure.'

'Goodbye then.'

'Bye.'

Birdie broke the connection and put the phone down on the chest of drawers. Out of habit she switched it off. Then she switched it on again and turned her back on it.

'What's all this about journos?' asked Jude abruptly. 'Sorry. I didn't mean to listen. I just . . .'

'Listened,' Birdie finished for him. She padded across the room, suddenly acutely conscious of her state of relative undress, and sat down on the bed again, pulling her kimono more tightly around her.

'Seems your friend Trev's been talking in gaol,' she went on. 'Hinting that he's going to spill some sort of beans. Dad heard. He was ringing to tell me. Beth Bothwell's been trying to get onto me, too. About the same thing, I guess.'

'No one rang from my office,' said Jude gloomily. 'That'd be right. Naturally we'd be the last to know.' He lifted the blind again, peered out into the darkness. 'His light's still on, I think,' he said. 'He's still up.'

Birdie leant forward, watching him, struggling to pull herself together. 'You had no idea?' she asked. 'He didn't say anything to you? Before?'

'Not a thing. Not a bloody thing. Kept it all to himself.'

'Probably thought it'd be more fun that way.'

He nodded. 'Probably. I told you he'd been a bit strange. I thought he had something on his mind. But I never imagined anything like this. Birdie, the worst of it is, I can't think what he's got into his head. I mean, I've been over the evidence a million times. I've seen all the photographs. I've read all the reports. There was nothing there. I mean, nothing that incriminated anyone in particular, including Trevor himself. That was the whole point, really.'

He let the blind fall, and started pacing the room, hands again stuck deep in his pockets.

'If the first trial had been anything other than a kangaroo court, he'd never have been convicted. It was a scandal. The defence was a scandal. Well—you know.'

'Yeah. But Jude—Lamb's got something, hasn't he? Has he had access to all the stuff you have?'

'Yes.' Jude stopped, and frowned.

'He must have seen something you missed.'

'I can't believe that!' Jude started pacing again.

'You think he's mistaken, then,' Birdie said, finally. She was a little amused to witness Saint Jude in the grip of professional pique. And a bit disappointed, too. She had to admit that. But she pursued it, pushing him. 'You think he's got some crazy theory that won't hold water. That he's going to cause a lot of trouble for nothing. Make wild accusations. Make a fool of himself.'

Jude turned to face her. 'He's not likely to make a fool of himself,' he muttered. 'Trevor wouldn't put himself in that position. He likes people to think he's smart. Really smart. He wouldn't risk looking stupid. It's the last thing he'd do.'

'Well, what are you saying?'

Jude ran his hands through his hair. 'I don't know!'

At that moment he looked exactly as he had looked at twenty-two, when things went wrong, when everything seemed black and hopeless. Birdie watched him. Saw the expression in his eyes. Recognised it. And finally, a certainty penetrated the mellow haze that had enfolded her ever since that double Scotch burned its way down into her stomach. She realized that with all this talk about evidence Jude was circling around the main issue. He wasn't piqued, embarrassed, professionally insulted, or anything else. He was worried. Worried to death.

If Trevor Lamb didn't kill his wife, who did?

'Listen, Jude. If Lamb really knows something, why has he waited till now to tell it? It doesn't make sense. there'd be no reason. Why wouldn't he use the information to get himself out of gaol more quickly?'

'I've known Trevor Lamb for quite a few years now,'

Jude said slowly. 'And if there's one thing I've learnt about him, it's this: he never does anything without a reason. The reason might seem strange or twisted to other people, but that's irrelevant. It's reason enough for him. And he often thinks things out way in advance. He's known for quite a while that it was ninety-nine per cent certain that he was going to get out. I think, knowing that, he just bided his time.'

'You wouldn't think he'd want to spend one day longer in gaol than he had to.'

'After nearly five years I guess he thought a couple of extra months were worth it.'

'Worth it?'

Jude came and sat on the bed beside her. He clasped his hands between his knees, and stared at the door.

'Worth it from his point of view. Trevor's very into revenge. He can't stand being crossed, by anyone. He never forgets a slight. And a big part of his recreation is planning exactly how he'll get back at his current enemy. Thinking about the most exquisite possible revenge on some guard who'd been heavy, some other prisoner who'd stolen something from him, or got him into trouble—or even just said the wrong thing.'

He sighed wearily. 'He used to talk to me about it when I visited him. Endlessly. Sometimes it was hard to get him to concentrate on his case.' He ran his hands through his hair again, then he straightened up, and turned to Birdie.

'But the point is, Bird, he liked to gloat. That's the point. The plans always included the victim knowing he was the one who'd brought them down. If possible, actually seeing him sneering at them from the sidelines as they were taken off to solitary or sacked, or whatever. That was the satisfying part, for him.'

'Must have made him popular,' Birdie murmured.

Jude's tired face relaxed into a smile. 'Anyway, you see what I'm saying? If he has something on someone here— someone who let him go down for something they themselves did, he'd move heaven and earth to make sure he was on the spot when they got what they deserved. It wouldn't be enough for him to just organize it from gaol, at arm's length, nice and quiet and clean. It wouldn't satisfy him.'

'At least in gaol he'd be safe,' Birdie said quietly.

'Thank God you're here, Birdie,' said Jude. 'You're the

only sane thing in the place.' Impulsively he reached over and gently laid his hand on her bare ankle. 'You always were. In the old days. The only sane thing in my life.'

For a moment, the only sound in the room was made by the moths beating against the light fitting. Birdie sat perfectly still. She knew she only had to laugh, make a joke, casually change position, and the moment would pass. Then her life would remain the same. She knew she only had to reach out, and Jude would reach out too. Then her life would change.

She did nothing. Said nothing. Waited.

If he really wants to, he will.

Jude put out his other hand. The backs of his fingers caressed her cheek. Her skin tingled under his touch. Her face began to burn. He leant towards her.

'Birdie . . .?'

The phone rang.

They jumped, sprang apart.

'Shit!' Half-laughing, Jude stood up. 'Oh, shit!'

He rarely swore. Birdie watched as he strode over to the chest of drawers, picked up the shrilling phone and came back. He put it into her hands, and sat down on the bed again, throwing his hands into the air to signify jokey dismay.

She shook her head, answered the phone.

'Birdie? That you?'

Dan Toby. She couldn't believe it. She closed her eyes for a moment. Opened them again.

'Who else would it be?' she snapped.

'You sound funny. Where are you?'

'None of your business. What are you doing, ringing me this time of night?'

'Did I wake you up?'

'None of your business.' Birdie shook her head again. This was getting nowhere. She gritted her teeth. 'What do you want, Dan?'

She felt Jude's eyes on her. Looked up and watched him get up from the bed and walk over to the window. He lifted the blind and looked out.

'No need to be crabby,' Dan Toby said in an injured voice. 'I'm doing you a favour. I'm ringing to tell you something.'

'Trevor Lamb's threatening to expose the real killer of

his wife.' Birdie closed her eyes again. The memory of Jude's hand on her cheek rose up and closed her throat.

'You *know*?' Dan sounded disappointed.

Birdie's eyes snapped open. 'Of course I know. I'm here, aren't I? I've been with him all day. He's told everyone.'

'He *named* someone? For God's sake, Birdwood. Why didn't you call me? Who ., . . ?'

'He hasn't named anyone.' Birdie looked over at Jude, by the window. He was frowning, staring out into the darkness. 'He says he's going to, that's all.'

Dan swore. 'Big-noting, conceited bloody bastard! What's he playing at? Is he serious?'

'Jude thinks so.'

Jude turned around, at the sound of his name. She smiled at him, and raised her eyebrows. He shrugged, grimaced, and leant against the window. At least he was facing in her direction again.

Dan's voice changed. Became jeering. 'Jude, huh? Well, he'd know. Knows everything, that bloke, doesn't he? Far as you're concerned.' There was a moment's silence. 'He's with you now, is he?'

'Don't be ridiculous.' Birdie pressed her lips together in fury. Then, suddenly she registered the background noise at the other end of the phone.

'You in the car?' she asked. 'You on duty?'

'That's right, detective. Milson and I are taking one of our little trips together.' Dan's voice was cold.

'Where are you going?'

'I'd say it's none of your bloody business, except it suits me not to. We'll be with you in the morning. But in the meantime I want you to—'

'*What?*' Birdie sat forward, hunching over the phone. Jude watched intently, questions in his eyes. 'You're coming here? To Hope's End?' she said, for his benefit.

'That's right. Coming to have a look-see. Special orders from on-high. Milson's thrilled. Aren't you, Milson? We're staying at some flea-trap motel they've booked us into. In some hole called—what is it, Milson? Sassafras, or something. Anyhow, it doesn't matter. The point is, it's just up the track from Hope's End, they tell me. If we stay there overnight we can get into Hope's End first thing. On-high was keen for that to happen.'

'Why, Dan?'

Toby sighed heavily. The sound wooshed breathily through the phone. 'On-high's been embarrassed, Birdwood. On-high wants to head off further embarrassment at the pass. On-high wants Lamb's cooperation. Get the picture?'

'Yes. But it's hopeless, Dan. It won't work. Lamb's not likely to cooperate with you. Quite the reverse.'

Birdie rolled her eyes at the watching Jude. He shook his head slowly, half-smiling.

'Birdwood, you take the words out of my mouth,' said Toby. 'But, unlike you, we humble policepersons have to follow orders. However bloody stupid the orders are. What, Milson?' He broke off. Birdie heard Milson's voice speaking in the background. Then Toby came back on the line. 'Milson tells me Sassafras is up ahead. He saw a sign. No flies on Milson. Now, look. I want you to do something for me.'

'Dan, I can't help you,' said Birdie firmly. She'd been waiting for this. 'I can't persuade Trevor Lamb to do anything. I've got my own job to do with him, and I can't jeopardise it. And Jude's leaving tomorrow, early, so he can't help you either. Even if he wanted to.'

'God, talk about jumping to conclusions! Have I asked you to persuade anyone to do anything? Well, have I?'

'No. Not yet. But—'

'But nothing. I only want you to do one thing for me. You've got my mobile number. I want you to call me, straight away, if anything happens there before tomorrow morning. Could you do that? Would that be too much of a problem to you? Interfere too much with your love life?'

'Dan, it's the middle of the night! Everyone's gone to bed. Nothing's going to happen now.'

At that exact moment, Birdie saw Jude turn around to the window again, heard the sound of a car. Someone had pulled up outside the pub. A car door slammed. What was going on?

'Maybe not,' Toby was grumbling. 'But if it does, you call me. And you keep right out of it. Understand? And tell your mate Jude to keep out of it, too.'

'I can't tell Jude—' Birdie slipped off the bed and went to join Jude at the window. She peered outside, but could see little in the darkness.

'You tell him. Lamb's news. Bad news, as far as I'm concerned, but he's having a love affair with the press, and we can't afford another balls-up.'

'Dan—'

'I'm going to hang up now, Birdwood. Milson seems to have located the motel. God. Traveller's Rest. Looks more like Traveller's Ruin. I'll see you in the morning.'

The phone clicked, and went dead. Birdie and Jude looked at one another.

'What's happening?' they both asked, at the same time.

Jude laughed. 'Keith Lamb's come back. He must have had a fight with Lily. I think he's paying Sue Sweeney a visit.'

'What for?'

Jude raised his eyebrows. 'Oh, come on!'

'She wouldn't be in that!'

'How do you know? Anyway, what did your copper friend have to say?'

'His bosses have heard the goss. They're sending him here to troubleshoot.'

'Oh, no. I've got to go and tell Trevor.' Jude ran his fingers through his hair. Suddenly he looked tired to death.

'Jude, you can't do it now. It's so late. And he might have someone with him. Bearing in mind the open invitation—though who'd be mad enough to take him up on it I don't know.'

'I have to, Birdie. I've got to get away on time tomorrow morning. And he has to know the cops are on their way. So I'll have to tell him tonight. Hey! Looks like you were right.'

A light had gone on as someone opened a car door opposite. Birdie saw the figure of Keith Lamb climb into the car. The door slammed. Then, after a few seconds' delay, the engine started, the headlights lit up, the car reversed, swung around and sped away, roaring over the bridge and off into the distance.

'She sent him packing,' said Jude. 'He must have decided to try his luck in Sassafras or Gunbudgie.'

'He shouldn't be driving. He's drunk so much beer.'

'Yeah. More than most of us. Which is saying something.' Jude peered into the darkness. 'Look,' he said pointing. 'Trevor's light's still on. I'll have to go. It won't take long.'

'He doesn't have to know, Jude. I mean, he hasn't done

anything wrong himself. He's not going to get in any trouble. They're just going to try to persuade him to tell what he knows. So they can control the situation.'

'And get the credit,' said Jude grimly. 'I know them. No, but that's not the point. He'd want to think it over. Decide how he's going to handle it. I can't know they're coming, and not tell him. He'd find out I knew, eventually. He'd see it as a betrayal.'

'Does that really matter now?'

'It matters to me. I just want to finish this thing with him clean and sharp, with no mess, or confusion, or misunderstanding. Look—I don't know, it's hard to explain. Trevor and I aren't friends. But we have a relationship all the same. Quite intense. Sometimes it's been tricky. Awful. There've been times when I wished I'd never started the whole thing. Wished I'd never written *Lamb to the Slaughter*. Just wanted to forget it. Because then I could get Trevor Lamb right out of my life.'

He was pacing again. 'But I stuck with it,' he went on. 'I couldn't leave it. The injustice of that trial—it was too much. I couldn't turn my back on it. On him. However loathsome I found him some of the time—a lot of the time. That wasn't the issue.'

'I know,' said Birdie. 'And what you did was right. It was really—admirable.'

This time he didn't brush off the compliment. He stopped pacing and his eyes softened as he looked at her. 'That really means a lot to me,' he said. 'And you understand why I went on with it, don't you? You really do. Because you would have felt the same.'

'Yes,' she said quietly. 'I *have* felt the same, about things I've been involved in myself. I've had my own obsessions.' She was silent for a moment, remembering. Other times, other places. Agonising choices. 'After a certain point, personalities don't matter,' she said at last. 'For you, justice is what counts. With me, it's the truth.'

'Aren't they the same thing?' He was watching her closely.

She wrinkled her nose, pushing up her glasses. 'I don't know. It's too late at night to think about stuff like that. They have a close relationship, anyhow.'

He moved closer. Smiled teasingly. 'Maybe justice embraces truth. Or does truth embrace justice?'

'Jude, are you going, or not?'

The smile broadened. 'Yes I am. Apart from everything else I might be able to convince him to let the cops in on whatever he's got without making a meal of it. Then I can get away tomorrow with a clear conscience.'

'You'll do your car on that track in the dark, for sure. Then you won't get away tomorrow at all.'

'I'll walk it, Bird. It'll only take ten minutes.'

She sighed. 'Take my torch.'

'Thanks. I'll be back here in an hour, tops. Could you stay awake, to let me in? Floury'll be asleep by now. And I shouldn't really leave the door unlocked.'

'Of course. I mean, of course you shouldn't leave the door unlocked. And of course I'll wait up and let you in.'

'Thanks, Birdic. Then maybe I can come back up here?'

'Maybe you can.'

He raised his eyebrows. 'And then do you know the first thing I'm going to do?'

'What?'

'Turn off that bloody phone.'

Twelve

Birdie peered through her window. Black. Black, pierced above by a million stars. No streetlights, to mark the road, or shine on the hulking pepper trees. No moon to pick out the shape of the old wooden bridge, or light Hewitts' paddocks beyond.

There was no sign of Jude. She checked her watch. One-twenty. He'd left her at ten to twelve. He'd said he'd be back in an hour. Tops.

Trevor's keeping him talking, her rational mind said.

But he knows I'm waiting up for him, the other part of her mind argued. He wouldn't stay away so long, knowing that. Something must have happened.

You call me, if anything happens . . .

Nothing's happened. Don't be a fool. Toby's spooked you. Stop looking out the window. You can't see anything out there.

You can't see anything out there.

Birdie's hand gripped the blind. Too hard. The brittle fabric cracked in her fingers. She should be able to see something. A gleam of light. Back there in the bush. She'd seen it just before Jude left, but now there was nothing. The light from the shack had gone.

Jude's left. That's all that means. Jude's on his way back right now. Trevor's gone to bed. Jude will be here in five minutes. Ten at the most.

She wandered back to the bed, picked up the folder of notes she'd been reading, and sat, listening. But in ten minutes she was back at the window, checking her watch.

How long had the light been off? She'd looked out the window before, and hadn't noticed then whether it was shining or not. She just hadn't thought about it. It could have been off for an hour or more, for all she knew.

Maybe it hadn't been the shack light Jude had pointed out at all. Or maybe Trevor and Jude had simply moved into another room, a room from which light didn't show. Or maybe . . .

She had to do something. The inactivity, the waiting, was driving her crazy. And she couldn't go to sleep. She'd never felt less like sleep in her life.

Then she remembered the kitchen. 'Tea and coffee,' Sue Sweeney had said. Biscuits. Anytime.

She'd make herself a cup of tea. She'd love a cup of tea. And a biscuit. Two biscuits. Presumably 'anytime' included one-thirty in the morning. And no one was going to hear her, anyway.

Birdie stripped off her kimono, pulled on some clothes and let herself out of her room, into the dark corridor. Then she had a thought, returned to the room, and grabbed her mobile phone. Just in case Toby took it into his head to ring again.

Back in the corridor, she looked cautiously both ways. Floury Baker's room was at the far end, next to the bathroom. Room one. No light showed under the door. The bathroom, too, was in darkness.

Birdie tiptoed to the stairway. There was a light switch there, somewhere. Sue had used it. Birdie fumbled on the wall, found the switch, and flicked it on.

Dim yellow light illuminated the stairway. So far so good. She crept down the stairs.

At the bottom, she hesitated. To her left was the back door. Through its glass panels a dim light glowed. Birdie craned her neck to see where it was coming from. The flat above the garage. Sue Sweeney was still awake, then.

For a moment Birdie considered going to see her. It would be good to talk to someone. They could have a cup of tea together, maybe. Then, immediately, she realised that this was a stupid idea. For one thing, Sue was probably in bed, reading or something. She might even have gone to sleep with the light on. For another, even if she was awake and eager for company, the moment Birdie got involved with her, Jude would come back for sure. That was the way these things happened.

Birdie turned quickly away from the back door, and switched off the stair light. If Sue was awake, and saw it, she might come over to investigate. In the darkness Birdie turned towards the front of the building and felt her way along the right-hand wall of the corridor. Behind the doors on the left, she knew, were a storeroom and Floury's office. The kitchen was on the right. Her fingers found the door without difficulty, and she slipped inside. She pulled the door almost shut, then turned on the light.

The kitchen was old-fashioned, but clean. Floury made his meals here, she knew that. And sometimes he or Sue made chips for the pub crowd here, too. But there was no sign that anything substantial had been cooked tonight. A single upturned saucepan on the draining board of the sink was the only evidence of domestic activity.

She put down her phone and trailed around, trying not to make noise, finding kettle, tea, teapot, a mug, making the tea, fossicking for the biscuit tin in the cupboard. There was a hard wooden chair drawn up to a narrow table near the sink, and she sat down to drink, with the biscuit tin close to hand.

It was so silent. Everything was so silent. No traffic noise, of course. That was it. No lights, no traffic noise. Just dark, and quiet.

She sipped her tea, nibbled biscuits, sitting at the table in the corner of the lighted kitchen. Behind her, outside the kitchen door, there was only blackness. In front of her, outside the window, blackness. The world had shrunk. It was like being on an island. It was as if nothing else existed.

The minutes ticked by. She poured herself another cup of tea. Drank it. Washed her cup. Put everything away. Looked at her watch. It was ten to two. Now what?

She knew, really. She was going to have to go and see what was happening at the shack. She couldn't wait any longer. In fact, she'd probably waited too long already. Ten minutes there. Twenty minutes to talk to Trevor. Ten minutes back. Forty minutes. Maybe fifty. Maybe a whole hour, if Trevor was in a garrulous mood. But not two hours. That was too long. Much too long.

Her heart pounding, she picked up her mobile phone, walked quickly to the kitchen door, swung it open, then hesitated. Should she really go out into that darkness alone?

Without a torch? Should she wake Floury Baker? Ask him to go with her? Or should she go and get Sue?

They'll think I'm crazy. Crazy, spooked city girl, fretting over some bloke who's an hour overdue. What if nothing's wrong at all? What if I call out the troops and we get to the shack and find Trevor and Jude working out some computer problem, or just chatting over a cuppa? I've got to hang round in this place for a few days. I can't afford for them to think I'm an idiot.

Call me. If anything happens . . .

Nothing's happened.

Moving quickly, before she could change her mind again, she stepped back into the kitchen and went to the cupboard where the biscuit tin had been. She'd seen candles there. And matches. Floury's preparations for a blackout. Well, there was a blackout out there, all right.

She took a candle that was already stuck into an old-fashioned candle-holder. I'll look like Wee Willie Winkie carrying this around, she thought. But the holder would protect her fingers from hot, dripping wax. She lit the candle, and stuck a full box of matches into her pocket. Then she left the kitchen again, and turned off the light.

The candle flame flickered on bar, mirror, bottles, beer taps as she walked slowly to the front door. Her conscience pricked her at the thought of leaving the door open, but really she had no choice. And in fact, there was little danger that there'd be a robbery in the short time she'd be away. The locals all knew the pub was locked at night. And any stranger to the district would almost certainly arrive by car. Down the track, over the rattling bridge, shattering the silence of the night. Floury would hear that. Sue Sweeney would hear it.

She put the door on the snib, and pulled it closed behind her as she stepped out onto the verandah. There was no wind to blow the door ajar. It would look locked as normal, from the road.

Any stranger to the district would almost certainly arrive by car.

The prosecution had made much of that at Trevor Lamb's trial. No one could arrive in Hope's End by car at any time without being seen or heard by the people in the pub. And even on foot, a stranger would be seen during pub opening hours. So the idea of a wandering burglar-turned-murderer, put forward by Trevor Lamb's defence counsel, was patently ridiculous.

And that meant . . .

Birdie crossed the road and began to walk beside the pepper trees, towards the hidden gap that was the start of Trevor Lamb's track. The trees hunched blackly beside her. The candle flame wavered, barely moving. Out here, it made little impression on the darkness. But it was better than nothing. A lot better.

She passed Jude's car, moved on. Sounds. The creek. Tiny rustles and clicks from the undergrowth. A flutter above her head. Somewhere, in the distance, the bark of a dog.

The mouth of the track yawned ahead now. Pitch dark. She held the candle out in front of her, and with the other hand gripped the phone, smooth and reassuringly hard. Then she turned into the track, and started walking.

The trees rose up beside her and met over her head, blotting out the stars. She walked slowly, watching her feet. The track twisted and turned. The air was very warm and still. And thick, like air in a tunnel. It hung around her, still and heavy, full of the smells of earth, and leaves, animals, and the sluggish creek.

A twig snapped in the undergrowth. somewhere off the track to her left. Birdie paused. Listening. She held up her candle, watching her hand tremble so that the small flame dipped and swayed, danced over blackness, without penetrating. The sound of her own breathing filled her ears. So loud. Too loud. *Too loud.* Her throat closed up. Her heart began to beat faster, harder.

She wasn't alone. There was someone else here. Someone else, very near, crouched hidden in the undergrowth. Breathing with her.

Move on.

She forced herself to start walking again. Her knees were weak. They were shaking. She looked straight ahead. Her ears strained, listening for the slightest movement.

A tiny sound, behind her, to the left. The faintest rustle, as someone or something changed position, eased a cramped muscle. She spun around. 'Who is it?' she shouted. Her voice sounded thin and childish.

Silence. And then, a groan. Low, anguished. Not behind her, but ahead. Ahead.

Her heart pounding, Birdie turned and began stumbling forward again. Away from the silent watcher in the undergrowth. Towards the sound. The skin on the back of her neck prickled and crawled. She panted, expecting with every step the rush of noise and movement that would mean attack from behind.

Half-sobbing with fear and tension, she reached the place where the track curved sharply around the great tree. The shack was just ahead, through this avenue of trees. She knew that. But she could see nothing. She wet her lips. Called.

'Where are you? Jude? Is it you? Are you all right?'

'Here. Please.'

The voice was unrecognisable, lost in the darkness. She ran forward, holding the candle flame too close, almost blinded by its light. And she nearly missed him. Nearly passed him by in her forward rush.

'Here.'

The voice, masked by pain, was at her feet. She swung the candle. Saw the figure lying sprawled on its back, one leg bizarrely twisted. The white face gleamed in the candlelight. Black eyes. White face, twisted in agony.

'Oh God! Jude!' She flung herself down beside him. She reached out a hand. Blood had trickled down his neck. The back of his head was sticky wet.

'Leg,' he moaned. 'Doctor, Birdie.' His eyes closed.

The phone. Thank heavens for the phone. She punched the emergency numbers with fingers that barely operated. Spoke in a voice she barely recognised as her own. Ambulance. Accident. *Accident?* Man hurt. Leg. Hip. Something like that. Head wound. Back of the head. Concussion. Hope's End. Down a track. A little track. Just past the pub. To the right.

'Jude, they're coming. Soon. What happened? Who did this? How long have you. . .?'

But he was out of it. Her thoughts raced, collided. Concussion. Broken leg. Shock. Shock kills. A blanket.

'I'll be back in a minute, Jude. In a minute,' she whispered, in case he could hear her. And then she was running blindly ahead. To the shack she knew was there, though still she couldn't see it.

Quite soon, the clearing. And over to the right, the shack. Inside, she realised, music was playing softly. The candlelight flickered over the verandah, the door, hanging half-open. Darkness with him.

'Trevor?'

She crossed the verandah, kicked at the door. It slammed back against the wall.

'Trevor!'

Her voice echoed through the house. She held up the candle, looking for the light switch. Shadows danced on the walls, the ceiling, the floor, the crooning transistor and computer equipment on the table.

'Trevor!'

Then she saw him. He'd been there all the time. And she needn't have shouted. He couldn't hear her. Couldn't hear anything, down there on the floor, face buried in the small, inky shadow that wasn't a shadow.

Her fingers found the switch. The room lit up.

She crouched, crawled, reached for the outflung hand. It was still faintly warm. But there was no pulse. She hadn't expected to find one. The back of the head was misshapen, a caved-in mess of wet hair and splinters of bone. The dark blood had trickled down on both sides, pooling on the floor, soaking into the thirsty old boards.

Birdie crawled backwards, back to the door. 'Let me love you,' throbbed the radio, sickly sweet. 'Let me love you, sweetheart!'

There was something she had to do. She staggered to her feet, stumbled to the bedroom and pulled a blanket from the bed. Half-dragging it behind her she got back to the kitchen. The candle. Remember the candle.

Out into the the clearing again. Back to Jude. Quickly. As quickly as you can, without putting the candle out. Don't think about the body in the shack, cooling to music. Don't think about the watcher in the bush. Jude, lying helpless there. You'll be with him soon. It's not far. On your right, about halfway along the avenue of trees. Watch out for him. He's over at the side. Watch the bases of the trees.

But again she nearly missed him. Went a few steps past.

Had to turn back. She knelt and pulled the blanket over him. He groaned faintly, grimacing with pain.

'I'm here, Jude,' she whispered. 'It's all right. I'm here.'

But it isn't all right. Trevor Lamb's dead, Jude. He's dead. Did you see it? Do you know? How long have you been lying here? Was it going, or coming, that this happened to you?

If anything happens . . .

The phone was lying where she'd left it. She picked it up, punched in some numbers.

In less time than she'd expected, the phone was answered.

She spoke. And again, she barely recognised the thick, breathy sound of her own voice.

'Dan? It's me, Birdie. Something's happened. Please come.'

Thirteen

Jude lay still. His breathing was shallow and uneven. Birdie hunched beside him, wanting to do something for him, but knowing she could only wait. With one part of her mind she wished desperately for him to wake. Then at least she could talk to him. Find out what happened. Reassure herself that he was going to be all right. Stop herself feeling so alone. But she knew that if he did wake he'd be in pain again. Awful pain. It was better for him to be unconscious.

'It won't be long,' she whispered, as much to herself as to him. Gently she brushed away fallen leaves and tiny sticks from his chest, neck and face. He sighed in his sleep. An insect rasped in the undergrowth. Then another. The back of her neck prickled. But if insects were calling, that must mean there was no one hidden there in that darkness. If there were, the insects would know, and keep silent. Whoever had been watching her from the scrub had either gone, or at least hadn't followed her around the bend, to where Jude's body was lying.

Light from the shack streamed into the clearing ahead. The door gaped open, and the tinny music of the radio floated out into the night. She should have turned off the light. She should have shut the door. Moths and other things would get in. They might disturb the evidence.

They might disturb the evidence? Moths? She closed her eyes, heard the sound of her own half-hysterical snort of laughter. She'd undoubtedly done a thousand times more damage to the murder scene by blundering into the shack, going to the body, and then the bedroom, pulling the blanket from the tumbled bed, dragging it along the floor and out the door. Not to mention hauling it into the clearing and down the track. Everywhere she went, she would have been adding, removing and obscuring footprints, fingerprints, hairs, threads, fibres . . .

But she hadn't had a choice. And at least she'd been alone.

The candle flickered. She looked at it anxiously, suddenly noticing how far it had burnt down. Its flame was long and wavering and very yellow. And there was soot smearing the waxy stub that sat, dripping in the holder. No—not soot. Blood.

She looked at her hands. The fingers were bloody. She wiped them vigorously on her shirt. Jude's blood? Or Trevor's? Could be either, or both.

If anything happens . . . you stay out of it.

Sorry about that, Dan. When you get here, I'll explain. How it was.

The ambulance would be here first. And the local police. Birdie glanced at her watch. No, it was still too soon even for them. The minutes were crawling by. The local police and the ambulance were at Gunbudgie. Twenty-five to thirty minutes, the operator had said. Twenty-five minutes from Gunbudgie to Hope's End. As the ambulance flies. Toby and Milson would follow. Thirty minutes from Sassafras to Hope's End, at normal speed. If you didn't miss the turning, where the sign pointed straight to the ground. If you turned right, not left, where the track forked. If you didn't speed, and run off the road. If you didn't get behind a crawling Bobcat. Well, *that* wasn't likely, at least.

Was it only yesterday that Bull Trews had escorted her into the Hope's End pub? It seemed so much longer ago. It seemed she'd been in this place forever. Its ambience had enclosed her, swallowed her up.

At least the ambulance drivers would know the way. They should, anyway. This was their general area. And people must have needed emergency help in Hope's End before. But there was still no sound of a siren, even in the far distance. Where were they? She'd told them it was an emergency. She'd begged them to hurry.

Should I try to turn him on his side? He's on his back. I'm afraid . . .

Only if he starts vomiting. Otherwise, best not to move him.

When they came, Jude would be all right. They'd be able to give him something for the pain. Do something about his leg. Move him out of that terrible, twisted position without causing further damage. They were experts. They did this sort of thing all the time.

She was an expert, too. Or she was supposed to be. But so far she'd done nothing except mess things up. She could hear Dan's voice, now. Deep, suspicious.

'What was your boyfriend doing going to see Lamb in the middle of the night?'

'He wanted to tell him you were on your way.'

'How did he know we were?'

'I told him.'

Silence. Accusing silence. *That was privileged information, Birdie. I trusted you.*

She hadn't thought about it like that at the time. But sitting here, waiting, she could see how it would look to Dan. Changing sides. Currying favour with Jude Gregorian, betraying a trust. An unstated trust, but a trust nonetheless.

Jude stirred, moaning. Birdie put her hand on his cheek. 'Just lie still. It wont be long now,' she promised. He quieted immediately, as though he understood and was reassured.

Her heart felt as though it was being squeezed. She turned her face away from him, and looked out into the bush. She didn't want to confront what she was feeling. Instead, she started to berate herself. She was the expert. The great investigator. The piecer together of puzzles, the noticer of clues, the logical thinker. And here she crouched, helpless, over a guttering candle, waiting for a whole lot of men to take over, save her, take the responsibility, put her out of her misery.

She imagined Toby's voice. Flat, heavy, almost bored. 'All right, Birdwood, you were first on the scene. What did you notice about the shack? Lamb's body? The track? The scrub? What did you hear? What did you see?'

Her voice. Thin, whispering. 'I don't know. I was so rattled. Jude was hurt. It was dark. I was frightened.'

Toby's face, peering at her, disbelieving.

Birdie shivered, drawing her arms protectively over her

chest. She forced her mind away from the vision of that face, that expression. But her mind veered back to it, cringing.

She knew she had to pull herself together. She had to concentrate. Get her brain working again. Or rather, get back in touch with it. Just because she had been absent, it didn't mean her mind hadn't been recording, noting, just as always, she told herself. It was just a matter of calling back the information. Step by step.

What did she know? She knew that Jude had left her at about ten to twelve to walk to Trevor's shack. Outside, it had been dark. From her room you could see the nearest glimmer of light, deep in the bush opposite the pub. That could have been the shack. Jude had thought it was. He had taken her torch, and gone.

The torch! She held up the candle. Shadows and light flickered on the earth as she peered around, looking for the gleam that would betray the presence of a little tube of black plastic in the undergrowth, on the rutted dirt of the track, among the leaves and stones. When Jude was attacked the torch would have fallen from his hand. His right hand, presumably. And it was probably somewhere quite near where he was lying. She could see no sign of a vigorous fight, around or along the track. Even in this feeble light, scars of a moving struggle would have shown in the leaf-strewn earth. It looked as though Jude had been taken by surprise, felled by a single blow. Maybe kicked, once he was down. Only he could tell them that. But, for the moment, he wasn't talking.

She fixed her mind on the torch. She should be able to find it. She frowned, concentrating on Jude's position. He was lying on his back, his right hand flung outwards. His feet were towards the shack. So he'd been facing in that direction. He'd fallen backwards, his leg awkwardly twisting under him, snapping as he crashed heavily to the ground. After that, he wouldn't have been able to move. So the torch could be . . .

Carefully, she lifted the blanket away from Jude's right side and brought the candle down to ground level. With a satisfied grunt, she saw the gleam of the torch. It was lying just where she'd thought it might be. By his right thigh.

She picked it up gingerly, praying it was still working, and nearly cheered as its strong beam snapped on without hesitation, lighting up the track and even piercing the undergrowth as she shone it around.

Absurdly pleased by this modest success, she sat for a moment, flashing the torch here and there, feeling its small, reassuring weight in her hand, conquering the darkness like a child. She put the candle out. Now she didn't need. Now it didn't matter that there was no moon, no streetlight. She was equipped again.

She eased the blanket back into place and started picking up the threads of her story, trying to remember all the details. Jude had left. She had waited. She'd read, stared out the window. She'd seen nothing, heard nothing. At some point she'd realised that the gleam of light from the bush had gone out. But she didn't know when. It could have gone out long before she registered its absence. At about one-thirty she'd left her room to go down to the kitchen. Floury Baker's room was dark. Sue Sweeney's light was on. She'd made a cup of tea. She'd left the pub at—about five minutes to two.

After about five minutes of walking, she'd heard someone in the undergrowth. To her left. Her skin crawled again as she thought of that breathing, those tiny sounds. Whoever it was must have been quite close. But whoever it was had been content just to watch, hidden. They hadn't followed her.

Was the watcher Trevor Lamb's murderer and Jude's attacker? If so, why had he or she waited around? And why hadn't Birdie been attacked, in her turn?

Because she didn't see anything. Because she presented no threat. The watcher had heard her coming, and had managed to slip into the undergrowth before she came into view.

So, if the watcher and the murderer were one and the same, and you couldn't take that for granted, of course, we weren't talking here about some crazed killer rampaging around Hope's End in the grip of bloodlust, seeking out victims just for the hell of it. We were talking about a selective murderer.

But, of course, she'd always known that. Whatever she had thought when she found Jude by the side of the track, the sight of Trevor Lamb's body lying face down in the kitchen, blood pooled like a black shadow around his head, soaking into the floorboards, had cleared her mind of any doubt.

Someone had executed Trevor Lamb. He'd been killed, in fact, in exactly the same way as his wife. His skull had been smashed by a heavy blow, from behind. He could have been arguing with his killer, then turned away. Or his killer could have crept into the shack and . . . no, that wouldn't have been possible. The front door squeaked far too loudly for anyone to have been able to enter that kitchen without being heard. The back was bolted.

So, Trevor had let his killer in. Unless—the killer had been hiding in the shack already, when Trevor arrived back from the pub. The shack was locked. A new lock, and Trevor had the key. But windows can be forced—especially old, ill-fitting windows. The killer could have got in that way, by a back window, and waited in the hot, stuffy darkness, the weapon, perhaps, already clutched in a sweating hand.

The weapon. Something hard, and heavy. Something that could crack the back of a man's skull.

Birdie screwed up her eyes, trying to recall everything about that scene in the kitchen. In her mind, she scanned the stained floor. She could remember nothing lying there except some beer cans. The floor had been bare otherwise. She was sure of it.

The killer had taken the weapon away, then. Hidden it somewhere. Or thrown it into the bush, or the creek. But Toby would find it. Even if it were cleaned, there would be traces forensic could pick up. It wasn't so easy to wash away blood. It remained, for years, invisible to the naked eye, but there, waiting to be exposed. Like guilt. Toby would find the weapon eventually, and the weapon would lead him to the killer, if nothing else did.

They didn't find the weapon last time.

Last time.

Birdie looked back at the shack, where now two people had died. At last her mind was working rapidly. It was important not to jump to conclusions. The two deaths could be entirely unconnected. Or not. If not, if the deaths were connected, intimately, was Trevor Lamb's death an implacable revenge killing? Had someone thought, an eye for an eye, a tooth for a tooth, and carried out the sentence without thought of the possible repercussions?

Or had Lamb's death been a necessity, to protect the

identity of his wife's murderer? Had Daphne Lamb's killer come out of hiding to kill again?

Lamb had had his own reasons for coming home to Hope's End. Some twisted plan of revenge had formed in his mind, and he was carrying it out. He'd seemed to have a grudge against everyone. But he'd had one particular victim in mind, if what he'd said in the pub about revealing Daphne's killer was true.

Why hadn't he seen his danger? Surely he'd realised that the murderer might kill again, to prevent exposure? Birdie stood up and began to move restlessly. Trevor Lamb wasn't a stupid man. Yet he'd declared himself in front of everyone at the pub. That would seem foolhardy in the extreme.

Trevor never does anything without a reason.

That declaration. In the pub. It was the best publicity possible in a place like Hope's End. Better than plastering signs on every tree. Better than taking an ad in the local newspaper. People talk. The Lambs, Floury Baker, Sue Sweeney, the silent, watching men. All of them would spread the word. And Phillip Hewitt had been there, too, Birdie remembered. He would have told his parents.

She winced at the thought of that, of them. According to Jude, Les and Dolly Hewitt still believed in Trevor's guilt. They had never wavered from their conviction. This—all this—must be, would be, agony for them.

Yet would it? Now? With Lamb's death, hadn't they finally got what they'd wanted all along?

She shook her head, stuck her hands in her pockets, and paced, a few steps up the track, a turn, a few steps back, a turn . . . She reminded herself of Jude, pacing in her bedroom, and made herself stop.

There was a sound, drifting, bell-like on the air. The last chime of a town hall clock, perhaps, from far away, echoing to this lost place by a freak of wind.

And then she became conscious of another sound. The sound of a car engine, out in the hills, beyond the creek. It was muffled by the bush; she couldn't tell exactly how close it was. But it was getting louder.

And there—a flash of light, through the trees. A red light. The ambulance, travelling fast, without its siren. Of course, it wouldn't need a siren out here. And of course, that was good. This way it would attract no attention, rouse no one, except perhaps Floury and Sue at the pub.

The light flashed, moving downhill, beside Hewitts' paddocks, towards the creek. She could follow its progress easily. The trees weren't impenetrable, then. At least in this direction. They just seemed that way, in the darkness.

The rattle, loud, as the vehicle crossed the bridge. Still the occasional flash of red light. Then, a slowing purr. And finally, a man's voice, shouting, from the mouth of the track.

'Hello? Ambulance here. Is this where—?'

'Yes!' called Birdie, starting to run towards the sound, the torchlight bobbing in front of her. 'Yes! Here! Here!'

She had reached the sharp bend when the screams started. Hysterical, shrill and terrified they echoed around the clearing behind her, where the shack still glowed with light.

Birdie spun around. There was a thud, a crash, and a burst of loud, static-filled sound from inside the shack. The radio on the kitchen table had been knocked over. Someone was . . .

A figure flew from the door, tripped and went sprawling onto the veranda. And the screams went on, and on, and on.

Fourteen

After that, all was chaos. Or so it seemed to Birdie. Grace Lamb, stumbling from the verandah, crawled to the middle of the clearing, screaming, screaming. The awful sound of a radio blaring between stations, volume turned up full. Dogs, near and far, barking from all sides. Lights, suddenly switching on, shining like beacons through the darkness. From the Lambs' hill. From the other side of the creek, the Hewitt house. From the road, where the pub must be, and further along, as households woke to curiosity or fear. From the ambulance, parked at the mouth of the track. From the paramedics' torches, mini searchlights scanning the bush as they hurried in answer to Birdie's calls.

And people came. The paramedics themselves, young and eager, one tall and fair with slicked-back hair, the other shorter and chunkier, with an earring and a five-o'clock shadow, rushing to Jude's side, crouching over him, ignoring her, talking only to each other. Rosalie and Punchy Lamb, appearing immediately afterwards like shadows through the scrub of the clearing, skirting Grace, rushing into the shack, despite Birdie's calls for them to stop. Jason, left behind, whooping from the hill, crashing through the bush, thinly wailing, 'What's up? What's up? Wait for me. Wait for me. Mum? Mum!'

Birdie ran for the clearing, her torch beam bobbing up and down, her knees feeling as though they were about to give way. 'Rosalie, Punchy, don't touch anything!' she bawled as she ran. She heard the radio noise stop.

Grace was lying on her side in the dirt, howling, shuddering, crying. Birdie ran up to the verandah, halted at the door.

Rosalie and Punchy were standing by Trevor's body, looking down at it. They were holding hands. Punchy, barechested, in unbuttoned jeans and elastic-sided boots, had tears rolling down his cheeks. Rosalie, tidier but just as pale, was dry-eyed. Both of them had blood on their hands and on their clothes. They must have knelt beside the body when they first came in, as she had. The battered little transistor radio, its case cracked open, lay on the table, silenced at last.

'Rosalie, I'm sorry, but you should come outside,' Birdie said gently. 'The police are on their way. And a doctor. You should come outside, and shut the door. You don't want to disturb any evidence.'

Rosalie's mouth stretched open. She started to laugh. Shrill, gasping laughter. 'Doctor?' she gasped. 'He doesn't want a doctor. What evidence? Evidence that he's dead? Look at the blood. Look the back of his head. It's cracked open. His brains are showing through. Isn't that enough?'

Birdie stepped forward rapidly, but already Rosalie had quietened. She sank into a chair and sat there panting, still gripping Punchy's hand. He looked sheepishly at Birdie.

'Come outside, Rosalie,' Birdie said. 'Grace needs you.' The woman shook her head.

'She won't go,' said Punchy. 'And if she doesn't go I won't go.' He stuck out his bottom lip stubbornly.

'Well, look, don't let anyone else in. And try to remember not to touch anything,' Birdie said, giving up. She'd done her best. She had to get back, to Jude. She backed out of the kitchen, and stepped down into the clearing just in time to see Jason bursting into the open from some hidden bush trail.

He was wild with excitement. 'What's happening? Where's Mum?' he screamed at her. 'What's wrong with Grace?'

'You talk to Grace,' said Birdie. 'You stay with Grace, and don't leave her.'

She turned and left him, with little hope that he'd take the slightest notice.

She ran back up the track, through the avenue of trees. The paramedics were still working efficiently over Jude, manoeuvring a stretcher, a drip and various other bits of equipment Birdie didn't recognise. They looked up as she approached.

'There's been a murder. There's a dead man in the shack,' she said. Somehow she felt they ought to know.

The paramedics, interrupted in the smooth performance of their scheduled task, looked at one another. Here was a complication.

'We weren't told about a murder,' said the fair one angrily. He frowned. His Adam's apple jiggled up and down. He was worried.

'I didn't know about it when I called you. I found the body afterwards.'

'Sure he's dead?' asked the chunky one, after a moment. He fiddled with his earring.

Birdie nodded.

'Cops know about it?'

She nodded again.

'They shouldn't be mucking round in there. You're supposed to leave things the way they were, if there's a murder. Even accidental death.'

'I know. I can't make them leave.'

'Sure he's dead?'

'Yes.'

With a resigned look at his colleague the fair paramedic got up and started to jog towards the shack. To have a look-see. Better to be safe than sorry. Birdie watched him go. He had a strange, loping way of running. The back of his neck was stiff with resentment and tension.

Birdie crouched by Jude's side, trying to screen everything else out. She'd done her best. The paramedic's authority would carry far more weight than hers. Maybe he could get Rosalie and Punchy out of that terrible room with its smell of blood, old and new.

In the absence of his partner, the chunky paramedic became friendlier, chattier. Jude's leg was broken. Badly sprained arm. Spine seemed okay. He had concussion. Severe concussion. Did she know what happened? No, she didn't. No, she wasn't his wife. She was no relation. Just a friend. Yes, she knew his name. Of course she knew his name. No, she wasn't sure of his address. She only knew his office phone number.

'Could you follow us to the hospital?'

Could she? Birdie was confused. Should she go and leave all this, for Dan to find?

You keep out of it.

She became aware of voices. She looked up. Floury Baker, big-bellied, red-faced and tousled in jeans and white singlet, was standing by the bend, murmuring to two other men and a sharp-faced old woman with her head done up in pins. They'd obviously just arrived. They stood there, taking in the scene, staring at the paramedic and Jude, then turning their eyes towards the clearing. As Birdie watched, Sue Sweeney, carrying a powerful flashlight, wrapped in a red-flowered dressing-gown with pink runners poking incongruously from below its flapping hem, joined them.

The gang's all here, Birdie thought, getting up and walking towards them.

But it wasn't. Annie wasn't here. Yet. Keith hadn't come back. Lily was missing, too.

And none of the Hewitts had made an appearance, either. That was strange. They must have heard the screaming. They must have seen the lights—the flashing red light of the ambulance, in particular. It was surprising that they hadn't come to see what was happening.

Unless they already knew.

The group stared at her as she approached. 'There's been an—a death," she said. She'd been going to say 'accident,' but at the last second had baulked at the euphemism. Under the circumstances, even 'death' was a euphemism. It implied natural causes.

Sue's hand flew to her mouth.

'Is it Lamb?' snapped the sharp-faced woman with the hair pins.

Birdie nodded, her eyes on Sue. Sue made no obvious movement. But her knuckles whitened as she pressed her fingers hard against her lips, and above her hand her eyes were wide and black.

The woman smiled, thin-lipped and turned to Floury Baker. 'Told you!' she said triumphantly.

He shrugged. 'Never argued with you, Peg, did I?' he drawled.

'Who did it?' she demanded, fixing Birdie with a beady eye.

'I don't know.'

Peg peered at the paramedic working over Jude.

'Anyway, what's he mucking around with him for?' she demanded. 'He's dead, isn't he?'

'That's—not—Trevor,' mumbled Sue. Hand still pressed to her mouth, she stared wildly at Jude's sprawled body, then at Birdie.

'No, no,' Birdie said, as calmly as she could. 'That's not Trevor. Trevor was killed in the shack. That's Jude, there—Jude Gregorian—you know?'

Floury's heavy face was wooden. 'What happened to him?'

'Doesn't look so good,' Peg opined, narrowing her eyes.

Birdie kept her voice steady. 'They say he'll be all right. He's got concussion and a broken leg. But they have to get him to hospital. They want me to go with them.'

'To fill in the forms, and that,' Peg nodded knowledgeably.

'But the police are coming. The local police, I guess. But also Detective-Sergeant Dan Toby and Detective-Constable Colin Milson, from Sydney.'

One of the men gave a short laugh. 'Sydney coppers? By the time they get here—'

'No.' Birdie fixed her eyes on Floury. She had to get his attention, 'They should be here soon. They've been staying in Sassafras. If I go with the ambulance, could you tell them where I am? The hospital at Gunbudgie. Tell them I'll get back as soon as I can.'

He nodded. 'No problem,' he said slowly. 'I'll leave the back door open for you.' If he was wondering why two city cops had been staying at Sassafras, how Birdie knew they were, or why they'd particularly want to see her, he didn't give any indication of it.

But the sharp-faced little woman's nose twitched. She, at least, was bristling with curiosity. At the same time her eyes kept darting towards the shack. She wanted to go down there. See things for herself.

Birdie noticed that the tall, fair paramedic had returned. He'd closed the door of the shack, and Punchy, Rosalie, Jason and Grace were clustered together in the clearing looking after him. At least Grace had stopped screaming. What a white coat and an air of authority, however spurious, can do, thought Birdie, hurrying back to where Jude was lying.

He was on a stretcher, a hospital blanket tucked around

him, a drip in his arm and an oxygen mask over his face. He looked like a stranger. He was terrifyingly still.

'He's all right,' said the chunky paramedic, seeing the expression on Birdie's face. 'He's stabilised. We'll take him now. You'll follow?'

'Yes. I'll have to go and get the car keys.'

'You do that. We'll get on. Gunbudgie Hospital. Know where that is?'

'I'll find it.'

They picked up the stretcher. Chunky at the front, tall and fair at the back. They were going to carry Jude to the ambulance.

'Better than bumping him over this lot,' said the fair one. 'Even if we could get the vehicle down this far. Which I doubt.'

'Do you want me to hold the torch for you?'

'Nah. It'll be right,' the chunky one said cheerfully. 'We're used to this. Working round here . . .'

She nodded, and started walking uncertainly beside them, shining her own torch in front of her feet. Its beam looked pitifully inadequate beside the strong one thrown by chunky's professional job. She hardly needed it. But it made her feel independent.

Floury, Sue, Peg and the others pressed back into the scrub as they passed. Peg looked avidly at Jude's face, obscured by the oxygen mask, and nudged the man beside her.

'Looks bad,' she said in a stage whisper. 'Terrible colour.'

Birdie looked at Jude. She stumbled slightly, bumping into the stretcher and rattling the drip.

'You go and get the keys,' chunky suggested kindly. 'Go on. Your friend'll be okay. He won't know you're gone. Doesn't even know you're here, does he? What you say his name was?'

'Jude. Jude Gregorian.'

'Yeah. Jude'll be okay. You leave him with us. We'll see you at Gunbudgie.'

He was being breezy and tactful, but having her hanging around was worrying him. He wanted her to leave them to get on with their job. Or maybe he wanted to talk to his friend without her being there.

Birdie glanced behind her. Floury, Peg, and the two men

were slowly, inevitably, making their way down the track towards the clearing. Sue Sweeney was standing alone, looking after them, her arms crossed over her chest, hands clutching the shoulder seams of her flowered gown. What was she thinking? What was she feeling? Was she glad, or sorry, that Trevor Lamb was dead?

'I'll go then,' Birdie said aloud, and moved on quickly, slipping in front of the stretcher, and walking on ahead.

'. . . back of the head,' she heard the fair one saying, when she was nearly, but not quite, out of earshot. 'Been a few hours.'

'. . . tell them . . . not to go in again? Till the cops . . .'

'Yeah. But soon as we're gone I'll bet . . .'

Their voices faded away as Birdie hurried on.

The flashing red light was just ahead now. It appeared and disappeared as she stumbled around the bends of the track. She realised she must have already passed the place where she heard the watcher in the scrub. She hadn't given it a thought. Her mind had been too full of other things. But now she remembered, and again her throat closed up. The claustrophobic air of the track was nearly choking her. She was suddenly frantic to escape it.

She scurried around the final bend, expecting to see open road ahead. But the mouth of the track was closed. The ambulance had been backed into it, leaving little room on either side. Birdie squeezed past it, pushed frantically through the overhanging pepper trees, making for the road.

A heavy hand grabbed her shoulder.

With a scream, she tore herself free. She spun around. A light flashed into her face.

'Where do you think you're going?' Dan Toby demanded.

She stared at him, speechless, her mouth open, her heart beating wildly. He was frowning thunderously. Behind him Colin Milson hovered, his dark, thin face a mask of disapproval.

'Well?' growled Toby.

She licked her lips. 'I'm going to the hospital, Gunbudgie Hospital, with Jude,' she managed to say. 'He's unconscious. I've come to get the car keys. Everyone else is—in there.' She pointed to the track.

His eyebrows shot up. '*Everyone else?* What d'you mean, *everyone* else?'

'Trevor Lamb. Dead. Jude. Unconscious. The ambulance guys. Rosalie Lamb, Punchy Lamb, Grace Lamb, Jason Lamb, Floury Baker, Sue Sweeney, a woman called Peg, some other men . . .' Birdie heard her flat voice beginning to tremble, felt her control giving way, as she watched his expression change from severity to almost comic dismay. She could read his mind. *Not again.*

Poor Dan. It was so funny. So terribly funny, really. She fought down the hysteria.

'There was nothing I could do,' she choked. 'One of the paramedics tried, but . . . The mention of the ambulance reminded her of what she was supposed to be doing. The car keys. She started to turn, to move away. Again he stopped her, with a hand on her arm.

'What about the Gunbudgie police?' he asked grimly.

'Not here.'

'The doctor?'

'Not here.'

Milson made a disgusted sound, barely suppressed.

'Go, Milson,' snapped Toby. 'I'll be along.'

Milson stalked to the mouth of the track, squeezed past the ambulance, and disappeared.

Again Birdie tried to move. He tightened his grip on her arm, shaking it.

'Get a hold of yourself, will you, Birdwood?' he muttered. Then he looked up the road, beyond the pub. Voices. A rattling sound. Two bicycles suddenly sailed into view, emerging from the dark into the light thrown onto the road by the brightly-lit houses next to the post office.

The bikes swerved to a halt beside the ambulance in a spray of dust. Two boys leapt from them and in an instant had plunged into the darkness of the bush.

'Hey, you! Stop!' Toby roared.

But there was no reply. Only a cracking, thrashing noise and then the sound of running feet as the kids reached the track and sped towards the action.

'Little bastards!' Toby took a step, changed his mind. 'Milson'll deal with them,' he reminded himself.

There was a banging sound from the back of the ambulance. The paramedics had arrived with the stretcher.

'I have to go!' Birdie struggled to free herself. 'Can't you hear? They'll be going in a minute. Let me go, Dan.'

'Birdie, stop it.' Toby's voice was level, and cold. 'I don't know what's been happening here. I don't know where the Gunbudgie cops are. I don't know why I've been chosen by fate to preside over yet another colossal balls-up. But what I do know is this. The man I was supposed to question is a bloody corpse. And so far you're the only source of information I've got. So there's no way I'm letting you out of my sight. You're staying right here. You're not going anywhere.'

Fifteen

Milson was standing with his back to the shack door, being menaced by Annie Lamb. His face was carefully expressionless, but he was bending slightly backwards, obviously in an effort to protect himself from the full effect of her breath, no doubt a noxious combination of stale beer fumes, cigarettes, spittle and rage.

'God,' muttered Dan Toby, as he and Birdie approached through the crowd of onlookers gathered in the clearing. There must have been a dozen of them now. Quite a few people had arrived since Birdie left. They must have come through the bush. Except for the two boys on the bikes she'd seen no one enter the track from the road.

People fell back to let them pass, giving them plenty of room. Among the strangers, familiar faces seemed to leap out at Birdie. Floury Baker, stolid, Sue Sweeney, fearful, Rosalie, frozen-faced, fumbling with the buttons of her shirt, Jason, frightened, half-excited, Punchy, worried, uncomprehending, Grace, a pale little ghost. They were as familiar as old friends. Yet she'd known them for less than a day.

'Don't madam me, you skinny-faced git!' screeched Annie, thrusting her red, sweating face forward.

Milson winced, and leaned back a little further, but stood his ground.

'I got a right!' she shouted. 'I got a right to see me own son, haven't I? I should've been the first to be told. The first, not the last. Bloody cops. Think you're going to get away with this? I'll get the law onto you.'

She thrust a massive arm around Milson's narrow back, and felt for the door handle.

'You tell 'im, Annie!' shouted a man's voice from the crowd.

'Mrs. Lamb, please step back,' said Milson coldly. 'If you continue to obstruct me in the course of my duty I'll have to put you under arrest.'

He sounded ridiculous, but Birdie had to admire his sangfroid. Annie Lamb, grey hair on end, gums bared in rage, huge body quivering with fury, was a formidable assailant.

'Grandma! Birdie's here!' shrieked Jason.

Annie spun around and saw Birdie walking towards her. 'Ha!' she spat. She turned back to Milson and lifted a huge fist, shaking it in his face. 'Now! Now we'll see. This girl's from the ABC. She's a friend of our lawyer that you got rid of so convenient. That puts a spoke in your wheel, doesn't it? You're not going to get away with your dirty copper tricks so easy with her around, are you? She'll put you on TV.'

Milson remained impassive. What he was thinking was impossible to guess.

Annie pursed her lips, then turned around again and stomped off the verandah. She ploughed her way over to Birdie. She was still wearing the pink-and-mauve-flowered dress, Birdie noted. She'd probably slept in it.

Annie shot one hard look at Dan Toby, then turned her back on him and bent towards Birdie. 'They got Trev, love,' she said rapidly. 'They got him, and they packed Jude off to Gunbudgie in an ambulance.'

'I know,' Birdie said. She pointed at Dan. 'Annie, this is Detective-Sergeant Dan Toby.'

Annie ignored Toby completely. She took Birdie's arm, and drew her a little aside.

'Don't you be taken in, love. They'll be trying to put one over you. You listen to me. You gotta get on to your boss and get us onto TV. We gotta make a big stink. It's the only way.'

'The only . . . ?'

'The only way. Don'tcha see?' hissed Annie. 'A cover-up. That's what this is going to be. Why d'ya think these coppers are here? The blokes in suits? Local coppers aren't here. They're being kept out of it. It's hush-hush, isn't it? See?'

'You think . . .'

Annie's lips worked. 'They got Trev,' she whispered. 'I should've known. I thought it was funny, them letting him out. I said to Rosalie.' Her red-rimmed eyes brimmed with tears. 'But they planned it all, the bastards. They let him get right back here, then they fixed it. And if we don't do something, they'll get away with it. That bastard Hewitt'll get away with it like he always does. He'll pay them off. And Trev's dead. My boy's dead!'

She clutched at Birdie, and bent over, sobbing. The tears were rolling down her cheeks now, falling unheeded onto her chest.

'Annie—' Birdie began. But she knew it was no use. Whatever she said wouldn't be believed, wouldn't comfort, wouldn't help.

Someone came up behind her. It was Rosalie. In the light glimmering from the windows of the shack Birdie could see that her face was still and pale. The skin under her eyes was grey-blue. She put out her arms and took her mother by the shoulders, gently moving her away from Birdie.

'Come on, Mum,' she said. 'We'll see Trev later. Come on home.'

Annie shook her head. She couldn't speak.

'Yes, Mum,' said Rosalie. 'It's better. Jason shouldn't have woken you. There's nothing you can do for Trev. Come on home. Birdie'll watch the cops for us. She'll do it, just like Jude would've. Remember what he said? She's a lawyer too. She's his friend. She'll stand in for him. Won't you, Birdie?'

She looked into Birdie's eyes over Annie's heaving shoulders. The look was steady, almost without expression. But Birdie knew what was required.

'I'll do what I can,' she said. 'I'll do the best I can. I'll do whatever Jude could have done.'

That, at least, was the truth, she thought, as she watched Rosalie lead Annie away. I'll do the best I can. I'll do whatever Jude could have done. Briefly she thought of Jude, being sped, unconscious, to Gunbudgie. She had wanted to go with him. But she knew Dan's claim was stronger. She'd fought it, but half-heartedly. In the end, logic had triumphed over emotion. As always. I was right to stay, she thought. But the knowledge didn't comfort her.

Punchy, Jason and Grace followed as Annie and Rosalie disappeared into the bush to toil up the hill to the old house.

At the edge of the clearing, Punchy turned and lifted his hand to Birdie. A silent gesture of confidence, camaraderie and farewell. She nodded to him, and raised her own hand as he melted into the shadows.

Birdie looked at Dan Toby. He raised his eyebrows quizzically, conspiratorially.

Like your new friends, Birdwood. Right up your street, aren't they?

She didn't smile. She didn't change expression. Suddenly, with Punchy's wave, her mind had cleared. She knew what she had to do. For Annie. For Jude. For herself. Not just what Jude could have done. Jude was the defence expert. Saving and protecting the innocent was his specialty. And that wasn't what was needed now.

What was needed now was another kind of expert. Her kind. The kind who sought out the guilty.

With new eyes she scanned the watching crowd. And she knew the process was beginning. The process that would eventually lead her to Trevor Lamb's killer, and to that killer's exposure and punishment. However long it took. Whoever the killer might be. Whatever the motive. Whatever the cost.

'You all right?' Toby hitched at his belt. He'd adjusted his expression. He was trying to look friendly now.

'Sure. You going inside now? To look at the body?'

'He'll keep. Not going anywhere, is he? Got to get rid of this lot, first.' He jerked his head at the muttering crowd. Then he raised his voice.

'Milson?'

Milson moved away from the door and stepped down from the verandah, dusting the back of his jacket with a fastidious hand.

'Get rid of them, will you?' said Toby brusquely. 'Names and addresses first, of course. Park the car across the track. Tell them no one's to set foot near here till they're told otherwise. Ring the local police again too, will you? See what in God's name they think they're doing.'

'Yes,' said Milson. 'Sir.' He stalked off towards the crowd of people. A woman at the back began to edge away. Two boys—the two who'd come on their bikes—frankly turned and ran.

Toby turned back to Birdie and rubbed his hands with

an air of complacency that was completely unconvincing. 'Better late than never. That'll give forensic a bit of a go, anyhow.'

Birdie shook her head. 'It's hopeless, Dan. Most of those people been tramping round here for half an hour already. There might have been others we haven't even seen. Who skipped off through the bush before you arrived. And anyway, I don't think you're going to find anything you can use.'

He scoffed. 'What's that? Private dickess's intuition?'

'No. Local knowledge.'

'Local knowledge? You've only been here half a bloody day!'

'Long enough to know that just about everyone in Hope's End is here, or has been here. You'll find traces of them all. And I'll bet most of them have been inside the shack as well. Between when the paramedics left and Milson arrived.'

He scowled. 'The local coppers are a dead loss. They should've been here long ago. Kept everyone out. Sealed the area. We've got no equipment. Nothing.'

'They must have run into trouble on the way.'

'What could be worse than this? God, Sydney's having kittens.'

'I can imagine. Bit embarrassing for them. Losing their star released prisoner in less than twenty-four hours. Be even more embarrassing for them once Annie starts spreading her conspiracy theory around the place.'

'You'll have to stop her doing that.'

Birdie felt a small flame of anger flare in her cheeks. 'Is that so? I'm working for you now, am I?'

He looked her up and down. 'What's the matter with you, Birdwood?' he growled. 'Has this place got to you or something? I'm not your enemy, for God's sake. Don't you see that if that woman goes shooting her mouth off to the press about Les Hewitt she might wreck our case? Not that I'd care too much, really,' he added.

She looked at him curiously. 'You've made up your mind who did this, then? Without even seeing the body? After talking to no one? You think Les Hewitt did it?'

He shrugged. 'Who else?'

'It could have been anyone else, Dan. Anyone here. A lot of people had motives, of one sort or another. You only had to spend a few hours with Lamb to realise that. And everyone had the opportunity, too.'

'No one could've had a stronger motive than Hewitt. He worshipped his daughter. He swore he'd kill Trevor Lamb if he ever had the chance. Well, I'm betting he got his chance, and he took it. And I'm a copper, so I'm going to have to do something about that. But you know what?'

'What?'

'If I wasn't a copper, I'd say good luck to him.'

'Dan, have you forgotten why you came out here?' Birdie said slowly.

He stared at her.

'Have you forgotten why they sent you?' she repeated. 'Wasn't it because of what Trevor Lamb said, in gaol?'

'All that big-noting shit about telling who killed his wife?'

'Yes.'

'What about it?'

'Hasn't it occurred to you that Daphne Lamb's murderer might have heard about it?'

'No, it hasn't.'

'Why not?'

'Because Daphne Lamb's murderer's lying in that shack right now, dead himself. And good riddance.'

'Dan, I can't believe this!' Birdie was honestly aghast. 'If you really think that you shouldn't even be here. You shouldn't have been sent to question Lamb. You shouldn't have agreed to come.'

'I didn't have a choice. Like I told you, we humble coppers can't make choices about which cases we will and won't dirty our fingers on. Not like classy lawyers who talk like social workers and wear handmade suits.'

'Dan!'

He shrugged. 'It's the truth. Like it or lump it.'

'It's only part of the truth. It's not fair!'

Is truth the same as justice?

I don't know . . . They have a close relationship, anyhow.

Birdie realised that Toby had been watching her. She quickly put a guard on her expression. But it was probably too late. Because his own expression was sour as he turned and stumped towards the shack.

'You come with me,' he shouted to her over his shoulder. 'I want you to tell me if anything's been moved. That is, if you can remember more than your own name, the state you're in.'

'What's that supposed to mean?' she called after him angrily.

But he didn't answer.

Sixteen

Toby opened the door with his handkerchief. A pretty pointless exercise, Birdie thought viciously, considering the number of people who had wrenched at that knob since Trevor Lamb was found dead. But of course he had to play the thing by the book. And of course if under the mass of other prints, one of Les Hewitt's, or Phillip's, was found, he'd regard his theory proved.

And if she didn't come up with the goods for him he'd regard his other theory proved as well. Insulting, one-eyed . . .

He's jealous, she told herself. Jealous as a kid. He resents Jude. He's being ridiculous.

Still simmering, she followed him inside, listening to the piercing creak of the door, remembering that she hadn't yet told Toby about Phillip Hewitt's outburst at the pub. She found herself reluctant to do so. He seemed to be in the mood for jumping to conclusions. Les Hewitt, by reputation at least, could look after himself. His son was another matter.

The room smelt vile. Even worse than it had when she had been in it last. Of course, then, the door had been hanging open. In the short time since it had been shut, the smell of blood, dust and general mustiness had thickened and condensed.

At least there are no flies, Birdie thought. If it had been daytime, there would have been hundreds of flies. Especially in this heat. The thought made her feel queasy.

'Well?' Toby asked.

She looked around. Swallowed. 'The door was half-open when I got here. The light was off. I turned it on, and left it on. The transistor radio was playing. I didn't touch it, but I think Grace Lamb—that teenage girl who was out there—knocked it off the table later, and then her mother—the woman who was out there—turned it off.'

'What were they doing in here in the first place?'

'I think Grace just slipped in while I was sitting with Jude up the track, waiting for the ambulance. She didn't know I was there. I didn't see her come. First I knew she was hurtling out the door, screaming. She must have thought her uncle was there. The light, the radio, and so on . . .'

'Well, he was there, wasn't he?'

'Rosalie and Punchy, the brother, came after that. They just rushed into the shack. I couldn't stop them. A lot of these blood smears on the floor, and so on, are theirs. Some are mine. Some are probably other people's. I don't think there were any before.'

Toby was crouched beside the body now, his face impassive.

'Wouldn't be, if the killer was lucky,' he said. 'Just the one whack. That's all it took, I'd say. Hammer, maybe. What do you reckon?'

Callous bastard, she thought. Not a flicker out of him.

Then, as she watched him, her anger faded and died. If she'd seen dozens of dead bodies, he'd seen hundreds. In far worse circumstances than this. He was hardened to it. He rarely felt sorrow for the human beings he saw ravaged, destroyed, decomposing in shallow graves, stiffening in suburban living rooms, tossed like garbage in the dark corners of city streets. He didn't think about their lost hopes, opportunities, loves, ambitions. Didn't think about their struggles and joys. Didn't imagine what they might have been like had they escaped this fate and lived on.

It wasn't that he was incapable of it. Or incapable of pity. She knew that. He just automatically reserved that part of himself when he was working. He couldn't afford to expose it, if he was going to survive. If he was going to do what he had been trained to do. Day after day, week after week, year after year.

This was the dark side of justice. Her side. Suddenly Birdie was glad Jude wasn't with them. Glad he didn't have to see this. Glad he didn't have to see her dealing with it. He would have been sickened.

It was as though Jude had been taken out of her life, just as Toby came back into it. As though the two couldn't coexist. Darkness and light.

I'm tired, thought Birdie. I need sleep.

'I took a blanket from the bedroom, to cover Jude,' she said. She barely remembered doing it, but she knew she had. Toby sighed heavily, but said nothing.

Birdie wrinkled her forehead. At the edge of her mind was a feeling that there was something else she ought to tell him. Something she'd noticed, without consciously registering it. Something about the bedroom . . .

Toby stood up. 'Can't do much till the doctor gets here,' he said casually. 'And the bloody photographer and the clowns with the vacuum cleaners and plastic bags and tweezers. Milson can look after them. He loves all that. God, we'll have to be bloody careful on this one.'

He stuck his hands in his pockets, looking around the room. He didn't move. Just looked. She looked with him. At the bolted back door. The dusty stove. The kitchen sink, splashed with a few drops of water. The two crumpled beer cans lying by the red waste bin. The third, on the floor near the body. The computer equipment, neat, grey and silent on the kitchen table. The bloody smears on the floor, the table edge, the ruined transistor radio, the doorframe, one of the chairs. Smears left by fingers and feet. Hers. Grace's. Rosalie's. Punchy's. Maybe even Jason's. Floury's. Sue's. Peg's . . .

The only one who hadn't been in this room was Annie. The very one who'd had the most right.

Where's Keith?

The thought struck her suddenly. She opened her mouth to say something to Toby, but he was looking over her shoulder, out the door.

A rangy man, with a thick thatch of greying fair hair, was stepping onto the verandah. He was carrying a doctor's bag.

He walked into the room. He looked at Toby, Birdie and the body of Trevor Lamb, and his mouth turned down at the corners. A habitual expression, Birdie thought, looking at the grooves that marked the face from the corners of the lips to the sides of the chin.

'Lanky,' he said, nodding to Toby, staring at Birdie.

Lanky was his name. Dr Lanky. It had taken a moment for Birdie to understand that. The way he said it, it had sounded like a comment. Not that 'lanky' described Trevor Lamb. Or Toby, or Birdie—not possibly. But it was a perfect name for the doctor himself, so perfect that it had probably caused him a little grief in his youth.

Dr Lanky was in his fifties, probably, but his thin, suntanned face, with its bony nose, deep-set eyes, wide, thin-lipped mouth and small chin was heavily lined and creased, like the face of a much older man. Combined with his features this gave him an almost comically lugubrious look. It was as though he'd been caricatured, and the cartoonist's jokey black lines had somehow transferred themselves to the real man.

'Dan Toby,' Toby said, holding out his hand.

Dr Lanky shook hands with Toby, bending over slightly and holding out a long, long arm, preserving the distance between them.

'This is Verity Birdwood,' Toby said. 'She discovered the body.'

Dr Lanky nodded slowly, and decided to shake hands with Birdie as well, repeating his name as he did so, in case she hadn't caught it the first time.

Then he turned his attention to the body on the floor.

'So,' he said, looking down at it. 'Finally.'

It seemed a very odd thing to say, and he must have realised it. Without taking his eyes from the floor, he went on. 'Been heading for this since the day he was born, this bloke.' He sighed, deeply. 'Still, his troubles are over now, aren't they?'

By now Birdie had remembered that she'd read Lanky's name before.

'Weren't you the doctor who examined Daphne Lamb's body, the first time?' she asked.

Without haste he turned his head to look at her. 'That's right.'

He turned away, then slowly bent over the body from his great height, his hands on his knees. He looked for a long moment.

When he straightened up, he had a curious expression on his face. Almost startled.

'Anything wrong?' Toby asked, rather irritably.

'Nup,' said Dr Lanky absently. He sighed. 'Don't want me mucking round with him till you get some snaps, I suppose?'

'Not really. What's the hold-up, do you know?'

'Car smash. On the track. Had to stop. Do what we could. I left first. They're right behind me.'

As he spoke, there were sounds outside. Voices, tramping feet.

'There you are,' said Dr Lanky. His mouth turned down at the corners.

Milson was escorting a group across the clearing. One man in uniform, two others in plain clothes. All of them tall, tanned, thin-lipped, expressionless. For a wild moment, on first catching sight of them, Birdie thought she'd seen them before—in the Hope's End pub. They looked exactly like the men who'd stood there wooden-faced throughout each scene as it occurred, propping up the wall, unsurprised, sipping beer, saying nothing.

Could they be the same men? Could part of the pub audience simply have changed its boots, put on jackets, and in one case, a uniform, and moved from the front stalls to the stage?

No, of course they couldn't.

Dan was right. This place was getting to her. Birdie's eyes prickled, and she rubbed at them, under her glasses.

Toby moved out onto the verandah, and Birdie took the opportunity to slip outside too. She leaned her back against the wall, decided to sit down. Her legs were aching. Her back was aching. Jude would have arrived at the hospital by now. Soon she could ring. Ask about him.

Through half-closed eyes she watched the policemen meeting. Like dogs circling one another, waiting for the wrong move, the slightest sign of aggression. More handshakes, from a distance. No smiles. Then they were all walking towards the shack, carefully casual, carefully apart.

Birdie closed her eyes. The approaching voices droned in and out of her consciousness, refusing to be screened out. The Gunbudgie police didn't seem at all apologetic for their delay. Instead they were regaling Toby with the tale of the reason for it with a great deal of relish.

'. . . off the edge. Right into the scrub. Must've been . . . bat out of hell . . . Drunk as a skunk. Been there a while.

Bloody near bled to death . . . miracle we saw the car down there . . .'

'Pity we did . . . save a bit . . .'

'. . . soaked . . . impossible . . . whose blood . . . sent a uniformed bloke . . . ambulance. He'll get the clothes . . . Got the tyre jack in the back . . .'

They were clumping onto the verandah now. Pausing by the door. Birdie kept her eyes closed. She wasn't wanted for the moment. Toby would come for her when he was ready. In the meantime . . .

'So. Looks like you'll be able to get home quick smart. That suit you?' Satisfaction obvious.

'Don't quite follow you.' Toby's voice. Wary.

Silence.

'Didn't Lanky tell you?'

'What?'

Snort of laughter. 'Bloody Lanky. Thought he'd have told you.'

'What?' Toby's voice was dangerous now.

'Can't believe he didn't tell you. Close-mouthed bastard. Bloke in the car. Doing a runner. What I've been saying. He's your boy. We got him for you. Keith Lamb.'

Birdie opened her eyes. Toby was standing with Milson and one of the men in plain clothes. The uniformed police-man and the other detective were nowhere to be seen. Pre-sumably they'd gone inside to start taking the 'snaps'.

'You think he killed his brother? Has he said so?' Toby.

'Nah. 'Course not. He's not saying anything, mate. He's out to it. An' he'll deny it till he's black in the face once he's awake. But he did it all right.'

'What makes you so sure?'

'He had the chance. He had a motive. A beauty. He's a bad bastard, anyhow. And he was running. Take it from me. He's the one. I can smell it.'

'Since when has your nose been a legal argument?' snapped Toby.

Birdie stirred, but he didn't look at her.

' 'Scuse me?'

'We need proof he did it.'

'Ah.' The detective flapped his hand dismissively. 'Like I told you. Forensic'll have a look at his clothes and such. Covered in blood, of course. Might be his brother's as well as his, if we're lucky. We'll give them his tyre jack, too. He might've used that. Had it in the back of his car.'

'Isn't that where they're usually kept?'

'Yeah. So what?'

Birdie clambered to her feet. Milson looked down his nose at her. The detective noticed her for the first time.

'Who's this?' he asked, jerking his thumb at her. Then he looked more closely. 'Oh, the woman from the ABC. The one who found the body. Right?'

'Right,' Toby grunted.

'Well, she'll tell you there was no love lost between Keith and Trevor Lamb. She was in the pub when Trevor told Keith what he thought of him. She saw the whole thing. Didn't you, love?'

'How do you know I was at the pub?' asked Birdie sharply. This man was getting on her nerves.

The detective shrugged. 'Word gets round,' he drawled.

'That's the motive, is it? Bit of a dust-up in the pub?' growled Toby.

'Nah. The girlfriend's the motive, mate. Haven't you heard? Trevor was making a line for Keith's tart. Think he'd know better. More or less asked Lily to come back to the shack and give him one, so I heard. She probably did it too. Real little slut. And if anything would've driven Keith Lamb over the edge, it'd have been that. He's got a problem with women.' He grinned slyly. 'The locals know all about it. You ask Floury Baker what he thinks.'

Birdie felt Toby's eyes on her. Accusing. *What do you mean by letting me get shown up? Why didn't you tell me all this?*

She looked coldly back at him *(You didn't give me the chance!)* and then turned to the detective.

'Well, if you heard about Keith and Trevor and Lily you must have heard about everything else that happened at the pub, mustn't you?' she murmured. 'Including the fact that Trevor Lamb was offensive to just about everyone there. Including Phillip Hewitt.'

The detective snorted with contemptuous laughter. 'You don't know Phil Hewitt. Phil Hewitt wouldn't hurt a fly. Doesn't even eat meat 'cause he's sorry for the little lambs. He was just pissed.'

'He was very drunk, yes. Like everyone else. But it

doesn't follow that he didn't mean what he said. And I'm not just picking on him. There are other people round here who weren't too happy to have Trevor Lamb back. You probably know who they are. And added to all that, there was Lamb's carry-on about naming his wife's murderer.'

The detective sneered. 'That was just—'

Birdie raised her voice and spoke over him, looking directly at Toby. 'I don't blame you for keeping an open mind, myself, Dan. Given what happened last time the police round here jumped to conclusions.'

Off the hook, he turned a bland face to his Gunbudgie foe. 'Best to keep an open mind,' he said.

Milson sniffed. Whether in triumph or in disgust at his superior's hypocrisy Birdie couldn't tell. His usual expression of well-bred distaste hadn't altered.

'Whatever you like,' said the detective airily. 'But you're wasting your time, mate. Keith Lamb did it, all right. I can smell it.'

Seventeen

Toby leaned over the railing of the Hope's Creek bridge. It creaked ominously, and he jerked back.

'I don't think the railing's safe,' said Birdie, rather late.

'Thanks for the warning.' He stuck his hands in his pockets and looked gloomily at the faintly pink-stained sky. 'Going to be hot,' he remarked.

There was weary silence, broken only by the gurgling of the creek and the bleating from Hewitts' paddocks as the lambs woke and butted their frowsy mothers for milk or skittered off through the grass.

'Nice little things, aren't they?' Toby squinted at the nearest of the gambolling, white, woolly dots. 'Full of life.'

'They're going to the abattoir, soon,' said Birdie drearily.

'Oh.' Toby looked thoughtful for a moment, wiped his mouth with the back of his hand, then frowned.

'Now. You've told me everything, have you? From start to finish?'

'Everything I can remember. Some of it's a bit of a blur. But you've got the gist.'

'The gist'll do me for now. You'll have to do a formal statement later. You're not planning to push off, are you?'

'No. I think I'll be hanging around here for a couple of days.'

'Thought so.' Toby hitched at his belt. 'You keep out of our way,' he warned. 'I've got to be careful on this one.'

'I know. But you could bear in mind that the way the Lambs feel about cops I could be quite a bit of help to you. If you want information from them, that is.'

He grunted. Looked at his watch. 'I'd better get back

and see how Milson's getting on. See if we can get the body moved before the locals are up and gawking.'

'Most of them did their gawking last night.'

'Maybe they'll sleep in, then.'

'I doubt it.' Birdie followed him as he left the bridge and started walking slowly back towards the pub. He was dragging his feet. He looked tired and discontented. He doesn't want to do this, she thought.

'So you're here for the duration yourself, are you?' she asked.

'According to on-high, yes,' he said sourly. 'On-high's carrying on like a chook without its head. On-high wants both a quick result, and cast-iron proof. For a nice neat, conclusive, no probs, no embarrassments, no excuses, no arguments, no questions, press release—by lunchtime. That's what on-high wants. Never mind the wait for forensics. Never mind the extra blokes from Sydney won't be here for hours. Never mind the problems with the locals. Huh! What does that matter?'

'They can't ask the impossible.'

'They can. And guess who's in the gun if they don't get it?'

'So what are you going to do?'

'What do you think? Try to get a confession. It's possible, if Les Hewitt is the one. He's not the type to run away from a thing like that. Not if he's confronted the right way. For all I know he's waiting for me with his overnight bag packed right now.'

'You still think he did it. What about Keith Lamb?'

'The Gunbudgie mob are going to work on him. I wish them luck. But I don't like their chances. They're wrong about him. Doesn't make sense he'd run like that if he did the murder. He could've just gone home to bed and been safe as houses. And why do it, anyhow? The motive's pathetic. Who says he'd kill his brother just out of gaol, because of a flirt in a pub? But the Gunbudgie blokes see it differently. So they're going for him. Leaving Hewitt to me.'

'You're each going to ride your favourite? You've made a deal?' Birdie shook her head. This would be funny if it wasn't so bizarre.

'You can put it that way if you like.'

They reached the pub, and Birdie stopped.

'What if neither of you gets a confession?'

'Then we're stuffed, aren't we?' Toby kicked angrily at the dust.

'Dan—'

'Ah, all right. Not stuffed. Just back to square one. And the old recipe. Take statements from every Tom, Dick and Harry. Dodge the bloody press. Try to find the bloody weapon. Wait for Milson's hairs and seeds and specks of fluff and God knows what to be looked at. Hang out for the post-mortem results . . .'

'Wasn't Dr Lanky any help?'

'Some. Said Lamb almost certainly died of a single, very violent crack to the back of the head with something hard and oddly-shaped, by the look of the damage to the skull and the skin surrounding the injury. No enormous strength necessary, he said. Just a lot of anger and a bit of luck. Couldn't see any fragments of wood or anything else in the wound. With the naked eye, anyhow. So he's betting the weapon was metal.'

'Something like Keith's car jack?'

'Yeah. Something like that. But it could have been any-thing. And a car jack—it's hardly oddly-shaped, is it? Seemed pretty sure Lamb died sometime between midnight and two a.m. But frankly I don't see how he's so certain. It was hot last night. That would've made a difference. He could've died earlier.'

'When Jude left the pub at ten to twelve, there was a light showing from the shack,' Birdie reminded him. 'I no-ticed it was off at about one-twenty. But it could have gone off long before that. Almost immediately, as far as I know. And besides, Jude was attacked on his way to the shack. He never got there. He'd been lying on that track for hours.'

'You don't know that.'

'Yes. The more I think about it, the more sure I am. Lit-tle sticks and bits of bark and stuff from the trees had fallen all over him. And anyway, he was facing the shack.'

'He could've turned around, for God's sake. Defending himself.'

Birdie shook her head. 'I don't think so. It was the way he was lying, Dan. He'd obviously been knocked for six with one hit—he'd fallen flat on his back, heavily enough to break his leg. No struggle or anything. As if he'd been taken completely by surprise. As if someone heard him coming, and hid, then jumped out and hit him. The back of his head was bleeding.'

She paused. Swallowed. It seemed incredible that she could be talking about it so coldly. Toby waited. Birdie heard her own voice speak on. Flat. Expressionless.

'Either someone cannoned into him from the front, suddenly and really hard, so he fell backwards and knocked his head that way, or they hit him from behind. It was probably that. After all, it had worked with Lamb. It was just lucky whoever it was didn't hit Jude hard enough to kill him, too.'

She stopped, and nibbled at her lip. Then she would have found Jude dead by the side of that dark track. The thought made her stomach turn over.

'The point of all that being,' drawled Toby, kicking at the dust, 'that Lamb was killed around midnight?'

'Yes. It's a reasonable theory.'

'Presuming lover boy was in fact jumped by the escaping murderer, not just some stray lawyer-basher out for kicks. Then there's your heavy breather in the scrub. Same bloke, you reckon? Hung around a while, didn't he?'

Birdie finally lost her temper. 'Dan, do you want my help, or not?'

'Not particularly,' he said coolly. 'I just wanted what you knew. Well, you've given me that, now. So you can toddle off to Gunbudgie whenever you like to hold the boyfriend's hand. Sorry I held you up. I'll be following in due course. To have a chat to him. What's the story on that, by the way?'

'Sometime this morning, they said.' Birdie was suddenly too tired to argue with him any more. 'They've set his leg. He's asleep now. Well, he was when I called. They said he mightn't remember much, though. When he last woke he was very disoriented.'

'Great! I might have known he'd continue his unbroken run of being a pain in the arse.'

'Dan, you're being really illogical, you know,' she said quietly.

He turned away, looking vacantly towards the police cars parked under the pepper trees.

'Any idea where I could get a cup of tea in this hole?' he asked, as if she hadn't spoken.

'There's the pub,' she said. 'You could ask the publican.'

'Allan Baker.'

'They call him Floury.'

'They would. And he won't be up for hours.'

'I know where the kitchen is. I'm allowed to use it. I could have a pot of tea made by the time you get back from checking with Milson.'

'What's the catch?'

'I was thinking that you'd be going on to the Hewitts' place afterwards.'

'So?'

'I'd like to come with you.'

'Thought you'd be buzzing off to Gunbudgie straight away.'

'No. I want to go to the Hewitts' place with you.'

She saw a look of satisfaction pass briefly across his face. But when he turned to her his expression was sardonic.

'Bribed with a cuppa,' he growled. 'Come cheap, don't I? Okay. You're on. Can't hurt. Might help. Stranger things have happened. You can get the missus out of the way for me, anyhow. I'll see you in twenty minutes. Could you find me something to eat?'

'There are some biscuits.'

'That'll do.'

He spun around and strode on towards the mouth of the track, leaving her standing there. But she noted that he was no longer dragging his feet. That was something, anyway, she thought. She needed Dan Toby's full cooperation if she was going to do what she had in mind. She needed to keep him sweet. Never an easy task at the best of times. And very difficult now with the chip he had on his shoulder about his orders, the problems to come, and Jude.

She stepped off the road, onto the pub verandah, and then stepped off again. All the pub lights were off, as was the front light of Sue Sweeney's flat above the old stables. There was no sign that anyone was up and about yet. But Floury had told her he'd leave the back door open.

Birdie skirted the verandah and moved along the side of the old building. She reached the backyard, and glanced up at the side window of the flat—where she'd seen the light last night. But that window, too, was black. Sue was asleep. Or lying awake in the dark. Birdie wondered which. She'd have to talk to Sue, sometime soon. Sue was going to be an important witness for her. But first things first.

The back door was unlocked, as Floury had promised. Birdie let herself in, and crept to the kitchen to put the kettle on. Then she went out again, and tiptoed upstairs.

She looked longingly at the bathroom at the end of the hall as she let herself into her room. But she knew she didn't have time for a shower. Not now. She'd have one later, she promised herself, as soon as she'd seen the Hewitts. A shower, and a proper breakfast.

Inside the room she stripped off her grubby, blood-stained clothes, and pulled clean ones from her bag. Fresh underwear. Another white shirt. Another pair of jeans. At this rate she'd start running out of clothes. She should have brought more. Still, she hadn't banked on finding dead bodies or crawling around on the ground looking after unconscious men when she'd packed, had she?

She pulled the clothes on, then found her comb and went to do her hair in the speckled mirror on the back of the door. Her reflection stared back at her as she struggled with the tangled curls. She barely recognised herself. The thin, pointed face seemed unnaturally pale. The eyes behind the thick glasses were huge and dark. She looked worried. Which she was. She looked as though she hadn't slept all night. Which she hadn't.

Her leather handbag lay where she'd left it on the bed, contents spilling out onto the black and green triangles. Wearily she pushed them all back, added the mobile phone, snapped the bag shut and threw the strap over her shoulder. Like an old warhorse, she thought, lugging it out into the corridor.

Back downstairs, and into the kitchen. The kitchen, filled with steam from the furiously boiling kettle. Birdie made a pot of tea, put it on a metal tray with two mugs, milk, and sugar for Toby. And a teaspoon. And some biscuits on a plate. The least wholesome-looking biscuits she could find.

Yes, what she had to do now was keep Dan sweet. And if that meant playing Little Miss Housekeeper, she'd do it. She needed his help to get to the Hewitts. They wouldn't talk to her if she turned up alone. And she needed to talk to them.

Birdie picked up the tray and began to carry it towards the front door. She and Dan would drink their tea on the verandah. Just in case Floury objected to her entertaining a copper inside.

She knew she didn't have a hope of getting much more information than she had on the killing of Trevor Lamb. She wouldn't be allowed back on the murder scene. And the results of forensic testing wouldn't be available for a long time.

But if she was right, she wouldn't need that, except as final proof.

She put the tray down on the bar, and went to open the front door. She saw with pleasure that the sky was lightening. There was a tiny breeze. The air was filled with the sounds of carolling magpies.

She went back for the tray and carried it carefully to the front step of the pub. Then she sat down, to wait for Dan. To her left, the road stretched on, lined for a short way by small, closed houses, then disappearing into the thick bush that covered the hills where it finally died. In front of her the pepper trees stirred. To her right, the railings of the old bridge framed a view of Hewitts' paddocks, golden-green, undulating, peaceful, beautiful.

It was all just as it had always been. It was as though time stood still in Hope's End.

Dan could relax out here. She hoped he'd arrive before Floury or Sue got up to complicate things.

They'd have their tea, then they'd go to see his suspect. And he'd persuade, and bully and talk tough to Les Hewitt, hoping for a confession. And while he was doing that, the Gunbudgie police would be sitting by Keith Lamb's bedside, with their notebooks, persuading, bullying, talking tough, hoping for the same thing.

They'd both be disappointed. They'd both end up back at square one. With the interviews, with painstaking searches, with waits for forensic, with routine. And it was unlikely they'd let her into all that.

But she didn't want it. She didn't need it. Interviews with certain people were all she needed. Or rather, the chance to chat. The conversations wouldn't seem like interviews, the way she'd handle them. Because she wouldn't be asking about Trevor Lamb, or the events of last night. She'd be asking about Daphne.

She was going to ride her own favourite. Track her own killer. And the police couldn't prevent her doing it. She already had a mass of evidence. More than the police would get on Trevor Lamb's murder in a year. It was up there, right now, in her hotel room. Beth's file on the murder of Daphne Lamb: the huge dossier full of begged questions, and woolly thinking, grim photographs and lists of names and times. And Jude's book, *Lamb to the Slaughter*.

The trail was cold. Five years old. But nothing much changed in Hope's End. The information she needed was all still there, locked up in people's minds, as well as in the papers upstairs. And Daphne's killer was still here, too. Daphne's killer, and Trevor's.

The clues that would lead to Trevor Lamb's murderer lay not in the present, but in the past. She was sure of it.

Eighteen

'That's the gate, up ahead, I think. On the left,' Birdie said from the back seat. Milson made no reply. His lean jaw was set as he slowed the car, turned the wheel and eased over the crossing. He thoroughly disapproved of Birdie's presence. But as usual he'd said nothing. She knew, as Dan did, that he'd save his complaints for later. And he wouldn't complain to Dan directly. He'd just make sure Dan's superiors were fully briefed on this, as on every other disciplinary lapse in the past. 'Fully briefed.' That's how he'd put it. He'd be responsible, serious, concerned, as he made his report, his undertaker's face composed and re-gretful, his eyes veiled to conceal the spite that otherwise might show.

It had happened before. So often, that Birdie wondered why Dan Toby continued to risk official displeasure by arbi-trarily letting her tag along when Milson was around.

She got out of the car and trudged around it to open the gate. It was very early, but already the gloss had gone from the morning. Already the air was warming. The little breeze had died. The colours of the land were bleaching out, and contours were losing definition.

She lifted the heavy metal ring from its peg on the rough timber gatepost, and let the fastening chain slip through the wire and fall. It clattered against the post as the gate swung wide. Milson, staring straight ahead, let the car move for-ward and through the gap.

Birdie pushed the gate shut again, threaded the chain through it and made sure the ring was firmly pushed over the peg. It wouldn't do for Les Hewitt's lambs to escape their fate. That would certainly add an unwelcome touch of colour to proceedings—and to Milson's report.

She climbed back into the car and slammed the door. Milson drove on. Sheep looked up uncertainly, panicked and began milling around, as they passed. Lambs bleated in the crush.

'Take it steady, Milson,' said Toby comfortably. 'You're in the country now.'

His eyes were closed. He smiled to himself. Nothing he liked better than irritating Milson.

And that's the point, isn't it? Birdie thought. That's why I'm here, right now. Dan's in a bad mood, and I'm a perfect way of irritating Milson. I'm his way of rebelling.

Not that Toby's animus was all directed at this one man. It was what Milson represented that pricked Dan on to torment him. The four 'Rs'. Rules, regulations, routine, rigidity. Dan couldn't stand them any more than she could have done. And so far, so far, he'd got away with his minor acts of rebellion. So far the people he called 'on-high' had been content to let him go his own way.

It had been a rather eccentric way, curving and twisting and going off at tangents, like a country road. It wasn't mapped in official guidebooks. It had been potholed with disciplinary infractions and blunders, occasionally blocked suddenly and completely by the falling debris of disastrous miscalculation. But, more often than not, it had led, finally, to success. And that was Toby's salvation.

She, Birdie, had been part of that success. She knew it, he knew it. To a certain extent, 'on-high' knew it. Their partnership was unusual. There was no provision for it in the rule book. But it worked, and so, with a wink and a nod, 'on-high' listened to the complaints brought to it by Milson and others, contented itself with minor reprimands, reminding Toby of his place, and basked in the good publicity that flowed from cases solved.

But Milson was always there. He was the safeguard. And if one day Toby should slip and fall on his chosen track, it would be Milson who'd yap the alarm, then go in for the kill.

And this time, of all times, Dan couldn't afford to slip. Couldn't afford to deviate too much from the official line, either. This time the whole country was watching.

Another closed gate ahead of them. The car slowed, and stopped. Birdie heaved herself out, to deal with another metal ring, another heavy chain.

Ahead the road curved upward to climb the small hill above the creek. And there, in startling contrast to the surrounding countryside, was what looked like a lush oasis of green, studded with trees and flowering bushes, and precisely defined by a white-painted fence. The house was in the centre of the oasis, half-hidden by the trees—a big old timber bungalow, painted white, with a bull-nosed, vine-shrouded verandah all around it, and a green corrugated-iron roof. Behind the house, there were some outbuildings, also white, with green roofs, and beyond those, in a separate paddock fenced by white rails, three horses, looking intelligently towards the road. Beside one of the outbuildings, there was a ute.

Dogs were barking furiously.

'Well, they'll know we're on our way, anyhow,' Toby said quietly.

He was tense. Working up to the confrontation to come.

'You get the woman aside, Birdie,' he said, as the car moved forward again. 'Ask her about the chooks or the curtains or something. Milson and I need Hewitt on his own. Don't want her fluttering round. It'll put him off. She's sick, or something, isn't she?'

'Not physically, I don't think. Nervous illness. Very anxious. Never goes out. Agoraphobic, maybe.'

'Agor-what?'

'Fear of leaving home,' said Milson coldly.

'Ah.' Toby peered at the house as they approached it. Two cars were parked side by side in an open garage next to the house, at the end of a driveway neatly finished with double gates painted to match the fence. The Hewitts, it seemed, were home.

'Nice place,' he commented. 'Nice view, too. And the creek's just a hop, step and a jump away, isn't it? Wouldn't take five minutes to run down there, would it? Cross over. Pop up through the bush to the shack. And no one any the wiser.'

He was right, of course. But . . .

The road ended at a bald patch of ground in front of the white-painted fence. A turning circle, for visitors not invited to park inside the perimeter. Milson pulled up, and turned off the engine. The barking became a crescendo. But the dogs were nowhere to be seen.

'All right,' said Toby. 'We're away.'

He heaved himself out of the car, slammed the door and strode to the front gate, where pink roses climbed over a wire frame. He let himself in and walked towards the house. He didn't look back at Birdie and Milson. He knew they'd follow. And shut the gate for him, too.

Birdie let Milson go first. She stood back, effacing herself, as he strode under the roses and up the front path without a glance right or left. Then she entered the garden herself, and leant back against the gate, hearing the soft sound of its catch clicking into place.

On this side of the fence it was another world. A world of coolness, shade, colour and scent. All sense of inappropriate contrast disappeared. Memories of paddocks, hills, raw-sided dams, winding, unmade roads, wire fences, faded away. Tall shrubs concealed the white-painted boundary. Big trees—not gum trees, but soft, graceful exotics—jacarandas, golden elms—spread their canopy over fine green grass, clusters of shrubs, drifts of flowers.

Milson was knocking at the front door. Birdie moved. Down the front path, lined with lavender and rosemary bushes that scented the air as she brushed against them. Up the front steps, onto the dim verandah with its twisting fringe of jasmine and wisteria.

She turned to look back the way she had come. From the verandah, two steps higher than the path, you could see the countryside again. But the view was controlled and framed by roses, wisteria and arching trees. You couldn't see the gully through which the creek ran. Just trees, and sky, and distant hills.

Yet below, very near, Trevor Lamb's shack huddled in its clearing.

Imagine going from this, to *that*, she thought. Not for the first time, she wondered about Daphne Lamb.

Milson knocked again. But the door remained firmly closed. No one twitched the lace curtains at the windows. No footsteps sounded in the hall.

'No one's answering, sir,' he said.

'I can see that, Milson,' snapped Toby. 'But there must be someone here at this hour.'

'They might be still asleep. It's only six o'clock.'

'If they were they'd have heard us. Bedrooms are usually at the front, in a place like this. Anyhow, Milson, you're forgetting. You're in the country, now. Man like Hewitt'd be up at sparrow-fart. Up and doing. Let's go around the back.'

They stepped down from the verandah, and followed the path that circled the house. Dogs barked ceaselessly.

'God, how many are there?' muttered Dan. 'Sounds like they've got a hundred of them back there.'

But there were only four. Three kelpies, one border collie. All half-strangling at the ends of their chains beyond the garage, pawing the air as they heaved, leapt and flung themselves forward in their efforts to get free and defend the home paddock.

Nervously, Birdie wondered what they would do if they did manage to break their chains. Leap upon the intruders and tear their throats out? Or, embarrassed to find their bluff called, run away?

Milson stopped and frowned. 'They look savage,' he said.

'It's okay, boy,' called Dan to the dogs, showing his teeth in an ingratiating smile.

The dogs redoubled their noise and their efforts, slavering at the mouth.

The door to one of the outbuildings was flung open. 'Get down there!' bawled a voice.

The dogs fell silent, and lay down, pawing at the dust. A man stepped out into the light. A big man of about fifty, heavy-set, wearing boots and working clothes. He put his hands on his hips and stared at the three strangers.

'C'n I help you?' he shouted.

'Ah—Mr Hewitt?' called Toby, beginning to walk towards him.

'Yes.' The man didn't move.

'Police, sir,' Dan shouted, feeling for his identification. 'Like to have a word with you.'

'Yes?'

Birdie heard a sound behind her. She spun around and saw a small, middle-aged woman staring from an open screen door at the end of the house. The woman's grey hair was pulled into a knot at the back of her neck. A crisp, very clean blue apron enveloped her, covering a printed cotton dress and tied neatly at the back. She had soft, blue flat-heeled shoes on her feet. Her face was a mask of terror.

'Mrs Hewitt?' Birdie said softly.

But the woman didn't hear her. Her whole attention was concentrated on the jacketed figures of Dan Toby and Colin Milson, walking away from the house, past the crouching dogs, towards her husband.

One of the kelpies lost control, sprang to its feet and let out a growling bark.

'Down!' thundered Les Hewitt furiously.

The dog dropped, and whined.

The woman by the door winced.

'Mrs Hewitt?'

The woman's eyes turned vacantly in the direction of the sound. She blinked at Birdie, unsurprised, small hands gripping the frame of the door.

'My husband's over there,' she said. Her voice was soft and young-sounding. At odds with her strained, lined face.

Birdie nodded. 'Do you think I could possibly have a drink of water, Mrs Hewitt?' she said.

The woman smoothed her apron with a nervous hand. 'Water?' He brow puckered, and she glanced behind her, into the house.

'If that would be all right.' Birdie smiled, shrugged. 'Actually, I've been up all night. I'm not feeling so well.'

'Oh. You'd better come in, then.' The response was quick, automatic. As Birdie had hoped, a direct appeal for help had worked where bright conversation, however cleverly begun, would almost certainly have failed. This woman was beyond normal intercourse with strangers. Maybe even with friends.

Dolly Hewitt could have said, 'There's a tap over there,' pointing out into the garden. She could have said, 'I'll get a glass of water for you,' and disappeared back into the house. But the courtesy that once she'd lived by had been too strong for her.

Already she was regretting her offer. You could see it in her face. But the offer had been made. Birdie was walking towards her, smiling gratefully. She had no choice but to swing the screen door open further.

'Come through here,' she said. 'Be careful you don't slip on the floor. It's wet.'

Birdie stepped into the room beyond the door. It was the laundry. Impeccably neat. Spotless white cupboards, shining taps, large washing machine, stainless-steel tub where something lay soaking under a froth of suds, tumble-dryer set underneath a white bench-top. Blue vinyl-tiled floor, still gleaming and slippery by the door where it had been cleaned, white ceramic tiles on the walls, each one printed with a small blue flower. The smell of washing powder and bleach. White-painted cane soiled-clothes basket. A small window beside the door, looking out over the back garden.

'I was just putting on some washing,' said Mrs Hewitt. She pulled a knob on the machine, and water began rushing through the pipes. She plucked at the strings of her apron, and started to take it off.

'Don't let me disturb you,' said Birdie. 'I don't want to be any trouble.'

The woman shook her head. 'It's no trouble,' she said. Again, it was an automatic response. There'd been a time when nothing was too much trouble to Dolly Hewitt, and old habits were hard to break.

Carrying the apron over her arm, she led the way into a spacious kitchen.

'Excuse the mess,' she said. She half-shut the door to the laundry as the machine finished filling, and, sloshing and thudding efficiently, began to wash.

There was no mess that Birdie could see. Nothing she'd define as mess.

The kitchen was a pleasant room, the window above the sink looking out over the vine-hung side verandah and beyond it, to the garden, where an old swing hung from the branch of a tree. The verandah dimmed the window, but light streamed through a skylight in the centre of the room. Birdie noticed that the skylight was fitted with a blind so it could be shut off as the day's heat increased. Everything had been thought of, it seemed.

A scalloped blue pelmet stretched across the top of the window, hiding the tight roll of a matching holland blind that was presumably pulled down at night. The floor tiles, blue like those in the laundry, were shining. Fitted timber cupboards and white benches scattered here and there with decorative nick-nacks filled the available wall space on three sides of the room. On the remaining wall, the wall opposite the back door, was a large dresser stacked with blue and white china, and near it stood a plain timber table and six straight-backed chairs. There was probably a formal dining room somewhere, Birdie thought. There would be, in a house like this. It would be in the front of the house, behind the closed door near the dresser. But she'd bet that most of the family's meals were taken here. Why go anywhere else?

The lingering scent of toast and bacon hung in the air. Dishes, greasy cutlery and a frying pan half-filled with water were stacked on the sink, ready to be washed. A big teapot covered by a tea-cosy in the shape of a hen stood on the table which was still spread with a blue and white checked tablecloth, speckled with crumbs. These things, presumably, were what Dolly meant by 'mess'.

The Hewitts had already breakfasted. As Toby had said, men like Hewitt were up and doing at sparrow-fart. Early to bed, early to rise . . .

'Sit down, dear,' said Dolly Hewitt. Quickly she gathered up the tablecloth, crumbs and all, and took it, and the teapot, to the sink. She left them to pick a clean glass from a cupboard, and fill it from a jug she took from the refrigerator.

Birdie sat at the table, feeling troublesome, and a fraud. Feeling something else, too. This kitchen—spacious, comfortable, well-appointed—was a world away from the kitchen in Trevor Lamb's shack. And yet, in a way, the two were similar. In their careful attention to detail, their tidiness, their colour-coordinated accessories, their combination of a homey air with the necessary efficiency of a workplace. One end of the room for preparing food, the other for eating. Separated, but linked by colour and ornament.

In the shack by the creek, Daphne Lamb had tried to re-create, in her own way, and with her own apparently meagre resources, a place that reminded her of home.

Playing house, thought Birdie suddenly. She looked up as Dolly Hewitt placed a glass of water in front of her.

'Thank you,' she said, and sipped. It was deliciously cool. She closed her eyes with pleasure, and sipped again.

'What are they doing here, those men?' asked Dolly abruptly. 'Who are they?'

Birdie opened her eyes. Somehow she'd assumed Dolly knew.

'They're police,' she said.

'Not local police. They don't look like local police.'

'No. They're from Sydney.'

'But what are they doing here?'

'They—well, they just wanted to ask—your husband, mainly—about—' Birdie hesitated. The woman's brown eyes were fixed on her, the lined face taut with anxiety.

'Had you heard—that Trevor Lamb was dead? That he'd been murdered?'

The woman clutched at her throat. She sank down into the chair closest to her. Birdie half-stood. 'Are you all right, Mrs Hewitt?'

She nodded, swallowing.

In the laundry, the washing machine finished agitating, and clicked.

Dolly Hewitt's head jerked up.

'Excuse me—it's going to—I've left—I have to—'

She rushed for the laundry door. Very concerned, Birdie followed.

The woman was heaving a plug from the tub beside the washing machine. Letting the water out. Wringing the dripping floor cloth that had been soaking in the suds between her small, brown hands.

'I nearly did it again. Let the laundry flood. I was just soaking this,' she chattered, her eyes wide and frightened. 'Only meant to leave it for a minute. The water from the machine runs away into here . . . silly system, but I've never got around to . . .'

As she spoke, the machine clicked again, and water began belching out through a pipe hooked over the tub. Rising, half-filling the bowl, and rushing away down the drain.

Birdie stared. The water was cold, and red. Pinky-red.

'It's all right,' whispered Dolly Hewitt, twisting the floor cloth in her sudsy hands. 'It's all right. It's only blood.'

Nineteen

'Blood?'

Birdie knew she was gaping. She couldn't take her eyes off that rushing, crimson tide rising, bubbling, in the tub.

'My husband. He slaughtered a lamb last night. Blood pumped all over him. Does that. Sometimes. If he's not careful.'

'Lamb's blood.'

Their eyes met. The bloody water running from the pipe slowed to a trickle. The level in the tub went down. No stain was left behind on the shining stainless steel.

'I had to wash the floor, first thing after breakfast,' said Dolly Hewitt. 'It put me behind. Blood was dried on, from where he'd dropped his clothes last night. It was very late. I was already in bed, or I'd have been able to fix it then. He'd been to Gunbudgie. Killed the lamb after he got home. Stupid, really. Should have left it. He didn't get to bed till half-past twelve.' The words were tumbling out of her, as if they were substitutes for thought. 'He's careless,' she rushed on. 'Doesn't think. Just drops them on the floor. You know how men are. Some men.'

Birdie didn't know. But she'd heard.

The last crimson drops fell into the tub. The machine hummed and clicked, started to fill again.

'Two rinses in cold, then a cold wash usually does it,' said Dolly absent-mindedly. 'We'll see.' She hung the squeezed-dry floor cloth over the washing machine taps, and moved back into the kitchen. Birdie followed her, then went to the table and picked up her glass. Her mouth was dry.

'Sit down, dear,' said Dolly, in exactly the same tone as before. 'You're looking peaky.'

Peaky wasn't the word for the way Birdie was feeling. She sat obediently, and sipped her water. Follow your own plan, she thought. Don't ask any more. Leave that to Toby.

'Phillip—my son—doesn't like blood either,' said Dolly. She put on her apron, went to the sink, put the plug in and ran hot water. It was as though Birdie had never mentioned Trevor Lamb's death. Somehow the incident with the washing machine had helped her disengage again. She wasn't going to talk about Lamb. Ask how he died. Wonder what was happening between the three men outside. She was going to talk about anything else but that. Think about anything else but that.

'Phillip hates it when his father kills a beast. He won't eat the meat. Won't touch it.' Dolly Hewitt bent for the detergent in the cupboard under the sink, squeezed the liquid into the steaming water, put the container back. Neatly. In exactly the same spot as it had been before.

Birdie took a breath. Now. She'd try it now.

'Was your daughter the same? Daphne?' she asked gently.

Dolly's head jerked slightly. Her hand flew to her throat again. It was as though the mention of the name had jolted her like an electric shock. Her forehead wrinkled. But she answered. Slowly and painfully.

'Daphne—didn't mind. She always ate what her father killed.' She slipped some dishes into the sink. Began to wash them, mechanically.

'She didn't mind about the lambs?'

'Oh, no. Not that she was hard-hearted. She was kindness itself. Raised plenty of poddy lambs in her time, and you can't imagine how gentle she was with them. She loved them. But she was a real farm girl. She knew—well, she learnt—' Dolly Hewitt looked up, her hands stilled in the foamy water. The brown eyes filled with tears.

'I'm sorry, Mrs Hewitt.' Birdie bent forward. 'I didn't mean to—'

But you did mean to. You did.

'It's all right.' The woman shook her head, wiped her hands on her apron, and felt for the handkerchief tucked into her belt. 'It's all right. It's been five years. I should talk about her. I should. Otherwise she's really dead, isn't she? If no one talks about her. If no one remembers.' She rubbed her eyes with the white linen, dragging at the loose, puckered skin ruthlessly, as if by doing that she could force the tears back, or even wipe away the memories causing them.

'Les won't talk about it,' she said. 'Phillip will, but it upsets him. I don't like to upset him. He comes home from school so tired. It's the last thing he needs, to be upset, when he comes home. I remember how it was.'

She tucked her handkerchief back in her belt and returned to the washing up, as though talking about her other child had calmed her, reminded her of her duties.

'You used to teach at the school yourself, didn't you?' Birdie asked.

The woman nodded, washing dishes, putting them into the smaller side sink, ready to rinse. 'That's how I came here, to Hope's End. Thirty-one—thirty-two years ago,' she said slowly, as if she couldn't believe it.

She looked out the window, her eyes lingering on the swing, hanging still from its branch. Her voice, flat and listless, went on.

'I came full of plans and ideas. You know. I was only young. But it was nothing like I'd thought. I hated it. I hated it so much. I stayed on for a while after I married my husband. But then I left. He wanted me to leave. Wanted me here, at home. And anyway, I'd started Daphne.'

She paused. That name again. Then she went on, driven by a flood of memory. 'I was so happy,' she said. A touch of wonder entered her voice, glazed her eyes, as she watched the swing.

So happy. It's hard to believe, now, that I could ever have been so happy. But I was. I remember . . .

'The baby coming. The house to look after. My husband. The garden. And I had my books. My painting. Photography. I used to take photographs, in those days. I didn't miss the teaching. Not at all. It was a relief, such a relief, not to have to go to that place day after day, getting nowhere, feeling a failure. I might have done better somewhere else. I don't know. I sometimes wonder. If I'd never come here . . . if I'd been posted somewhere else . . .'

I wouldn't have met Les Hewitt. I wouldn't have married him. I wouldn't have had Daphne. Daphne wouldn't have married Trevor Lamb. Daphne wouldn't have been killed. I wouldn't feel like this . . . half-dead, half-alive . . . if I'd never come here . . .

Her hands moved mechanically, washing dishes. 'That school. There were a few children I could have done something with. A few. But most of them—they didn't want to learn. Didn't want to be—to do—anything, as far as I could see except get old enough to drink, and drive, and leave school. They were very disruptive. I couldn't manage them.'

'You must have taught some of the Lambs. Annie's children.' Birdie didn't mention Trevor's name. She didn't want to break this mood, but she had to know.

The woman frowned. 'Oh, yes.' Cutlery clattered in the sink. 'Bridget, Mickey, Johnny, Brett. And Keith. He started just before I left. Sometimes we had Cecilia, too. The baby. Poor Bridget would bring her along. Little skinny thing lugging this big baby. "Mum's sick today, Miss," she'd say. Well, we all knew what that meant.' Her lips tightened.

'The other children would laugh. Poor little Bridget. I can still see her, blushing up to the roots of her hair. It didn't worry her brothers. They'd laugh along with the others. But Bridget felt it. She hated the way her parents drank.'

With a sudden, vigorous movement she turned the cold water tap, sluicing the washed dishes, knives, forks and spoons piled in the small sink. Her lips were a hard line, now. The clean water gushed onto the dishes, washing away the detergent foam, splashing upwards onto the front of her apron. 'People like that shouldn't be allowed to have children,' she said.

She plucked the plates and bowls from the sink, and stacked them in the dish drainer, followed by the cutlery.

'I'll do the frying pan later,' she said, more to herself than to Birdie, and wiped her hands on her apron.

Birdie had finished her water. She watched the small woman moving around the kitchen, wiping benches, taking the tablecloth outside to shake it, folding it and putting it away. Taking the teapot outside to empty it, putting it on a tray near the electric kettle, ready for her husband's midmorning break. Following a routine. Drugging herself with it.

How was Toby going? Birdie wondered. How soon would he come back to the house, wanting to talk to Dolly, or wanting to leave?

The washing machine was gushing out rinse water into

the tub again. It wouldn't be red any more. Maybe just the palest pink.

Don't worry. It's only blood.

She'd have to find a way of telling Toby about the blood before they left. Discreetly.

She twisted restlessly in her chair, pretending to drink from the empty glass. She hadn't achieved what she'd wanted to achieve here. Soon Dolly Hewitt would indicate, politely, that it was time for her to go. She'd had her rest. She'd had her water. What could she do now, to keep the woman talking?

The school. She's interested in the school.

'I heard the school was closing down soon,' she said.

'Oh, yes,' said Dolly. 'Soon. There aren't enough children round here to make it worthwhile any more. That's what they say. The children will go to Gunbudgie School, on the bus. With the high school children. Makes a long day for them. But there you are.'

'The end of an era, then.' Birdie knew she was talking rubbish. Just making conversation. But her time was running out. Dolly Hewitt was hovering, wiping her hands on her apron, getting ready to ask if Birdie was feeling better now, because she had to get on with her work, and if Birdie would excuse her . . .

'Do you have any photographs of the school in the old days? When you were teaching?' Birdie asked, suddenly inspired. 'If you do, I'd love to see them.'

The woman looked surprised. 'Would you?'

'Oh, yes. I'm—' Birdie searched her memory for anything, anything that would justify her interest. '—I'm interested in local history. I did it as one of my options, at university.'

The smallest glow of interest in those dull eyes. 'Oh. University. Where did you go?'

'Sydney.'

'Oh. I went to the University of Sydney, too. Did you do an arts degree?'

'Arts-law.'

'Arts-law,' repeated Dolly Hewitt. There was a moment's silence. 'That's a hard course to get into. You must have done well. Daphne didn't do well enough for that. But she could have gone to university. Could have done an arts degree. Or agricultural science. She would have liked that. She could have boarded. Come home at the weekends, like Phillip.'

'But she didn't?'

'No.'

'Why was that, Mrs Hewitt?'

Silence. Then, slowly, the answer.

'Her father. He didn't want her to go. Wanted her here. Said there was no need for her to go away. He said he could teach her all she needed to know about farming. But it wasn't that.'

The woman shook her head, helplessly. 'It wasn't that. I just wanted her to get away from Hope's End for a while. Of course we'd miss her. Everyone would miss her. Everyone loved Daphne. But—she needed to see more of life. See—that there was more than this, than Hope's End, and the people she knew here, and their attitudes, and this way of life. She needed a chance to grow. She'd been so protected. She seemed so practical, but she was a romantic. And so young. I told him. I told him. If only he'd listened to me, and let her go . . .'

The voice went on, and on. The floodgates had opened at last, and bitter regret, contained for years bubbled up and out into the light, bright kitchen. A torrent of words. Birdie listened, careful not to move, not daring to make a sound, afraid of damming up the stream with a wrong word, a gesture out of place.

A story took shape. A story the newspapers hadn't told. That Jude's book hadn't told. The story she wanted to hear. Daphne's story.

Daphne grew up loved, protected, admired, happy. A little princess, in Hope's End. But not spoilt. She could have been, but her nature was too naturally sweet, her sense of irony too well-developed, her practical streak too strong. She went to the local school, the local high school. She did well, she worked hard. If she didn't love the classics, as her mother did, if she played the piano only to please, if she preferred magazines to books and riding to listening to concerts with her mother on the radio—well, that was the way she was.

But she was cloistered in Hope's End. She knew little of the outside world. If only Daphne's father had let her go. To see a bit of life. Perhaps then she wouldn't have fallen for the spurious charms of a man like Trevor Lamb. Perhaps then she wouldn't have mistaken his bullying machismo for strength, his sullenness, selfishness and paranoia for worldly wisdom, his conceit for pride, his practiced seduction techniques for tenderness.

Little did her father know the trap he was preparing for his daughter. Her mother sensed it. But her feeble struggles to encourage Daphne to continue her education did little to combat the father's warm, undisguised wish for the girl to stay with the family on the farm. Les didn't want to lose Daphne—his little mate, his daughter, the light of his life. She was good as any man with the sheep. She was equally at home on a horse's back, at the wheel of the ute, sitting on a fence rail. And for all that she was a real little woman too, he often used to say—neat and quick in all her movements, loving and sweet and generous, good to her mother.

Let her younger brother Phillip follow his mother's ambitions, he said. Phillip had never liked farm work anyway. The business sickened him. He didn't even like horses. He was actually scared of them. He never rode the pony Les had bought for him. Even the dogs knew they didn't have to obey him. Let him go to university, become a teacher or whatever. That was okay by Les. Maybe the boy would be better with kids than he was with animals. But Daphne was different.

So Daphne stayed. Les Hewitt rejoiced in his triumph. But within a year or two his happiness had turned to baffled outrage. A thing he had never imagined, had happened. He couldn't believe it was possible. Daphne had fallen in love with Trevor Lamb—a man she'd known since childhood. A man not fit to clean her boots. Daphne was going to marry Trevor Lamb—and nothing her father could say would change her mind. Daphne had married Trevor Lamb, and gone to live with him in a miserable hutch of a place on his own clan's run-down property.

It was with grief-stricken satisfaction that Les Hewitt saw his daughter battling with the results of her ill-advised marriage. He saw little of her. Too many bitter words had passed between them. But Dolly, her mother, kept in touch and did what she could. She had wept for her daughter, had begged her not to marry in haste, but Dolly had never threatened Daphne's independence the way Les had done.

There were no barriers of pride standing between mother and daughter.

'I couldn't do much for her,' Dolly whispered. 'I don't have any money of my own. Just what I can save out of the housekeeping. She spent a lot of what she had on doing up the shack. Making it fit to live in. Getting the roof fixed, and so on. Her father put the electricity on. But that's all he'd do. He said, she's made her bed. Now she can lie on it. He thought she'd leave Trevor Lamb, you see. Thought she wouldn't be able to stand it. But he didn't know Daphne. He thought he did, but he didn't. She wouldn't give in. Not like that. She wouldn't run home. Not after what he'd said to her. I knew that. He trapped her there, with that man, as surely as if he'd tied her down. And then—she died.'

Her voice trailed off. She blinked at Birdie, as if waking from a trance.

'I don't even know your name,' she said, after a moment.

'It's Verity. Verity Birdwood.'

Slowly, Dolly Hewitt undid her apron and took it off.

'Verity means truth,' she said. She turned away. 'The photo albums are in the study. Do you still want to see them?'

'Yes, I do.'

'Just come through,' the woman said. 'While I find them. You'll have to excuse the mess. I haven't dusted for a few days.'

She hung her apron on a hook behind the door, and led the way inside.

Twenty

Cool dimness. A clock ticking. Soft carpet underfoot. The smell of furniture polish.

Birdie blinked, trying to take everything in while her eyes adjusted to the dull light.

A blue-flowered couch, with armchairs to match. Cushions, pink, blue, pale green and beige. Gleaming old wood, a fireplace, shielded by a brass wire guard, mantelpiece cluttered with ornaments: Wedgwood vases, Royal Doulton figurines, statuettes in marble and bronze. On either side of the fireplace, glass-fronted cabinets filled with books, china cabinets filled with yet more ornaments.

French doors leading out to the verandah. Beside them, a piano. Paintings on the beige walls—some original, very pastel, watercolours—perhaps by Dolly herself—some prints of old masters. In front of the French doors, several smaller armchairs, with woven cane arms and tapestry backs and seats, arranged around two small occasional tables.

Dolly Hewitt ran her finger over one of the tabletops. 'Dust,' she said apologetically.

Birdie looked around. Dusting would take hours in this room. Every surface was cluttered.

'You're a collector,' she said. She bent to look at a bronze figurine on one of the tables: a woman and a bird. The bird's huge wings were almost covering the woman's body. The woman was cowering, her hands crossed over her breast. With a slight shock she realised she was looking at a rape scene.

She straightened. 'Leda and the Swan,' she murmured.

'Yes,' said Dolly Hewitt. She paused. 'Daphne gave that to me,' she said, with difficulty. 'For my birthday. She saw it in a magazine. It was one of a series I'd been getting for my-self. Greek and Roman legends. I like the legends. I've al-ways liked them.'

She gestured around the room. Birdie looked obediently. Yes. There was Perseus triumphantly holding up Medusa's head, on the mantelpiece. An effeminate-looking boy bend-ing over a miniature pool surrounded by bulrushes—Narcissus—on one of the bookcases. On one of the low tables a girl kneeling beside an intricately-carved box, just beginning to open it. Pandora. The girl whose curiosity un-leashed evil and misery on the world.

'Lovely,' murmured Birdie insincerely.

'I wasn't going to get the Leda,' said Dolly. 'I thought it—well, the subject probably isn't quite right for a lounge room.'

And a cut-off head writhing with snakes is? Birdie thought.

'But when Daphne gave it to me, of course I didn't say,' the woman went on. 'I don't think she even knew the legend, in fact. Didn't know—you know—what was happening in the scene. She just knew I'd been buying the series. She was so thrilled with herself, bless her heart. So thrilled she'd thought of a birthday present I'd really like, and surprised me. Cut out the coupon, took the money out of her bank ac-count, sent it off, all without me knowing. She loved to sur-prise me, on my birthday.'

Again tears welled in Dolly Hewitt's eyes. She fumbled for the handkerchief in her belt.

'I'll be back in a minute,' she murmured, turning aside. 'I'll just get the albums. They're in the study.' She turned and walked clumsily away, pushing open a door at the side of the room. Birdie glimpsed a polished table and chairs, the glis-tening of silver and glass on a sideboard. And another door. Dolly went through that door, and disappeared.

Birdie prowled to the fireplace, inspected a porcelain figurine of an old woman selling balloons, another of a boy herding geese, a painting of a jacaranda tree in full bloom, a slow-ticking antique clock. Beside the clock, bronze Perseus, snarling in triumph, held up Medusa's head. The gorgon's eyes were closed. But the snakes that crowned her head lived on, writhing, hissing, depicted in loving detail.

Birdie prowled on. She looked up the picture-lined hall-

way that led to the front door. There were four doors off
that hallway. Bedrooms, for sure. But the doors were closed.
And in one of those rooms, presumably, Phillip Hewitt was
sleeping off his hangover. She couldn't risk snooping. She
turned her back on temptation, wandered on.

She stopped by the piano. Standing on it, beside a vase
of dried flowers, was a photograph in a silver frame.
Daphne. The same photograph that had appeared in Jude's
book, and all the newspapers.

It was a soft studio portrait. Taken, Birdie recalled, on
Daphne's twenty-first birthday. Five months before her marriage. Had her parents known, then, what she was planning
to do? Had she?

Birdie stared. Before, she hadn't understood. Daphne
Hewitt. Trevor Lamb. It had seemed such an anomaly. Now
it seemed horribly inevitable.

The girl in the photograph, brown hair curling on her
shoulders, smiled out at the world, eager and untroubled.
She wasn't beautiful, but her face was sweet, intelligent,
lively and warm. And determined. And innocent. A terrifying
combination. The photographer had tried his best to smother
her real-life charm with an overlay of glamour, posing her
looking sideways over her shoulder, her hands lifted to
her face, showing the small diamond ring, the birthday present, that had been found missing in the days following her
death. But the life in her, the energy, sparkled in her eyes despite his efforts.

Everyone loved Daphne.

But Daphne had married Trevor Lamb. The man nobody loved. Except, perhaps, his mother, his sister . . .

Birdie turned away from the piano, the photograph. She
looked around the room, then out through the French doors,
to the garden.

This had been Daphne Hewitt's home. This, she had left,
at twenty-one, for life in the shack by the creek with Trevor
Lamb.

Just as long as we're together . . .

She thought she had loved Trevor Lamb. She thought
nothing else mattered.

*Better is a dinner of herbs where love is, than a stalled
ox, and hatred therewith . . .*

But there hadn't been hatred here.

'Oh, sorry.'

Birdie spun around to see Phillip Hewitt staring at her from the door to the hallway. He was dressed for work. Jacket, shirt, tie, immaculately pressed slacks. His hair, wet from the shower, was slicked back. He was sickly pale. There were shadowed half-moons under his eyes. He looked ill. Haunted.

'I didn't know anyone was here,' he said, coming into the room uncertainly.

'I'm just waiting for your mother,' said Birdie, with a friendly smile. She wondered if he remembered seeing her in the pub. Probably not. He'd been very drunk. And he'd been concentrating on Trevor Lamb.

'I was in the shower. I didn't hear.' He stood, irresolute, waiting for her to speak. Tell him what she was doing in the house.

'Phillip!' It was Dolly, carrying three photograph albums. Matching. Pale blue trimmed with gold. She thrust them at Birdie, tumbling them into her arms, her eyes on her son. 'You're up. I thought you weren't well. I thought you were staying in bed today.'

He shook his head, glancing at Birdie, the albums, back to his mother's worried face.

'What's happened?' he said quickly. 'Mum? What's happened?'

'It doesn't matter,' she said. 'Nothing that need bother you, Phillip. There's been trouble, in town. That's all.'

She ushered him into the kitchen.

'You just have your coffee,' Birdie heard her say, as the door swung shut behind them. 'Your father's dealing with it.'

'Mum . . . ?'

'Your father's dealing with it.'

'Mum . . . !'

The door was firmly closed.

Left alone, Birdie took the albums to one of the tapestry chairs by the French doors. She sat down, and stacked the albums on the table, beside Leda and the Swan. The girl's terrified face, turned and uplifted, stared out from behind a tangle of hair, as the swan's wing curved around her bare shoulders, on the point of covering her and bearing her to the ground.

Birdie stretched out a finger to touch the bronze. Cold,

hard, smooth as glass in some places, seamed, scrolled and rippled with painstaking detail in others. Hair, feathers, dress torn from the shoulders and falling in folds, bare feet twisted in a base of writhing grass.

I like the legends. I've always liked them.

Perseus and Medusa. Narcissus. Pandora. Leda. It was strange that these images didn't worry Dolly Hewitt. Didn't prey on her mind every time she walked through this museum of a room, with its soft carpet, ticking clock, and invisible, drifting dust.

But she didn't seem to see them as images of violence, terror, human frailty, fatal mistakes. For her they were simply representations of cultural icons—links with the grandeur and romance of another time, another place, another culture, rich and strange.

Birdie flipped open the first of the albums, leafed through the pages. There were dozens of photographs. Some black and white, self-consciously arty, enlarged and displayed singly—a little weatherboard school seen through pepper trees, close-ups of fences, old desks, a deserted classroom, a cracked school bell—some in colour, grouped on the pages and more straightforward—children sitting under trees, eating lunch, children in lines, girls skipping, playing clapping games, boys swinging on a rope.

One child seemed to appear in more of the photographs than all the others. A thin, serious-faced little girl with long brown plaits. Noticing this, Birdie turned the page only to find the girl again, this time in black and white, and larger. A proper portrait. The photograph was simply captioned 'Bridget.'

It was an interesting study. The girl's face seemed to shine from a shadowed background, her eyes wide and dark, her flesh almost translucent. Birdie wondered if it had happened by accident, or if Dolly had worked hard to achieve it.

Out of the corner of her eye she saw movement. Movement in the garden, beyond the verandah. Turning her head quickly she saw male figures walking beyond the trees, towards the house. Toby, and Milson. She stayed where she was, flipping over the pages of the album, staring at the photographs, without really seeing them. Waiting.

In a moment or two, the kitchen door swung open.

'You're wanted outside,' said Dolly Hewitt. 'Your

friends are going. They said they'd meet you at the car.' Her voice was flat and colourless again, all animation gone. Her eyes were wary.

Birdie stood up, closing the album and putting it carefully with the others.

'Thank you for showing me these,' she said. 'I haven't finished. Maybe I could come back another time.'

The woman's lips twitched into the parody of a smile, but she said nothing.

Birdie walked past her, to the kitchen, and picked up her handbag. From his place at the table Phillip Hewitt watched, unsmiling. In front of him was an untouched bowl of cereal, a small jug of milk, a spoon. A film of sweat gleamed on his high, white forehead. He'd been talking to his mother, she guessed. Telling her who Birdie was. Who Birdie must be, if she'd come here with the police. Telling her Birdie was taking advantage of her. Slipping under her guard.

She nodded to him, turned to the woman standing by the sitting-room door.

'Goodbye, Mrs Hewitt,' she said.

'Goodbye.'

Birdie walked through the laundry, and out into the open air. The screen door slammed behind her. She paced slowly along the back of the house. As she reached the corner, and turned to walk towards the front gate, she heard the washing machine start filling again.

'Lamb's blood, eh?' muttered Dan, as they drove away. 'Pumped all over his clothes. Which lamb do you think she meant?'

'The one hanging upside down in that shed on a chain, presumably,' said Milson, breaking his rule of silence for once.

'Don't remind me.'

'He killed it last night,' Birdie said. 'They skin them and take out the intestines and then let the body hang overnight. Before they cut them up.'

'So he told us. *While* he was cutting it up. While he was telling us he hadn't seen Trevor Lamb, knew nothing about any murder, was out in Gunbudgie from nine till midnight last night, witness, a Miss Posy Delius, do you mind, to prove it—'

'He wasn't too happy about giving us the name,' said Milson.

'No. 'Course he wasn't. You can just imagine who and what Miss Posy Delius is, can't you? He wouldn't want his wife to know about it.'

Milson's thin lips thinned further, until they almost disappeared. 'Rather odd to visit a prostitute last night, wouldn't you say? The first night Lamb's home?'

Toby glanced at him. 'Can you think of a better way to forget your troubles, Milson?'

Milson obviously could, so he preserved a disapproving silence. Toby allowed himself a small smile. A mere twitch of the lips. Then he continued.

'Hewitt got home about midnight, changed into working clothes, slaughtered the lamb, which takes fifteen to twenty minutes, he says, dumped his clothes in the laundry, showered and went to bed, witness, wife, to prove it. Says she mentioned it was gone twelve-thirty when he climbed into the cot. Saw nothing after that. Heard nothing. Neither did his wife, or his son, both whom were at present ill, and not to be disturbed. And why didn't we piss off and let him get on with it? All the time he's telling us this he's carving at this bloody corpse with a knife sharp as a razor and long as my arm. God!'

'Messy business,' said Milson, looking down his nose. 'Unhygienic.'

'Good way of covering up blood on your clothes, though, isn't it? Soaking yourself with more blood. Then getting the missus to wash the lot, whiter than white.'

'Forensic testing could still . . .'

'Quite so, Milson. Don't worry. We'll be back. With a search warrant. Then we'll see. Get the clothes for testing. Comb the place for the weapon. The Gunbudgie cops can get a statement from Posy Delius.'

'If that checks out it clears him till about midnight,' Milson pointed out. 'But after he got home . . .'

'Quite. After he got home, he could've done anything. Changed into his work clothes, say. Nicked down to the shack. Slaughtered one Lamb. *Not* the wooly one. Then come back and taken care of the other. *Then* dumped the bloody clothes, showered quick-smart, and gone to bed.'

'Couldn't have done it all in thirty minutes, Dan,' murmured Birdie from the back of the car.

'Maybe not. But let's face it, it doesn't have to be that way. He could've slaughtered the lamb in the shed before he went to Gunbudgie. Put on the same clothes when he came back.'

'No. Dolly would've washed his clothes straight away. She wouldn't have left them there all night, to be washed this morning.'

'Why not?'

'She just wouldn't leave them. I know she wouldn't. They must have been put into the laundry after she went to bed. She said they were, and I'm positive she's telling the truth.'

Toby sighed gustily. 'Okay. So he could've killed Lamb, showered, gone to bed, then waited till his wife went back to sleep, then got up, put on the same clothes and slaughtered the lamb in the shed. Or the whole twelve-thirty thing could be a put-up job between them. She'd say anything he wanted her to say, wouldn't she?'

'I don't know.'

'Well, it's a relief there's something you don't know, Birdwood. You get anything from her?'

'Nothing that would help you. We didn't talk about Trevor Lamb's murder. We didn't talk about last night at all. Except she did say her husband came to bed at twelve-thirty. She didn't seem anxious about it. It was quite natural, the way she said it. I'm sure she was telling the truth.'

'We'll see,' Toby grunted. 'We'll have a word with her. And the son, Phillip. When we go back.'

'Phillip's going to work. At the school.'

'Ah. Miraculous recovery, eh?'

'He was just hungover, I think. And he's the conscientious type. It's a one-teacher school. If he doesn't turn up, school's out.'

The car stopped at the first gate. Birdie wearily climbed out to open it. She looked back at the house. Nestled in its patch of fertile green, it had turned into an exotic oasis again.

The car drove on. Sheep drifted, panicked, wheeled in a wooly mass. Birdie lay back, eyes closed. She'd decided not to do the next gate.

'Did you get on to Gunbudgie? What did they say?' she heard Dan murmur.

'They've got nowhere with Keith Lamb,' Milson said. 'He won't say anything except he didn't see his brother after he left the pub. He left Hope's End at about eleven-thirty and didn't come back. And he wants a lawyer. Wants Jude Gregorian.'

'That right? Doesn't he know Gregorian's out of commission? In the same hospital he is?'

'Apparently not.'

'Doesn't that worry them at all? The Gunbudgie mob? Don't they think that if their man bashed Gregorian on the head on his way out from killing Trevor Lamb, he'd know it?'

'They seem to think he does know it. Trying to bluff them.'

Toby snorted disgustedly.

'Could be right,' said Milson.

The car pulled up again. Toby waited for a moment and then, finding that Birdie didn't move, heaved himself from the car and dealt with the gate.

Birdie kept her eyes closed as Milson eased them over the crossing, and onto the road. She heard the door slam as Toby climbed back into his seat, with much martyred groaning and puffing.

'It's all right, Birdwood. I've done it. You can open your eyes now,' he said.

'Thank you, Dan,' she murmured.

'S'pose you'll be going back to the pub for breakfast and a nice hot shower, will you?'

'I guess so. What about you?'

'Oh, Milson and I'll probably have a nice sit down and a game of cards,' he growled. 'Why not? This case is going so well. Everything in the garden's lovely. To sum up: no confession from Les Hewitt. No confession from Keith Lamb. No information worth two bob from anyone else involved. Except your good self. And you weren't exactly a mine of information.'

'What about Grace? Rosalie? The rest of the Lambs? And Lily Danger, Keith's de facto? You haven't talked to them yet.'

'Our Gunbudgie friends have. The whole lot of them say

they were home all night. Till the alarm was raised, that is.
Paul, Rosalie and Jason Lamb claim to have been asleep in
bed from the time they got home from the pub till when they
heard the little floosie screaming. The little floosie herself
says she woke up after a bad dream, went out to get a breath
of air, saw the light on in the shack, and went down to chat
to dear old Uncle Trev, only to find him deadibones. Hence
the screaming that woke Paul, Rosalie, Jason and the rest of
the town. Except Mum Lamb, who slept like the dead, quote
unquote till Jason Lamb came back up to the house and
woke her up with the good news. And the improbably
named Lily Danger, who nobody bothered to wake. And the
Hewitts, who, according to the man with the big knife, were
tucked up tight in their fancy house like the three wise mon-
keys all night. Gregorian's still off with the fairies. None of
the other worthy citizens saw or heard anything. We can't
find a weapon, or anything like a weapon. The whole town's
been tramping on the murder scene and feeling up the body.
The press'll be descending on the town like a swarm of blow-
flies any second. And it's going to be bloody hot. Is that
about the size of it, Milson?'

'Yes. I'd say so,' said Milson coolly. And slowed the car
to a crawl, as they crossed the Hope's Creek bridge.

Toby undid the top button of his shirt, and loosened his
tie. 'Before we do anything, I want to go back to that shack,
Milson,' he said. 'Take another sniff around.'

'The scene is being—'

'I know the bloody scene's being vacuumed and scraped
and dusted and tested, every leaf and hair of it, Milson. I just
want to take another look. You know. With my eyes? The
old-fashioned way?'

Birdie sat up. Something had suddenly clicked in
her mind.

'Dan!' she exclaimed. 'I've just thought of something.'

She saw Milson cast up his eyes resignedly as he pulled
the car into the shadiest parking spot he could find.

'Oh, still awake, are you?' snapped Toby.

'The shack—the bedroom of the shack.'

'What about it?'

'It was different—when I saw it last night. In the afternoon, it was tidy. The bed had been freshly-made. But last
night the bed was all messed up.'

'It was messed up because you dragged a blanket off it, Birdwood!'

'No. It was messed up before that. The blanket was half on the floor. The bedspread was pushed down to the end of the bed. The pillows weren't straight.'

'He'd been in there, then. Gone to bed. Fair enough. He'd had three beers, on top of what he'd had at the pub. That's interesting. He was woken up. Heard a noise maybe, and—'

'No, Dan. I don't think that was it. The bed didn't look like it had been slept in exactly. It looked more like . . .'

Toby swung around, violently, to stare at her over the back of the seat.

'You're saying he had a *woman* there?'

'I think he might have. The more I think about it . . .'

'God Almighty, Birdie, why didn't you tell us this before?'

'I didn't remember before. I didn't register. I'm sorry.'

'The testing would have picked it up,' Milson put in, staring through the windscreen at the pepper trees. 'The post-mortem would have—'

Swearing, Toby leapt from the car. 'God, don't you bloody understand we can't wait for all that, Milson? Come one. Get your arse into gear.'

He lowered his face to Birdie's window, and glared at her.

'I'll see you later, mastermind,' he growled. 'Don't leave town.'

Twenty-one

The front door of the pub was still locked. Of course. It was still very early. Five to seven. Birdie trailed around to the back door, and wearily let herself in.

The light was on over the stairs. She hadn't left it like that. Someone was stirring here, anyway.

The corridor light was on, too. And the bathroom light. Floury Baker, no doubt, starting the day. Damn! She'd have to wait for her shower. And she wanted to have it, quickly, so she could go to Gunbudgie to see Jude without any further delay. She had no intention of obeying Toby's final instruction. There was no reason to do so now. She'd told him everything she had to tell. And with any luck she'd be back in Hope's End before he even realised she was gone.

Perhaps she should skip the shower after all. But as she wearily felt for her key, contemplating this, the bathroom door opened, and the figure of Sue Sweeney, head wrapped in a pink towel, appeared through a cloud of scented steam.

'Oh, hi,' said Birdie. 'It's you.'

She turned off the bathroom light and walked towards her. She was wearing her red-flowered satin dressing-gown. It clung to her full body, showing every line and curve as she swayed along in open-toed, high-heeled white slippers, trimmed with swansdown. Her fingernails and toenails were painted bright red. But she was carrying a bulky pink sponge bag decorated with kittens, and her face, framed by the tightly-turbaned towel, was pink, soft, scrubbed clean, the eyes, minus shadow, eyeliner and mascara, round and slightly startled-looking, with short, light lashes. She looked like a kind, wholesome, country girl wearing someone else's clothes.

'Have you been up all night?' she asked.

Birdie nodded.

'You must be exhausted. How's Jude?'

'He's going to be all right. That's what they told me. I haven't been able to get to the hospital myself yet.'

'Oh. I thought that's where you must have been. I thought you were going with the ambulance.'

'That's what I thought, but it didn't work out that way.'

Sue looked down, fiddling with the zip of her sponge bag. 'Has he said anything, yet, did they say? About—last night?' she asked off-handedly.

'Not yet. They're letting him sleep. Or they were, when I spoke to them last. I'll ring them again in a minute. After I've had a shower.'

'Are you going to have a sleep, then?'

'No. I can't. I want to go to see Jude.'

'You poor thing.'

There was a moment's pause. Then, impulsively, Sue put a plump hand on Birdie's arm. 'Listen. You have your shower, make your call and then come up to the flat. I'll make you some breakfast before you leave. How about that? You should eat.'

'Oh—' Birdie thought rapidly, revised her plan for the morning with lightning speed, then nodded, and smiled. 'That's really nice of you,' she said. 'That would be great. If it's not too much trouble.'

'No trouble.'

'I'll be twenty minutes, then.'

'Twenty minutes.' Sue squeezed the arm she was holding, and let go. 'I'll be waiting. Coffee, or tea?'

'Coffee, please.'

'Okay.'

With a pleasant smile Sue swayed off down the corridor, clutching her sponge bag under her arm.

Birdie watched her click down the stairs in her high heels, holding tightly to the railing. Then, rushing now, she let herself into her room, grabbed her own sponge bag, towel and kimono, and made for the bathroom.

It was still warm, misty with steam, and faintly perfumed. Birdie felt slightly uncomfortable as she locked the door and stripped off her clothes. The scent, so reminiscent of Sue's alien femininity, somehow made her feel as though she was in someone else's private space. But under the shower, with water as hot as she could bear it beating on her back and shoulders, and the familiar smell of her own soap rising in the steam, she forgot all about it.

She couldn't relax, though. Pictures flipped into her mind one by one. Jude on a stretcher, an oxygen mask strapped over his mouth and nose. Dark blood on a timber floor. Dr Lanky, bending from the waist, with his hands on his knees. Annie Lamb's angry, anguished face. Punchy, lifting his hand at the side of the clearing. Scarlet-coloured water rising in a tub. A woman in a blue apron, washing dishes, staring out of a window at a motionless swing. A slaughtered lamb, swinging upside down in a shed. A big man with a long knife. A photograph in a silver frame. A bronze wing, curved round a crouching figure, dimly shining . . .

'No!' Birdie said aloud. Her voice echoed over the noise of the shower. She took a deep breath. She had to stop this. If she couldn't sleep, she had to rest. Rest her mind. For just a few minutes. She knew how to do it. She'd done it before, many times.

Deliberately she banished the pictures that plagued her. Cleared them away, till her mind was a drifting blank. She closed her eyes and turned her face up to the water. Taking herself far away. To another time, another place. A time and place she had often visited, like this. A time when life had been simple, though it seemed complicated. When she had been very young, though she had felt so very old. When choices had seemed infinite, though the days were rushing by so fast.

She stood motionless in the warm stream. And drifted. Far away from Hope's End, and death, and heat and pain. To the time when she was twenty, and sat talking through long afternoons, over lamb with rice and a bottle of wine, with Jude, at the Greek place.

Fifteen minutes later, clean and much refreshed, Birdie was walking across the pub courtyard and climbing the stairs beside the old garage. She'd made her phone call. It had been brief and unsatisfactory.

Resting comfortably.

What did that mean? It meant Jude's condition was

satisfactory, that he wasn't in danger, that he wasn't in pain—or at least, what the hospital regarded as pain worth mentioning.

Soon she could go and see him. See him for herself. As soon as she had had breakfast with Sue Sweeney. It would have been foolish not to take advantage of the invitation. Sue was one of the people she'd planned to talk to. Infinitely easier and more natural to do it like this, in Sue's own home, at Sue's invitation.

'That you, Birdie?' called Sue. She'd been listening out for the sound of footsteps on the stairs. 'Come in! Water's just boiling.'

The screen door was closed, but behind it the green-painted front door stood open, wedged in place by a shining brass cat with green eyes. Birdie slipped through the screen, and stepped inside. She found herself in a quaint little sitting room with a steeply-sloping ceiling, and an uncurtained, tree-top view of the pub backyard. The walls were cream, and covered in posters: a rainforest scene, whales spouting, a panda chewing a bamboo shoot, kittens playing with a ball of wool. A multicoloured cotton rug covered the cream carpet on the floor.

Opposite the door, against the wall, was a couch gaily patterned with tropical flowers, palm leaves and parrots. In front of that was a long, low coffee table, spread with a batik runner, and set with plates, knives, paper napkins, a milk jug, bright yellow with white spots, butter on a yellow dish, and pots of jam and honey. A single cane chair, painted green, stood beside this, and a TV set sat on a small table close by.

At the end of the room, under the window, there was a small refrigerator, a sink and a narrow cupboard under a bench-top. The kitchen. Sue, hair dried and fluffed on her shoulders, dressed for work in tight red skirt, strappy red sandals and a white blouse, was standing at the bench, pouring water into mugs that matched the milk jug.

'It's instant coffee. Hope you don't mind,' she said. 'Sit down.' She waved to the couch.

Birdie edged around the coffee table and sat. She looked around her, and found herself smiling. There was something very engaging about the little room. She approved of it highly. None of the pieces in it matched, except the china. It had the air of being lived in, willy-nilly, by someone impulsive, energetic, busy and, occasionally, thoughtful. But lived in. Not kept, like a museum, for people to see. Or struggled over, with ferocious determination.

'This is a nice place,' she said.

'Thanks.' Sue brought the coffee over and put it on the table. 'Do you take sugar?'

'No, I don't.'

'I don't either. Used to, but I gave it up. Trying to lose weight. Much good it did. Help yourself to milk. I'll just make the toast.'

She went back to her tiny kitchen and Birdie heard the sound of bread clicking into a toaster. 'Feel better after your shower?' She called.

Birdie sipped her coffee. 'Much better,' she called back. 'Almost human.' She looked around. Through a partly-opened door that led to the front of the flat she could see the gleam of peach-coloured satin, and part of a mirrored wardrobe. The bedroom. 'You don't have your own bathroom here, I gather.'

'No. Worse luck. I've only got the two rooms. Still, I suppose I'm lucky to have those—and the kitchenette, too. And in another way, if this place did have a bathroom I wouldn't have been given it. It'd be used for paying guests. Which is what it was built for, years ago. The publican before Floury thought he could charge more for motel-style accommodation. That's what he called this, according to Peg McCann at the post office.'

She laughed. 'But he didn't have the money to put in a bathroom, poor old bugger. So no one was interested in this place. The sort of people you usually get round here— salesmen and odd-jobbers and such—just want a convenient place to flop. Cheap. Close to the bar. Close to the loo. So this place didn't appeal to them. The honeymooners and dirty weekenders want a private bathroom. So they wouldn't take this place either. They turned up their noses and stayed at Gunbudgie or Sassafras. So this was just a white elephant. The old bloke ended up having to stay in it himself. He didn't like it either. He had a weak bladder, Peg reckons. Peg reckons the whole thing broke his heart. It's what made him sell up to Floury, retire to Sassafras. Still, it's good for me. I don't mind popping over to the pub to have a shower, and the loo's just outside the back door. It's no problem. I haven't got a weak bladder. Well, not yet, anyway.'

She laughed again, and came over to the table with a yellow toast-rack. 'Help yourself,' she said, and sat down in the chair opposite Birdie.

Birdie realised she was starving. She reached for a plate and a piece of toast, buttered the toast liberally, and bit into it.

'Don't you want some jam?' asked Sue.

Birdie shook her head, chewing.

Sue sipped coffee. 'What did those Sydney police want with you last night?' she asked suddenly. Then coloured, realising she'd been too abrupt.

Birdie shrugged, pretending not to notice. 'I know them,' she said. 'People in my business get to know cops sometimes. That's the way it is. We need them. They need us.'

Up to a point, Birdwood.

'Do they know who killed Trevor?'

'I think they're still investigating. They've got a long way to go yet,' Birdie said vaguely. She put down her cup. 'Didn't the Gunbudgie police talk to you? Take a statement?'

'Oh, sure.' Sue picked up a piece of toast, and started nibbling at the crust. 'They were mainly interested in Keith. He came to see me last night, you know. About eleven-thirty. I didn't have much to tell them. He didn't stay long. The cops said he'd had a car accident afterwards. Could have died. Did you hear about that?'

'Yes, I heard something about it. Why did he come to see you?'

'Oh,' Sue tossed her head, and her cheeks flushed a darker red. 'He was—you know—trying it on. Have some more toast.'

'Thanks.' Birdie helped herself. Toast, butter, and this time, a generous spoonful of honey from a yellow pot with a striped bee sitting on the lid. 'You mean he wanted to—'

'Yeah!' Sue frowned, hunched over her coffee. 'You wouldn't believe it, would you? That anyone could be so stupid as to think I would? I don't know who these guys think I am. I mean, I'm not the town bike. I might like a good time, but, you know, I choose who I'm going to have a good time with. Know what I mean?'

'Of course I do. But maybe he was—I mean—you were on with his brother for a while, weren't you?'

Sue's eyes hardened. She put down her coffee mug with a sharp crack. 'What if I was?'

Alarm bells. Delicacy required. Birdie chose her words carefully, brought them out breathily, as though she was slightly flustered. 'Oh, I'm sorry. I just thought, last night, well, Trevor was making a line for Lily. She's Keith's girlfriend, isn't she? Keith might have thought you'd be angry about that. Like he was. So maybe you'd . . .' She let her voice trail away to confused silence.

Sue smiled, bitterly, a trifle wearily. 'Oh, don't worry. I'm not insulted. Not really. You're probably right. It's the sort of pathetic thing Keith would think of. In fact, as I recall, it's just about what he said to me. Before I told him to get nicked. He's a real wrong-drummer where women are concerned. Hasn't got a clue. Keith and Trevor, they're—they were—like chalk and cheese. Trevor knew exactly which buttons to push. Always got what he wanted with women. Look at Daphne. She could have had anyone. Done anything. And she married him. Look at me. I was her friend, and I still—' She broke off, picked up her coffee mug, and drank deeply.

Birdie dropped her flustered manner, and leaned forward. 'You know, Sue, you don't seem too unhappy that Trevor Lamb's dead,' she said bluntly.

Sue Sweeney looked up over her mug. Slowly she lowered it, cupping it between her hands. 'No. I'm not,' she said, almost in surprise. 'Yesterday I didn't know what I thought about him. But today I know. I hated him. I'm glad he's dead. How about that?'

She stood up quickly, pushing back her chair so roughly that it almost tipped over on the ruckled cotton rug. 'More coffee?'

'Yes, please. If it's not . . .'

'It's no trouble. I'll fill mine up, too.'

She took Birdie's mug and went to the kitchenette. She ran water into the electric kettle, plugged it in, stared out the window.

'I'm going to leave this place,' she said. 'I should have left years ago.'

'Where will you go?'

The plump shoulders lifted as Sue shrugged. 'I don't know. Somewhere. Soon as I find another job.'

'You'll miss this flat.'

'Yes, I will. In a way. But . . .' She turned and leant her back against the sink, surveying the bright, cluttered room. 'I don't know. In a way I won't.' Her eyes moved to the bedroom door, flicked away. 'There are a few too many memories here,' she said.

She swung back to the sink, and began rinsing the mugs. After a moment she went on. In a determined, cheerful voice. Talking herself up again.

'Maybe next time I'll even get a little house. I've got money in the bank. A bit of money. Enough for a deposit. Houses are cheap as chips around here. Or maybe I'll go to the city. To Sydney. Plenty of jobs for barmaids there.'

The electric kettle boiled, and clicked off. Sue spooned coffee into the rinsed mugs, poured in steaming water. 'Anyway, whatever I do, I'll be well out of this,' she said, bringing the mugs back to the table. 'There's no one here I care about any more. No one who cares about me. Hasn't been since Daphne died.'

'You really liked her.'

It was a statement, not a question.

'Oh, yes. I loved Daphne. Everyone loved Daphne.'

Everyone loved Daphne.

But Daphne died.

Sue sat down heavily. 'I s'pose you think I'm a prize bitch,' she said.

'Why?'

'Having it off with my friend's husband.'

'It happens.'

'Yeah.' Sue reached for the milk jug, picked it up. 'Daphne gave me this,' she said. 'This and the sugar bowl. The set. For my birthday. To match my cups.' She poured milk into her mug and put the jug down. 'She gave me that honey pot, too,' she added. 'For Christmas.' She touched the striped bee with a gentle finger.

'I gather she liked giving presents. Daphne.'

'Oh, yes.' Sue smiled, still looking at the bee. 'She was like a kid about it. Went to so much trouble. Loved thinking up things her friends would really like. Planned it all, ages in advance.'

Her brow furrowed. 'She had to be careful with money, though. She was trying to fix up the shack. Make it more comfortable. More like a proper home, she said. It wasn't easy for her. She and Trevor were always short of cash. She had a bit in the bank when she married him. I think she thought they could build on it, save up and buy a little farm. That's what she really wanted. And Trevor had said he wanted it, too. He was always on about how Les had taken all the Lambs' good grazing land. You'd have thought Les stole it, instead of buying it from Milton.'

Sue sighed, restlessly turning to look out of the window again, at the shimmering tree tops. 'But the money in the bank went, bit by bit, till there was nothing left.'

'What were they living on, then?'

'The dole. Daphne didn't like it, but it should've been okay. They had the shack rent free. But it costs to drink like Trevor did. And Floury doesn't give credit. Well, he'd be a fool to, round here.'

Her mouth twisted in a bitter smile. 'They had this gas-guzzling old wreck of a car, too. It was always breaking down, or getting dinged, and having to be fixed up. It ate money. It should've been on the scrap heap. But Trevor wouldn't be without a car. Somehow they had to find the money, every time. It worried the life out of Daphne. I said to her, go and ask your dad for a loan. Get a new car. But she wouldn't do that. Said Les wouldn't give it to her anyway. He was trying to starve her out. Get her to come back home. Give up. But he didn't know Daphne.'

He didn't know Daphne.

'She wouldn't tell her mother how bad things were. Never told her the money in the bank was all gone. She wouldn't take money from me, either. I offered it often enough. But she wouldn't take it, even as a loan. Just wouldn't.' Sue shook her head. 'She hoped she might be able to get some sort of job. But she wasn't trained for anything except farming. And there are no jobs round here, anyway. She sold things, after the money in the bank was gone. Little bits and pieces of jewellery she had. Sold it all, bit by bit, except for one diamond ring. She held onto that, as long as she could. She always wore it. I suppose she thought that way Trevor couldn't nick it without her knowing. But it went in the end. At the trial they said a burglar must have taken it.

But that was all bull. She hadn't had it for a month at least before she died.'

Birdie sat forward. This was new.

'Are you sure?' she asked.

'Oh, yeah. I noticed it was gone. I asked her where it was. She just mumbled something about leaving it off for a while. But I knew she'd sold it. She'd never had it off her finger as long as I'd known her. And then I thought she might have needed the money for—you know—an abortion, so I didn't say anything else about it. I didn't want to make her any more upset than she was.'

'You knew about the baby?'

'She told me, that day. I think I was the only one she had told. She hadn't told Trevor. I know that. She hadn't told her mother, either. She was going to, later, she said. When the time was right. I don't know if she ever did. But she didn't have an abortion, did she? She was still pregnant when she died, they said. So the money went on something else. Some bill or other, I guess.'

'Her parents gave her the diamond ring, didn't they?'

'Yeah. For her twenty-first. That's why it meant so much to her. She really loved them, you know. It made her so unhappy, not seeing her dad, and everything. But she was determined to make a go of it with Trevor. She was sure her dad would come round, when she'd got Trevor sorted out. Got him away from Hope's End, fixed up with a job. Got that farm she thought they were going to have.'

Sue sighed, sipped coffee, staring at the bright, yellow china on the table. 'She didn't realise, you see. Thought—I don't know—she had this idea that people didn't understand Trevor. That if she could get him away from his family, show him a different way of life, he'd change. Like his sister, Bridget. She got away. Started fresh, somewhere else. And it was Daphne's mother who lent her the money to go. Mrs Hewitt had taught Bridget at school. And later Bridget used to babysit Daphne, sometimes. Daphne really liked Bridget. She often talked about it. How Bridget had made good, because someone took an interest in her, helped her. Mentioned Bridget's name every time she mentioned Trevor, just about. But she didn't understand. Didn't see the difference. Trevor wasn't like Bridget. Wasn't like Keith. Or even poor old

Punchy. He didn't want to do, be, any different to what he was. Except to have money, of course. He wanted that.'

'Maybe he got the money from the ring.'

'Maybe. I doubt it, though. He was skint. Living from fortnight to fortnight on the dole money. Couldn't even bail out his bloody car, the last time it cracked up. He'd gone to Sassafras one Friday afternoon to buy Daphne some medicine. She had the flu. Car started smoking and banging, so he took it into the Sassafras garage. Guy told him it wasn't worth fixing. But did he listen? Oh, no. He said fix it anyway. I've got the cash. Big man. Next dole day he got Rosalie to drive him to Sassafras, picked up him money, paid out practically the whole lot to the bloody garage, then drove the car back here, came straight into the pub, and spent the rest on getting drunk. God, he was a bad bastard. What were they supposed to live on for the next two weeks? I asked him. Fresh air? He just laughed and said something stupid about getting the money off Daphne.'

'What *did* they do?'

Sue's face changed. 'Nothing,' she whispered. 'It didn't matter. That was the night . . .'

She shivered, cradling her cup in her hands.

'The night Daphne died?'

'Yeah. And Trevor crashed the bloody car on the way out, so it was smashed up all over again. It's a wonder he wasn't killed. Better if he had been.'

'You think he killed Daphne?' Birdie spoke quietly, but Sue's head jerked up.

'I'm not saying that,' she burst out. 'I'm not saying that. I don't know who killed her.' She gripped her cup so hard that the knuckles shone white. Her voice dropped to a low murmur. 'All I'm saying is that if anyone deserved to die, it was him. And when I saw him lying there, dead, on that floor last night, in that room where poor little Daphne worked so hard and tried so hard . . . lying there with his bloody new, expensive, crash-hot computer stuff all set up and ready to go, I felt . . . good. For the first time in five years. I felt good. The radio was playing "Poison". You know that song? And I looked down at him and I thought. That's right. You're poison. But not for me. Not any more. I'm out of it. I'm free of you. I'm . . .'

She faltered. Her eyes widened. The tip of her tongue crept out, moistening her lips. She'd realised her mistake.

Slowly, Birdie put down her mug. 'The radio wasn't playing then, Sue,' she said. 'By the time you arrived with Floury and the others, it had been turned off.'

'Oh, yes.' Sue's face was burning. 'Oh, sorry, I wasn't thinking. I had it wrong,' she gabbled. 'I was thinking about something else . . .' She jumped up, backed away from Birdie. Tears of shock and fear welled in her eyes, spilled over and rolled down her cheeks. 'I didn't mean it,' she sobbed. 'I was . . .'

But she knew it was too late. The truth had tumbled out of her. More truth than she had intended to tell. And now there was no taking it back.

Twenty-two

'It's not how it looks! Honestly. Birdie, listen, it's not how it looks. I was there—before I said. I admit that. But I didn't kill him. I didn't! Don't look at me like that!'

'Sue—'

'No! Listen to me, and I'll tell you. I'll tell you the truth. But you have to promise, *promise*, you won't tell anyone else.'

'I can't promise that, Sue. You know I can't.'

Sue nibbled at her lip. Her eyes darted around the room, as if looking for a way out. 'The police—if you tell them, they'll think I did it. Because I lied in the beginning.'

'Why did you? If you just found Trevor Lamb dead, why on earth didn't you tell anyone?'

If you're innocent, why are you scared?

'That's what happened to Trevor. He found Daphne. And they said he'd killed her.'

'That won't happen again, Sue.'

'Why not?'

Good question.

'Because they'll be much, much more careful this time. They wouldn't dare make the same mistake again. No way. This time they'll check and re-check before they go to court with anyone. They'll make sure they've got hard evidence. Or a confession.'

'Are you sure?'

'Absolutely.' Birdie kept her gaze level. She hoped she was right. Then she remembered something she'd almost forgotten. Her trump card. Especially in Hope's End. 'And remember, Sue,' she added. 'Jude's mixed up in this. He'll be watching the cops' every move. As soon as he gets back on his feet. If he thinks they're jumping the gun he'll say so. And he'll defend anyone he thinks is innocent.'

That was the clincher. The story came out. Slowly at first, then faster, till it was tumbling out in a stream of words. Birdie listened, absently stirring the sugar in the happy, yellow bowl. The gift from Daphne.

Sue had gone to her room after the pub closed, feeling numb. The evening had been for her a deadening anticlimax. Standing behind the bar, she'd watched proceedings as though entirely separated from them. It had taken her a while to sort out how she felt about it all. But when she had, she'd realised that all her mixed-up thoughts and feelings about Trevor Lamb had been a waste of effort and time. Trevor had ignored her all afternoon, all night. He'd left the pub without a goodbye—just a conspiratorial wink in her general direction. But that wasn't what had bothered her. Not really. It was Trevor himself. It was as though she'd suddenly seen him with new eyes.

He'd seemed somehow diminished. Smaller than she remembered. In every sense. Seeing him brawling with poor, scared Phillip Hewitt, big-noting himself in front of Jude, sneering at Floury Baker, and even hurting poor old Annie's feelings, he wasn't the Trevor Lamb of her memory—some powerful, unpredictable, dangerous giant, striding her world. Suddenly he was just a mean-minded, selfish, vain, self-indulgent man, determined to re-establish himself in the minuscule society he thought he had a right to dominate. No wonder he'd wanted to come back to Hope's End. He had to be a big man. And where else could he be one, but there?

And the worst of it was, he hadn't changed. She knew that. Standing behind the bar she watched him draw out every weapon in his armoury, and recognised it. Every gesture, every expression, every gambit, was familiar to her. She saw how they affected other people. But realised, with bitter satisfaction, that they no longer affected her.

She was the one who had changed. In five years of grieving for Daphne, working at arms-length with the silent, detached Floury Baker, vainly looking for warmth in brief, unsatisfying sexual encounters with strangers, sleeping alone, she had grown older, sadder, colder and, without knowing it, wiser. If world-weariness counts as wisdom. She knew she was seeing Trevor Lamb now as he'd always been, seeing him for what he was. She was filled with sick shame. For this worthless man, in her blindness, she'd deceived her lover, her friend, herself . . .

Floury Baker—terrible, shocked hurt on his heavy face, staring from the pub door. Daphne . . .

Safely back in her flat, door closed and locked, Sue had made herself tea, sat and stared at the wall. Then a car had stopped outside the pub, and a moment later there were footsteps on the stairs. For a moment she thought it was Trevor himself, and her stomach turned over.

But it was Keith. Keith, drunk and in tears. Wanting to be taken in. Wanting comfort, of a very specific kind. Lily had locked herself in the caravan, and was telling him to get lost. Lily was saying his brother was ten times the man he was. Ten times as interesting to women. A man without hangups, for a change. That was what Lily needed. According to Lily. And surely Sue would give him a bit of love. Surely she needed comfort, too. Trevor had given her the arse, hadn't he? The bastard. The low, rotten bastard.

'He went on and on. "C'mon, Sue, c'mon. Let us in." ' Sue, leaning forward in her chair, chin cupped in her hands, raised her voice in mimicry of a pathetic, whining drunk. She straightened, and shook back her hair. 'But I wouldn't let him in. Of course I wouldn't. I was sorry for him, but it's not as if he only wanted a cup of tea and a pat on the shoulder. I'm not a charitable institution, and anyhow, it wouldn't have worked.'

She grimaced, looking at Birdie. 'I didn't want to give him a hard time. I've got nothing against Keith. But he's not my type. I'm not his, either. He'd never have come near me, if he'd been sober, and if it hadn't been for Trevor. He likes them skinny and flat chested and mean, like Lily. His wife, Yvonne, was like that, Peg said.'

'His wife left him, didn't she?' asked Birdie.

'Yeah. Just before I came here. That's why—oh, well, it doesn't matter. Anyhow, I said no, and no, and no about a hundred times, and I finally got him to go.'

'About eleven-thirty.'

'Something like that. How do you know? Oh, of course, you would have seen him. Right. Well, he left. And I sat here, and started thinking again. I thought, Keith really believed I'd let him in because I'd be in fits about Trevor and Lily. And Trevor expects me to go to his place. That's what that wink meant. I know him. Arrogant bastard. He didn't look at me, he didn't speak to me, but that's what that wink was all about. He's waiting there, right now, thinking any minute I'll turn up, hot and wet, excuse me, Birdie, with my tongue hanging out, busting a gut to jump into his bed.'

She'll keep.

Sue's pale face flushed. 'And the more I thought about it the colder I felt. And I thought, I will go down there. But not for what he thinks. I'll go down there and tell him exactly what I think of him. I'll tell him how pathetic, and low, I think he is. Then I'll leave him standing. With aching balls, I hope. And if he thinks Lily Danger can help him out there, he's sadly mistaken. From all I've heard.'

The fierce light in her eyes went out. Suddenly she was ashen again.

'So I went,' she said flatly.

'What time was that, Sue?' Birdie spoke calmly, but as the other woman considered, she held her breath.

'I'm not absolutely sure. But I think it was about a quarter past twelve. About then. I remember standing up and looking at the clock and it was twelve-fifteen. But then I took a couple of minutes to find my torch and change my shoes.'

Silence. Stretching into a long minute.

'So you went to the shack,' Birdie prompted. 'Did you see anyone, on the way?'

'Not a soul. I half-ran all the way. I don't like that track in the dark. I got to the shack . . .'

'Was the light on, or off?'

Sue stared. 'Off. But the transistor was playing in the kitchen, and the door was half-open. I thought, he's sitting there in the dark, waiting. He used to say he could see in the dark. All bull, of course, but he liked the idea of it. So I went in. I had my torch. And I saw him. Lying there, on the floor. I knew he was dead.' She shuddered.

'Did you touch him?'

'No. I didn't go near him. I just looked at him. "Poison" was playing on the radio. I just looked at him. I thought—well, I told you what I thought. Then I just got out of there, and ran. All the way back here.'

'Did you meet anyone? On the track?'

Sue stared, swallowed. 'Of course not. If I had—'

If you had, you couldn't have pretended you'd been home all night. But . . .

'I got back in here. I was shaking all over. I thought, he's dead. He's dead. And everyone thinks I was pissed off with him, because he'd thrown me over. If I say anything, say I was there, they'll think I killed him.

'I felt—filthy. I wanted a bath or a shower. But I didn't dare go over to the pub and have one. Floury would have heard me. His room's right next to the bathroom. It was too late. It would have looked suspicious. So I just washed my face and hands in the sink, and changed into my nightie. In case anyone came.

'I didn't go to bed. There was no point. I knew I couldn't sleep. So I stayed here. Drank wine. Watched TV. Well, sort of watched. I couldn't tell you what was on. It was just something to do. Then, after a while there was this screaming. And I knew—someone had found him. All the lights went on in the pub. I waited a while, then I went into the bedroom and looked out the window. Floury was on the road, walking towards the track. Some other people, too. There was a flashing red light there, behind the pepper trees. I thought it was the police. I didn't think of an ambulance.'

'So you went out, too.'

'It would've looked funny if I hadn't. So I went. I didn't want to. But I had to. Anyway—you know the rest.'

'Yes.'

'I didn't kill him! I didn't. I saw him dead, that's all. I ran away. I didn't tell anyone. But that's not a crime, is it?'

Birdie said nothing. She didn't quite know what to make of all this. She became aware of Sue's anxious eyes upon her, and stirred. 'You ran to the shack at about twelve-fifteen,' she said, slowly. 'You ran back here straight away. You didn't see anyone, going or coming.'

'That's right. So there was no harm done. No one need ever know . . .'

They hadn't discussed Jude. Sue didn't know that Birdie was certain he'd been attacked on the way to the shack. Midnight, at the latest. Birdie had mentioned that only to Dan Toby. And Jude himself was safely away in Gunbudgie

Hospital, talking to no one. So Sue couldn't realise the trap she was setting for herself. And Birdie knew she couldn't tell her.

Could Sue have run past Jude's crumpled body, twice, without seeing him? She could have done. Birdie herself had nearly missed him. He had been lying right over to the side. And with inadequate light, Sue could have run straight by.

Or—was she lying about her times? She could have started off for the shack much earlier than she claimed. Soon after Keith Lamb left her, in fact. Then she would have reached the shack at about eleven-thirty-five.

The light in the shack was on, then. It was a reasonable supposition that Trevor Lamb was alive at eleven-thirty-five. So what might have happened then?

Birdie thought of the tangled sheet, the blanket kicked aside in Trevor Lamb's bedroom. That's one thing that could have happened.

And what then? In the bitter aftermath, the sullen awareness of having fallen prey to someone despised, yet again? Because Sue's contempt for Trevor Lamb was real. Birdie would swear to it.

Murder?

She looked at her hands, unwilling, yet, to meet Sue Sweeney's eyes. The woman seemed so open. So honest. And yet—she'd lied once already, about her movements last night. She'd taken pains to cover her tracks. She'd got through her interview with the police perfectly. It was only here that she'd relaxed and made the slip that had betrayed her.

Why would she lie about the time she left here?

Because somehow the timing was important.

Was it Sue Sweeney who had heard Jude approaching as she hurried back along the track after killing Trevor Lamb? Was it she who, panicking, had attacked him?

It could have been. But something didn't ring true. The motives were all wrong. For the attack, and the murder, and even the lying about the time. Sue was impulsive, yes. She'd felt a genuine loathing of Trevor Lamb, yes. But if her tone of voice, her expression, were to be trusted, the loathing had been cold, not hot. And Sue Sweeney kept her head in a crisis. That had been obvious from her behaviour behind the bar, and her comprehensive diddling of the Gunbudgie police. It was hard to believe, under the circumstances, that a woman like this would have killed Trevor Lamb in a passion of rage, then, in panic, attacked Jude as well, risking a double murder.

Birdie knew she'd been silent too long. She looked up and met Sue's troubled eyes. 'I think you'd better talk to Detective-Sergeant Toby about this, Sue,' she said firmly. 'I'm going to call him now. Get him to come and see you.'

'*No!* Please, I—'

'Listen, Sue. You may as well tell them. They're going to find out anyway. There's all sorts of scientific testing being done. They'll be able to tell you were in the shack, in your day clothes. They'll be checking everything out. From the bed linen to the dust on the kitchen floor. It'll take a while but in the end they'll come back to you. And then it'll look a whole lot worse. And Toby's okay. He won't give you a hard time. Just tell him the truth. Like you've told me.'

If you have told me the truth.

Sue slumped forward in her chair. She put her hands over her eyes.

'All right,' she said. 'Call him.'

Twenty-three

Birdie waited till Dan arrived. She cleared away the breakfast things, while Sue put on her make-up, arming herself for the encounter to come.

By the time Toby toiled up the narrow steps to the green front door, Milson stepping carefully, well behind him, Sue's coffee table was bare of its welcoming clutter of china, and Sue herself was the perfect hard-as-nails barmaid, her plump, vulnerable face transformed by black eyeliner, blue eyeshadow, long black lashes and lips that matched her skirt and her nails.

Birdie made the introductions, then moved for the door. Sue had asked her to stay, but she knew Toby wouldn't be happy with that.

'I'll hang around for a while. I won't go to Gunbudgie just yet,' she promised. 'I'll see you after Toby's finished talking to you.'

'If I'm not in the lock-up by then,' Sue said, only half-joking.

'You won't be,' Birdie assured her. 'They'll just take a statement from you. All you have to do is tell the truth.'

But as she escaped from the little flat, saw Toby's eyes flick thoughtfully over Sue's seductive figure, and Sue's eyes, beneath their disguise, widen slightly with fear, she felt like a rat taking the last lifeboat.

She hoped she could trust Toby to see the woman under the mask.

She ran over their phone conversation in her mind. It wasn't reassuring.

'She didn't notice your boyfriend on the track?' he'd asked.

'No.'

'Then either you're wrong about when he got thumped, or she'd lying about the times.'

'Not necessarily. It was very dark. She was running. Anyway, we didn't discuss that.' With Sue's anxious gaze on her, Birdie could say no more.

'You've been discreet for a change,' he'd said ungraciously. 'Okay. What we need is Gregorian's confirmation on times. Rung the hospital lately?'

'About half an hour ago. He's still asleep. But like I told you, they said he mightn't remember much.'

A grumbling sigh. 'Anyhow, if we can trust her, Lamb was dead by twelve-thirty at the latest.'

'That's right.'

'And she wasn't the woman in the bedroom?'

'We didn't discuss that. But according to Sue, obviously not.'

Sue's eyes, worried.

What's he saying?

But Toby was speaking again. 'We'll be right along. Ten minutes. Stay with her. Don't let her leave.'

'She won't.'

'Stay with her.'

Back in her bedroom, Birdie considered ringing the hospital again. Then she abandoned the idea. It was too soon. They'd have no more to tell her. All she'd achieve by calling again would be to irritate them. The sister hadn't been too accommodating last time. She'd been brusque, and had sounded harried. Hassled, Birdie supposed, by the presence of police in the hospital. Or maybe just hassled permanently.

If I hadn't accepted Sue's invitation to breakfast, I'd be pulling into the hospital car park right now, Birdie thought, glancing at her watch. Then I'd have been able to see Jude for myself, instead of sitting here twiddling my thumbs, waiting for Toby to finish his grilling session.

Not that she regretted her decision. She learnt a lot from Sue over that toast and coffee. More than Sue had wanted her to know, in fact. Birdie sighed. If she didn't regret accepting the invitation, Sue must certainly be regretting having extended it.

Was Sue lying or telling the truth? Toby would no doubt form an opinion. Some parts of the story were plainly true. Notably Sue's description of looking down at Trevor Lamb's body while 'Poison' played on the radio. That had been too vivid to have been fabricated. And it had spilled out of her, before she thought about its implications.

But *when* that moment had occurred, and what came just before it, were not so certain.

So . . . Birdie sat a little straighter. So the police could check out the local radio stations. Find out which one of them had played 'Poison' last night, and when. It wasn't a new song. It was what disk jockeys called a classic hit. It would be a coincidence if more than one station had played it last night. Especially within the relevant period.

She reached for her phone again, and had it in her hand when again she changed her mind. Toby wouldn't want to be disturbed now. She'd talk to him about it later. Tell him about 'Poison'. It was unlikely Sue would mention it to him herself. She wouldn't think it was important.

But the phone was there. And she had nothing else to do. Sadly, there was nothing to stop her from doing her duty by poor Beth Bothwell. With a sigh, she punched in Beth's home number.

'Birdie! At last! How's it going? There's been a development. I tried to get you yesterday for ages, then I had to go out. Did you try me last night? Sorry.' The voice was loud, the words tumbling over one another. Birdie blinked, forcing herself to concentrate. Had Beth always talked so fast? Or was Hope's End getting to her already?

'Birdie? You there?'

'Yes, Beth.'

'Well, say something. Go on. Tell me. How's Trevor Lamb?'

'Ah—not so good, Beth.'

The rapid voice sharpened. 'What? Isn't he being cooperative? After all that? Listen, Birdie, you just tell that bastard from me that we—'

'Beth, he's not being uncooperative. He's dead.'

Silence. Then . . . 'What did you say?' asked Beth cautiously.

'I said he's dead. He's been murdered. Bashed on the head.'

'You're joking.'

'No, I'm not. Listen, Beth, I'm going to hang around here for a couple of days, and . . .'

'*Dead?* I haven't heard about any of this. It wasn't on the news this morning. Are you sure . . . ?'

'Beth, I saw him. I found him. He's dead. Dead as mutton. Believe me.'

An astonished snort of laughter. 'Dead as mutton. How appropriate.'

'It's not funny, Beth!'

'No, sorry. Lawks-a-daisy. What a turn-up. Who did it? When? Where? How? Tell, tell!'

'I don't know. No one knows. It was sometime in the middle of the night. We don't know when exactly. In his shack. It could have been anyone. They haven't found the weapon yet.'

'Just like last time,' murmured Beth.

Birdie's scalp prickled.

Just like last time.

'What's going to happen to the book advance? Does the publisher get it back?'

'I have no idea. Listen, Beth, I can't talk long. I just rang to fill you in. Like I said, I'll be staying on for a couple of days, and—'

'I don't know if we can fund you after this, Birdie,' Beth interrupted hastily. 'I mean, from our point of view the story's dead, isn't it? Oh, sorry, bad choice of words. I mean, it's not us any more. It's News, I guess. Well, I'm sure it is. So—'

'That doesn't matter. I'll pay for myself if I have to. I don't imagine the Hope's End pub is beyond even my slender means. And I can probably cadge a meal here and there.'

'Well, there's no need to be sharp, mate. I can't help it, can I? I mean, with the budget cuts I have to be awfully careful, and—'

'Beth, I understand.' Birdie closed her eyes. 'Don't worry about it.'

'Do you want me to get on to News and ask them if they want to use you?'

'No! No, thanks, Beth. I'd really rather be a free agent from here on. Honestly. They'll be sending their own people anyway. So just let's leave it. All right?'

'All right. We'll pay up to now, of course. The agreed expenses. Including this phone call. I mean, it's not your fault he got killed, is it?'

'No. Thanks, Beth. I'd better go now.'

'All right. Will you get the file back to me sometime? Archives are fussy about—'

'Sure. Soon as I get back to town. See you then, Beth.'

'See you, mate. Thanks for everything. Sorry it didn't work out. Keep your notes. You never know, they might come in handy. Talk to you again soon.'

'Sure. Bye.'

Birdie cut the connection before Beth could think of anything else to ask. Like, what does Jude think about all this? Could we profile him instead of Lamb? How does he feel about his protégé being knocked off the same day he gets out? Does he feel guilty? Does he feel the last five years have been a waste of time? Is he devastated?

Jude. Birdie checked her watch. At eight-thirty she should try Jude's office. Tell them what had happened. Tell them that Jude wouldn't be back in Sydney today. He wouldn't be able to go to court tomorrow. They'd have to seek an adjournment.

Her eyes drifted to the file on the chest of drawers. The file, and the copy of *Lamb to the Slaughter*. While she was at it, she'd ask them to do a bit of research for her. Jude wouldn't mind. It wouldn't take them long. It was just a little thing, but she was curious about it. She'd been curious about it ever since yesterday.

She sat, her hands on her lap, bouncing slightly on the creaky bed, staring at the wall. The roses climbed their lattice, fencing her in. She looked again at the phone. She stood up. This was hopeless. She couldn't just sit here, waiting.

She rifled in her bag for her notebook, tore out a page, and scribbled a message. Then she pushed her phone back into her bag and, holding the scrap of paper between her teeth, let herself out of her room again, locked the door, and made for the stairs.

As she reached the bottom, she heard the chinking of china from the kitchen. She went towards the sound and discovered Floury Baker sitting at the table, eating a bowl of cornflakes. He looked around, loaded spoon in hand.

'Morning,' he grunted. 'Help yourself to breakfast. I'll be out of here in a minute.'

'I've had breakfast, thanks.'

'Up at Hewitts?'

She looked surprised. How did he know where she'd been?

'Peg, lady from the post office, mentioned she'd seen you go up that way,' he explained. 'You and the Sydney coppers. I saw her earlier.'

She nodded, feeling a little discomforted at the idea that her movements had been so carefully monitored.

He went back to his cornflakes, carefully filling his mouth and chewing slowly, staring straight ahead at the blank wall.

'Will you be staying downstairs now, Mr Baker?' Birdie asked.

He turned slowly to look at her again, his mouth still working. 'Probably,' he mumbled.

'Would you mind telling anyone who wants me that I've gone up to the Lamb place, and I'll be back soon? I wrote a note, but since you're here . . .'

She moved forward and put the scrap of paper on the edge of the table.

He swallowed. 'Don't need that, love. I might be old and stupid but I can remember that much.'

She wasn't sure if he was insulted, or joking. Then she saw him smile as he lifted another heaped spoonful to his mouth.

'It's got my mobile phone number on it,' she explained. 'In case anyone wants me urgently.'

'Oh, right.' Again he smiled, enjoying the private joke. 'In case they want you urgently.'

City people. Can't help themselves.

'Does the post office in Gunbudgie have a fax machine, do you know?' she asked. May as well complete his picture of her as a driven, machine-dependent city type.

He put down the spoon, finished his mouthful without haste.

'The post office here's got one,' he said at last, staring at her.

What d'you think we are? Hicks?

'Oh, I didn't realise. Well, that's handy,' Birdie heard herself gabbling inanely. 'I'm—I will be—expecting a fax. I'll have to get the number. What time does it open? The post office.'

'Post office opens at nine. Shop part of the place at eight-thirty. On the knocker. Peg lives next door, but she won't open up earlier.'

'No, of course not. It's not so urgent that I can't wait till eight-thirty.'

See? I can be laidback too.

He nodded. 'That reminds me. There was someone wanting you urgently yesterday,' he said. 'Left a message. Two messages, if I remember rightly. Did you get them?'

'Yes. Thanks. Sue gave them to me last night.'

'Right. Went clean out my head. What with one thing and another.'

His mouth clamped firmly over another spoonful of cornflakes. He chewed. Swallowed.

'It was a long night,' said Birdie. 'Well, I'd better . . .'

'Yeah. Off to see the Lambs. Pay your respects before you go, eh?'

'Sort of,' Birdie answered evasively. Then she realised the question was double-barrelled. He was asking her if she was going back to Sydney. 'Well, actually, I'm not leaving just yet, Mr Baker. I'll be staying on in Hope's End for a couple of days, as planned.'

'Floury'll do,' he said. He put his spoon into the bowl, and pushed himself away from the table. 'Right-oh. What about Jude, d'you reckon?'

'I don't know. Well, he won't be back here, I guess. I hope to talk to him later. I'll let you know what to do with his stuff after that.'

'Those Sydney coppers want rooms,' he rumbled, moving to the sink. 'But I've only got the three upstairs, plus mine. The empty one's got two beds in it. But they don't seem too keen on sharing.'

Birdie thought rapidly. Of course Toby would want to stay on the spot. Milson, too. And it would be handy for her to have them nearby. But they'd rather go back to the Traveller's Ruin at Sassafras, or move to Gunbudgie, than share a room.

'Let's move Jude's stuff into my room for now,' she said. 'He'd only have an overnight bag, wouldn't he?'

'As I recall.' Floury rinsed his bowl and spoon, shook off the excess water, and left them to drain on the side of the sink. 'What about his car?'

'We can't do anything much about that. I'll have to ask him what he thinks. Probably someone from his office'll come and get it. He won't be able to drive.'

'Bad luck, that, wasn't it? Doesn't seem like a bad bloke.'

There didn't seem to be an appropriate reply to that, so Birdie made none. But Floury, having wound himself up to talk, continued without further stimulation.

'Not a bad bloke. Not what I expected. Thought he'd be some smooth-talking spiv. But he's not. Is he?'

'No.'

'Made a bad blue, though, didn't he? Getting mixed up with that bastard Lamb. Getting him off.'

'You still think Trevor Lamb killed his wife?'

Floury Baker hunched his massive shoulders. 'Not my business to think anything, is it? All I know is, no one came into town that night without me knowing abut it. No strangers. And there wasn't a soul in Hope's End who didn't think the world of Daphne Lamb.'

Everyone loved Daphne.

'But someone killed her,' said Birdie quietly.

'Yeah.' Floury pressed his lips together and stuck out his chin. She thought he'd said all he was going to say, but then he spoke again. 'And if it wasn't her bloody swine of a husband, who was it?'

If Trevor Lamb didn't kill her, who did?

'Were you surprised when she married him, Floury?' asked Birdie lightly.

The big man stirred uncomfortably, as though he wasn't used to being asked his opinion on matters he regarded as personal.

'Put it this way,' he said at last. 'I was, and I wasn't.'

Perhaps he thought this would satisfy her, but she went on looking at him enquiringly, her head on one side.

As the silence lengthened, he was driven to explaining himself.

'I been publican here for ten—twelve—years. Daphne

Hewitt must've been about sixteen when I first come here. Knew her, and her mum and dad. Knew the Lambs, too. 'Course, Milton, Annie's husband, was alive then. And most of the kids were still at home.'

He paused, gathering his thoughts.

'You'd have thought, then, there was no way a girl like Daphne Hewitt'd look twice at one of the Lamb boys. They went to school together, like, in Gunbudgie, and mucked around together and such. Everyone knew that. But you just took it for granted, like, that when the time came, Daphne'd be looking to marry someone more her own kind.'

He glanced at her impassive face. 'Not rich, I don't mean,' he hastened to add, in case she misunderstood. 'Daphne was no snob where money was concerned. And Dolly wasn't, neither. Dolly was a great one for saying it was the person who counted, not how fancy their duds were, or where they lived, or what they done to earn a crust.'

He paused, pondering. 'True enough. But maybe that was the problem. When it come to how Daphne thought about Trevor Lamb. See, Dolly's shrewd, for all her talk about art and that. You ask Peg at the post office. Peg'll tell you. She's known Dolly thirty years. Dolly was young when she come here, but she'd lived a bit in the world, moved around, taught school before that. Know what I mean? She knew people. Look how she picked up on Bridget Lamb. She was the best of the bunch, they say. Clever little thing. Just needed a chance. And Dolly gave it to her. But my point is, it was because she could see Bridget had something going for her. Daphne, she was different. Heart soft as butter. Always thought the best of every bugger. And I reckon that's how Lamb got her in.'

'She thought he was—better than he was.'

'That's it. He spun her a line. God knows what he told her. And 'course, at that age—well, you know what kids are. He was good looking, I s'pose. An' she didn't have anything to compare him with, did she?'

His eyes were troubled. 'Used to bring her in here, sometimes. When his family weren't here, 'course. He knew to keep them away from her. She'd have lemon squash. Or a coffee. Out on the verandah. I'd see them talking, heads together. Her eyes'd be all wide and dark and soft. An' I'd think, here's trouble. An' I was right. It was trouble. Next, she's telling her parents they're going to get married. God, then there was hell to pay.'

'I can imagine what the Hewitts thought. What about the Lambs?'

He stared, as if he'd hardly thought about that. 'I dunno,' he said finally. 'Well—I don't reckon they were too pleased about it either, to tell the truth. Annie hates Dolly Hewitt like poison—because of Bridget, 'course. Don't really remember about the others. Had a few other things on my mind, at the time.'

His face darkened.

The silence in the kitchen lengthened. Birdie could see that whatever memory was now plaguing him had turned his thoughts inward, drying up the flow of reminiscence. She'd done her dash with him.

'Well, I'd better get on my way,' she said brightly, moving towards the door. 'I'll see you later.'

He looked up. 'Listen, come on into the bar, will you? If you're going up to Lambs' . . .'

He led the way into the front room of the pub. The front door was still firmly closed, but light streamed through the two front windows, making the beer taps and the bottles behind the bar gleam. Enticingly, no doubt, to any thirsty Hope's End resident pressing their noses against the windows, waiting for opening time.

Floury bent and fossicked under the bar. After a moment he stood up again, with a bottle of sweet sherry. It was slightly dusty, and he wiped it on his shirt before holding it out to Birdie.

'Give this to Annie for me, will you?' he said. 'Tell her I thought it might come in handy. Tell her, no charge.'

'Okay.' Birdie took the bottle.

Floury hitched at his belt, in a way that reminded Birdie of Dan Toby. 'No one else drinks sherry round here,' he mumbled, apparently anxious not to appear soft-hearted. 'Annie buys cheap flagons in Sassafras. This bottle's been here for donkey's years. She may as well have it. Probably needs it by now. And I can't open till ten.'

'Not with so many police around, anyway,' said Birdie jokingly.

Flourty's eyebrows drew together, and for a moment he looked quite severe. 'Pub opens at ten, closes at eleven,' he said. 'That's what's allowed. I'd be risking my licence if I did anything else. And I don't. Ever.'

Birdie nodded meekly. Obviously it didn't do to joke about pub rules.

Floury opened the front door to let her out. 'See you later, then,' he said. 'And I'll tell the copper he can have Jude's room, as well as the other one.'

'Right.' Birdie heard the door close behind her as she walked over to her car, still sitting with its nose pressed obediently into the pepper trees. She could walk up to the Lamb house. But she wasn't going to. Driving would make the whole thing quicker.

As she unlocked the car, a thin woman with tightly-curled grey hair and a nose that was very red at the tip, came out onto the minuscule verandah of the house next to the post office. She stood, arms folded tightly across her chest, watching.

Birdie recognised the sharp, curious features of Peg McCann, the Hope's End postmistress, guardian of the fax machine.

She waved, and the woman nodded without smiling.

Birdie considered going back across the road and speaking to her. Then she could get the post office fax number, ready for her phone call to Jude's office. And she needed to talk to Peg sometime, anyway. The woman was obviously a classic small-town gossip. She'd be a mine of information.

But she'd have to be handled carefully. She probably wouldn't open up to a stranger—not straight away. Better, perhaps, to see the Lambs first. Then Birdie would have an in with her. Information to trade.

Birdie slid into the car and started it, busily arranging her thoughts. She'd spoken to Dolly Hewitt. She'd spoken to Sue Sweeney. And Floury Baker. Slowly a picture was forming. And a few ideas were drifting around it, in her head. But none of them made sense yet. A visit to the Lambs, the remaining Lambs, had been high on her agenda. She had been going to seek them out as soon as she got back from Gunbudgie.

Well, she was going to see them now. And, thanks to Floury, she was going bearing gifts.

She moved the bottle and her handbag from her lap to the passenger seat, and backed out of her parking spot with high hopes.

Then she drove on towards the Lambs' turnoff, waving to Peg McCann again as she went by.

Twenty-four

Annie was kicking at the caravan door, and screeching at the top of her voice.

Her shouts were piercing enough to be heard a hundred metres away. Even over the sound of the car engine. The words weren't perfectly clear at first, but that didn't matter, since Birdie realised, once she had pulled the car up at the fence and leapt out to stare in amazement at the scene, that Annie was repeating herself over and over, punctuating the phrases with kicks.

'You come out, you little bitch!' (Thump, crash.) 'Come out and take what's coming to you!' (Crash, thump.) 'You come out!' (Thump.) 'Come out!' (Thump, thump.)

She was a terrifying sight. Grey hair loose on her shoulders, pink and purple dress riding high on her great, veined thighs as she raised a foot to kick the shuddering caravan again and again—Birdie wasn't surprised that whoever was locked in there was refusing to come out.

Jason, hair sticking up in a brush, barefoot and wearing only a t-shirt and red underpants, was dancing around Annie, eyes wild with excitement. The dogs were yapping on their chains. Punchy, magnificently bare chested, black hair rumpled, looking like a sex symbol in a television advertisement for jeans, was grinning from the corner of the house. It looked as though the family had only recently woken.

Annie drew herself back for another assault.

'Mum, stop it!' shouted a voice. 'You'll hurt yourself. You'll break the door.'

Rosalie had been standing behind her mother, hidden from Birdie's sight. Now she stopped into the open, pulling at her mother's arm. But Annie took no notice of her whatever.

'Come out of there!' she roared. 'You little bitch! You slut! You get out of our caravan. Get out!'

'Birdie's here!' screamed Jason, running madly across the yard towards the sagging gate. 'Hey Mum, Birdie's here. Mum? Mum!'

Rosalie looked around helplessly.

Jason beckoned to Birdie. 'Come on!' he yelled. 'Come and help Mum get Grandma off Lily. Lily's locked herself in the caravan 'cause Punchy saw her having it off with Uncle Trev, and—'

'Jason!' screamed Rosalie. 'You get back here!'

Jason threw open the gate and grabbed Birdie's arm. 'C'mon!' he insisted. 'C'mon!'

It was a bizarre social situation. The decent thing to do would be to retreat. But this was more than an ordinary family brawl. Birdie couldn't slink away and leave Annie to it. Not after what Jason had said. Punchy had seen *what*?

The woman in the bedroom of the shack. Lily! Lily Danger, who'd said she was at home all night. Hadn't gone out. Hadn't seen Trevor Lamb after he left the pub. This went a long way towards letting Sue Sweeney off the hook, didn't it? If it was true. And the timing—if Sue was speaking the truth, Trevor Lamb was dead by about twelve-twenty. If Punchy saw his brother alive sometime after eleven, that narrowed the timing considerably.

She let Jason half-lead, half-drag her into the yard and over to the caravan at the side of the house. Annie barely looked at her. But Rosalie, fumbling with the buttons on the gaping bodice of her short cotton nightdress, greeted her with a cold glance that sat oddly on her pleasant face.

'Can't keep away from us, can you?' she drawled. 'Sure you can cope with this? You've left your candle at home this time, I see.'

'I'm sorry,' said Birdie breathlessly, holding up her hand to show Jason's firm grip on her wrist. 'He insisted.'

'Come out of there!' roared Annie. 'I heard what you did. Punchy saw ya!' Again the caravan shuddered as the sole of her thong-clad foot slammed against the door. Birdie saw that the thin wood was starting to splinter.

'Get away from me, you crazy old drunk!' came a muffled voice from inside the caravan. 'Piss off.'

Annie howled with rage and kicked again.

Jason squealed with excitement. 'She's gonna break the door down!' he yelled, crouching down the better to see the cracking wood.

Rosalie dropped her mother's arm, and put her hands up to her face. 'I don't know,' she muttered. 'I just don't know.'

From his vantage point at the corner of the house, Punchy guffawed. Rosalie rounded on him. 'I dunno what you're laughing at!' she scolded. 'If Mum gets her hands on Lily she'll break her in half. Why on earth did you say anything? Couldn't you keep it to yourself?'

Punchy looked confused. 'I only told her what I seen,' he said. 'I didn't know she'd go mad as this. I never even finished—'

'Well, what were you doing creeping round at night, spying on people anyhow? I thought you'd stopped all that. Mum said you had.'

His eyes grew shifty. Suddenly he looked more like Jason than his usual genial self.

'You know I don't sleep good, Rosalie,' he whined. 'And if I can't sleep I get pains in my legs, just lying in bed. I don't do anything bad. I just walk around. I can't help it if I see things.' Then his voice grew more self-righteous. 'Anyhow, I wasn't even in bed yet. An' I wanted to see where Lily was going,' he said. 'She wouldn't let Keith in when we got home, would she? An' he took the car and went? Then she went out? I just wanted to see where she was going. Keith would've wanted me to.'

'That's right!' panted Annie, wiping the sweat from her forehead with the back of her hand. 'You leave your brother alone, Rosalie. He did the right thing. Keith's got a right to know what the little slut was up to after she'd sent him off to half-kill himself.'

'It's not my fault he smashed himself up, you old hag!' screeched Lily from the caravan. 'It's his own bloody, gutless, stupid fault. Like everything else that's ever happened to him. Christ, no wonder his wife turned lesbian and pissed off. He'd turn anyone off men. Him and his creepy brothers.

God knows what their old man was like. Glad I never met him.'

'You watch your filthy tongue, or when I get my hands on you I'll tear it out and stuff it down your scrawny little neck!' Annie banged at the caravan door with meaty fists.

Inside, and, for the moment, safe, Lily laughed. 'God, what a trio. My three sons. A gutless wonder who can barely get it up, a dim-wit who pervs through windows, and a murdering slimeball with a mind like a sewer. Christ, did I get lucky, coming here.'

Annie's face turned from scarlet to maroon. She stepped back. 'Punchy, get the axe,' she muttered.

'Punchy, no!' ordered Rosalie, as he began to turn away obediently. He stopped, bewildered.

'Get the axe,' spat Annie. 'Rosalie, you keep out of this. Paul Lamb, do you hear me?'

'Punchy, no!'

Punchy hovered uncertainly.

'I'll get it,' Jason offered.

Birdie put a firm hand on his shoulder. 'You stay right here,' she said. He frowned, and wriggled, but quieted.

'Annie,' she said loudly. She waited until the woman looked at her. 'Annie, don't let Lily get you into trouble. If you hurt her, the cops'll have you in the lock-up so fast your head'll spin.'

'Think I care about that?' the woman shouted.

'You're needed here,' murmured Birdie, deliberately lowering her voice so that Annie had to lean towards her and concentrate, to hear. 'Everyone here needs you. Punchy, Rosalie, Jason. And Keith's in hospital. He's badly hurt. He's in a lot of trouble. He's going to need help. From you. You can't do much for him in custody, can you?'

Slowly the colour began to fade from Annie's trembling cheeks, forehead and breast. She stood there, panting. 'What d'you mean, Keith's in trouble?' she said.

'The police seem to think—that he might have been the one who killed Trevor.'

Annie gaped at her, seemingly unable to speak.

'The Sydney police don't think so,' Birdie said steadily. 'And I'm sure everything will work out, Annie. But you can understand, it's not a good time for you to be getting on their bad side, by kicking up rough with Lily. Why don't you just go inside, now, with Rosalie?'

'I want that scheming little slut out of there,' mumbled Annie. 'I want her off my property.'

Birdie drew her a little aside, and lowered her voice even further. 'Listen, Annie. There's something else you have to think of. Lily told the police she didn't leave the caravan all night, last night. But she did, didn't she? She lied to them. I think they'll want to talk to her about that.'

A look of cunning stole across Annie's face. 'You mean—' she began loudly. But Birdie put her finger to her lips, and she stopped.

'You mean,' she breathed in a hoarse whisper so redolent of alcohol that Birdie nearly reeled back, 'that if we keep her here, and just tell the cops what Punchy told us, the cops'll come and get her?'

'I think it's very likely.'

Annie nodded with satisfaction. 'Bloody little liar,' she muttered. Then her brow creased. ' 'Course, Punchy didn't mention to the cops he'd been out, either.'

True. Looking for a way out, Birdie decided prevarication was justified in this case. Jude wouldn't have agreed. But Toby would. 'No,' she agreed. 'But they probably won't worry too much about that. I mean, they'll understand Punchy'd be embarrassed. His brother's girl behaving like that.'

She glanced at Punchy, who had been listening with interest. He nodded solemnly, as though his motive for lying to the police had indeed stemmed from the highest motive, rather than being an automatic response to questioning by anyone in authority.

Annie looked with loathing at the locked caravan door. 'Bloody girls. Been nothing but pain and misery for my boys. Wanting this, wanting that, wanting the other. Out for everything they can get. Pain and misery. Never satisfied. First it was that dirty little piece Yvonne, with Keith. Then it was Daphne Hewitt, with Trev. Always trying to interfere with everything. Just like her mother. And then getting him into gaol. Now it's this little slut, cheating on Keith with his own brother, and getting Keith in trouble. It's criminal.'

She wiped the back of her hand over her mouth. 'I was never like that with Miltie. Never gave him a moment's trouble. Never played up on him when he was away. Never once. Had his kids. Cooked his food. Never complained.'

'Yes you did, Mum. You complained the whole time.' Rosalie put her hand on her mother's shoulder, and smiled tiredly. 'Come on. Come inside. I want to get dressed.'

'I want a drink,' said Annie. 'I'm dry. What's the time?'

'Pub won't be open for hours, Mum. I'll make you a cup of tea.'

'Tea,' Annie repeated gloomily.

Birdie had a thought. 'Floury Baker sent you a bottle of sherry, Annie. No charge, he said.'

Annie's eyes widened with something like joy. 'That right? Where is it?'

'In the car. My bag's still there too. I'll go and get it.'

'Nah. Don't you worry, love. Punchy'll get it.' She raised her voice. 'Hey, Punchy! Get the bottle and Birdie's bag out of her car. Will ya?'

'I will, I will!' shouted Jason, already running.

'Not you!' Annie shrieked. 'You might break it.'

Like a dog flattening its ears and speeding up when its owner calls it away from a fascinating quest, Jason ducked his head, leapt over a pile of half-burnt rubbish and swung through the gate without looking back.

Annie sighed heavily. 'Little bugger,' she said. 'If he breaks that bottle, I'll—'

'He won't break it, Mum,' said Rosalie. 'Come into the house.'

Twenty-five

With Rosalie leading the way, they climbed the single step and crossed the verandah to the front door of the old house.

The door led directly into a large living area, furnished with sagging couch, TV set, and a long table with chairs at either end, and wooden benches along each side. Half the table was covered several layers deep with the sort of mess that accumulates on horizontal surfaces in any room where children and exhausted or apathetic adults spend much time—piles of paper, plastic bags of long forgotten miscellaneous objects, odd items of clothing, dried-up felt-tip pens, toys, rocks, a belt bearing a row of plastic hand grenades, collector cards from cereal boxes.

In pride of place was a bright-green papier-mâché dinosaur, gruesomely realistic as to teeth and bloody jaws. It had obviously been brought home from school, since there was a printed blue card stuck to it with adhesive tape. 'Merit Award' Birdie read. And in small, neat handwriting below. 'Jason Lamb, papier-mâché sculpture, subject of choice. Well done, Jason.'

Birdie sighed for poor Phillip Hewitt. Tyrannosaurus rex, blood dripping from its fangs, probably hadn't been the sort of subject he'd had in mind when he'd initiated this project.

The other end of the table was cluttered with the evidence of a half-eaten breakfast. Milk, sugar, cereal, mugs of cold tea, a metal teapot. It seemed that Punchy had thrown his bombshell about Lily while the family was eating.

Pop songs belted from a small radio standing beside one of the places. Punchy walked over to the radio, turned it up, then sat down at the table. He picked up a spoon and started scooping up what was left in a bowl, chewing ravenously. Rosalie disappeared through another doorway, presumably her bedroom.

'Sit down, love,' said Annie to Birdie. Absent-mindedly she pushed some comics and a cracked plastic Dracula mask further along the table, to clear a space.

Birdie took the offered seat, and looked around. At the barbecue last night she'd only caught a glimpse of this room through the open doorway. The shabby couch, the TV set, part of the table, a scrap of tinsel left over from Christmas dangling from a nail on the wall. Then it had looked alien and unwelcoming. But now, smelling of toast, in the morning light, it didn't seem any of those things.

This big table—once it had been filled, at breakfast time, at dinner time. Filled with chattering, fighting, laughing children, competing for food and attention. Annie would have sat at one end—there, where she was sitting now. The chair at the other end would have been Milton's—when he wasn't 'away'.

The narrow mantel over the fireplace, cluttered, like every other surface of the room, was dominated by two silver trophies. Both were crowned by two small figures in boxing gloves. Unlike anything else in the room they had been well and lovingly cared for, polished to a high shine.

'Are they yours?' Birdie asked Punchy, raising her voice slightly to compete with the radio.

He nodded, scraping up the last of the cereal, then up-ending the bowl to drink the remaining milk.

'You were a champ, weren't you, Punchy?' Annie said encouragingly. Her eyes were soft.

'Yup,' he said briefly, and got up to put bread in the toaster that stood, obviously in its accustomed place, on a narrow side table.

Jason appeared bowed down under the weight of Birdie's bag which he'd slung crosswise over one narrow shoulder. He was clutching Floury's bottle.

'Good boy,' said Annie, holding out her hand. He trudged across to her and gave her the sherry, then, deeply sighing, took himself, and his burden, to Birdie.

'It's real heavy,' he complained, as she untangled him

from the strap and heaved the bag over his head and onto her lap.

Birdie took out her mobile phone. Jason eyed it with respect. 'Are you going to call the cops?' he asked. 'Have you got a hot line?'

'No. Not exactly,' she said.

Annie stirred. 'What I want to know is, why's my Keith in the gun, and that bastard Hewitt still running around free? The Sydney coppers were up there at Hewitts' earlier. Saw them going up the track, then back again. Didn't stay long.'

'They haven't got enough evidence for an arrest, yet, Annie,' said Birdie carefully. 'Anyway, this new information of Punchy's—of Lily's—might help. I'm just going to ring them.'

'We got a phone. You can use that,' said Annie, jerking her head to the side table.

Somehow Birdie hadn't expected there'd be a phone here. But there it was, sitting beside the toaster.

'Use it,' muttered Annie, pouring sherry into a mug. 'Go on. I want them to know it's us reporting that little bitch. It'll be more official if you use our phone. I want them to know it's us.'

Her voice was flat now, and her face was grim. She looked very tired and worn. Her skin hung heavily from face and arms. Her hair had settled around her face in stringy tails. It was as though her anger having left her, she had deflated. She sat there at the head of her depleted table and looked vacantly into the fluid in the mug. Not drinking yet. Just staring. Thinking, perhaps, of Trevor. Or of Keith. Or maybe of Milton. Or of the others—Johnny, Bridget, Cecilia, Mickey, Brett . . . all gone. So many lost children, thought Birdie, watching the bent head. How must that feel?

She slid off the bench and went over to the offered phone. Before she dialled, she looked up. 'Punchy, do you know exactly what time it was when you saw Lily with Trevor last night?'

He shook his head, spreading toast thickly with peanut butter.

'It's quite important,' Birdie said. 'I mean—' She hesitated, choosing her words carefully. 'They're trying to work out exactly when Trevor died. And if you saw him alive at a certain time . . .'

Punchy chuckled, deep his throat. 'He was alive then, all right. With Lily.'

'But when? When was it?'

'After Keith left,' Punchy said patiently. 'Lily wouldn't let him into the caravan, after we got home from the pub. So he went off in the car. He was real mad. Rosalie tried to stop him, but he just went.'

Rosalie had come back into the room wearing blue slacks and an Indian muslin shirt. She walked towards the kitchen. 'Must have been about quarter past eleven, then,' she said briefly, as she went through the door. 'Maybe twenty past.'

'How's Grace?' called Annie after her.

'Still asleep. Thank heavens.' There was the sound of water running into a kettle.

'Did Lily go out straight away, Punchy?' Birdie persisted.

'Soon as Rosalie went back inside, just about,' said Punchy. 'She snuck out, and went round the back of the house. Then she went down the paddock.'

'Did she have a torch?'

He looked surprised. 'Nah. What'd she need that for? She knew where she was going. Shack light was on. You could see it. I followed her. She didn't see me. I'm good at tracking.'

'I'm good at tracking, too,' boasted Jason. 'And no one ever hears me, either.'

'You'll get yourself into trouble as well,' said his mother, coming back out for the teapot. 'Anyhow, what are you doing still here, Jason? You should be getting ready for school. Go on, now.'

'Aw, Mum, I can't go to school today,' said Jason. 'Me uncle's been murdered, hasn't he? I got a right to stay home, haven't I? When Ryan Winchester's father fell under the tractor he got to stay home. For two whole days.'

She stared at him.

'Anyhow,' he added pathetically, 'I been up practically all night. I'm too tired to go. Sir says if you go to bed too late you can't concentrate.'

She sighed, and turned away.

'What happened then, Punchy?' Birdie urged. 'When Lily got down to the shack?'

He shrugged, crunching toast. 'She went up to the door, and Trev opened up. He was drinking a can of beer. She said something. I dunno what, I couldn't hear. Something dirty I reckon, 'cause Trev laughed and pulled her in and shut the door. And then after a while the bedroom light went on.'

Jason sniggered. Annie sipped sherry, shoulders slumped. She didn't appear to be listening.

'So that would have been about eleven-thirty, would it?' Birdie hazarded. She made a few quick calculations. Keith Lamb was just leaving Sue Sweeney's, then. She and Jude had seen his car going over the bridge. But he could have stopped the car at some point, and come back on foot. Slipped through Hewitts' fence, moved through the paddocks down to the creek, across it, through the dividing fence and up to the shack. Suspecting, maybe, what was happening inside.

Punchy shrugged again. 'Dunno what time it was,' he said. His brow wrinkled. Then, suddenly, his face broke into a huge smile. 'The news was on,' he announced.

'On the radio in the shack?'

'Yeah.'

'A proper news? Not just a news flash?'

'Yeah. Before Trev shut the door.'

The obligatory half-hour news. So eleven-thirty it was. Well, that was a start. But—Birdie frowned, her fingers tapping the phone. If Lily arrived at eleven-thirty, Jude was cracked over the head at about midnight, and Sue Sweeney supposedly arrived at twelve-twenty . . .

'How long was Lily in there, Punchy? About?'

'I dunno. Not long.'

Birdie felt a chill. 'Did you see anything?' she asked abruptly. 'Did you stay the whole time? Did you look through the bedroom window? What did you see?'

Jason sniggered again. Punchy stared, and coloured slightly.

'I wouldn't do that, Birdie,' he said, in strangely formal fashion. 'Look in the bedroom. That's private, isn't it?' Obviously troubled, he looked at her sideways, perhaps readjusting his opinion of her.

She felt her own face flushing. 'Sorry. I mean—I didn't mean—I'm trying to work out how long Lily stayed, Punchy, that's all. I mean, how do you know what they were doing, if you didn't see? And did you see her leave?'

His face cleared. 'Oh, yeah. I saw her leave.' He grinned broadly, as if remembering something that pleased him.

'Did you see Trevor?' Birdie held her breath. Rosalie came out of the kitchen with the filled teapot and put it on the table.

'Oh, yeah. Saw him. Heard him, too. Boy, did I hear him.' He snorted with laughter, spraying toast crumbs over the table in front of him.

Not long.

How long was 'not long'?

Annie looked up. 'What's so funny?' she asked. Her voice was already slurred.

'I was telling ya. Before you suddenly run out and started yelling at Lily.'

The phone rang, making Birdie jump. She stepped aside and Rosalie picked up the receiver.

'Hello? . . . Yes. That's me. Yes. That's right.'

'Who is it, love?' asked Annie.

Rosalie frowned, and waved at Punchy to turn down the radio.

'Is he?. . . Oh, all right then . . . yes, I'll try. It's just we haven't got a car at the moment because . . . yes. Anyway . . . yes . . . okay. Thank you. Bye.'

She put the phone down and turned back to face them. 'It's Keith,' she said dully.

Annie's hand flew to her face. 'He's worse.'

'No. He's okay. But he wants me to go and see him.'

'What for?'

'I don't know. They just said he wanted Rosalie. They were ringing to tell me.'

'Doesn't he want to see me?'

'Mum, all I know is what they told me. The sister says he keeps asking. Anyway, I'd better try and get to Gunbudgie. Find someone who'll give me a lift.'

'Oh, wow. Can I come?' gasped Jason.

'No!' snapped his mother. Pale and drawn, she looked at the end of her tether.

'I could take you, Rosalie,' Birdie offered. 'I'm going to Gunbudgie as soon as I leave here. Well, more or less. There are a few things I've got to do first, but they won't take long.'

'Oh, thanks.' But there was no animation in Rosalie's voice. And her hand shook as she picked up a mug, to pour tea.

'Dunno why he wouldn't want to see me,' grumbled Annie, frowning into her sherry. 'I'm his mother, aren't I?'

'He wouldn't want to worry you, Mum,' murmured Rosalie. 'He wouldn't expect you to make the trip. Not after last night.'

Annie nodded, only partially mollified. She took another drink.

Birdie dialled Toby's number. Engaged. You wouldn't believe it.

'Don't you tell Keith about Trevor and Lily, Rosalie,' Annie warned. 'Not while he's so bad.'

'Of course I won't, Mum.'

'Why not tell him?' asked Jason loudly. 'He said he'd finished with her, didn't he? When he went?'

'Yeah,' Punchy agreed. 'Keith's finished with her. He said. And Trev got her good. Shoulda heard him. Give Keith a laugh, wouldn't it?'

'What'd Uncle Trev say? What'd he say?' begged Jason.

'Punchy, stop talking crazy,' cried Rosalie. She was almost in tears. She gulped at her tea and stood up. 'Could we go now?' she asked Birdie.

'Sure.' Birdie stood up too. She didn't want any tea, and clearly she was going to learn little more here. Now wasn't the time for the rambling chat about the past that she'd planned. The affair of Lily was absorbing everyone's interest.

She said goodbye to Annie, and started for the door. She heard Punchy talking to Jason, taking what audience he could get.

'Trev says, "Okay, out," see,' said Punchy. 'He has her by the scruff of the neck, and he's pushing her out the door. She's got her tits hanging out and her pants down round her knees so she can't even walk properly. And she starts screeching. "You can't do this to me!" she goes. And Trev pushes her onto the verandah and he goes, "You asked for it, you got it. I didn't mind. Five years is a while. Needed to get the rough off, didn't I?"'

Birdie stopped, riveted.

'The rough off,' giggled Jason.

'Yeah. And she screeches, "What d'you mean by that, you bastard?" And he pushes her right off the verandah so she falls on the dirt with her bum in the air.

' "I mean you're not worth more than five minutes of anyone's time," he says. "Keith always was a hopeless picker. Now clear off."

'Then he slams the door. And she goes right off her brain. She screams and yells. "I'll kill you, you bastard," she goes, and bangs the dirt with her hands.'

'Punchy!' breathed Rosalie. But Punchy didn't hear her.

'And then she pulls up her daks and runs off, back through the bush.' Punchy laughed uproariously, slamming the table with the flat of his hand.

'Punchy,' said Birdie, her head reeling. 'Did you follow her after that?'

'Yeah, 'course. I wanted to see what she'd do.'

'And what did she do?'

'Just went back into the caravan. Could hear her banging around in there, tipping stuff over and that. Was pretty boring, so I come back to the house and went to bed.'

'Could she have gone out again? Would you have seen her?'

Punchy looked confused. 'No. But why would she? No point going back to the shack. After that.'

There was silence.

'Birdie, let's go,' said Rosalie urgently. 'Mum, you stay here. We're going to send the police. Don't leave the house. Punchy, Jason, you stay here too. Lock the door after me. Don't go near the caravan. Hear me?'

They nodded, wide-eyed. Annie stirred, but said nothing. She seemed to be turning something over in her mind. Her eyes were glazed.

Hurrying through the door, Birdie fumbled in her handbag for her keys. Toby. She had to get to Toby. Quickly. Wallet, comb, pens, mobile phone, calculator—where were the keys? Then she remembered. She'd left them in the car when she'd jumped out earlier.

She looked up at the fence, and blinked. For a moment she couldn't believe her eyes.

'Where's the car?' hissed Rosalie, behind her.

Birdie ran across the yard as if, somehow, the car was going miraculously to reappear.

But the grass in front of the collapsing front fence was bare. She looked back towards the house. Punchy, Rosalie, Annie and Jason were staring at her from the front verandah. The caravan at the side of the house stood silent, door gaping wide.

The car had gone. And Birdie knew, without doubt, that Lily Danger had gone with it.

Twenty-six

'She won't get far.' Toby rubbed a big hand over his face and sat down heavily on the pub step, next to Birdie. 'They'll pick her up on the highway on the way into Sassafras. Or Gunbudgie. Depends which way she went. They'll watch both. They'll get her. Take her in for questioning. Said they'd call me, soon as they did.'

'You think she killed Trevor Lamb?'

'How would I know?' he said irritably. 'She's certainly drawn attention to herself. But it's bloody unlikely.'

'Why?'

'Because I say so.' He stared out into the road, frowning thunderously.

'What about my car? How am I supposed to get to Gunbudgie now?'

'Well it's your own bloody fault. How you could leave the keys in the vehicle like that with characters like that around is beyond me.'

'I—'

'Oh, all right. I know the story. Anyhow, you'll get your car back. Just keep your shirt on. There's no rush. Your boyfriend isn't going anywhere, is he? He's still conked out, anyway, from what I hear.'

'Dan—'

'Birdwood, you'll get to Gunbudgie. I will take you personally if necessary. In an hour. Or two. When I'm finished here. For the moment, consider yourself marooned.'

'Rosalie Lamb has to go as well, remember.'

'Yeah. Well, I'll take her too,' snapped Toby. 'We'll all go to Gunbudgie, centre of the known universe, seat of all power, object of everyone's desire. When I'm ready. Not before. I've got a murder enquiry on here, in case you hadn't noticed. All right?'

'What's the matter with you?' Birdie turned to look at him. He was staring at the road, brow deeply furrowed. Suddenly she realised that he had something other than her car, and Lily Danger, on his mind. 'Has something happened? While I was at the Lambs'? It's not that Sue—'

'Miss Sweeney has made her statement,' he said bitterly. 'Whether it's the truth, this time, I couldn't say. But as you suggested we checked on "Poison", or whatever its stupid name is. It was played on one station only last night. At twelve-nineteen precisely.'

'So—Punchy saw Trevor Lamb alive at eleven-thirty . . .'

'After that. He saw him bidding farewell to your little car thief, after he'd had his way with her. Or she'd had her way with him. Whichever.'

'But we don't know how long after eleven-thirty that was, do we? Punchy just said "not long". That could mean anything.'

'About ten minutes, tops, I'd say. Maybe less. Maybe when he said she was only worth five minutes of anyone's time he wasn't joking.'

'But surely . . .'

'Surely what? Lamb was only twenty-nine. Been away from women for five years. The little tart comes along with hot pants, he gives her one, then he throws her out. Ten minutes, tops, I'd say. So that takes us to eleven-forty.'

Birdie looked at him with distaste. He returned her gaze calmly. 'Don't shoot the messenger, Birdwood. That's life. Said something about "getting the rough off", didn't he? How would you interpret that remark?'

'I don't know,' Birdie muttered, not looking at him, still gripped by a repugnance she knew was unfair.

'I do. He thought he was going to get another offer. From someone he'd want to take more time over. He wouldn't have got rid of Lily so quickly otherwise. Even if he didn't like her much. Any old port in a storm, as they say. So who do you reckon the other lady was?'

'Sue Sweeney said she thought he expected her.'

'But she'd decided not to play. At least, that's her story.'

'Do you think she's lying?'

'Do you?'

Birdie thought of Sue, hunched forward in her chair in the brightly-decorated sitting room. That naked, vulnerable face, the flood of words.

'I—don't know.'

'Neither do I. We know Lamb was alive at about eleven-forty. We know, or at least we've got good reason for believing, that he was dead by twelve-nineteen.' Toby paused. 'And Sweeney was Lamb's old girlfriend, wasn't she? She testified at his trial. Didn't do him much good, as I recall.'

'Dan, what are you saying? Why are you so down on Sue? Lily could just as easily have come back and killed Trevor Lamb before Sue even arrived.'

He looked thoughtfully at the backs of his hands. 'You reckon Lily Danger could've ambushed your boyfriend on the track? I know he's no muscle man, but you said she's just a skinny little thing.'

'Well—yes. But anyone can hit anyone on the head, if they aren't expecting it. Lanky said whoever killed Trevor wasn't necessarily very strong, just maybe very angry. And it depends on the weapon, too, doesn't it?'

'Ah, yes. The weapon.' Toby turned his hands over, and studied the palms.

'And leaving aside Lily and Sue, what about Les Hewitt? I thought he was your main suspect. You seem to have forgotten all about him, suddenly.'

'He didn't arrive home till midnight. He couldn't've. Posy Delius checked out. He left her at eleven-thirty. On the knocker, she said. Appropriate phrase, they tell me. She's a well-endowed girl, apparently.'

'He still could have killed Lamb before Sue arrived. He could have met Jude on the way. Knocked him out then, so Jude couldn't stop him.'

'Saint Jude'd have Buckleys stopping Les Hewitt doing anything he wanted to, I'd say.'

'Well, maybe Hewitt knocked him out to stop him seeing what was going on, then. I don't know.'

'No, you don't.' Toby stood up, and stretched. 'You don't know the half of it, mate.'

'Dan what are you on about? What's going on? Tell me!'

Toby squinted down the road to the right, beyond the bridge, to the crest of the hill.

'Car coming,' he drawled, hitching at his belt. 'First of

the press, I'll bet. Well, I'd better get on.' He started moving back into the pub. Birdie darted ahead of him to the door. He pushed at her half-heartedly, but she stood firm, barring his way.

'Dan! Tell me! Why have you lost interest in Les Hewitt? And why don't you think Lily's the one? I mean, why is Sue a possibility, not Lily? Have you had something from forensic already? Or have you had some early medical stuff? Isn't it too soon?'

'Too soon for any old murder, Birdwood,' he said bitterly, 'Way too soon. But this isn't any old murder, is it? On-high can move mountains, if they want to. No expense spared. If they want to. If they're embarrassed enough. And they are. In fact, it's possible, Birdwood, that on-high've never been so embarrassed as they are right now. And that's saying something.'

Birdie stared at him. His mouth was grim. And his eyes—full of baffled anger. He looked as if he'd been cheated, somehow. But cheated of what?

The approaching car slowed, preparatory to rattling over the Hope's Creek bridge. Toby looked at it over his shoulder.

'Birdie, move,' he said in a different voice. 'I want to get inside before I get buttonholed.'

She stepped out of the way and let him through the door. He slammed it shut, closing them in.

'What a bastard,' he muttered.

'Who?'

'It. This situation. Everything. Life.'

'Dan—'

'Oh, give it a rest. You make me tired. I'll tell you. Why not? Everyone's going to know eventually. You may as well know now. Have your own private celebration, in Gunbudgie, at our expense.'

'What do you mean?'

'Trevor Lamb's head wound. Remember what Lanky said? About it being oddly-shaped? The weapon probably metal?'

'Yes.'

'Remember what they said about Daphne Hewitt's head wounds?'

'Same sort of thing.'

'That's right. Well, the boffins have compared pictures, got out their little tape-measures, had a confab. And you know what they reckon?'

'A similar sort of weapon was used on Lamb?'

'Oh, no. They're going further than that.'

She stared at him.

He nodded. 'That's right. They're betting London to a brick that it was the same weapon, Birdie. They're saying whatever was used to kill Trevor Lamb was used to kill his wife as well.'

'They can't know that,' Birdie breathed. 'Not for sure.' But as she spoke, she was remembering the look on Dr Lanky's face as he straightened up after looking at Trevor Lamb's body for the first time. He'd been puzzled. Something had disconcerted him.

Lanky had been the one to examine Daphne, five years ago. He'd seen the similarity. He'd wondered about it. But he'd said nothing. He knew that if he was right, the truth would come out soon enough. Why should he put his reputation on the line, jumping the gun? That wasn't the way of a man like Lanky, fond of keeping his own counsel.

Still, she repeated her words. 'They can't know that for sure.'

'No. Not yet. But they're sure enough to be bloody concerned. And to put pressure on me. Because in the end everyone and his dog's going to hear about what Lamb said in stir. And in the pub last night. And then . . .'

'They're going to know he was telling the truth, all along. And that someone here killed him.'

'Exactly. Someone here killed him. Like someone killed his wife. With the same weapon. The weapon the bumble-foot coppers can't find. That they haven't been able to find for five years. That must be here, under our noses. That must have been here all along. In Hope's End. With a double murderer who's been watching us stuff around, wasting time with the last people on earth who'd be involved, keeping mum, laughing up their sleeve.'

'I don't think they'd be laughing.'

'Why not? Wouldn't you?'

'No. I'd be scared.'

For the second time you look down on a crushed skull, sprawled limbs, dark blood, seeping into an old wooden floor. The weapon is in your hand. For the second time, you have to hide it. Hide your guilt. Only then can you hide yourself, behind the mask you've worn for five long years.

Where? Where will you hide it?

Where you hid it before. Of course. Where it's stayed, waiting, all this time.

Did you know it would be brought out, to kill again? Were you ever drawn to its hiding place, not looking, perhaps, not touching, but knowing it was there? How did you feel, when you did that? Smug? Nervous? Sickened? Tormented? Afraid?

Did you think about Daphne Lamb, dead at twenty-two? Or her child, dead before it had lived?

Did you think about Trevor Lamb, waiting out the long years in prison?

Or did you just think about yourself, and your guilt, and hurry away from the hidden weapon that you knew one day might betray you?

'I'd be scared,' Birdie repeated.

'Nothing to be scared of, is there?' muttered Toby. 'Whoever it was got away with murder before. Why shouldn't they get away with it now? Nothing's changed.'

'Yes it has,' said Birdie slowly. 'You're here this time, aren't you?'

He snorted. He knew what she was thinking. 'And so are you, is that it?' he growled.

Yes. And so am I.

Twenty-seven

'So that girl took your car without asking? Saw her drive past. Thought, "that's funny," ' said Peg McCann. 'Never thought she'd stolen it, just thought, "that's funny. What's Lily doing driving the ABC lady's car?" Thought you might have lent it to her, to go and see Keith in Gunbudgie. But it did seem funny. I mean, you'd want to be going there yourself, wouldn't you? To see Jude Gregorian?'

Birdie, busy scribbling the post office fax number in her notebook, murmured something meaningless. She wanted to talk to Peg McCann. But not about Jude.

'Heard you haven't had any sleep. You'd be tired,' Peg continued, apparently impervious to any snub. 'You look tired. Wrung out. Exhausted, I'd say.'

'Oh, I don't feel so bad, considering,' said Birdie untruthfully, glancing up from her notebook.

Peg's gimlet eyes bored across the counter, straight into the middle of Birdie's forehead. The tip of her sharp nose was as red as a tiny beacon. Maybe it throws a target beam. Like on one of those high-powered guns they use to assassinate people, thought Birdie wildly. She certainly felt under attack. Her plans to pump Peg McCann seemed to have gone awry. The woman was cornering her, instead of the other way around.

'You don't sleep if you've got things on your mind,' Peg went on relentlessly. Again that gimlet look. She turned to flip the calendar on the wall to the correct date.

'That's right,' Birdie murmured. 'Some night, last night, wasn't it?'

' 'Course, you went up to bed early,' said Peg, refusing to be diverted. 'Had your bath and all, Floury Baker says.

But then you got disturbed, poor soul. Jude Gregorian, wasn't it? Saw him looking out the window. Thought, he's keeping that poor girl up—talking and carrying on. And she needs her sleep. But men are thoughtless sometimes, aren't they? And maybe you didn't mind all that much. You're an old friend of his, I heard.'

'Did you?' snapped Birdie, very ruffled.

'Oh, I hear most things. Eventually,' said Peg McCann ominously.

With enormous relief, Birdie heard someone come through the door behind her. She turned, and was confronted by the bony white face and enormous eyes of Phillip Hewitt.

He started like a nervous horse when he saw her, then turned in confusion to the post office counter, where Peg waited, eyes ravenous.

'Come for yesterday's mail, Phillip?'

He nodded.

'How's your poor mother, dear?'

'Not so well. She's got one of her headaches this morning.'

Peg clucked sympathetically. 'That'd be the police visiting, for Les, wouldn't it?'

He made no answer.

'It's such a terrible thing to happen, isn't it? Not that I don't think that Lamb deserved it. I do. I'm a law-abiding woman, Phillip, but . . .'

Birdie slipped just outside the door, keeping it open a little with her foot, and dialled Jude's office number. It answered almost immediately.

'It's Verity Birdwood here,' she said. And immediately, as rapidly as she could, began to explain the reason for her call while the woman on the other end of the phone exclaimed and questioned.

'So that's the story. Sorry to be so brief. The hospital will be able to tell you more. I just wanted to let you know.' Birdie knew she must sound abstracted. And hurried. But she wanted to keep this call short. She'd been presented with a perfect opportunity to corner Phillip Hewitt alone, and she didn't want to miss it.

She saw Peg McCann go behind a small screen plastered with post office information posters. She was about to get the mail. Any minute Hewitt would be leaving.

'I have to go now,' she said, cutting short another bout of astonished and horrified expostulation. 'But there's another quick thing. Could you please organise to fax me the list of items removed from the Lamb shack by the Hewitt family? Jude said you'd have a copy of it in your files . . . Thanks. Soon as you can, please. I'll give you the number.'

She repeated the number as Peg returned from behind the screen with a small bundle of letters.

'Nothing very interesting, dear, by the look of it,' Birdie heard her say, handing it over.

Phillip mumbled something, and began backing slowly toward the door, as she talked on. He was preparing his getaway.

Birdie flicked her eyes across the street. There was a small, white car parked there. Phillip's car. She'd seen it before, in the Hewitts' garage. It was neatly parked beside Jude's. An idea occurred to her. Jude's car. It was possible, just possible, he'd have brought some spare keys. If he had, they'd be in his room, upstairs. She turned her attention back to the phone.

'Thanks very much. Oh, and one more thing. Jude's car is here. I just want you to know I'll probably be using it when I go to see him . . . Don't think he'll mind, do you? . . . Well, no . . . I haven't had a chance to see him yet. But I will. For sure . . . I don't know. Soon as I can. I'll call you after and tell you how he is . . . Bye,' gabbled Birdie, and cut the connection. Jude's devoted assistant would think she was a very cold-hearted little piece indeed, she thought. She could almost hear her saying it. But it couldn't be helped. She edged back into the post office. She didn't want Hewitt running out on her.

'You're not looking too rich yourself, Phillip,' Peg was saying, red beacon and gimlet eyes working overtime. 'Had a bad night, did you?'

'Not too good,' he said.

'It worries your mother when you aren't well. You should be more careful.' She wagged her finger at him playfully, then lowered her voice. 'Mind you, I understand how you must have felt, Phillip. I really do. Everyone understands, dear. Don't you feel too bad about it. Everyone's behind you a hundred per cent.'

He coloured, and escaped, mumbling, ducking blindly past Birdie. She turned to follow him.

'Poor Dolly,' said Peg to Birdie, with a gusty sigh. 'I can imagine how she must be feeling now. What that woman's suffered! I can't tell you! And now the Posy Delius business is going to come out. Cruel, isn't it?'

It was the opening Birdie had been waiting for. But the timing was terrible. If she stayed to hear Peg out, Phillip would get away. She'd have to put the post-mistress on hold.

'I'll be back. For the fax,' she gasped, and escaped in her turn.

She ran across the road, to where Phillip Hewitt was climbing into his car.

'Excuse me! Mr. Hewitt! Phillip!' she called.

He hesitated. He was too polite to ignore her. Too full of fear and dislike to smile. He just stood there, awkwardly crouching, half-in, half-out of the car.

'I was wondering if it was possible for me to see over the school,' she said. 'While I'm here. I mean—' she shrugged, ruefully, '—the story I was supposed to be covering doesn't exist any more. I thought, considering, I might have a look at the school, if that's all right. It's closing, isn't it? You never know. There might be a story in it.'

Sorry, Jude. All's fair in . . .

Phillip's smooth forehead wrinkled. He was suspicious, but didn't know how to say no.

'I wouldn't get in the way,' Birdie urged. 'Just have a quick look. A very quick look. Okay?'

'Oh, yes, well, all right,' he said reluctantly. 'Do you want to do it now?'

'Now would be fine,' she said.

'Well, follow me, then. It's no distance.'

'I haven't got a car at the moment,' said Birdie, flashing what she was sure was a most unconvincing smile. 'Could you give me a lift?'

'Oh—yes. Of course.'

Birdie slipped into Phillip Hewitt's very clean car with the certain knowledge that she was unwanted and he was intensely uncomfortable. But she settled back in the spotless passenger seat with a sigh of contentment.

'Oh, it's good to sit down,' she said. 'This is a nice car. Is it new?'

'Three years old,' he said briefly. His knuckles, on the wheel, were white. He bared his teeth briefly, in what seemed to be an involuntary grimace, then he spoke, looking straight ahead.

'Look, do you really want to see the school? Or do you just want to pump me about last night?'

Birdie hesitated. 'Both,' she said, after a moment. She realised it was pointless to lie. She could hardly deny she wanted to ask him questions, then start asking him questions. But there was no sense in telling the unvarnished truth, either.

His Adam's apple jiggled nervously. 'I know what you were doing talking to my mother,' he said. 'You took advantage of her. She's not well, you know. I didn't think the police were allowed to spy like that.'

'I'm not police,' said Birdie. 'Your mother and I weren't talking about last night. Didn't she tell you?'

'Yes.' He turned his head to look at her. The tip of his tongue crept out and moistened his lips. 'She said you talked about Daphne. She said it did her good.'

'Well, then. Look, are we going to go? That woman at the post office is probably staring at us through the window. She'll be wondering what we're doing, sitting here. She'll be spreading rumours about us, soon.'

He whispered something under his breath, started the car, and backed out into the road. As they moved away, Birdie looked towards the post office window. Sure enough, sharp eyes were watching through the highly-polished glass.

'Can't do much around here without being noticed, can you?' she remarked.

Phillip shook his head. Carefully he turned the car off to the right, in the direction of the Lambs' house. But instead of going straight ahead, he took the first left-hand turn, drove along a little way, then pulled up.

There was the school: a tiny weatherboard building with a red corrugated-iron roof, standing in a grassy paddock with knots of trees at the sides, and, at the back, a small red-brick toilet block, and a patch of asphalt marked with faded white lines. Birdie recognised it easily from Dolly Hewitt's photographs. It hadn't changed in thirty years. Almost certainly it hadn't changed since it was built, except for the addition of the toilet block and asphalt, and different choices on paint colour for the main building.

Just now it was a faded brown. Sepia, Birdie thought. Appropriate, for a slice of history soon to vanish. She looked at the old brass bell, still hanging on the rickety timber frame in the playground, where Dolly Hewitt had photographed it all those years ago.

A few children played on the grass towards the back of the yard. They looked up half-heartedly as the car drew up, then went back to their game. At this distance, fading into the bleached grass, they could have been any children from any time.

Les Hewitt had played here as a child. Milton Lamb, too. Maybe Peg McCann, Bull Trews. And later Daphne Hewitt, Phillip Hewitt. And all the Lambs. Bridget, Johnny, Mickey, Brett, Keith, Cecilia, Rosalie, Trevor, Paul . . .

Ghost children . . . Birdie shivered.

But by the front step of the building, shattering the illusion, lay a tumbled pile of backpacks, bright pink, luminous orange, black, covered in labels and stickers. Messy. Aggressive. A relief.

Phillip got out of the car, took a pristine briefcase with shiny brass clips from the back seat, and waited on the grass for Birdie to join him before locking and testing each door of the car in turn.

They walked up the cracked concrete path, and around the side of the building. 'We don't use the front door,' Phillip explained. 'White ants in the frame. They haven't bothered to do anything about it, of course, because the place is closing.'

He unlocked a red-painted side door, and they went inside. They crossed a small side passage, with pegs on the walls for bags and hats, and went through another door into the main room.

Phillip Hewitt carefully closed the second door behind them.

'Now,' he said, with a twisted smile. 'You can talk to me at the same time as seeing the school. This is all there is to it. What do you want to know?'

Twenty-eight

It was extraordinary, thought Birdie, how schools, no matter what sort of schools they were, always smelt the same. Old bananas, leather, chalk, sweaty socks—and something else. She'd never been able to work out exactly what that something was. Children, maybe.

This school was very different from any she'd seen before. But only because it was so small. Otherwise, with its tall windows, blackboard, battered books in the 'reading corner', spelling posters and art projects on the walls, and mobiles made of painted egg cartons and paper hanging from the ceiling, the classroom was very similar to those she remembered from childhood.

'We don't have much equipment', said Phillip, putting his briefcase down on a battered table at one side of the room. His 'work station' presumably.

'You've got a computer,' Birdie said, pointing to the single machine perched beside the briefcase.

'Oh, that's mine,' he said diffidently. 'I brought it in so the children could use it. They should be learning computer skills, and the P and C around here isn't very active. Well, it's moribund. No way we'd get anything that way. Anyway, at Gunbudgie they've got computers. So next year . . .'

His eyes had a far-away look.

'Will you be sorry to leave?' asked Birdie.

He shook his head.

'Where will you go next?'

'I don't know. They'll relocate me if they can, but I haven't applied for anything. I haven't decided what I'll do. Don't even know if I'll stay with teaching. Don't think I'm cut out for it, really.' He smiled wryly. 'Kids are like horses.

They can smell your fear. If you're weak, they run rings around you.'

'You were just about to start uni when Daphne was killed, weren't you? And when you finished you asked for this school so you could be close to your mother?'

'That's right. But it wasn't just that. I mean, I didn't think I was making any huge sacrifice. I thought, it would be quiet here. Good for my writing.' His pale face flushed pink again. 'I write poetry,' he said.

Birdie nodded.

'But it hasn't really worked out,' Phillip went on. With long, nervous fingers he plucked at the clasps on his briefcase. 'This school—the farm—they don't suit me. The farm never did, really. I just forgot that. I'd been away, except for weekends and holidays, for years. I forgot what living here full time was like. And without Daphne—'

His face was suddenly swept with a look of inexpressible sadness.

'You were here, when she died, weren't you? You'd finished school by then?'

He nodded. 'I was here. Waiting for uni to start. But I hadn't seen Daphne for a few days. For nearly a week, actually. She had the flu. She was in bed. Mum was going over to see her every day. Sometimes twice. When she knew Trevor was out, of course. She wouldn't go while he was there. He didn't like it. Peg at the post office used to ring Mum to tell her when Trevor arrived at the pub. Mum'd go across the creek and see Daphne then. Once he got to the pub he never went home for hours.'

'Didn't Daphne ever go home? To your place, I mean?'

'No. Because of Dad. She wouldn't.'

'They were very close, weren't they? Daphne and your father? Before?'

He smiled sadly. 'Oh, yes. That was the tragedy of it. He just couldn't understand why she'd want to marry Trevor Lamb. He couldn't cope with it. He tried to order her not to. But of course that was stupid. She just got more determined, then.'

'What did you think about it? About Daphne and Trevor?'

'I—' His top lip twitched. He looked down at the desk, at the shining briefcase. 'I was just a kid. I think—in a way—I was glad.' He looked up swiftly, to see her reaction. She returned his glance with calm interest.

'I'd always been the problem one, you see,' he went on, with difficulty. 'I don't mean naughty. Trouble at school, or anything like that. I was never naughty. Of course not. Wouldn't have had the guts.' He gave a small, bitter laugh, and his lip twitched again.

'I was shy, and I was scared of horses, and I didn't have any friends—well, not real friends. For years I wet the bed. I used to go into hysterics when Dad killed a chook, or a lamb, even as a teenager. He despised me. Still does, I guess. Mum worried about me. Still does.

'But Daphne had always been perfect. The perfect daughter. She could ride, and cook, and sew. She loved animals. She was confident, and happy, and kind. She did well at school. She was popular. Everyone loved her.'

Everyone loved Daphne.

'When she said she wanted to marry Trevor Lamb it was as though she'd blotted her copybook for the the very first time. Just for once, everyone was worrying about her, instead of me. Mum was beside herself. Dad was—well, I can't think of a strong enough word. They both went on and on at her, endlessly. But she wouldn't give in. She just kept saying that they didn't understand Trevor. That they were prejudiced against him, just because he was a Lamb. She said she and Trevor were going to save up, buy a farm. As soon as they were on their feet. They had it all planned. Mum and Dad told her it'd never work. That Trevor wasn't up to it. But she—just wouldn't listen. She thought she was the only one who really knew him.

'She married him. For once, I was the one who was the good child. Mum started talking to me. Properly. Like she used to talk to Daphne, when she was still at home. So I liked it. I loathed Trevor Lamb. I kept as far away from him as I could. But in a way, I enjoyed the situation all the same. Pathetic, isn't it?' His face twisted in a grimace of self-disgust.

'I think that's why I didn't go to see her when she was sick,' he went on. He'd obviously been over and over this in his mind, Birdie thought. Pulling it out and picking at it compulsively, torturing himself. 'I told Mum I didn't want to risk bumping into Trevor by mistake. That was true, in a way.

But also, I had my nose out of joint, because Mum was running after Daphne again, instead of me. Cooking little meals for her, behind Dad's back. Worrying about her. Saying she was sicker than she should be, just with the flu. And too quiet. She thought Daphne had something worrying her. Maybe Trevor had hit her again. Or he was in trouble with the police. Something like that. I was going to be leaving home, practically, in a couple of weeks. I thought I deserved more attention. Can you believe that?'

The door flew open and a skinny boy in shorts and a t-shirt that came down to his knees, appeared.

'C'n I have the key to the toilets, Sir?' he asked, looking curiously at Birdie.

'Oh. Yes, Jonathon. Knock next time, will you? Try to remember.'

The boy ducked his head, grabbed the offered key, mumbled, and departed as rapidly as he'd come, leaving the door slightly ajar.

'You tell them, but they don't listen,' said Phillip Hewitt fussily. He pushed the door closed, then, without hesitation, began talking again, quickly slipping into the monotone of the compulsively self-absorbed.

'So, I didn't go to see Daphne. All week. Mum particularly asked me to go, that last day. Trevor had gone to Sassafras in the afternoon. He was going to pick up the car, and collect his dole money. She knew he wouldn't be home after that till the pub closed. She knew we'd be safe. She wanted me to see Daphne, see if me being there would make Daphne talk more about what was wrong. But I wouldn't go. I said I felt sick because Dad had a lamb in the shed, and he was going to kill it. I locked myself in my room. She knocked a couple of times, but I wouldn't come out. Wouldn't even answer her. She gave up in the end.'

He shook his head. 'I stayed there sulking. Went to bed hungry, out of spite. Childish spite. Wanting Mum to worry. About me, instead of Daphne. And the next morning . . .' His bottom lip trembled. '. . . In the morning, the police came. And told us. Daphne was dead. So I never saw her again.'

His big eyes filled with tears. Furiously he wiped them away with his fingers, wetting the long, thick lashes.

'I often think,' he whispered, 'that if I had gone with

Mum, like she wanted me to, if I hadn't been so selfish and self-indulgent, Daphne mightn't have died. I mean, we might have been able to persuade her to come home with us. Leave him—Trevor—for good and all. Then everything would have ben so different. I keep thinking it's all my fault. Mum knew something awful was going to happen. If I'd listened to Mum . . .'

Birdie turned her face away to give him a chance to recover himself. 'You're still assuming Trevor Lamb killed your sister,' she said crisply, looking out the window on the opposite side of the room.

'Well, he did, didn't he?' Phillip's voice trembled. 'They released him because of lack of evidence. Because they said his trial was unfair. Not because they thought he was innocent, necessarily. Of course he killed her. Who else would have done it?

If Trevor Lamb didn't . . .

Birdie ran her hands through her hair. Suddenly she felt exhausted. Wrung out. Bad enough to content even Peg McCann. 'Anyway, whoever did it you can't blame yourself, Phillip,' she said, turning back to him. Forcing herself to look into those swimming eyes. 'You must know that, really. Your mother was upset because Daphne was sick, that's all. She was probably extra concerned because of the pregnancy. If Daphne was badly morning sick as well as having the flu—'

He shook his head. 'Mum didn't know Daphne was pregnant. None of us did. Till—afterwards. I can remember feeling really strange about it. Somehow it made that marriage—which really was grotesque, you know—seem real for me, for the first time. It was as if I'd woken up from a dream, when I heard about it. I mean—to me—it meant they did it. Had sex. Of course I must have known they did, really. But I'd never really imagined it, till I heard about the baby. Then I couldn't stop thinking about it. I wrote some poems about it. Trevor Lamb and my sister, in bed together. Daphne with a big belly, swollen up with Trevor Lamb's child. Then, when it was born, some little thing with Trevor Lamb's eyes, staggering around with a runny nose and its nappy sagging, like Grace and Jason used to do, calling Annie Lamb Grandma, chewing on empty beer cans . . . It was sickening.'

He looked up at her, his face twitching, looking for her disapproval and disgust. Maybe even hoping for it.

'I can understand that,' said Birdie, very weary of this endless self-flagellation. 'You were only eighteen or something.' She glanced at her watch. 'Look, it's a quarter past nine. I'd better not hold you up.'

That list might have arrived at the post office by now, she thought. Don't want it lying around for everyone to read. Not that most people would make much sense of it.

'We start at twenty past,' Phillip Hewitt said listlessly. 'We're supposed to. But some are always late.'

'Jason Lamb won't be here to trouble you today, anyway,' said Birdie. 'He's taking another day off. Because of his uncle.'

Phillip nodded, fiddling with the papers on his table. 'Don't you want to know about last night?' he asked.

There was a knock at the door. It opened, and a freckled-nosed little girl with brown hair and a fringe poked her head into the room.

'Five minutes, Lucy,' said Phillip automatically.

She nodded, and withdrew.

'She's one of the bright ones,' he said. 'She'll do well. Anyway, don't you want to know about last night?'

Suddenly he seemed anxious to talk. Birdie suspected there was something particular he wanted to tell her. Probably something demeaning. She didn't really want to hear it. But she knew she had to encourage him. He mightn't be so forthcoming for Toby. Not that Toby was too concerned about the Hewitts any more. But he'd get around to Phillip eventually. Leaving no stone unturned.

Even worms turn.

She'd said that to Jude. So long ago, it seemed. But it was only yesterday.

'You saw what happened at the pub, didn't you?' he asked. 'You were there.'

She nodded, impatient to be gone.

'I was very drunk,' he said, hanging his head in a way she found incredibly irritating. 'I'd had an argument with my father at dinner. About the lamb. Not Trevor Lamb. The lamb he had in the shed. I asked him to let it go. Just this one. Just that night. In memory of Daphne.'

His lip twitched. 'It was stupid of me. Melodramatic.

Stupid to think he'd understand. Even mentioning Daphne was stupid. He never talks about her. He told me I was a weak-kneed little twerp. That's what he said. So I left. I went to the pub and got drunk. Then I tried to take on Trevor Lamb. Well that turned out a miserable failure. Like everything I do. I went home. My mother was there, on her own. Just sitting in the living room, in the dark. My father had stormed off to Gunbudgie. To see this woman he's got there, I suppose. Of course he wouldn't have told Mum that. But she'd have known. Imagine him leaving her alone last night. I don't know how he could have done it.'

You left her, to go and make an exhibition of yourself at the pub.

Almost immediately, as if Birdie had spoken aloud, Phillip echoed her.

'I'd left her, to go and make a fool of myself in the pub. Dad had left her, to play the big man with some prostitute. And she was sitting there in the living room by the French doors, all on her own, in the dark. The only sound was the clock ticking. It was awful.' He shuddered. 'She never sits there. If she's on her own she usually sits in the kitchen. I think she'd gone into the living room because of Daphne's picture, and because the room's full of presents Daphne gave her.'

Leda and the swan. The girl's face, lifted in helpless terror. The huge wings, bearing her down . . .

'She just sat there, when I came in. Didn't get up, or anything. She must have realised how drunk I was, because she told me to go to bed. Told me I should go to bed because when Dad got back he was going to slaughter the lamb. I said I was going to stop him. But she just looked at me. Even she knew I wouldn't have the guts.

'I went outside again and went over to the shed. Stumbled over, I suppose you'd say. The dogs went off their heads, barking. They were already excited. Always are, when there's a lamb in the shed. They know what that means. Fresh meat. The head to fight over.' His face twisted in disgust.

Birdie squirmed inwardly.

'I went into the shed, and the lamb was there. It was asleep. Just lying there asleep. It had forgotten all about its fright when it got picked out of the flock. It was quite calm.

Just like Dad wanted it to be. When a beast is killed when it's frightened the meat's tough. I looked at it. I was going to let it go. Then, as I was standing there, I thought, if it's not this one, it'll be another one. So what's the point? If I save this lamb, another lamb will die in its place. And that death will be my fault. So I just turned around and left it. I went into the house. I made Mum a cup of tea. I made her go to bed. Then I lay down on my bed and I went to sleep. Just like that. The alcohol I suppose. I usually don't fall to sleep easily.

'I woke up with a sort of shock. It was nearly half past twelve. I could hear water running in the pipes. I guess that's what woke me. I know what it meant. I got up and went into the laundry. I didn't turn on the light. There were clothes lying on the floor. A pile of them. They smelt like blood. I went outside, and over to the shed. The lamb was hanging there, skinned, dripping. I stood there and looked at it. I made myself look at it. Then I made myself go over and touch it. It was all floppy. Not like meat. Like flesh. Your own flesh.'

He turned tormented eyes on her. 'There was no point in saving it,' he muttered. 'If I had, another one would have died. It just goes on, and on, and on . . .'

Birdie's stomach was churning.

There was a furious knocking at the door. Phillip's head jerked. He ran his hand over his forehead. 'What's the time?' he muttered.

'Time for me to get out of your way,' said Birdie. 'Past time. I'm sorry, Phillip.'

'Oh, don't worry,' he said, and began to unclip his brief-case with shaking fingers. 'We're supposed to start at nine twenty. But someone's always late. Why shouldn't it be me? Just for once. And it won't hurt the kids. They don't care. They don't care about anything. They just live day to day. Eating, sleeping, playing. As if there's no tomorrow. Like the lambs.'

Birdie opened the door and pushed her way carefully through the small, jostling crowd of children waiting there.

Like the lambs.

'Bye, Miss,' called one boy, small and chunky, cheekier than the others.

'Bye,' she said, and smiled at him, grateful for his cheek, his sturdy independence, his happiness, his life.

She let herself out into the playground. The red-painted door closed behind her. She walked quickly to the road. Then, turning her back on the school, and the bell, the ghost children of the past, and the strident children of the present, she strode off in the direction of the pub, as fast as she could go.

Twenty-nine

Birdie reached the main road, and looked down towards the pub. There were a few men and women standing around on the road outside the verandah, now. Some had cameras. One man, his hair caught back in a ponytail that reached halfway down his back, was filming the pub. As Birdie watched, he turned slowly to his left, panning across the street to show the bridge, circling further to take in the cars under the pepper trees.

Just like the last time.

Birdie remembered seeing shots just like that on television news items over the last five years. During Trevor Lamb's trial, and afterwards, during the mounting campaign for his release. The cameraman could have saved himself some film. News could have used footage from the archives. Nothing in Hope's End had changed.

Jude had often been featured in the later news items. Walking along to his office with a folder or two under his arm, getting out of his car, giving a statement with microphones marked with the symbols of various radio stations pushed under his nose.

Jude. She must get to Gunbudgie to see him. Soon. As soon as she'd talked to Toby about what Phillip Hewitt had said. As soon as that fax arrived and she'd had a word with Peg McCann. As soon as . . .

She crossed the road and walked, as unobtrusively as possible, towards the pub. She saw a few of the journalists look in her direction, but they quickly lost interest. They probably recognised her as not being a local. And, trudging along with her heavy bag over her shoulder, she was plainly not one of the police either. Therefore she was of no account in their hunt for a story.

She passed the post office, and glanced involuntarily through the window. Peg McCann was dealing, thin-lipped, with two people with notebooks, and one buying what appeared to be flavoured milk and a packet of biscuits. Breakfast, morning tea or boredom? Birdie wondered. She was almost past the window when Peg's eyes flicked up and met hers. Birdie raised her eyebrows. Peg shook her head slightly. No fax had arrived yet, obviously. Birdie moved on.

She moved into the pub grounds, and walked around to the back. Sue Sweeney's door was firmly closed now. She must be in the pub, preparing for opening time. There'd be many more customers than usual today.

The back door of the pub was shut, and there was no key in the lock. Birdie knocked. After a few moments there were heavy footsteps and Floury Baker opened up, thrusting his red face forward, ready to repel any unauthorised entry. His face changed when he saw her.

'In yer come,' he said, ushering her through the door and closing it after her. 'Sorry I had to lock up. Bloody press've been driving me bonkers. Won't take no for an answer, some of 'em. Bloody vultures.'

'Is Detective-Sergeant Toby here, Floury?' asked Birdie. 'He said . . .'

'In here,' rumbled a voice from the dimness of the corridor.

'I give them the office for the morning, till they get themselves fixed up,' said Floury. 'I won't be using it, will I? Be up to me ears in boozers all day, the way it's shaping up. And they need a bit of a hand. By the look of the big bloke they've got about as many leads as a one-armed swaggie's dog. Anyhow, let Sue or me know when you're ready to move Jude's stuff. Soon as you like. Need to change the sheets and that. Be good if we could do it before opening time.'

'I'll just be five minutes. I have to see Detective-Sergeant Toby first.'

He nodded slowly. 'Bad luck about your car,' he said. 'That Lily Danger's been bad news ever since she come here. Still, good riddance to bad rubbish. She won't be back. Well's dried up round here for her, I'd say.'

'You'd think so.'

He paused. 'Been up to the school, have you? Saw you in Phil Hewitt's car. Looks shocking, doesn't he?'

Birdie murmured something noncommittal.

'Tragedy, what's happened to that family,' he mumbled. 'Bloody tragedy.'

'Birdie, you coming in here or not?' shouted Dan's voice. 'Got some news for you about your car.'

Floury patted her arm. 'There you are, love,' he said. 'Looks like you're right.'

He lumbered away towards the front of the building.

Birdie went to the office and stuck her head inside. 'What news?' she enquired.

Toby was sitting at Floury's big old desk, frowning.

'Where've you been?' he asked abruptly.

'Round and about. Chatting to the postmistress. Looking at the school. Picking up some local colour. And some info for you. Anyway, what's this about my car? Is it okay?'

'Not too bad,' he said evasively.

'What d'you mean—?'

'They had a bit of a chase. It skidded off the road. Got a few dings, apparently. Tyres might be a bit the worse for wear. One of the doors got a thump.' He straightened some papers on the desk in front of him. 'Anyhow, they've towed it back to Sassafras.'

'*Towed* it—'

'The good news is they picked up Lily. Charged her with theft of a motor vehicle, driving without a licence, driving in a manner dangerous to the public, and murder.'

'*What?!*'

'Yeah. She got them riled up enough to get their arses into gear and check her out. Seems she's been wanted in Queensland for a few years. Five years, two months, to be exact. She and a little mate kicked an old woman to death. Old bag lady. Someone sprung them putting in the final boot. The little mate got done, Lily did a runner. Anyhow, they've got her now. Trouble is, she was a juvenile at the time. Only thirteen.'

'*Thirteen?* You mean she was only thirteen when she came here? She's only eighteen now?'

'Apparently.'

'Only thirteen when she killed the old woman?'

'That's what they tell me.'

'Why did she do it?'

'Money. Poor old duck had a few bucks on her. 'Spose Lily and her mate thought they had a better right to it than she did, but the old lady didn't agree. So they decided to take it anyway, and then got a bit carried away once she was down. Lily got off with the cash when they were sprung. That's the main reason her mate dobbed her in, I'd say. Her mate was only twelve.'

Birdie felt sick.

'What's Lily's real name?'

'Leanne Dee. D for Danger, I suppose she thought. She says her father abused her as a child. 'Spose that gives her a licence to kick old ladies to death, does it? Well, some lawyer like your mate Jude'll make sure everyone thinks so, anyhow.'

'Dan—'

'Still, that's not my affair, is it? I just bring them in. Someone else gets them off. That's the game. Right?'

He stared at the wall, fiddling with the papers under his fingers, his face a blank.

'You can't generalise like that, Dan. It's not fair.'

'It's the truth.'

Birdie decided to go on the attack. It was the only way, when Dan Toby got like this.

'Dan, why didn't they pick up on this before? I mean, when Lily first got here? Surely she'd have been checked out then?'

'Yeah. Well, someone slipped up. She looked different, of course. Had long black hair, in Queensland. No tats. She must have got herself fixed up on the way here. She had the old lady's money. I'd say the local coppers didn't bother much with her. She'd only been in town a few hours. She'd been in the pub all night—well, except for going to the loo. And . . .'

'And no one really wanted to look past Trevor Lamb, anyway.' Birdie wasn't going to let him off the hook.

'Maybe a bit of that, too.' Toby rubbed his hand over his eyes, slipped it down to feel his chin. 'I need a shave.'

'You need sleep.'

'So do you. Anyway, moving right along, what did you have to tell me? How was school?'

Birdie thought of bitter remorse, a twitching lip, tortured eyes, a man storming off into the night, a woman sitting alone in the dark, a dead lamb swinging on a chain. She decided to stick to the basic issue.

'It's about Les Hewitt's alibi. According to Phillip Hewitt, that lamb was still alive after his father left for Gunbudgie, but it was dead by twelve-thirty. I'm certain Phillip wasn't lying. So unless Les Hewitt arrived back in Hope's End before he said he did—'

'He didn't. Keith Lamb's remembered he saw him at the turnoff to the highway at eleven-forty. He remembers looking at the clock in his car. Lamb was turning out, Hewitt was turning in. Hewitt confirms this. Milson just spoke to him on the phone. It takes twenty minutes to get from here to the main road turnoff. That means Hewitt couldn't have got here before midnight. So if we say Trevor Lamb was killed between eleven-forty and twelve-nineteen, and it takes fifteen or twenty minutes to slaughter a lamb . . .'

'Hewitt is out of it.'

'Right. Not that he was really in it, any more, from my point of view. Since we found out about the weapon. Anyhow, it's ironic. Keith thought he was giving himself an alibi, but he was really giving Hewitt one. Bet he'd never have opened his trap if he'd known.'

'It doesn't give Keith an alibi at all. He could still have doubled back and got to Hope's End in time.'

'Sure. And the Gunbudgie blokes are working on that. Trying to find out if anyone saw Keith's car parked on the track running up to Hope's End round about midnight. But they're getting no joy so far. And the car jack's clean. Well, I knew it would be. Though what the bloody weapon was—I'd give my right arm to get a clue on that.'

'No possibles so far?'

Toby picked up a pencil from the desk and began to draw on the back of an envelope. Question marks. 'Nothing within a bull's roar. But let's face it, how many sheds and rubbish dumps and dams and haystacks and God knows what else are there round here? We just have to keep looking. It'll take time, that's all. The pub yard alone's taking forever.'

Sue Sweeney. That's why they're looking in the pub yard. Sue.

'I didn't see anyone out there,' Birdie said aloud.

'Milson pulled them off to work on the caravan up at Lambs'. Seemed worthwhile, given Lily's history. Sorry, Leanne Dee's history. What d'you reckon?'

'Well, obviously you have to do it. But what would her motive have been? To kill Daphne, I mean. Not Trevor. I mean, she'd never even met her.'

'That's what I thought. But I had a bit of a clue when I was talking to your mate Floury Baker earlier. Lamb was buying Lily drinks, that night, I heard. Running through what was left of his dole money. Baker reckons that when Sue Sweeney asked Lamb what he was going to live on for the next fortnight, he laughed and said Daphne could take care of it. Maybe our Lily thought Daphne was a source of income. And just trotted on down the track to get it, while she was supposed to be in the ladies'. Quick bump on the head, she might have thought, and there'll be a bit of cash in my pocket again. But when she got there, saw the shack, nice and quiet, tucked away, she might have thought: I need a nice, quiet place like this to lie low in for a bit. And that Trevor Lamb's a fanciable bloke. I could do worse than him. Why don't I just get wifey out of the way? Then I can have her money, and the house, and Lamb as well. So she could have found herself a suitable weapon, and done the job.'

'That's insane. She couldn't have thought—'

'Does Lily Dee sound in the pink of mental health to you, Birdwood? Or does she sound like a sociopathic little monster who thinks that other people exist only to serve her needs?'

Birdie was silent.

'What I can't understand is why Keith Lamb put up with her for so long,' Dan went on. 'By your account she didn't exactly give him an easy time.'

'No. But he was hung up on her. And at least she stayed with him. Maybe that's how he looked at it, till it all got too much. I don't think he's the kind of man who really expects much. Hasn't got much confidence. His wife left him for another woman. And—'

'Yeah?' Toby's mouth twitched in a fascinated smirk. 'Poor bugger.'

Birdie averted her eyes abruptly. She'd been going to say, scathingly, that round here having your wife take a lesbian lover seemed to be some sort of rather amusing slur on a man's masculinity. But apparently this view wasn't confined to Hope's End.

'By the way, your boyfriend's starting to stir, they tell me,' Dan said. 'There's someone sitting with him, but Milson and I'll be off to Gunbudgie after a while, if you still want a lift. I must say I thought you'd have cadged a ride by now. You seem to be coping with your natural impatience quite well, Birdwood.'

He stuck the end of his pencil in his mouth and chewed it. 'In fact,' he added, grinning maliciously at the wall, 'if I was Jude Gregorian I'd think you'd decided you had better things to do with your time than visit him.'

'That's not fair, Dan!' she exclaimed hotly.

He shrugged. 'It's the truth.'

It's the truth.

Birdie moved to the door. 'As a matter of fact, I'm going right now,' she said, without turning around.

'What are you going to use for wheels?'

'Jude's car.'

'Oh. I see. Good thinking. And you're going right now, are you?'

'Yes.' Birdie hesitated. 'Well, as soon as I've seen Sue Sweeney, and been upstairs, and gone to the post office, and picked up Rosalie.'

'We'll end up getting there before you, Birdie. Just how keen on this cove are you, anyway?'

His guffaws of laughter followed her down the corridor.

Thirty

It didn't take long to talk to Sue. Wide-eyed and frightened, she'd decided, belatedly, to keep her own counsel. She answered Birdie's enquiries in monosyllables, then turned away and said she had to get on with her work. It was Floury who accompanied Birdie up to Jude's bedroom, unlocked the door, and helped her carry Jude's few belongings to her own room.

It felt odd, to be rifling Jude's jacket for his spare car keys, then putting the jacket on its hanger into her wardrobe. It hung there, lonely. Birdie hadn't bothered to hang any of her own clothes. It felt strange to put his bag beside hers, on the faded carpet.

Then she realised something. Of course, he would want the bag at the hospital. It would have his pyjamas in it, if he wore them. Maybe a robe, a change of clothes. And his shaving gear, and all that. It would be best to take it with her.

She felt irritated that she hadn't thought of this before. A more domestic-minded person would have thought of it instantly.

She took the jacket back out of the wardrobe, carefully folded it and slipped it through the handles of the overnight bag. Then she left her bedroom with a sense of relief. She knew it would have unsettled her, keeping Jude's things.

She lugged the bag downstairs. As she reached the dim little corridor, Sue Sweeney came hurrying from the front room.

'I'm glad I caught you. I'm sorry about before. I really know it's not your fault. I won't blame you, whatever happens,' she breathed, glancing nervously over her shoulder as if Toby might be listening from the little office. 'All you did was make me tell the truth. There's no point in me being angry about that. Whatever happens, at least I know I didn't do anything wrong.'

That's the sort of thing I would say, if I wanted to be considered innocent. To get the right people on side. That's the sort of thing I would say . . .

'Nothing's going to happen,' Birdie managed to say.

But as Sue pressed her hand and turned away her mind, somehow always and forever in some part divorced from her heart, went on flickering warnings.

Toby was nowhere in sight. She let herself out the back door, and, hampered as she was by Jude's overnight bag and jacket, walked as quickly as she could out into the road and next door to the post office.

She saw Peg McCann's nose before she saw Peg. At least, that's how it seemed.

'You leaving us after all, love?' Peg asked, peering bird-like at Jude's bag. 'Thought you were staying a few days.'

'Oh, yes. I am. This is someone else's bag.' Birdie hesitated. 'Jude's,' she added. She had this urge to tell Peg McCann nothing. But it was ridiculous to be mysterious about things that didn't matter.

'You'll be taking it to him, at the hospital. Going to see him now, are you?'

'Yes, I am. I'm using his car.' May as well tell her the lot. She'd find out anyway.

'Rosalie Lamb's trying to get to Gunbudgie. They say her brother's asking for her,' Peg remarked, still peering at the bag. Memorising exactly how it looked, working out how much it had cost, how expensive the jacket slung through its handles was, no doubt.

'Yes. I'm taking Rosalie with me. I'm supposed to be picking her up right now. I just popped in to see if my fax had arrived.'

'Oh, yes.' Peg picked up some folded sheets of paper lying on the counter, and handed them over. 'Came in about five minutes ago. Three pages. I folded them to keep them private for you, love.'

Sure. Birdie unfolded the faxed pages and glanced at the top one. A cover sheet with a bland, typed message.

Dear Ms Birdwood,
Faxed following please find the list you requested.
Kind regards,
Helen Miskin

The remaining two pages were unheaded, except for Birdie's
name and the page number. Helen Miskin had blanked out
any reference to Daphne Lamb that might have been on the
original list. Clever, discreet Helen Miskin. The perfect personal assistant. Another Madeline. Thanks to this morning's
conversation she now almost certainly disapproved of Birdie
as wholeheartedly as Madeline did. But this hadn't affected
her efficiency. No way could Peg McCann or any accidental,
unauthorised recipient of this communication have been able
to work out what it was.

Birdie glanced quickly at the listed items. Clothes, shoes,
cosmetics, photograph albums, letters, Bible . . . Whoever
had compiled this list had been punctilious. It was exhaus-
tive, right down to the smallest items: '1 hair brush, 1 pkt
wrapping paper and card, 1 straw hat.' But the possessions
were few. Pathetically few, for the daughter of the house of
Hewitt.

And the item she was looking for wasn't there. Or not
that she could see. Acutely aware of Peg's sharp eyes boring
into the top of her head, Birdie looked up, refolding the
pages. She'd study them again later.

'What you were after, is it?' asked Peg, unable to contain herself any longer.

'Yes thanks.' Birdie smiled and stuffed the refolded list
into her bag, snapping down the catch decisively, hiding it
away for good.

Gotcha, she thought, relishing the frustrated gleam in
the other woman's eyes.

But Peg simply changed tack.

'Was speaking to Dolly Hewitt earlier. Just rang to see
how she was. Phillip said she wasn't so well. She tells me you
were asking her about poor little Daphne. Says it did her
good to talk. Probably did, too. She bottles things up far too
much, Dolly. Always has.'

'You've known her a long time.' Birdie tried to sound
sympathetic but still casual. It was important that she didn't
put the woman on her guard. But it was hard to hold back.

There was something fascinating here. Something in Peg McCann's eyes when she mentioned Daphne's name. A softness, quite at odds with her normal expression.

'I've known Dolly Hewitt, Dolly Macguire as was, since she first came to Hope's End. I was her bridesmaid when she married Les.'

Birdie tried to imagine this woman as a bridesmaid, and failed.

'That was a long time ago,' said Peg sharply, as if reading her thoughts. 'Lot of water's gone under the bridge since then. You know, I stood godmother to Daphne?'

'No, I didn't know that.'

'Well, I did. It made us close. She always called me Auntie Peg. Nice for me, since I had no family of my own.'

14 November Auntie P's b'day . . .

Peg nodded, her mouth primmed as though she was determined to keep it steady. 'I said to Dolly, when she asked me to stand godmother: "It'd be an honour." And it was. A sweeter child than Daphne never walked this earth.'

Everyone loved . . .

'Mind you, I wasn't keen on the name. "Daphne?" I said to Dolly. "What do you want to give the poor little thing an old-fashioned name like that for? She won't thank you for it later. What does Les think of it?" She said he was leaving the name to her. And she liked Daphne. She said it was the name of some girl in a story. Some Greek thing. Or Roman, or something. I forget now. One of those legends, anyway. Some poor girl whose father turned her into a tree because some god was chasing her. Have you heard that one?'

Birdie nodded absently.

I like the legends . . .

'Right. "Well," I said to her, "that's a miserable sort of story to name a baby for, Dolly." And she went on with some claptrap about how beautiful it was about the girl's dad loving her so much, and not wanting her to be violated, and I said, "Well, if you ask me, Dolly, he had a hide. If I had to make the choice, and please God I never will, I'd rather be raped than turned into a tree any day."

'She just laughed. Said I didn't understand. Well, maybe I didn't. Anyway, she stuck with the name. Very determined woman, Dolly, about some things. And Daphne didn't seem to mind. Even as a teenager, and you know what they're like. Said she thought the story was romantic. I can't see the romance in it myself. But there you are.'

She sighed. 'Well, we were all happier in those days. Town had a bit more life, seemed to me. Daphne'd come in for a chat most days. Dolly too, to pick up the mail, buy little bits and pieces. But she never comes in now. Never comes into town. So I never see her. She may as well be in another country. And she's just across the way. See, I don't like bothering her at night when Les and Phillip are home. She's got her hands full with them. And in the day I've got this place to look after. We talk on the phone, of course. But it's not the same.'

The door opened and a red-haired woman came in, darting a curious look at Birdie as she moved to the counter beside her. Peg darted behind the screen and came out with an envelope and a postcard. She handed them to the woman.

'There you are, Freda. Something from Kristin, by the look of it. Beautiful beach, isn't it?' She turned to Birdie. 'Freda's daughter's in Bali,' she told her.

The other woman nodded, apparently unworried by this wholesale discussion of her private affairs. 'Bull never came in yesterday, Freda,' Peg went on. 'Too much excitement going on next door, I'd say. I saw him going, but I was serving, and by the time I got out he was at the bridge. I called, but he didn't hear me.'

'Came home full as a boot,' said Bull Trews' wife resignedly. 'I said to him, "You shouldn't be allowed out, William Trews. You're a menace to society. And you forgot the post. There might have been something from Kristin." And, there you are, there was.' She frowned and slapped the postcard against her arm, in a way that augured badly for Bull Trews' immediate future.

Peg clucked sympathetically. 'Like children sometimes, aren't they?'

'Worse than some children,' said Freda Trews grimly, and departed.

'Poor woman,' said Peg McCann, shaking her head at Birdie. 'There are times when I thank the good Lord I'm single.'

'Everyone around here collects their mail from you, do they, Peg?' asked Birdie. 'There's no proper delivery?'

'Not for Hope's End. Mail for Hope's End comes in to me on the Gunbudgie bus. The one the high school kids get home on. People come and pick it up.' She paused. 'Nothing wrong with that,' she then added, somewhat belligerently. 'Works fine. There's usually someone from a family in town at four o'clock. Meeting the bus kids. The men coming in to the pub after work. It's no problem for them. No one's ever complained.'

'Sounds fine to me,' Birdie hastened to assure her.

Mail for Hope's End comes in to me . . .

'There's not much these days. Only takes a few minutes to sort.'

'Did Daphne and Trevor Lamb get much mail?' Birdie asked, on impulse.

'Not much. The electricity bill. Those letters mail-order people send you till you're nearly mad, once you're on the mailing list. Birthday cards. Christmas cards—for Daphne, of course. Trevor Lamb never got anything like that.'

Letters mail-order people send you, once you're on the mailing list. Birthday cards. . . . Birthday . . .

'Ever any packages?' Birdie gripped the edge of the counter.

'Sometimes a parcel. Daphne liked to send away for things she saw in magazines. Like her mother. But Dolly's stopped all that now.'

Her mouth drooped.

Life was happier then . . .

'Did Daphne get any packages—just before she died?'

'There was one. I remember it, because it was the first one she'd had for a long time, and she'd been waiting for it. She wouldn't tell me what it was. Said it was a surprise. But I thought it was probably something for her mother. Dolly's birthday's in February, you know.'

'Yes, I know.'

February 16 Mum's b'day.

'I thought to myself, when I saw it, where'd you get the money to pay for that, Daphne, you poor little thing? She didn't have two pennies to rub together by then. I knew that. Where she got the money from I do not know.'

I do, Birdie thought.

Sold it all, bit by bit, except for one diamond ring . . . one diamond ring . . .

Daphne gave it to me, for my birthday ... took the money out of her bank account ...

'Do you remember exactly when it came? The package?'

'Oh, I couldn't say, love. Not after all this time. You couldn't expect me to. It's been five years.' Peg screwed up her face, nevertheless, obviously thinking back. It was clearly a matter of pride with her to have at her fingertips all the facts about Hope's End that anyone might require. She was so absorbed in her task, in fact, that she even neglected to ask why Birdie wanted to know. Pride had taken the place of curiosity.

'It was a Friday,' she said finally. 'The pub was full. I remember thinking, here's the parcel Daphne was waiting for. And she's in bed, sick. Wonder whether that no-good husband of hers'll be in to collect the mail? He never bothered, usually. I thought, he'll be in the pub for sure. Maybe I should go in and give it to him. But I don't like doing that. Then I saw him coming out and I went out as and gave it to him. He just grunted like the pig he was. As usual. But I thought, well, at least that'll cheer poor Daphne up, and I didn't say anything. I just went back inside.'

'Daphne died the following Thursday,' said Birdie, following her own train of thought.

'Yes,' said Peg McCann. 'Poor little love.' She pursed her lips. 'Say what you will, that man killed that girl. I've always said it, and I'll never swerve from it. Who else would kill Daphne Hewitt but that man? That pig of a man? I can't think of anyone else who'd want to harm a hair on her head. Everyone loved Daphne.'

Everyone loved Daphne.

Thirty-one

'It was good, when we were little kids.' Rosalie sat motionless, staring out the window through a mist of dust, as the hills, scrub and paddocks slipped by. 'You mightn't believe it, to look at us now, but it was good.'

'I believe it,' said Birdie, watching the road, easing her foot off the accelerator. Jude's car was very different to drive from her own. Incredibly smooth and obedient. It was easy to speed. Several times she'd been astonished by the figure on the speedo. And with these bends to contend with . . .

I'll be able to get back to Hope's End in a couple of hours. Then I'll talk it over with Dan. He'll decide what to do about it . . .

'We'd play, and eat, and sleep. Keith, and Cecilia, and Trevor and me. Sometimes Brett, but he was older, and didn't always want to come. Sometimes Punchy, but he was younger, and just tagged along. We'd climb trees, make cubbies, eat apples down by the creek. Play by the shack, watch the old possum who lived in a hole high up in a tree there, down along the track, cook sausages on a camp fire in the clearing, eat them half-raw, play murder in the dark in the scrub till Mum yelled for us to come home. That's all we did. That's all we thought about. We never thought about getting old, or dying, or having children of our own, or anything like that. We never thought where the money came from. We just . . . lived each day, as it came.'

Like the lambs . . .

The car jerked as Birdie braked too suddenly. 'Oh, sorry,' she muttered.

'That's all right.' Rosalie was abstracted, lost in the past.

Birdie moistened her dry lips. 'Rosalie,' she said off-handedly, 'it'll make the trip longer, but I'm going to go to Sassafras before Gunbudgie, if you don't mind. I want to call in to the Sassafras garage. My car's there. I want to ask the guy about it.'

'Frank Tellman. He's a bastard.'

'Is he?'

Rosalie stirred, looked out the window. 'Oh, I don't know. Trev always said so. He had his car in there often enough. He reckoned Frank was a rip-off artist. I don't know.'

The country rolled by. Hills, knots of sheep, clumps of gum trees, wire fences . . .

'Did you always believe what Trevor told you?'

'I suppose I did. He was always so positive, I'm never sure of anything.'

'I think it makes sense. Not to be too sure of anything.'

'Maybe.' Rosalie sighed. 'But it makes life harder.'

'How's Grace?' Birdie kept her eyes on the road, her hands steady on the wheel. But she was alert to the sudden tension in the body of the woman beside her.

'Oh, Grace is okay. It was a shock for her. And it's the second time it's happened.'

'She was with you when you found Daphne, wasn't she?'

'Yes. Jason was too. But Jason's tougher. Grace—well, maybe you wouldn't think it to look at her now—but she was a very gentle little girl. In a way, she reminded me of myself, when I was that age. Easily led. Wanting to please. You know?'

'Yes.'

'I don't suppose you've ever been like that? Easily led? Wanting to please?'

'No,' Birdie grinned. 'I think when I was a kid I was more like Jason. Conceited. A know-all. Into everything. A pain in the arse.'

'You like him.' Rosalie's voice was listlessly amused.

'Yes, I do, actually. Against my better judgement.'

Birdie glanced across at the woman sitting beside her. She was smiling faintly. Looking out the window.

'Rosalie, what you told the police about last night . . .'

The woman's head jerked around. 'What about it?'

'You weren't at home in bed, were you? Grace's screaming didn't wake you. You were out before that.'

'No, I wasn't,' said Rosalie sharply. Her cheeks red-
dened. 'I wasn't. I was at home in bed. Like I said. Are you
calling me a liar?'

'I guess so.' Birdie stared straight ahead, watching the
road, keeping her hands steady on the wheel. 'I know you
were out.' She decided to take a risk. Nothing ventured,
nothing gained. 'I know you were on the track to Trevor's
shack just before two a.m.'

Rosalie brought her hands together with a smack. 'How
can you possibly know—? It isn't true!'

'Yes, it is. This morning you talked about me carrying a
candle. How did you know I was, if you didn't see me? By
the time I saw you at the shack later I was carrying a torch.'

'Someone must have told me!'

'No. No one knew. Only the person hiding in the scrub
while I was walking towards the shack could have known.
You were that person. Why were you hiding?'

It was almost too easy. Rosalie buried her face in her
hands. 'Have you told the police?'

'Not yet. Tell me what happened.'

'I didn't kill him.'

'I didn't say you did. I just need to know the truth.'

'You won't believe me.'

'I might. You may as well try it.'

Rosalie pushed back her hair. 'It had been a terrible
night,' she began in a low voice. 'After we got home Lily and
Keith fought, and Keith went off in the car dead drunk. I
was worried about him. Jason was all hyped up, hard to
settle. And then Grace and I had a really bad argument.'

'About Trevor?'

Rosalie nodded. 'She—Grace—was fascinated with him.
Thought he was wonderful. Exciting. She couldn't stop talking about him. She and I sleep in the same room. I wanted
her to get undressed and go to bed, but she wouldn't. She
wanted to go down and see Trev, at the shack. She said if I
didn't let her go she'd wait till I was asleep, and go anyway.
She wanted to talk to him on her own. Ask him about gaol.
See the computer. He'd offered to show it to her anytime, she
said. I told her she was being stupid. I told her he wasn't
wonderful. He was dangerous, and conceited, and a liar, and

bad, and she had to keep away from him. She got really angry. She screamed at me. I hardly recognised her. Her face
was all twisted up, and she was looking at me as though she
hated me. She said I was jealous, because I was Trevor's twin
and I thought no one else should get close to him. And I
was jealous of her because she was young and pretty and
I was fat, and had stretch marks, and my boobs hung down.'

Rosalie took a shuddering breath. 'I slapped her. In the
face,' she whispered. 'I've never done a thing like that before
in my life. It was awful.'

'What happened then?'

'I went out of the room. Into the living room. I could
hear her crying. I took Jason back to bed. He'd come to see
what was going on, of course. Nothing Jason likes better
than a fight. I tucked him in, and ticked him off and by the
time I'd finished there wasn't a sound from the bedroom. I
thought, she's gone. Run away. Or gone down to the shack,
like she said she would. But when I went in she was in bed,
asleep. Fast asleep. All curled up. With her hand under her
cheek. And the tears on her face still wet. Like a little child.
Like a baby. I saw how young she was. I couldn't believe
what I'd done. I thought, she'll never forgive me. Things'll
never be the same between us, ever again.

'I changed, and crawled into bed myself. I was so tired.
But I couldn't sleep. It was hot. I could hardly breathe. My
head felt as if it was full of cottonwool. Thick, and heavy.
Any my heart kept jumping in my chest. After a long time I
got up again. Grace hadn't moved. She was sound asleep. I
put on some clothes, and went out. Into the air. I walked out
the front gate, onto the road.'

'Do you know what time it was?' asked Birdie quietly.

'No. I didn't look at the time. I didn't care about it. But
it was very dark. I couldn't see a light anywhere.'

'The shack was dark? The Hewitts' house was dark?'

'There was no light anywhere. I wanted to walk, but I
didn't want to go near the shack. The thought of Trevor
made me sick. I was sure Sue Sweeney was probably with
him, anyway. I didn't know about Lily then. Didn't know
she'd already been down there. That Punchy had followed
her. That must have all happened while I was getting Jason
to bed the first time, and then fighting with Grace.'

'Where did you go?'

'Along the road. Down to the main street. I thought I'd go as far as the bridge, then double back. I thought it might help me sleep. I'd got as far as the pepper trees opposite the pub, then suddenly the pub door opened, and you came out, with that candle.' Suddenly Rosalie shivered. 'It gave me a terrible fright. The light was shining up into your face. It looked really weird. You started walking across the road. I thought, what's she doing? Then I thought maybe you were going to get something from your car, so I backed off and slipped under the pepper trees, onto the track.

'I thought you wouldn't see me there. But you came straight for me. I realised you were going to come into the track yourself. I just panicked. I crept further in, going as fast as I could without making a noise. You kept coming. I got round the back of one of the trees and crouched down. There wasn't anything else I could do. I didn't want to meet you there.'

'Why not, Rosalie?'

'Well—' Rosalie fixed her eyes on the road ahead. 'I thought . . . I thought you were going to see Trevor. I saw him say goodbye to you at the door, at the pub. I thought maybe he'd . . . said something to you. Arranged a meeting. You know.'

'I see,' said Birdie, rather disconcerted. 'So you hid. And when I heard you, and called out, you just didn't answer. Did you follow me? See me find Jude?'

'Oh, no. Soon as you turned the bend in the track I got out of there, as fast as I could. I heard you call out, 'Where are you?' I thought you were calling to me. I went through the scrub to the pepper trees, then I ran up the road back towards home. I felt as though I was going to faint or something. I thought you were going to chase me. But once I reached the turnoff I realised you weren't. So I slowed down. I started walking. Then I came to the road that goes along to the school. And suddenly I thought, I'll go there. To the school. It's quiet there. I can sit down. No one will know where I am. I'll be safe.'

A smile trembled on her lips. 'Silly, isn't it? Why would I be safer there than anywhere else? And I wasn't in any danger, was I? But that's what I thought. So I went along to the school, and sat under a tree, on one of the benches. Where

I used to have lunch when I was little. And I did feel safe. I really did.'

Birdie thought of the tiny sepia schoolhouse, the grassy playground. She hadn't found them comforting. Only rather depressing. But then, she hadn't grown up here. She hadn't played basketball on that patch of asphalt, thrown her backpack down on those steps, played clapping games at recess on the grass. Time after time. With everything familiar, easy, uncomplicated.

It was good, when we were kids . . .

'I sat there for quite a while,' said Rosalie. 'I don't think I really thought about anything. Then I sort of came to, and realised I should get home. In case Grace woke up. So I walked out of the playground. I wasn't watching where I was going, and I bumped into the old bell, in the dark. It made a noise.'

'I think I heard it.' Birdie remembered the sound, the single chiming note, in the darkness.

'It seemed terribly loud to me. I was scared people might wake up, but no lights went on. So I just wandered off, taking my time. I've wondered since if the bell woke Grace. Whether she heard the bell, and got up straight away, and went out. Because only a little while afterwards, just as I was coming into the yard of the house, she started screaming. Down at the shack.'

Rosalie was breathing fast, kneading and pushing her hands together in her lap. 'I could see there was a light on down there now. And there was this screaming. I knew it was Grace. And I ran, I ran . . . oh, I was so scared. All I could think of was getting down there. I thought, "If he's hurt a hair on her head. If he's touched her. If he's said anything to her. I'll kill him." '

She broke off, and her hand flew to her mouth.

'It doesn't matter,' said Birdie. 'It's all right, Rosalie. He was long dead by then.'

Rosalie's head drooped. 'Dead,' she said. She closed her eyes. 'Yes. He was dead. Thank God.'

They reached the place where the dirt of the track met the bitumen of the highway.

Here Les Hewitt met Keith Lamb. Keith turning out, Les turning in.

Birdie stopped, then moved onto the highway, turning to the right.

'Grace was Trevor's child, wasn't she, Rosalie?' she asked quietly.

Rosalie didn't move.

'How long did it go on? A year? Two? Three?' Birdie kept her eyes on the road.

There was a long silence.

'No one knows.' Rosalie's voice was a breath, the barest whisper.

'Not even Annie?'

'No.'

'Not even Grace?'

'No!' This time the voice was stronger, louder. 'She'd be the last one—'

'Did Trevor know?'

'Oh, yes.' The voice was bitter now. 'He knew. He thought it was funny.'

'How did you manage? Didn't your mother ask who the father was?'

Rosalie shrugged. 'Oh, yes. But I just wouldn't say anything. She never really pushed me. She thought it was just—one of those things. She never knew what Trevor had made me do, down in that shack. How I used to fight, and struggle, and then give up and let him do it to me. And every time I'd come home and I'd think, never again. Next time I won't let him do it. But then I would. So I knew I was bad. He'd always say I made him do it. That he couldn't help it. And I really believed that, in a way. I thought it was up to me to stop it. But what could I do?'

Tears brimmed over in her eyes, and trickled down her cheeks. 'What could I do? I couldn't tell anyone. I felt so wicked, and ashamed. Then I found I was pregnant. I didn't even know what was wrong with me at first. Why my periods had stopped. Why I was getting fat. It was Trevor who told me. And from that moment on he never touched me again. He said mothers made him sick. And besides, he had better things to do than mess around with his own sister. So that was that. I was only fifteen, and pregnant. I'd never even had a boyfriend. I didn't even know where the baby came out when it was born. I think I thought it was your belly button. Even though we'd had classes at school. I think I just hadn't listened.'

She looked down at her hands. 'Anyway, Mum told me, once she found out. And she looked after me. And when Grace was born, she was such a pretty baby. Like a little doll. Of course, I was a baby myself. I didn't know what to do with her. But Mum helped me. Showed me what to do. She'd had so many she could do it all blindfolded, drunk or sober. She liked it. She liked having babies around.'

'And you've never told her, or anyone? All these years?'

'No. At first I was too scared and ashamed for myself. But by the time Grace was three or four, I'd realised what it'd mean to her if anyone found out. If I'd told Mum, for example, she just wouldn't have been able to keep her mouth shut. Everyone would have known, in the end. When Keith's wife ran off with Cheryl Baker, the year after Trevor married Daphne, the whole town knew all the gory details in five minutes. Keith tried to shut Mum up, but it was hopeless. Floury just had to put up with it, like Keith. Trevor egged Mum on. He loved the whole thing.'

Floury Baker's wife . . .

Trevor Lamb, sneering in the bar.

Floury hates my guts . . . because I'm twice the man he is, and he knows it. Because he's like Keith. Can't hold a woman, however much of a slag she is . . .

'I thought Grace's friends would think she was a freak, if the word ever got out, about Trevor. I thought that *she'd* think she was. That no one would ever want to marry her. Maybe that welfare would come and take her away. And I loved her so much. She was the only thing . . .'

Her voice trailed away. She turned her head to look out of the window again, biting her lips.

'Weren't you afraid Trevor would tell, Rosalie?'

She shook her head. 'Not then. He was too smart. He knew his girlfriends wouldn't like it. And once he started really making headway with Daphne Hewitt, there was no way he'd risk it. So I thought I was safe all round. Because by then I'd had Jason, and that sort of took the attention away from Grace. Everyone was too busy wondering who his father was to worry any more about hers. Keith had married Yvonne by then, and they had two kids. Cecilia had left. Dad and Johnny had been killed. Everything was different.'

'Who was Jason's father?'

'Just some guy. A contract fencer, who came to work at Hewitts' for a couple of weeks. After he left he rang me up a few times, from various places, but that petered out after a while. He never came back. He never knew about the baby. Didn't even know I could get pregnant. I told him I was on the pill. He was a nice guy. But he didn't love me or anything. He just liked me. Said I was pretty.' Rosalie smiled bitterly. 'He wouldn't want to see me now, would he?'

'How did you get on with Daphne, Rosalie? I mean, what did you think of her?'

'She was okay.' Rosalie changed position restlessly. 'Oh, I mean, she was nice. You couldn't say anything against her.'

'But . . .?'

'Sometimes she used to irritate me.'

'Why?'

'Because she was so—I don't know—she thought she knew about things. She always tried to fix things. Stop Punchy fighting. Fix up the shack. Get Trevor to stop drinking and get a job. Get things organised. She should have realised—you can't change anything. But she never did. It was like she didn't know what the world was really about. Just refused to admit it. Never gave up.'

She shrugged and looked sideways at Birdie. 'I'm a bitch,' she said. 'What I'm really saying is that she was too good. She was always nice to me, and the kids. I'm sorry she's dead.'

They began passing the houses on the outskirts of Sassafras.

Somewhere here, the police sighted Lily.

Birdie slowed the car, looking for the garage on the other side of the highway. She saw it, put on her indicator light, and prepared to turn across the road.

'You won't tell about Grace, will you?' asked Rosalie. Her voice was flat and colourless. 'You have to promise. Now Trevor's dead, there's no one else . . .'

Birdie swung the car across the road and into the garage driveway. She could see her own car in the workshop. Crumpled door, smashed-in nose—a mess.

The car insurance. Was it paid up? Birdie seemed to remember that it was one of those bills she still hadn't posted. One of the bills with URGENT stamped across them in red.

What if they wouldn't pay? She thought rapidly. She probably didn't have enough in her cheque account to cover this. She might have to leave the car here, till she could borrow some money. From Jude. Or her father. Or even, heaven help us, Toby. What a situation. Her car in hock. She was as bad as . . .

Couldn't even bail out his bloody car, the last time it cracked up . . .

'Grace'll leave soon,' murmured Rosalie. 'She hates me. Hasn't spoken to me since last night. She'll go. And then there's no reason for her ever, ever to know who her father was. Or for anyone else to know. Unless you tell.'

. . . in the garage at Sassafras for over a week . . .

Birdie stopped the car. There was a ringing in her ears.

'Unless you tell. Birdie?'

'I won't tell, Rosalie,' Birdie said slowly. 'If Grace ever finds out, it won't be because of me.'

Is truth the same as justice?

'Do you promise?'

'Yes.' Birdie sat for a moment with her hands on the wheel. She was aware of the garage proprietor slouching unhurriedly towards her. Aware that there were things she had to do, say, ask. One thing, especially. But she couldn't move. She felt as though all the energy in her body was draining away. Through her feet, down through the floor of the car, pooling on the concrete below.

'Are you all right?' she heard Rosalie ask. 'Is there anything I can do?' The voice seemed to be coming from a long way away.

She felt her own lips move. Heard her own voice, thin and strange. 'I'll be okay in a minute. It's all right. There's nothing you can do. Nothing you can do.'

Thirty-two

The man lifted his hand in farewell as Birdie turned back onto the road, and drove away. He didn't move. After a minute or so she glanced in the rear-vision mirror. He was still standing there, looking after her.

I have done this before . . .

But this time, Rosalie was with her. This time, when she reached the sign that pointed down into the earth, she drove past it, and on.

Only yesterday . . . I came here for the first time. Trevor Lamb was still alive. I'd never met any of these people . . . only yesterday . . .

Rosalie fidgeted, uncomfortable in the silence. 'What did he say?'

Birdie glanced at her blankly.

'How's your car?'

'Oh. It won't take as long as I thought. He'll just do the basics, so I can drive. He'll do it today. I can get the rest done in Sydney.'

'That's good.'

'Yeah.'

'It only takes ten minutes to Gunbudgie from here. From the Hope's End road.'

'I know.'

The road fell away, steeply, on the right. The occasional safety post stuck up like a tooth in a gappy mouth.

Somewhere along here, Keith went off the road. Maybe there. Or there . . .

Into Gunbudgie. A proper town, on its outskirts draggled ugliness: the abattoirs, billboards selling beer, trucks, underwear, a car yard complete with plastic flags in red, white and blue, drive-in stalls hung with sheep and cattle skins, fake boomerangs, straw hats and t-shirts emblazoned with the legend: 'I got it in Gunbudgie.'

What now? Does it really mean what I think it means? How can I be sure?

Cruising past houses, weatherboard and corrugated iron, red-brick and tile. Slowing, into Main Street. The old part of town. Gracious shopfronts with shady awnings stretching over the footpath. A town hall. A park. Trees down the centre of the road. Cars parked nose to kerb. People shopping.

'Where's the hospital?' asked Birdie.

'To the right. At Parkin Street. There. Where the lights are.'

Past a supermarket, a hardware superstore, a petrol station, a motel. The hospital loomed up ahead, neat lawns and bright annuals, the odd tamed tree.

Into the car park, neatly stopping within a yellow-marked space. Through the swinging glass doors. The hospital smell, strong in the nostrils. People in pale blue and white, at home, efficient. People in ordinary clothes, hesitant, or resigned. Patients in wheelchairs, patients on walking frames and crutches. Patients perambulating in tartan or flowered dressing-gowns and new-looking slippers. A flower stall, coffee stop, signs, vinyl-covered chairs, the dinging sound of the lifts.

Mr Gregorian, Mr. Lamb. Ward D. Fourth floor, turn right. A frankly curious look from the receptionist. It was a small hospital.

Up in the lift. To the fourth floor. Turn right. Enquire at the nurses' station.

For Rosalie, a smile. Rosalie. Sister. Family. He'll be so pleased. He's been asking for you. Right along there. I'll show you. For Birdie, a half-smile. Verity Birdwood. Friend. Doctor's with him at present. Would you mind waiting?

There was a small sitting area beside the nurses' station. Square, vinyl-covered chairs in rows. Magazines, and a few battered children's books.

Birdie dipped into *Floppy in Bunnytown*, moved on to a *Bulletin* published the year she left school, escaped into a pile of 'homemaker' magazines, soft at the corners but rather less ancient and still retaining some of their former glamour.

Donated by a grateful patient, perhaps. Or by a nurse finally sick of renovating.

Birdie glazed over, flicking through the impossible pages. Ads for carpet, bathroom fittings, paint and door handles mixed and matched with editorial heavy on the photographs. Every photograph with its indoor plant in the foreground, its perfect roomscape in the back. Not an old biro, an unpaid bill, a grotty paperback or a lamb's head anywhere to be seen. 'High Style by the Sea', 'Country Looks for City Cousins', 'Quick-Fix Tricks', 'Bold, Bright and Beautiful': '. . . this singing yellow living room brings a breath of spring to gloomy winter days . . .' What does it do in the summer, when you've got a headache? Maybe people who read these magazines never got headaches.

And suddenly, there it was. It would have been so easy to miss it. It was the title, the name, that made her stop. That, and the photograph.

'Miss Birdwood?'

This exquisite new limited edition acquisition to the Legendary Heroes collection can be yours. Poignantly cast in genuine bronze, to dignify any bedroom, study or living room . . . a lasting pleasure, the perfect gift for someone you love.

'Miss Birdwood?'

The girl, pleading face uplifted, delicate hands outstretched . . .

A hand touched her shoulder. She looked up, startled.

'You can go in, now, Miss Birdwood.' The nurse's young, good-humoured face was slightly impatient. She had a lot to do.

Birdie held up the magazine. 'Could I keep this?'

The girl looked doubtful. 'They're for visitors,' she pointed out. 'To read. While they're waiting.'

'Here.' Birdie fumbled in her bag, pulled out some money. 'Buy another one to replace it. Could you?'

'I guess so. Sure.' The nurse took the money, glanced covertly at the magazine open on Birdie's knee. 'You know that's over five years old, don't you?' she said tactfully. 'I mean, offers and things—they'd be closed by now.'

'Oh, yes, I know. That's okay.'

Birdie flipped the magazine shut and stood up, tucking it under her arm.

'He's in 5D,' said the nurse, as if reminding her what she had come for.

'Thanks.'

'There's a policeman with him. They say he's got to stay, even while visitors are there. Sorry about that.'

'It's all right. I just want to see him.'

'He's very sleepy. Still doped up. He won't make much sense, but he'll know you're there.' The girl looked more closely at Birdie's face, then put a hand on her arm. Acting on a professional judgement, perhaps. 'You won't be frightened, will you? He'll come good in a day or two.'

'I understand.'

Walking to room 5D, Jude's bag heavy in her hand. The sleeve of his jacket, trailing, brushing her jeans as she walked. The brain, like something outside herself, working, considering alternative options in order, rejecting them, one by one.

This isn't the time. Stop thinking. Just think about Jude.

But she had no control over the process. It went on without her.

The doorway. The small room, slightly dimmed by a blind pulled two-thirds down. Jude lying, white, in a stainless-steel bed. His leg elevated, in plaster. Tubes running into his nose, into his arm. In the corner of the room, a man in a suit, reading a car magazine. He looked up, nodded to her and returned to his reading, effacing himself.

Birdie put down the bag, went to the bed. Looked. Touched his still hand lying on the white sheet.

'Jude,' she said softly. 'It's Birdie.'

His fingers moved under hers, turned and held on. His eyelids fluttered. Opened halfway. It seemed a struggle, as though they were very heavy.

'How are you feeling?' she asked. Stupid question.

The lips moved.

'Fell,' he slurred. 'Leg.'

'Yes. But you're okay now. Don't worry about anything.'

The eyes closed again. But he held her hand. And the lips moved again. She bent down, to catch the words. Out of the corner of her eye she saw the man in the corner look up.

'How long?' mumbled Jude. 'Hospital.'

'Not long. Only since last night. I would have come be-fore, Jude, but I was . . .'

Was what? Too busy? Too busy tracking down a mur-derer to take the time.

He'd drifted away again. His breathing was even. The grip on her fingers loosened.

'Didn't say anything, did he?' murmured the man in the corner.

'No. He just wanted to know how long he'd been here.'

'He's been trying to say a name,' said the man. 'Just mumbling, like he was just then. I couldn't catch it. What's your first name again?'

'He calls me Birdie.'

He shook his head. 'Don't think it was that,' he said. 'Anyhow, he'll come good. We'll get it eventually.' He went back to his magazine.

Birdie stood by the bed, leaning over a little uncomfort-ably, crowded against the metal bedside cabinet. She could have pulled her fingers free and straightened up. But she didn't want to move.

It was very quiet. Outside the room there were sounds. Inside the room there was only breathing, the occasional rus-tle of a page turning.

The eyes watched the sleeping face. Fingers touched still fingers. One part of the brain, mechanical, sorted data. Times. Places. People. Facts. Estimations. Probabilities. The other part remembered.

She walks, the candle flickering, the shadows black. She's afraid. She hears a groan, and runs. Into the avenue of trees. Nearly missing the crumpled body lying at the side of the track. Because the candle light is dim in that darkness. If she'd had her torch she would have seen him. It's only small, the torch. Small enough to be hidden in the shadow of his twisted leg. But still powerful enough for that. When she switches it on, later, she's comforted. It pushes back the darkness.

When she switches it on . . .

Ahead, the shack glows with yellow light. The light spills into the clearing through the open door. But on the track, only the torch pierces the darkness. There is darkness behind, at the pub, where Floury Baker and Sue Sweeney huddle in their separate rooms. There is darkness to the

*right, beyond the creek, where the Hewitts sleep, or lie
awake. There is darkness to the left, through the bush, up
the hill, where the Lambs do likewise. Except for Rosalie,
sitting on the bench in the old schoolyard, finding comfort,
of a sort. And Keith, speeding to hospital in the ambulance
meant for Jude.*

Only the torch pierces the darkness.

*She is still afraid. But she has no reason to fear. Whatever happened here happened hours ago. While she sat waiting in her room. While dogs barked. While a lamb was
dying . . .*

Birdie sat very still. Looking inward. At a name. The
one name left, from a list of names. She felt cold.

The man on the bed stirred. His fingers moved,
pressing hers.

'I'm here, Jude.'

Again his heavy eyelids lifted. He blinked, trying to
force his eyes to focus on hers. And finally managing it,
looking deep. Too deep. She felt a flutter of panic. It was too
soon. She wasn't ready.

'Don't try, Jude. Don't try to talk. Do anything. There's
plenty of time.'

'Birdie. You know.'

She couldn't lie to him. 'Yes, I know.'

He sighed, holding her gaze.

'Toby?'

'Not yet.'

Again he licked his lips. 'I can't do it. You have to.
Toby—will do what you say. Go back. Do it. You. Before
anyone else is . . .'

His eyes began to close again. He fought against it, tossing his head in frustration.

'You don't have to do anything, Jude. Don't worry any
more. Don't worry about anyone else. It'll be all right. Just
sleep.'

His grip tightened on her fingers.

'Tell her I'm sorry. I didn't know. Promise. You.'

'I'll do it, Jude. I will.'

He relaxed, lying back with a sigh. After a moment his
breathing changed. He was slipping back into sleep.

The man in the corner had stood up, clutching his
magazine.

'What's happening?'

'He wants me to do something for him. That's all. I'm going now. Back to Hope's End.'

Jude's lips moved.

'Sorry, Birdie. Sorry I can't . . .'

The man came over to the bed.

'He's talking a lot. Didn't say who conked him, did he?'

'No.'

Jude mumbled. The man bent down, screwing up his face in concentration.

'There,' he whispered. 'He's saying it again. That word. Or name, whatever it is. Can you catch it?'

Birdie slipped her fingers away from Jude's. She bent and kissed his forehead.

Jude moved, sighed, spoke.

'There! That's it! Did you catch it?'

Birdie straightened up. 'Yes,' she said, looking away from his eager, excited face. 'It was, "Daphne".'

Thirty-three

It was easy to tell which tree it was. There was still a mark at its base where Jude's body had lain. The young constable climbed. He was still just a boy, lithe and agile. It was no trouble for him.

'There's something here!' His excited shout was muffled. He was leaning around to the back of the trunk, peering into a cavity they couldn't see.

'Be careful, Creel,' growled Dan Toby. He looked up, frowning. His mouth was set. Beside him, Birdie waited.

'My husband's out.'

The woman's hands gripped the waistband of her apron.

'He's coming. We saw him in town. He's on his way. We'll wait out here if you like.'

'No. That's all right. Come in. You'll have to excuse the mess.'

They walked down the silent hallway, into the sitting room where the clock ticked, the dust motes swirled.

You don't have to come, Birdie.

I promised.

'Please sit down.'

The small hands pulled at the apron strings. The apron was taken off, folded, put aside. The dress underneath was blue.

'What's happened?'

'Wouldn't you rather wait until your husband gets here? It might be—'

'No!'

On the table by the French doors Leda crouched,

looking around in terror as the great wing covered her. On the bookcase, Narcissus stood captured by his own reflection. On the mantelpiece, snakes writhed on Medusa's severed head. And Pandora knelt, everlastingly opening the box that would unleash evil on the world.

Birdie looked beyond them, as Toby's voice began. She saw a box, in Milson's gloved hands. Still complete with twisted tabs of tape and the name and address label, stained by rain and dirt.

Mrs Daphne Lamb
c/– Post office
Hope's End NSW

She saw the bronze figure, wrapped roughly in the bubble wrap that had once held it secure. Saw the plastic fall away. The figure was stained and clotted with dark blood. Some new. Some old. But still the shape was clear. The girl, frozen in flight, hands outstretched, pleading face uplifted, while leaves sprouted from the gnarled trunk her soft body was becoming, and lifted to the sun. Daphne.

This exquisite new limited edition acquisition to the Legendary Heroes collection . . . a lasting pleasure, the perfect gift for someone you love.

February 16. Mum's b'day.

The diamond ring is sold. In secret, so the husband won't know, and object. The special gift is ordered. Then the girl waits, impatient for it to arrive. She's given her mother something similar before. And then it had been a great success. But this is even better. She hasn't been able to resist it. The legend she was named for. The legend her mother loves. She will give her the gift. On her birthday. Then she will tell her about the baby. That will be the right time to tell her.

There is little money. Less all the time. Several times over the next few weeks she almost regrets what she has done. But when she thinks of her mother's pleasure, her doubts disappear.

She becomes ill. A bad dose of flu. Worse, because of the heat. And because of the nausea that comes on her morning and evening. She becomes weak, and listless. Has to stay in bed. Can't go to town to collect the post, or shop. But her mother visits. Brings her things to eat, makes her bed, washes her face, makes her comfortable. She is filled with love and gratitude. She wishes the gift would arrive. The special gift. She's glad she's given everything she has for it. She has the wrapping paper and matching card all ready. Ready, and waiting. She always plans birthdays far in advance.

She imagines her mother's face as she opens the present. Her surprise, and delight. A surprise and delight that will flow on, the girl hopes, to the news of the baby coming. Of course it will. Surely her mother will be glad for her. Surely . . .

There was a sound at the back of the house. Les Hewitt called, moved into the room from the kitchen. His face was ashen.

'Dolly . . .'

She held up her hand to him. Her tearless eyes burned. Toby went on speaking, slowly. Taking his time. Not looking at Birdie.

The package arrives at the post office. The postmistress gives it to the girl's husband, to take home to her. He grunts, throws it onto the floor of the car. What rubbish has she been buying now?

He drives to Sassafras. Irritated, because he has to leave the pub early. But he wants to buy some cough medicine at the chemist. Something strong. His wife's coughing is driving him crazy. Stopping him sleeping at night. Just out of Sassafras the car starts smoking and banging. He gets it to the garage. Just.

Frank Tellman, the rip-off artist, says it'll cost an arm and a leg to fix. Better to dump it. It's a rust-bucket. Just fix it, he snarls. I'll get the money. He rings his sister at the pub. She comes to get him and he leaves the car with Tellman.

And the package is still lying on the floor of the front seat. He never gives it another thought. When he gets home at closing time he's too drunk to remember anything much. He's so drunk he sleeps like a log. His wife's coughing doesn't worry him, for once.

He has to do without the car for a week. He's waiting for dole day. He doesn't say anything to his wife, about how serious the problem is. How much it will cost. She'll just say, 'leave it', the selfish bitch. As the days go by he gets angrier and angrier. He hates being without a car. It's all her fault. He was getting medicine for her when it happened. He is filled with self-righteous rage. He didn't marry her for this. Her dad's rolling isn't he? He thought he'd be on easy street, marrying Daphne Lamb. It hasn't worked out that way. It's all her fault.

Dole day comes. She's still sick, acting like a martyr. Hasn't cooked him a proper meal for a week. He gets his sister to drive him to Sassafras. Bails out the car with most of the dole money. Goes straight to the pub when he gets back. He's told his wife he'll be home for dinner. She's promised she'll cook him something. But she can wait.

There's a new girl at the pub. A little blow-in. Full of herself. He'd like to take her down a peg or two. Will, if he gets the chance. If she hangs around.

He spends the last of the dole money at the pub. Easy come, easy go. Sue Sweeney chips him about it. He laughs and says Daphne'll see them right.

That's the plan. She wouldn't sell that bloody diamond ring for the car. But she'll sell it to put food on the table, and pay the electricity bill. She'll have no choice.

At closing time, he goes home with a six-pack of stubbies. Driving, for the first time in a week. He's drunk. Fuzzy. He didn't mean to get so drunk. It'll put her in a bad mood. But at least he's got the car. She can make what she likes of it. She'd better not give him any cheek, or she'll get a taste of what she got last time.

He parks in the clearing. He leans over to get the six-pack. He finds the package lying on the floor. He'd forgotten clean about it. He shoves it under his arm and goes inside.

She's there, sitting at the kitchen table. She looks at the six-pack, gets up without speaking, and goes to the stove. She's been keeping his dinner hot. It'll be all dried up by now. But he doesn't say anything. He goes over to her and hands her the package. She smiles. She's pleased. She starts to open it, carefully tearing open the tape, taking out something covered in plastic bubble-wrap.

No time like the present. He tells her the car cost more than he expected. There's no money to live on for the next fortnight. She'll have to sell her ring. There's no choice. He makes himself smile, and put his arm around her shoulders.

She looks shocked. She shows him her finger. It's bare. He hasn't noticed. Hasn't looked at her properly for weeks.

His grip tightens on her shoulder. She winces. He asks her where the ring is.

She's sold it. For the bloody stupid thing she's holding in her hand. A brass-coloured girl turning into a tree. A present for her bloody mother.

He can't believe it. Again, she's done him down. He's speechless with rage. He grabs the thing out of her hand. She screeches at him to give it back, not to hurt it. And, snarling, he smashes it into the side of her head, throws her away from him, hits her again as she goes down. And then again . . .

And the blood spreads, making a pool on the old wooden floor. The back of her head is crushed. She twitches, like a lamb whose throat has been cut, then lies still. He knows he's killed her.

He backs away. Her blood is all over his hands, the front of his shirt. Blood and hair and tiny fragments of bone stick to the bronze thing he still holds.

The weapon. No one knows about it. No one's ever seen it but him. He rolls it quickly in the bubble-wrap, stuffs it back into the box. All he has to do is hide it. They won't be able to prove he did it, without a weapon.

He stumbles back out into the clearing. Looks desperately around, seeking inspiration. They'll search the creek. Under the shack. The scrub. They'll see disturbed ground, if he buries it. Where?

And then he remembers. The possum tree. The tree along the track, that he and Rosalie used to climb. Where the old possum used to live, till he poisoned it. He wanted its hole for himself. It was a useful hiding place for other kids' wallets in those days.

And it would be useful now. It was made for the job. He runs into the avenue. Not far. He climbs the tree. Harder now than it was when he was a kid. He nearly slips, a couple of times, leaning around to the hole, holding on with one hand, stuffing the box in place, covering it with leaves. He's lost condition.

But he does it. He climbs down. He's filled with pride at what he's done. He runs for his car. He'll tell them he got home and found her dead. Got the blood on him, trying to rouse her. He'll tell them her diamond ring is gone. Someone has come and killed her, while he was in the pub, and taken *the ring. They can't pinpoint the time of death exactly. He knows that. There's no weapon. They won't be able to pin it on him. As long as he acts fast.*

He's back in the car, his head spinning with beer, and shock. He revs the engine, pushes the accelerator to the floor, and flies. The last thing he remembers is the huge tree on the bend rushing into the windscreen at him. Next thing he knows, he's in hospital, with a pig in uniform watching his every move.

They get him on it, anyway. The bastards. No one helps him. No one believes him. They don't care they can't find the weapon. They don't care they've got no proof. Even his lawyer doesn't believe him. He can see that. Her bitch of a mother testifies he knocked her around. That finishes it. They put him in gaol and throw away the key.

Then Jude comes along. Saint Jude. Lamb to the Slaughter. *And a point at which he knows he's going to be free. And rich.*

He's read a bit, in gaol. He's got a degree. He's educated now. He's read law books. He knows he can't be tried for the same crime twice. He made an unsworn statement, in the dock. He can't even be charged for perjury.

He makes himself a promise. When he gets out, he's going to go back to Hope's End. And everyone's going to pay. Dolly Hewitt especially. He's not content for her to know he's there, living just across the creek, well-off, and happy. He wants her to know he really did it. He wants her to be sure. Dead sure. He's going to climb that tree, and bring out that box. He's going to pull that bronze monstrosity out and stick it in front of her nose, covered in her precious daughter's blood. He wants to see her face when he does it.

Birdie's thoughts ran on. Beyond Toby's voice. Beyond, to the end.

Is truth the same as justice?

She'd done what Jude said. She'd taken the responsibility he asked her to take. That he couldn't find the strength to take himself. Had she had a choice?

Trevor Lamb goes home from the pub. He's tipped Sue Sweeney the wink, and he's expecting a visit from her. She's gone off a bit, in the five years he's been away. But she was always good value. He remembers.

He drinks a beer, turns on the radio. Then Lily turns up.

*He thinks, why not, and gives her five minutes. Enjoys
throwing her out. Smart-arse little bitch.*

*He waits for Sue. She won't be along till she's had a
shower and prettied herself up, after closing time. He knows
Sue. Likes to come to a man fresh and done up to the nines.
He drinks another beer.*

*It's midnight. He opens another can of beer. There's a
knock at the door. It's not who he's expecting. But he's
pleased. This is the beginning. He goes out, climbs the tree.
At Hewitts' place, dogs are barking. Old Les is slaughtering
a lamb, he thinks. How appropriate. He brings down the
box hidden there. Takes it to the kitchen, under the light and
shows it, grinning his triumph. Mouthing his contempt, at
last. Laughing. Laughing at the shock, the sudden, blind rage
he sees, but thinks is impotent. He turns away, to take another sip of beer. . .*

*And is struck down. A moment of disbelief. A second of
horrifying pain. And blackness. That never ends.*

Birdie sat, hands still in her lap. The clock ticked.

'I'm glad he's dead,' said Dolly Hewitt. 'He deserved to
die. A thousand times. He deserved it. Justice . . .'

Her husband's arm tightened around her shoulders.

Toby stood up. Birdie moistened her lips. 'Jude said to
tell you he was sorry,' she said in a voice she barely
recognised as her own. 'He said to tell you, he didn't know.
He didn't know Trevor was guilty. He didn't know.'

'He was only doing what he thought was right.' The
woman stood up, straight in her blue dress.

'But he made up for it,' she added, lifting her chin. 'My
husband would have killed Trevor Lamb, I think, if he hadn't
been afraid for me. Of leaving me alone. I would have killed
him myself, if I'd had the strength. You can tell Jude Gregorian from me. And from my husband. And my son. Tell him,
thank you. For doing what it was up to us to do. For killing
Trevor Lamb.'

Thirty-four

Birdie sat in Sue Sweeney's living room, drinking coffee. Her voice was steady, flat and calm. Her eyes were expressionless.

'There was no one else but Jude, in the end,' she said. 'Once I realised that Trevor Lamb really had killed Daphne, because the weapon used was something he only brought home that night, I could see that there were only a few people who might have killed him. Lamb had taken the weapon out of its hiding place himself, to show someone.

'So I eliminated people one by one. Trevor wouldn't have bothered to show the figurine to Lily Danger. Or Annie. Lily didn't even know Daphne. Annie didn't like her. It wouldn't have meant much to them. And Trevor was after dramatic effect.'

'What about the rest of us?' asked Sue. She sipped at her coffee. She gazed at Birdie over her cup. Her eyes were watchful.

'The timing didn't work for Rosalie, Grace or Keith. Punchy was fond of Daphne, but I didn't believe he'd have hit his brother with a weapon like that. He'd have been more likely to strangle him, or beat him up with his fists. Trevor wouldn't have dared to make a scene like that alone with Les Hewitt or Floury Baker. They're too big, too tough. He couldn't be sure they wouldn't turn on him. I was certain it wasn't Phillip Hewitt. I really didn't think he'd have been capable of going down to that shack in the dark, alone, and confronting Trevor. He was absorbed enough in his own bravery at facing a slaughtered lamb.

'That left Dolly Hewitt, and you, Sue. Either of you could have done it. Either of you would have been capable of it, I think. Both of you had the opportunity. Dolly could easily have slipped out while Phillip was in his room, and Les was killing the lamb. In fact, for a while, a little while, I really thought she might have done both the murders.'

'You thought she might have killed her own *daughter*? How could you *think* that?'

'It happens. And that was before I knew about the "Daphne" figurine. Dolly told me Daphne had given her the "Leda and the Swan" for her birthday. I didn't know which birthday. For all I knew the "Leda" was the figurine Daphne got in the post the week before she died. I hadn't figured out then that Trevor didn't take the package home till a week after Peg gave it to him. The "Leda" figurine would have been just as effective a weapon as the "Daphne" was. And they would have left similar marks.'

'But didn't you say the "Leda" was sitting on a coffee table in Dolly's sitting room?'

'Yes.'

'That would have meant she'd walk past it every day. Every single day.'

'Yes.'

There was a heavy silence. Birdie felt Sue's eyes on her. She glanced, but Sue turned her eyes away, simply saying: 'How did you eliminate us in the end?'

'Dolly could have gone to see Trevor while her husband was slaughtering the lamb. She could have killed Trevor, on impulse, if he showed her the "Daphne" statue. But after all, she didn't know he had it. I just couldn't believe she would have gone to see him just to berate him in the middle of the night like that. She believed he was dangerous. She knew she was weak. There would have been no sense to it. And of course she would have gone to the shack through her own land, over the creek. She would have had no reason to meet Jude on the track. And it didn't seem likely she'd have chased him. I finally eliminated her as a probability on all those grounds.'

'And me?' Sue kept her gaze fixed to the window above the sink. Tree tops swayed through glass.

'You . . . well, the timing was a problem with you, too. Lily left the shack at twenty to twelve. Jude would have arrived, all being well, at midnight. If you'd left the pub earlier than you said you did, that still didn't leave much time for you to talk to Trevor alone. A bare twenty minutes. And in that time, I figured, you would have been either arguing, or making love. One or the other. Whichever, Trevor wouldn't have had any reason to show you that figurine so early in the piece. And if you went at the time you said you did, you would have seen Jude lying there on the track.'

'But I *did* go at that time. And I didn't see Jude.'

'No, you didn't see him. Even though you had a flash-light. I thought about that, at the hospital. It looked bad for you. Then I remembered something. When I found Jude's torch, it was switched off. I didn't think anything of it, at the time. But why was it switched off? Because he was there when you went past, Sue. But he didn't want you to see him. He was in that tree, Sue, when you ran past, to the shack, and back. After he'd killed Trevor, he'd panicked. He was horrified by what he'd done. He wasn't thinking. He'd climbed up to hide that figurine again. In the place where it had been hidden so long. The place Trevor had showed him. The possum tree.

'And when I'd gone past, he tried to climb back down. And he fell.' Sue's voice was a breath. A sigh.

'Yes. He fell.' Birdie almost smiled. 'He's not a great ath-lete, Jude. Never has been. He fell, flat on his back, and broke his leg. And so he was still there when I came up the track just before two. Lying there helpless, under the tree. And I thought he'd been attacked. Why not? The thought he'd been climbing a tree never occurred to me. And I didn't suspect Jude for a minute. Why would Jude hurt Trevor Lamb? The man he'd saved? The man he'd given five years of his life to save? The man on whose case, whose case of terrible injustice, he'd built a whole reputation?

'And then I found out Trevor had been guilty, all along. And, by a process of elimination, everyone else dropped out. And then I realised why Jude might have been the one. Must have been the one. Because that night he found out. That Trevor Lamb was guilty, and didn't care. He was guilty, and he was gloating and rubbing his hands because what Jude had done had made him free. And he was going to tell every-one. Everyone. Rub their noses in it. And Jude—he just saw red. He just lost it. He lashed out. And he killed him.'

He killed him. I found out. I told . . .

Birdie put down her cup, and stood up.

'I'd better go now, Sue,' she said. 'I shouldn't be talking about it. Dan's giving me a ride to Sassafras so I can pick up my car. Thanks for the coffee. Say goodbye to Floury for me. And Peg.' She bent to pick up her bag, and slung it over her shoulder.

'Birdie—' Sue put out her hand. 'Birdie, I thought you loved that guy.'

Birdie said nothing. What was there to say?

'Why didn't you just keep quiet? Say nothing? The cops would never have guessed. And it was justice . . .'

'Jude wanted it,' said Birdie. Her voice was utterly controlled, absolutely calm. 'He asked me to do it. He knew it had to be done. He wanted it done quickly, before anyone else was arrested, or even brought under grave suspicion. He couldn't have handled that. Trying to cover up what he'd done was just an impulse. I know him. It was a mad impulse. He couldn't have carried it through. He would have confessed himself, in the end. He wanted me to save him from that. And that was something I could do for him. The only thing. Tell the truth.'

Is truth the same as justice . . . ?

'I couldn't have done it,' said Sue.

Birdie said goodbye, and left. She picked up her overnight bag, walked down the rickety steps, and went out through the yard to the street. She knew Sue Sweeney was watching her, waiting to wave, but she didn't turn around.

I couldn't have done it . . .

The afternoon sun was shining down the main street, glaring into the horizon. Peg McCann was doing a brisk trade with kids wandering home from school. Cars, utes, trucks and Bull Trews' Bobcat were pulling in under the pepper trees opposite the pub.

Birdie saw that the Lambs were already sitting on the log on the verandah. Grace, Annie, Rosalie, Punchy. Jason played by the water tank, beating it with a stick, ignoring Annie's yells.

Rosalie looked across the road, said something to her mother and stood up. She stepped off the verandah and walked towards Birdie, her hair bouncing on her shoulders, her eyes crinkling against the sun.

'You're going?' she asked.

Birdie nodded.

'They're saying you found out what happened. They're saying Trev really did murder Daphne. They're saying Jude killed him because he found out. Is that right?'

'That's the theory they're working on at the moment. I can't really say much more.'

When will this be over?

Rosalie looked at her, her head on one side. Then, suddenly, she put out her hand and grabbed Birdie's. Her touch was warm and strong.

'Don't feel bad,' she said. 'You did what you had to do. Life goes on. You do what you have to do, and you put up with what happens after. I know how you must be feeling, though. I couldn't have done it.'

Her grip tightened. 'I know it probably won't help. But I thought you'd like to know. Grace has come good. Seems she thought I'd killed Trev. Because of her. Can you believe that? She says she was terrified I'd be taken away. She says she loves me.'

'Of course she does.' Birdie shifted her feet on the dry dust of the road. 'How's Annie taking it?'

'She's a bit put out about Trevor. But she doesn't blame you. And Lily's gone. And Keith's coming home tomorrow. That's cheered her up. Keith thought I'd done it too, would you believe? That's why he wanted to talk to me in the hospital. He wanted to help me cover it up. Nice to know your family thinks you're a possible murderer, isn't it?'

She turned back to look at the verandah. Birdie looked with her.

Annie drained her glass. Birdie watched as she held it out and Punchy took it. It was time for another round.

'I'd better get back,' said Rosalie. 'I just wanted to say . . .'

'Thanks, Rosalie.'

Punchy, on his way to the pub door, grinned and lifted his loaded hands. A gesture of camaraderie, greeting and farewell.

Birdie stood there in the road. Lifted her hand. Thought of Dolly and Les Hewitt, tragic, vindicated, huddled together in that silent living room. Phillip Hewitt, tormented, writing poetry. Jude, dreaming in his white, antiseptic bed.

Is truth the same as justice . . . ?

She turned and walked to the car. Before she got in, she

looked back once. Jason was still swinging on the tank stand. Rosalie was scolding. Annie was grinning gummily, calling Punchy for the beers. Grace was slouched against the verandah post, talking to a bare-chested boy. Inside, Floury Baker and Sue were serving drinks to tan-faced men.

Life goes on.

The car door opened. 'In you get,' growled Toby's voice. Gentler, it seemed to her, than usual.

Birdie slid into the car, slammed the door behind her.

The car eased out of its parking spot, drove past the pub, towards the bridge.

The people on the verandah, shoulder to shoulder, yelled and waved.

Birdie watched them, through glass.

Already, they seemed very far away.

ABOUT THE AUTHOR

JENNIFER ROWE is a multi-award-winning writer and devotee of the murder mystery genre. She enjoys reading these 'extended brainteasers' as much as writing them. Her 'Verity Birdwood' mysteries also sell in Europe and the USA and include *Grim Pickings, Murder by the Book, Death in Store, The Makeover Murders* and *Stranglehold*.

SANDRA WEST PROWELL

"Prowell has staked out her own territory somewhere between Hillerman and Grafton Country."
—*Alfred Hitchcock Mystery Magazine*

Tough as barbed wire and just as tightly strung, Phoebe Siegel is a cop turned private detective with too much past, too much family, and a talent for diving too deeply into a case....

BY EVIL MEANS
____56966–X $5.99/$7.99 Canada

THE KILLING OF MONDAY BROWN
____56969–4 $5.99/$7.99 Canada